The
GIRL ON
THE LIAR'S
THRONE

DEN PATRICK

GOLLANCZ

LONDON

The right of Den Patrick to be identified as the author of
this work has been asserted by him in accordance with
the Copyright, Designs and Patents Act 1988.

First published in Great Britain in 2016 by Gollancz
An imprint of the Orion Publishing Group
Carmelite House, 50 Victoria Embankment, London EC4Y 0DZ
An Hachette UK Company

A CIP catalogue record for this book is available
from the British Library

ISBN 978 1 473 20004 3

1 3 5 7 9 10 8 6 4 2

Typeset at The Spartan Press Ltd,
Lymington, Hants

Printed and bound in Great Britain by
Clays Ltd, St Ives plc

The Orion Publishing Group's policy is to use papers that
are natural, renewable and recyclable products and made
from wood grown in sustainable forests. The logging and
manufacturing processes are expected to conform to the
environmental regulations of the country of origin.

www.denpatrick.com
www.orionbooks.co.uk
www.gollancz.co.uk

For Simon and Gillian,
who took Landfall from my hard drive
and put it into books

'Then there will be war. And all of your feasts, your pretty gowns and your great halls will be turned to ash'
THE HERALD

'Anger can be an expensive luxury'
POPULAR LANDFALL PROVERB

Great and Minor Houses of Landfall

HOUSE DIASPORA

Dottore Paolo Allattamento
veteran, conspirator, survivor

Domina Russo Maria Diaspora
chief steward of Demesne, betrayer

Erebus
the former Majordomo, arch manipulator and aberration

Eris
an impostor, passing herself off as the Silent Queen of Landfall

Isabella Esposito
long-serving maid to the Great Houses

Marchetti
former Myrmidon and assassin, now outcast

HOUSE PROSPERO

Duchess Salvaza Prospero
leader of Demense's mercantile house, mother to an
estranged daughter, widow

HOUSE ERUDITO

Maestro Fidelio
head of the many *professori* of Demesne, struggling to fill the
shoes of his predecessor, Cherubini

HOUSE DATINI

Viscount Francesco Datini
his stature, much like influence, is dwindling, not so his ambition

Viscountess Margherita Datini
mother to slain and outcast sons, wife to a cold-hearted husband

HOUSE SIMONETTI

Viscount Simonetti
keeper of tomes, Archivist of the great library

HOUSE DEL TORO

Dirigente Draco Romanucci
elected spokesperson for the Del Toro estate, rabble rouser

THE CULT OF SANTA MARIA

***Marchesa* Medea Contadino**
now a canoness, vocal opponent of the throne

Agostina Desideria
disciple of Santa Maria

Anea Oscuro Diaspora
the Silent Queen, an Orfano of rare intelligence, now prisoner

HOUSE MARINO

Durante Corvino
Delfino's long suffering *aiutante*

Delfino 'Denari' Datini
outcast noble, sometime painter, sometime scout, often flat broke hence the nickname

The Herald of War
an unwelcome presence from the south, violence personified

Duke Lucien Marino
orfano, kingslayer, and ruler of San Marino, a town to the
south-east of Landfall

Duchess Rafaela Marino
voice of reason, a commoner made noble through her
marriage to Lucien

A Rescue from Darkness

The girl sat alone, burdened by forgetfulness and incomprehension. That she was a prisoner was not in question, but the reasons were lost to her, just as she in turn was lost to the darkness. The ever-present silence weighed heavily on her slender shoulders, at once oppressive and maddening. How long had she been here? How would she escape? Questions needed answers, answers lost in a mind that failed to recall the subtle and the obvious. What was her name? Why was she here?

Her stomach growled, a distraction from summoning memories that refused to return. Many hours had passed since the guards had brought her food – might they not forget her as she had forgotten herself? She shifted, sliding from a cross-legged position in order to draw her knees up to her chest. It wouldn't do to move too far lest she got wet. This much she did remember. A solitary island of packed earth, just a few feet in diameter, rose above a fetid sea. The simple mound offered a reprieve from the icy waters of her existence. Certainly her ragged shift offered scant insulation. Fingers numb with cold teased at the scrap of cloth tied across her mouth. The veil was a curious affectation for a prisoner, yet the reason for it eluded her. Was it custom? Was there something that required cover? She left the rag tied in place, trying to ignore the terrible thirst.

A tawny light appeared in the abyssal black. It came closer, bobbing with a hypnotic motion that soothed the nameless girl even as her stomach called out for sustenance. A form appeared, gliding across the freezing, filthy waters like a phantom. Robed and hooded, the figure made graceful motions with a pole, as if spearing slow-moving fish. The figure glided forward further still, the lantern revealing it stood aboard a gondola. It drew ever closer with eerie grace. A splash as the pole dipped beneath the water. It did not rise again. The gondola slowed just feet from the island of earth and foulness, the dark held at bay by the lantern's nimbus. The girl blinked and held a hand to aching eyes.

'It's very early,' said the figure. 'I couldn't sleep. There's no one to talk to up there besides Myrmidons.' The figure gestured with one hand at the heavens. The girl looked up to discover they were made of stone. But she'd already known that. Another fact in a constellation of truths that dimmed in the darkness of her mind.

'We used to to talk so much.' The words came from beneath the hood, spoken softly, the voice rich and strong. A woman's voice. 'We spoke of philosophy and politics, republic and feudalism, fears and sometimes hopes. And then you stopped speaking to me, busy at your machines, busy with Virmyre.'

The girl on the island shifted as memory failed her once more. What was Virmyre? she wondered. A hiss escaped her, but words would not come to form the question.

'You were my greatest student, the brightest mind not just of your generation but of all generations. Now look at you. One sip of the waters at your feet and you'll not remember a single word of this conversation come the morning. It's what makes you the perfect confessor.'

The nameless girl regarded the penitent, realising her robes were deep red. At another time this figure would have clutched a silver staff, yet now she held a simple wooden pole, adrift on a lake of forgetting.

'All those hours of education, and now Erebus has reduced you to a dumb animal, shitting in the darkness. One created to rule Demesne, one trained to lead. Not much of an ending for one like you.' The hooded figure sat down in the gondola, mindful not to rock the narrow vessel for fear of overturning it. 'I never thought it would it come to this. I've let him destroy you and diminish me by extension. Demesne and all of Landfall are suffering, because of this.' She gestured at the Stygian scene, disgust dripping from each word. 'They say Lucien is threatening trade sanctions. War will follow.'

A tiny sound, a sob quickly muted. When she spoke again there was steel in her voice, but it sounded tired and brittle. 'War is coming to Landfall, and there's nothing to be done about it. Erebus won't be turned and Eris is too selfish to care.'

A pang of sympathy afflicted the nameless girl, sympathy for the woman in the narrow boat. She did not understand the nature of her worries, nor recognise the names she referenced, but an anguish pervaded every syllable. The pain of those words haunted the space between them. She held out a hand, but the hooded figure snorted with contempt.

'How can anyone rescue us from this darkness?'

The question wasn't addressed to her, was just sour rhetoric to sink without a trace beneath the frigid water.

'Sometimes I think I envy you. How nice it must be to stay here and drink the waters. I'd take the sickness and the cramps to be free of the things I've done and the people we've lost. Just a few sips.' She slid her fingers over the side of the gondola and pierced the surface of the water. 'But not today.'

The woman rose, using the pole to steady herself, then turned the gondola back the way she had come. The nameless girl stood also, reaching out with both hands like an infant wanting comfort. None was offered. The figure on the gondola receded, taking the lantern light with her as she went. Only her words remained.

How can anyone rescue us from this darkness?

The nameless girl waited as hunger gnawed at her innards, thirst clawing her throat. The darkness magnified time, made a madness of it. No way of tracking the hours or the minutes of her incarceration.

One sip of the waters at your feet and you'll not remember a single word of this conversation come the morning.

Words eddied like unseen current. And then the silence was broken by a sound that had always seemed part of the background, but was now leaden with significance.

Drip, drip, drip.

3

Fresh water. She stumbled from her island cage, gasping as the mire chilled her calves, then her thighs. She waited for the swell and splash to abate.

Drip, drip, drip.

The sound was beautiful, a pure thing unsullied by the dank, sickened gloaming of her prison. She waded deeper, the chill rankness enfolding her waist, sucking down the mean fabric of her shift. She cast about blindly for the source, slowly, so as not to dilute the sound with her passing.

Drip, drip, drip.

Her heart raced. It was so close. A spatter on her forehead, and another. Her stomach became light with anticipation. She pulled the rag aside from her mouth, her head thrown back ecstatically.

Water, clean water.

Each drip sated a thirst long denied. She stood until she could bear it no longer, stood until her neck hurt with the effort of angling her head back. She stood until her legs were numb from the icy mire. The nameless girl stumbled through the water, keen to find the island of packed earth, but the darkness confounded her. Her legs cramped and froze, leaching away the joy she'd discovered. Her effort to drink clean water would see her freeze to death in the oubliette.

The oubliette.

The name of her prison. Something shifted in her mind. The nameless girl shivered. The oubliette, where people were thrown to be forgotten, out of sight and out of mind. Her legs gave out and suddenly she was on her knees, hands casting about for something, anything to steady her. Such a cruel irony her body should betray her just as her faculties showed promise of return.

New light appeared.

This time the gondola bore two warriors girded in plate and leather. Curving helms hid their faces, the lower sections crafted to resemble mandibles. The girl pressed a hand to her ragged veil, almost remembering something, elusive and dreadful. The warriors' helms sported visors in the shape of chevrons, a gauze behind concealing their eyes. Armour protected chest and forearm, thigh and groin, all painted a ruddy brown. The hilts of short flat swords jutted from hips, the weapons of Myrmidons.

Myrmidons.

Another word from distant memory. The nameless girl hoarded it in a corner of her mind, hoping it would remain sacrosanct from forgetfulness. The Myrmidons' voices broke her fractured wondering. They drew the gondola up close and chided each other not to fall in. The light they brought caught the mound of earth, an ugly silhouette above the water. The nameless girl regained her perch and shivered.

'She fell in,' said the first dispassionately.

'It's a wonder she hasn't died already.' The second Myrmidon had a softer, kinder voice, but not much. The timbre of their voices gave them away as women.

'It's not deep enough to drown in.' A note of pique from the first.

'Says you. I didn't mean drowning anyway. I meant on account of all the disease. It's not clean.'

'They say she has some magic on her though,' said the first. 'Maybe it protects her.'

'The *strega* princess.'

The first Myrmidon grunted. 'I heard they called her the Silent Queen.'

The nameless girl, eager to hear more, blinked in the lantern light as the Myrmidons handed over the food.

The Silent Queen. I am the Silent Queen.

'She looks different today,' said the kinder of the two.

'Of course she looks different. She's been up to her shoulders in all this filth. She'll freeze to death down here.'

'She's supposed to stay alive,' said the kinder. 'If she dies the Domina will kill us too.'

'*Figlio di puttana.* We'll have to come back with a blanket.'

The nameless girl, now reinvented as the Silent Queen, watched them leave, tearing into the meagre food provided while digesting all she'd learned. It had been the Domina who'd ventured down to confess her regrets. The fact they thought her capable of magic was laughable.

Still, it's ever the province of the ignorant to mistake technology for sorcery.

The food left her dry. The bread in particular was stale and absorbed the moisture from the cavern of her mouth. No matter. She steeled herself against the cold to come and waded into the mire once again, following the sound of water as it fell from the ceiling. The clean water spattered her cheeks. She drank it down, giving thanks for the Domina's words, now a chorus in her ears.

One sip of the waters at your feet and you'll not remember a single word of this conversation come the morning.

She shivered and drank. Oubliette. Myrmidon. Domina. She was drunk on names remembered, intoxicated at the prospect of recovering more, remembering others.

I am the Silent Queen. A thrill of relief and excitement swept through her. Not yet a name, but a title and certainly an improvement on being a shivering girl in the dark.

The Myrmidons returned to find the Silent Queen atop her mound of unlovely earth. They poled the gondola closer, the water lapping about the prow of the boat.

'I'm telling you, she looks different today.'

'Just throw her the blanket and let's go.'

The kinder of the Myrmidons leaned forward from the narrow boat extending both hands. There was a scratch across the top corner of her breastplate, the mark a memory of the armour preventing injury, perhaps saving her life.

'Try to keep warm. Careful now. It's heavier than it looks.'

The Silent Queen took the blanket, noting the weight inside the folds of coarse fabric. She gripped it to her chest, nodding in reply.

'Come on. We've been down here long enough,' said the second Myrmidon, fussing at the gondola pole. 'We're needed at the Ravenscourt.'

They pushed off, taking the lantern with them, leaving the Silent Queen to discover her contraband before the light faded entirely. A stoppered clay jug, the fluid inside scentless. More clean water. Another thrill of excitement. The gondola glided further into the darkness, the sound of muttered discontent fading. A half-loaf of bread, fresh from the kitchen. A cup of olives only slightly dry. All were gone in a matter of moments. Of the things the Myrmidons had brought, the food was a poor second.

The Ravenscourt.

The word rang like a bell. Once it had been the centre of her universe.

It would be again.

2

The New Order

Eris sat on the throne of Landfall, regarding the Ravenscourt with heavy, lidded eyes, lost in thought. The legs of that great seat were fashioned from four helms in the style of the Myrmidons lest any forget who supported her rule. The arms of the throne were two scabbards, holding the short wide blades of the soldiers who protected her, while the back of the seat was a Myrmidon breastplate. A sunburst made of beaten copper sat at the top, forming a halo behind her head. This was not a throne that had been crafted so much as welded together, assembled from the very fabric of violence. It was designed to awe, not for comfort. Eris drowsed despite the shortcomings of the throne; she had not slept the night through since her brother's death. The succession of hours lost to wakefulness had frayed her nerves, shortening her temper. Losing life to a blade in Demesne was unremarkable in times such as these. Losing kin to illness was unthinkable.

The Ravenscourt was a wealth of shadows. The many windows her predecessor had installed were now shuttered for the winter; the darkness suited her deception. Baroque candelabra on stands fashioned as twisting figures shed pools of golden light, the artifice at once stunning and unnerving. The pieces, each the height of a man, were set at intervals along the edges of the chamber between thick columns.

The doors at the far end of the Ravenscourt creaked open, the Myrmidons bowing to the figure who entered. Only two people inspired such respect, Eris, in her guise as the Silent Queen, was one of them.

'They tell me you've been visiting your favourite pupil,' said Eris, her voice loud in the emptiness.

'Once the spymaster, now the spied upon,' the Domina replied with a scowl.

Eris grinned, masked behind her turquoise veil. Less hidden was the gleam of spite in her green eyes. The Domina, attired in the rich crimson robes and square hat she had made her symbols of office, crossed the cream and jet tiles of the Ravenscourt. A silver staff almost her equal in height occupied one hand. She was a lonely piece on a vast board, pawns depleted, the loyal knight turned traitor. Even the rooks had retreated to the countryside to be spared the new order.

'Surely there are greater matters that require your attention than my whereabouts?'

'Perhaps.' Eris sighed, then shrugged.

'Why bother sending watchers after me?'

'I make a point of concentrating on the tasks that bring me the most amusement.'

The Domina drew close to the dais, her grip on the staff tight, the thin slash of her purple-painted lips the same.

'You're not supposed to be talking,' said the Domina. 'The Silent Queen doesn't speak, or had you forgotten that rather important detail?'

Eris rose from her seat, raised her arms, gesturing to the empty hall.

'And who precisely am I playing impostor for? Not you. Certainly not the Myrmidons – their loyalty is without question.'

'This whole charade will come to an end if you're discovered,' said the Domina, 'and not one of us will survive.'

'Survive?' Eris stepped down from the dais until she was face to face with the Domina. 'You should be grateful you survived the transition to the new order.'

'Without me there wouldn't *be* a new order,' whispered the Domina, her eyes straying to the vast black curtain on the gallery behind the throne. Bronze leaves decorated thick brocade, the effect autumnal. The drapes concealed the source of their power, and their enslavement.

Eris stepped back and shook her head. 'I suggest you put an

9

end to Anea before she remembers herself. The Orfani have an aptitude for escaping death.' She clasped her hands before her, chilly fingers laced together. 'If that happens all hell will be unleashed.'

'I'd say we're well acquainted with hell already,' whispered the Domina, 'but some are more reluctant to admit it than others.'

The doors to the Ravenscourt opened once more, silencing their argument. Viscount Simonetti wandered in, loose stride carrying him to the throne. He was tall in a way uncommon to the men of Landfall, fair of hair, with watery blue eyes behind optics perched on his nose. The archivist had enjoyed Anea's favour. She'd entrusted her library to him, and his diligence had been rewarded with a title. Eris struggled to tolerate the man.

Simonetti bowed. 'My Queen, Domina. The clocks have struck noon. The *nobili* wait.' There was a moment's pause. Neither of the women reacted, still seething from their many cross words. 'The Ravenscourt is still meeting today, I trust?'

Eris raised her hands and signed, *Yes, of course. I just needed a few minutes with my most trusted aide.*

Simonetti exchanged a look with the Domina, and Eris wondered if he'd picked up on the sarcasm. The Myrmidons opened the doors before archivist or Domina could comment. The first to appear was Viscount Datini. He regarded the world over a blunt beak of a nose, a look of affront on his lined face. Age, or perhaps anger, had turned his hair pure white. Datini kept his hands behind his back – Eris knew it was to steady his palsy rather than a patriarchal pose.

'Viscount.' The Domina nodded; Eris did the same.

'My lady, Domina.'

'Good morning,' said Simonetti.

'What's good about it?' replied Datini. His mouth was a downturned slash of sourness, eyes dark and deep set.

Is something amiss, Viscount Datini? signed Eris.

'No.' His frown deepened. 'Nothing. That is to say my wife . . . Never mind.'

Eris had no need to press the issue; the Domina's spies had reported just that morning. Viscountess Datini had sent a significant sum of money to their outcast son in the south.

'We'll speak afterwards,' said the Domina, the words calming the disgruntled old man.

'Never marry, if you can help it.' Viscount Datini shuffled away on unsteady legs.

Is there something I should know? Eris signed, keen to test the depth of Simonetti's knowledge.

'Only that his age exceeds his politeness,' replied the archivist. *And?*

'The Verde Guerra claimed the lives of two of their three sons,' said Simonetti in hushed tones. 'The viscount made their surviving son an outcast some years ago, much to the chagrin of the viscountess.'

I see. Simonetti wasn't telling her anything not widely known. The archivist was holding back or too busy with his books to keep abreast of the court.

'The viscountess is lodging with House Prospero and is now a confidante of the duchess,' added Simonetti, as if this too were a secret.

'Speak of the furies and they're sure to appear,' said the Domina in a low voice.

Duchess Salvaza Prospero walked the length of the Ravenscourt with her head held high, an earnest pageboy of ten summers struggling to keep pace. She wore a black jacket with military undertones, a riding skirt in a matching hue and smart boots. A sash of silk in purple encircled her waist. Purple and black, the colours of her house.

'Hardly attire suitable for the Ravenscourt,' said the Domina from behind her hand. 'She looks dressed for the hunt.'

Perhaps she is, signed Eris.

Once, the duchess had used her enviable figure to seduce Demesne, but she had adopted an altogether different wardrobe since the departure of her daughter, Stephania, three months ago. Salvaza curtsied and bowed her head to the Silent Queen. Her page sketched a low bow, a wary cast to his gaze.

'Good morning, all.'

The Silent Queen had yet to be formally crowned, so she was queen in name only. Technically, the duchess outranked her, but Salvaza didn't have the Myrmidons under her command.

'I do so look forward to news of our belated elections.' Salvaza Prospero's smile failed to reach her eyes. Anea Oscuro Diaspora, the real Silent Queen, had offered her fledgling republic the chance to choose a ruler; now Eris found herself burdened with the promise.

'That should make for an interesting session,' said Simonetti, earning him a sharp look from the Domina. Salvaza curtsied and retired to one side of the Ravenscourt.

Maestro Fidelio and his wife waddled in, followed by a dozen courtiers and aides of various houses minor. The *maestro* governed House Erudito, Demesne's seat of learning.

At least these two can be relied on to stay silent, signed Eris.

'They know which side their bread is buttered on,' agreed the Domina.

'Both sides if I had to guess,' muttered Simonetti, earning him another sour look, this time from both of the women. 'Yes, well, if you'll excuse me I need to ah...' Simonetti crossed the room to Duchess Prospero, who looked unsettled by the newest arrival to the Ravenscourt.

Marchesa Contadino, Medea to her confidants, and more recently canoness, entered the hall. She displayed great presence despite her small stature. The white and blue robes of her order lent her a luminous quality in the darkness. Another sister of Santa Maria walked at her shoulder, Agostina, who it was said had nursed Medea through grief-stricken days verging on madness. Agostina's eyes glittered blue and green in the candlelight, whereas the canoness's gaze showed only darkness. It was the look of revenge waiting to be unleashed. The canoness and the sister approached the Myrmidon throne and bobbed curtsies, not nearly deep enough for Eris's taste. Medea flashed a cold look at Duchess Prospero before retiring to the opposite side of the Ravenscourt.

'I wish she had fled Demesne with her children,' said the Domina, a note of regret in her whispered words.

The next man to enter was not of noble stock but a representative of House Del Toro. He had adopted Anea's dreams of a republic without a moment's pause. Drago Romanucci was nut brown in the way of men who worked through the seasons; he walked with a soldier's contempt. His tremendous disdain for the

Ravenscourt, worn so clearly on his face, was matched only by his physique. A grey and white cloak lay across one vast shoulder, battered boots reaching powerful thighs. A fine sword, which he wore to the Ravenscourt with a flagrant disregard for etiquette, rested in a white enamelled scabbard. The blade was a none-too-polite reminder that House Del Toro were militant supporters of Lord Contadino. And never more so since his murder.

Drago Romanucci gave a perfunctory nod as he crossed the room and stood close to Medea like a faithful hound.

Other houses – Elemosina, Sciaparelli, Shiavone, even the far-off Previdente – had sent representatives. They were second sons or daughters playing at the role of emissary, pursuing petty politics. They made furtive deals or sated selfish pleasures. Some were simply unwanted cousins, sent far from their estates. Various scribes and messengers filtered in, but few if any displayed enthusiasm. The *nobili* faked polite bows and curtsies when necessary, but the majority wore their feelings on their faces: disapproval, distrust, disappointment.

I see House Albero have failed to send a representative. Again.

'There are strong indications they're aligning with House Contadino of late,' replied the Domina from behind her hand. 'Word has reached me that the children were sent there following Emilio's death.'

Eris sighed, eyes scouring Landfall's finest. She struggled to find a single soul she had a kind word for.

I used to think Demesne was the arena for those who dreamed of power, signed Eris, turning to take the throne. The Domina stood before her, blocking her gestures from the few who could decipher them.

'And now?'

We seem to be a dumping ground for the dispossessed; a latrine for the waste others would flush away. Half the people in this room only care for themselves. The other half hate us.

'I'd say it was a good deal more than half.'

Which?

'That hate us,' replied the Domina, 'although the groups aren't mutually exclusive.'

13

Eris was tired of the Domina's constant complaints, of her sour demeanour, of the blank look that haunted her eyes. But there was one Eris loathed more than even the Domina. He was late of course.

Dottore Allattamento, veteran of the Verde Guerra, physician to any number of nobles in Demesne. He'd recently begun teaching a new intake of students at House Erudito. This alone was a source of disgust to Eris. The *dottore* had an impeccable bedside manner, but his skills were questionable at best. And there was the none-too-small issue that he'd failed to save her brother.

Sabatino. The name entered her like a knife.

Dottore Allattamento bowed at the throne from the far end of the Ravenscourt, wary of approaching. He was dressed in a severe frock coat of black damask and grey striped britches, clean shaven with hair cut short in the way of soldiers. The *dottore* took a position alongside Viscount Datini, who paid him a retainer for his services and provided an apartment in House Fontein. Eris found it difficult to drag her eyes away from the man. She wanted to make him suffer. She wanted to make him hurt in the way she did. She wanted him sleepless and despairing during the small hours.

'Do you want to start? Or should I wait for you to finish glowering at your subjects?' said the Domina, clutching her silver staff with impatience.

I may start by sending you to the oubliette, signed Eris, the motions short and sharp, *seeing as you are so fond of the place.*

'Wouldn't it be convenient if you could rid yourself of me so easily,' said the Domina through a sneer. 'Perhaps you'll find yourself there one day.' The Domina turned her back before Eris could respond, slamming the silver staff against the floor three times. The Ravenscourt dropped to one knee.

'This session of the Ravenscourt is open. You may bring your concerns before Lady Aranea Oscuro Diaspora.'

Eris fidgeted. How she hated that name. How she hated to be reminded of being merely a copy, a splendid fake, a counterfeit queen.

Duchess Prospero cleared her throat and the Domina nodded.

'Lord and ladies of Landfall, fellow *cittadini* of Santa Maria, select of Demesne, the elections we were promised back in *Otto-bre* have yet to materialise. Has Lady Aranea Oscuro Diaspora has reneged on her promise for a fair and democratic republic?'

Eris began signing immediately, the Domina giving voice to the words that tripped from her fingertips.

'As you are aware, our finances have not recovered from the formation of the Myrmidons –'

'And whose fault is that?' complained someone from the back of the Ravenscourt.

Eris continued, the Domina glowering at the heckler '– and we have yet to stabilise the economy or the conditions of those who work the land. The last thing we need is an election, throwing an already struggling system into flux.'

'My lady, Domina,' rumbled Simonetti. 'If I might add something?'

'Please do,' replied the Domina, failing to conceal a sneer.

'As archivist, I recommend we divert money from our extensive war chest to other pursuits, such as reopening the library and furnishing a new apothecary.'

Eris all but rolled her eyes. This was Simonetti's favourite song, and he never tired of it. She'd considered giving in just to silence the man.

'You can't eat books, and people can't afford medicine when they can barely feed themselves.' *Marchesa* Contadino had swept onto the floor, placing herself directly before the throne. 'None of this would have happened had you not formed the Myrmidons. How much money have you spent creating swords and armour for your new army?'

Eris's fingers flicked and danced; the Domina watched and translated.

'I rule Demesne and I decide how the treasury is spent, after taking advice from the Domina naturally.'

'How convenient,' shouted the *marchesa*, 'when it was you two who decided to arm these creatures and to spend our taxes feeding and housing them.'

A sickened hush fell on the Ravenscourt. It was no secret that the Myrmidons were not entirely human. Eris signed her riposte to the Domina.

15

Tell this bitch that Lucien Marino's strength grows by the day; we have to protect ourselves.

The Domina nodded, turning to *Marchesa* Contadino.

'Lady Aranea Oscuro Diaspora says she is greatly troubled by developments in the south, and that her only wish is that Demesne and Santa Maria stay protected in the years ahead.'

Eris shifted on the throne and skewered the Domina with a stare.

Marchesa Contadino took a step toward the dais, looking up at the women with cold fury. Eris realised her mistake. The Sisters of Santa Maria often took vows of silence, emulating Anea, even down to her use of the silent language.

The *marchesa* raised her voice. 'That's not what she said!' Medea Contadino turned to the assembled nobles.

'What did she say, ah, I mean, sign?' said Simonetti. Eris glowered at him.

'She signed, "Tell this bitch that Lucien Marino's strength grows by the day; we have to protect ourselves."'

'Oh dear,' said Simonetti and began to polish his optics.

'Lucien Marino's strength only grows because the *cittadini* are fleeing to him for better lives. The formation of the Myrmidons *caused* this; they were never a reaction to southern aggression.' She turned back to Eris and pointed a finger. 'Best remember that this bitch understands the silent language.'

Eris turned to the Domina and made a fist, pointing her thumb toward the floor. Moments later Myrmidons were dragging the *marchesa* from the Ravenscourt, and Agostina along with her.

Lock them up for an hour or two, then throw them out onto the street, where they belong.

'You shouldn't have done that,' said Domina. 'Opposing the church is dangerous, no matter how annoying their spokesperson.'

Just be grateful I did not send you with them.

The rest of the session dragged through the long hours of the afternoon, Eris struggling to bring her full attention to the task, haunted by the Domina's words.

I'd say we're well acquainted with hell already, but some are more reluctant to admit it than others.

3

The Forgotten

The stoppered clay jug was a reassuring weight in the darkness. It was as if more of her old life washed the empty corridors of her mind each time she drank. Each mouthful sluiced away the dust of forgetting. She knew the water was not blessed, yet it remained her talisman. She shivered under the blanket and clutched it tighter to her spare frame.

And still my name eludes me.

The lack upset her deeply. The Silent Queen had been a sobriquet she'd not chosen herself. Nor could she remember if the honorific had been applied from affection or derision.

How can a mind be so shattered to not contain this cornerstone of identity?

She clawed her way over the rubble of the past and began building her reality anew. Fragments came back. Here a face with a kindly smile, there a name or a title.

And do I become someone else if I reassemble these pieces of memory incorrectly? Will I be no more than a revenant? The dead come back to haunt the living?

Many memories were jagged and sharp, most were painful and broken. There had been another time in the oubliette, when Dino had appeared to rescue her. Where was her brother now? And if not Dino then ... She struggled to remember. Lucien. Another memory surfaced in the dank waters of her mind. He'd come to her chamber and seen her unveiled face. Her shame had been compounded with dread as the apartment burned. Dread transmuted to fear as he'd urged her to escape the searing heat of the flames. And then relief. This event, more than any other, came back to her in startling detail.

A sound disturbed the water behind her, something heavy falling in. The Silent Queen shifted on her island and blinked a few times, trying to rid herself of a purple smear that ghosted her vision. She balled her fists and pressed them to the arches of her eye sockets, rubbed and let out a long sigh.

It stands to reason I should see phantoms after spending so long in pitch darkness.

The purple glow wavered.

The Silent Queen stood transfixed, not by some figment her eyes had conjured, but by a light source. She gathered the stoppered jug and gripped the blanket, wading into the mire. The iciness was not unexpected. She pressed deeper into the mire, ignoring the unseen objects her naked feet encountered in the muck. The glow remained constant, yet seemingly out of reach. She urged herself onward, knowing there was no chance of finding her way back to the island. She'd freeze to death long before the Myrmidons returned.

Onwards, wading through the filth and stagnation until the shimmer had grown. What had been no more than a dash of colour had expanded to something akin to embers in a hearth. It rippled and flourished on the surface before her. She dipped a hand in, feeling the resistance of an undertow. Warily she entered the light until she brushed up against the side of the oubliette. She had reached a boundary, one with a ragged hole beneath the surface of the lake. The water that flowed here was clearer, translucent, unfouled. The stonework was rough, but an inspection below the waterline proved what she'd dared not hope for.

She shook with the knowledge of what would come next. This underwater tunnel would lead her out of this tumbledown Tartarus and deliver her into freedom, or she'd drown, frozen and alone. She didn't have long, already chilled to the marrow of her bones. Down to one knee, feeling the waters lap against her torso, swallowing her limbs. Shoulders next, a sob escaping as she lowered herself.

No time for that now. There will be time for weeping when I get free.

This sterner voice pushed her beneath the water, sucking in a breath before she went. Her eyes snapped shut, reluctant to be parted from the purple glow that beckoned her escape. The undertow pressed against her. She ignored it. Struggling on, half crawling, half swimming, feeling the rough caress of masonry on her scalp beneath the water. She tried to stand, but stone prevented a return to the surface and to much-needed air.

Lungs protested, crawling panic engulfed, her fingers were numb. Legs worked mechanically, mindlessly, pushing her on, the stoppered jug a relic in her hand. The blanket now a hindrance in the chill depths.

Surely I must be close. How thick can the walls be?

The urge to breathe was now a compulsion, an imperative difficult to ignore. Her legs had weakened. Soon they would fail her and she'd be trapped in this watery nether, or else the current would drag her drowned corpse back to the oubliette.

The Ravenscourt. I will get back there. I must get back there.

Her legs kicked and thrust against the mud, her free hand clawing above her, searching for the way out. Numb fingertips met chilly air and she surged forward. The surface parted, releasing her to the air above. Water streamed down her body. She gasped down heaving lungfuls of air, coughing and hacking at the foulness that lingered in her ruined mouth. Water from the jug rinsed out the worst of it, but she feared a further erosion of memory and waited. No noticeable change occurred, but how to tell the loss of something as subtle as memory? She clambered from the sink hole and took a moment to regain her breath.

What is this place? One long forgotten or one never known?

The low-ceilinged chamber thrummed with a basso frequency that moved the hollow place beneath her ribs. The amethyst glow was all around her, streaming from black rectangles standing in orderly rows, ten abreast, each several feet tall. They were extraordinary, undoubtedly artefacts of the king, larger than anything she had seen before.

And if anyone knows about the king's machines it should be me, only I cannot remember my name.

Breath steamed on the air, and her plight was not improved by the freezing fluid that dripped from every limb, saturating her clothes. She picked her way on numb feet between the onyx blocks, each one thicker than a coffin. She examined the nearest of them. Its surface was smoked glass, almost black. The light that had guided her from the oubliette issued from a single eye near the top of each construct.

Of each sarcophagus.

Something uncoiled, sleep-slicked, unhurried. An indistinct form writhed within. Curiosity lured the Silent Queen closer until her outstretched hand pressed against the blackened glass. A constellation of symbols bloomed at her touch, yet more of the amethyst light. The basso dirge of the room shifted a fraction higher. A look over her shoulder confirmed the other sarcophagi remained silent and unlit. She kept her hand pressed to the surface, as if paralysed, then regained control, fingertips dragging across the glass, provoking yet more of the amethyst symbols to appear. More motion behind the opacity. The glint of an eye, the faintest outline of a face, a muzzle. More lights, pulsing in sequence. What witchery was this?

It's ever the province of the ignorant to mistake technology for sorcery.

And she was ignorant, or failing to remember at least. Her every sense cried out with the wrongness of this. No good would come of being here when the dancing lights reached their coda. She grasped her stoppered jug tighter, hurrying to the wall, hoping for a way to escape her stumbling mistake. The sound of the sarcophagus changed further, in discord with the basso thrum that still permeated the chamber. She was desperate to be away from the dire noise and the event it surely heralded.

There must be a hundred sarcophagi, a hundred slumbering horrors in the darkness.

She hurried on, one hand brushing the surface of the wall until she reached the corner of the room. Her numb feet turned, awkward and unresponsive. The noise in the chamber had become the frequency of her fear, the meagre harmony matching her dread.

Onward, stumbling through the gloom, clutching the clay jug. She couldn't begin to imagine what would emerge from the sarcophagus, only that she had no wish to be near it. Lucien had intimated that the king was an unholy creation; it stood to reason that he would create others in his image. Wasn't she one of the king's own experiments, evidence of his playing god?

Long moments stretched away in the darkness as she felt her way around the chamber, never straying from the walls. Her patience was rewarded when a gap appeared, the edges describing a circle, a tunnel. Her gasp of hope broke the dirge. Tentative steps, a shaking hand held out, testing the way ahead as frantic eyes failed to penetrate the darkness. Agonising footstep followed agonising footstep. The more she withdrew from the basso thrum the less frayed her nerves became. The more distance she put between herself and the disturbed sarcophagus the safer she felt.

How long she walked she couldn't tell, only that her legs were leaden with weariness. Her arm ached from being held out like an antenna. Then her fingers met resistance so suddenly she flinched and hissed. She reached out again, fingers tracing the contours of wood, not stone. The darkness was absolute without the witch light of the king's machines. Impenetrable black pressed in on all sides, wrapping every limb, swathing her in unseeing. Her filthy fingers sought a handle, a keyhole, a latch or crossbar that would free her, yet the search yielded nothing and a breathless panic clutched at her chest.

The Silent Queen slumped to her knees in the darkness, dragging her fingers over the wood's rough texture, then lower until they met water, the timber a rotten ragged pulp.

She slammed her foot into the sodden wood, lashing out again and again with a single-minded intensity, heedless of splinters. A sliver of light speared the darkness. The shock of it made her gasp, forced her eyes shut.

When was the last time I saw anything other than lantern light?

She resumed kicking at the wood until she had made a sizeable hole. The sun did not bring warmth as she had hoped. She shivered and clutched at the blanket about her shoulders, then slithered through the wreckage of the wood, gaining her feet and standing with care.

She was outside.

The sky was a pale grey leached of all cheer. Snow descended, lazy and slow. She stood in the shadow of the outlet of a sewer she'd not known existed, one boarded up and long forgotten. The wind stirred and brought with it the familiar smells of hay and horse, leather and dung, the crispness of newly fallen snow. The Silent Queen headed toward some stables with nothing more than warmth in mind. She turned a corner, tracing her fingers over exposed beams, glad to be in the presence of plaster and thatch. Her time amid the stone and decay of Demesne was at an end.

The yard was small. A blocky stone building on one side, stables on another, a well in one corner. Townhouses made up the other sides. The Silent Queen crept forward on numb feet to lean heavily on the well, exhausted and shivering. She would not last long unless she found a welcoming hearth and a change of clothes.

'Revenant!' The word came from behind her. She turned to protest, shivering fitfully, her shoulders home to a smattering of snowflakes.

Three women were staring at her from wide eyes above their veils. The nearest of them stood in the yard and had mismatched eyes of blue and green. Two more sheltered beneath the arched doorway of the stone building. Pale blue cords encircled their waists, hair concealed by a scarf in the same colour. Their robes were unbleached wool, worn beneath scapulars of pure white. Sisters of Santa Maria.

A chapel, this is the chapel.

The Silent Queen looked down at herself, shivering and wet, smeared with foulness, rank with the waters of the oubliette. Small wonder they thought her risen from the grave. Not so very far from the truth. She set the clay jug down and tried to sketch out words on the air with her fingers, but the symbols would not come. She lurched forward a step, frustration emerging as a hiss. As one the sisters drew knives from their sleeves

22

and settled into a fighting stance, blades held high, free hands ready to ward off an attack.

Much has changed in my absence.

The Silent Queen held out placating hands and took a step back. The sisters matched her withdrawal, a snow-dusted vignette of four women in white. Minutes passed, and the Silent Queen thought she would surely die of cold if nothing meaningful happened soon.

'She's not a revenant, she's a beggar.' The voice came from a narrow archway. 'Look at the state of her. She's practically dead on her feet.' The figure who entered was petite, her face lined with grief. She wore no veil, but her elaborate garments paid lip service to the robes worn by the sisters. Her wrist and fingers were entwined with rosewood beads, while her other hand held a long knife. Eyes that had once brimmed with kindness regarded her, severe and curious. The Silent Queen experienced another lurching moment of recognition.

Marchesa Medea Contadino.

4

The Edict

Medea's expulsion from the Ravenscourt had been the highlight of the session. The rest of the afternoon was consumed by the minor houses. The nobles wrangled for additional privileges, discounted services, improvements in living conditions and so on. They pressed the Silent Queen for every asset except the thing they desired most, the one thing Demesne lacked: money.

Eris, who had been close to starvation before her current guise as impostor, found the whole business disgusting. Two figures entered the Ravenscourt as she clenched her fists with impatience. She shifted on the uncomfortable throne, eyes narrowing with interest. Two Myrmidons. They all looked the same of course, the helms hiding the faces beneath, the narrow slit obscuring even the colour of their eyes. And yet a groove scratched into the breastplate of the Myrmidon on the left caught Eris's attention. Not just any Myrmidons but an altogether rarer breed, two female Myrmidons. Eris gestured with the blade of one hand, two strokes across her throat. The session was at an end.

The Domina communicated this to the nobles, stammering twice before making her intent clear. The silver staff slammed against the dais three times, failing to silence the mumbled complaints of the houses.

'Such a short attention span,' called Duchess Prospero. 'Do you tire of us so easily, Lady Diaspora?'

Eris signed, Simonetti interrupting her before the Domina could translate.

'Apologies, Duchess,' said the Domina. 'A matter of security has taken priority.'

The duchess stifled an incredulous smile. 'An apology? From you? The matter must be grave indeed.'

'I think we have covered sufficient ground today,' said the archivist.

'You call this sufficient? You're as foolish as you are lazy.'

The archivist flashed an anxious smile.

Duchess Prospero shook her head before resuming her usual expression, her face a mask of disappointment, then swept from the room, her page almost running to keep up with her. Eris noticed the boy grimace, his gait uneven. Another damaged child sworn to serve the houses.

The nobles continued to file out of the Ravenscourt, needling competitors with poisonous glances or daring to sneer at the Silent Queen herself. Eris met each gaze with a look of utter contempt, yet it was mild compared to the stare she turned on the Domina. The steward didn't notice, sharing a few private words with Viscount Datini. The old man gave a cheerful grunt, satisfied by some concession, no doubt. The Domina nodded, gesturing toward the doors of the Ravenscourt. Eris grasped at the sword hilts protruding from the armrests of the throne as she watched him leave, wondering what business the viscount was about. The doors of the Ravenscourt edged closed as the viscount passed beneath the arch, followed by Simonetti.

'Report,' said the Domina to the two Myrmidons once they were alone. She cradled the silver staff in both hands. Eris noticed her knuckles were white. Understandable given the ramifications of what would come next. As one, the female Myrmidons dropped to their knees.

'My lady, Domina. We have serious news. We noticed a change in the captive this morning. We took it upon ourselves to check on her an hour ago.'

'We fear she may be lost in the furthest reaches of the oubliette,' said the second Myrmidon in a quieter voice.

'Are you sure?' asked the Domina.

'We detailed another eight Myrmidons to help us. We found nothing, not even a trace of her.'

'She's not in the oubliette,' said Eris with certainty.

The Domina stepped up onto the dais, jaw clenched. 'You're supposed to be mute.' The words came out as a furious hiss.

Eris had found the act of speaking in front of the Myrmidons an amusing act of rebellion at first. Now she spoke purely to give herself some respite from the silent language.

The Domina addressed the still-kneeling Myrmidons. 'If ten Myrmidons were not sufficient then take twenty.'

'She's not in the oubliette,' said Eris. 'Are you deaf or merely stupid?'

'There's no way out of that place without help.' The Domina's words sounded hollow. 'I was down there myself this morning. She is lost or drowned.' Yet none of them really believed their captive remained in the oubliette.

'We will take lanterns and conduct an extensive search,' said the Myrmidon with the scratched armour.

Eris rose from the throne, then lunged forward and pushed the Domina from the dais with both hands. The Domina stumbled into the kneeling Myrmidons, a sprawl of crimson robes and dark brown armour. The staff hit the floor at the same moment she fell to her knees.

'I told you this would happen.' The words that fell from Eris's lips were like thunder. 'If you weren't drunk on *tinctura* and regret you might be half useful.'

The Domina regained her footing, drawing the staff across her body to defend herself.

'You –' Eris pointed at the steward '– are going to the oubliette with these two.'

'You're out of your mind.' The Domina blanched.

'You'll stay there until she's found. I don't care if it takes you the next ten years. Find her and kill her.'

'Get the assassin.'

The words had not issued from either of the women or any of the Myrmidons present. Each syllable, from beyond the bronze leaves and black curtain on the gallery above, was an unsettling drone that silenced everyone. Eris looked down at her feet, feeling the familiar stab of old shame.

'You banished him, my lord,' said the Domina.

'Get the assassin,' the voice repeated.

'I'm sure there is another way, my lord,' said Eris.

'This is not a request,' droned the voice; 'this is an edict. Persuade the assassin to hunt and kill for us again.'

Eris gestured to the still-kneeling female Myrmidons. 'The Domina needs an escort into town.'

The steward sneered but did not contradict her dismissal.

'You will both seek him out,' said the voice behind the curtain.

Eris stepped down from the dais and bent until her mouth was just a handspan away from the Domina's face.

'I'm going to make you suffer for this,' she whispered.

'And how will that be different to any other day?' The Domina gave Eris a bitter smile before turning away.

The doors to the Ravenscourt inched apart, revealing Simonetti and Dottore Allattamento. The men stood apart, wary and anxious, each lost to his own concerns. The *dottore* wrung his hands, while Simonetti polished his optics, shoulders hunched with tension beneath antiquated robes.

'We, ah ... Well, I mean ...'

While I am still young, Simonetti, signed Eris, before folding her arms.

'I heard voices and thought I might be needed,' said the archivist, placing his optics back on his nose and blinking. 'I hoped to be of some assistance.'

Eris almost shouted at the man to drag his rake-thin carcass back to his beloved library, remembering herself at the last second. She was the Silent Queen, the luxury of speaking denied to her. The doors to the Ravenscourt were no longer sealed. She had a role to play, no matter how much she loathed it.

'Thank you, Viscount Simonetti,' said the Domina. 'Perhaps you could dispatch a messenger to the stables to ask them to prepare two horses.'

Eris hissed, one of the few sounds she was allowed to make as the Silent Queen. The Domina turned to her.

'Yes, my lady?' None could miss the note of impatience in the Domina's voice. Eris flicked out some orders.

'Dottore.' the Domina smiled politely. 'Please go to House Fontein and ask for eight Myrmidons to await us in the Contadino courtyard.'

The *dottore* turned a sour look on Eris, unimpressed with being treated like a common messenger. Eris returned the look with an inclination of her head, a silent challenge. To refuse the queen would be a gross breach of etiquette.

'It will be as you ask,' said the *dottore*.

'Thank you,' said the Domina, flashing a look of warning at Eris. Allattamento turned on his heel and marched into the lingering gloom of Demesne, pausing only to liberate a lantern from a sconce before resuming the errand.

'My lady, is there any other way I may be of assistance?' rumbled Simonetti.

'Horses will be fine.'

'As you wish, Domina.' The archivist departed, leaving Eris with the Domina and the two Myrmidons.

I do not trust either of them. Perhaps they were listening at the door?

The Domina shook her head and rested the staff in the crook of her elbow before signing.

If you stopped speaking in public, as I keep asking, we wouldn't have this problem.

Eris rolled her eyes and gave a sigh of frustration.

I will post Myrmidons inside and outside in future, added the Domina.

It is not the future I worry about, signed Eris, her eyes searching the corridors for imagined eavesdroppers. *It is what they have already heard. And who they might be working for.*

'I hardly think Simonetti a dangerous conspirator,' said the Domina, dropping the silent language now the two men were out of earshot. 'And Dottore Allattamento's ambitions only extend as far as his own safety and comfort. You wouldn't remember, but the Allattamentos are famously self-serving. Opportunistic at best, mercenary at worst.'

Eris listened to the woman's counsel. The power of the Myrmidon throne was impressive, but there was no power quite like knowledge and experience. The Domina possessed an abundance of both.

*

They rode out into the late afternoon. Night darkened the skies all too soon at this time of year. Snow fluttered on the breeze, heavy cloud obscuring the stars. These were the very streets that had seen riots, violent opposition to the formation of the Myrmidons; now they were empty. The horses' hooves were muted by the snowfall, trampling the white to black and brown on cobbles that had run red with the blood of *cittadini*.

Do you think they distrust me? signed Eris, dropping her reins.

'The *cittadini*?' The Domina's reply was laced with boredom.

The Myrmidons.

'Why do you ask?'

Because I am not one of them.

'I doubt they care.' The Domina pouted. 'You are the voice of Erebus in Landfall. That should be enough. Perhaps you should ask them if it worries you.'

Eris regarded the eight soldiers who marched ahead, identical in their dark brown armour, curving helms with the hint of mandibles in their design. Once they had merely boasted breastplates, now their forearms were clad in vambraces, while spaulders of hinged chevrons covered their shoulders, all paid for by the taxes of the few *cittadini* who remained.

Do you wonder if they resent us for being human, for wielding power?

'The formation of the Myrmidons would never have occurred without us.' The Domina shrugged. Eris remembered the day well, sick with nerves and feeling unprepared for the act of impersonation. Her first time in the Ravenscourt had been a jarring, stilted affair. She endured the tension of the *nobili*, the many clamouring voices, the guarded glances and knowing looks, all to keep her brother safe, so she told herself. The familiar pain of Sabatino's passing rose in her chest, but she had no time for mourning now.

'Don't forget that you were instrumental in their formation.' The Domina sounded bored, the look in her eye glazed. 'Legitimising them as a people of Landfall was your first act as impostor.'

Eris regarded their escort, no more than detritus from the many experiments of the king. His lust to create strange

29

cross-breeds had resulted in the Orfani, anything but perfect specimens. And for every Orfano there had been a glut of underkin, twisted, misshapen creatures.

'You're not so very different to the underkin. They used to live in squalor, on the edge of starvation. Not so very different to the *cittadini*, especially those in the countryside.'

Being underkin is hardly the same as being an impoverished farmer.

'True. Many underkin made their home in the oubliette itself.'

And what happens when they decide they have no further use for us?

'You were threatening to have me thrown in the oubliette just an hour ago,' said the Domina with narrowed eyes. 'Forgive me if I'm not unduly concerned with your safety.'

The *taverna* was one of only three that remained open in Santa Maria. It smelled worse than it looked – stale beer, unwashed bodies and the tang of night soil. Woodsmoke covered the worst of it. A dozen patrons looked up from their drinks, surprised and afraid in equal measure. The Myrmidons were reviled; the wounds of the riots had healed but the memories of those times still festered. Two of the soldiers stood by the door; another positioned himself by the bar. Eris strode into the room and gestured for the Domina to interrogate the owner. A tall woman, she towered over the man, her staff and hat adding to her presence in the low-ceilinged room.

'We're looking for a man with a scar through his left eye. He wears a veil and is mute. Do you know of whom I speak?'

The owner had broad shoulders and a bull neck, long hair tied back. He bore scars of his own, not limited to the backs of his arms and hands. He'd likely served with House Fontein. The set of his jaw and the sour cast to his eye said as much.

'I know him.'

'And he's staying here?'

'He is. And beyond strange he is too. Writes down the things he wants. Never has any guests. Never drinks wine. Never takes any whores to his room.'

'Is that really so terrible?' The Domina curled her lip.

'A lot of my patrons think him *invertito*. I had to stop them lynching him last week. They'd all had too much to drink.'

The Domina turned to stare into the patrons' faces. 'I find it strange that your obsession is with beer when what you really need is soap and water.'

They were a gaunt and ragged crew, hardship worn in the lines of their faces, eyes dulled by sin and disappointment.

'A word to the unwise,' said the Domina. 'The man who lives upstairs could kill every last one of you.'

'Is that so?' said the owner with a sneer.

'Without breaking sweat or shedding a tear.'

'So why hasn't he?' growled the owner, crossing his arms.

The Domina leaned over the bar. 'Because no one has paid him to. Yet.'

Eris followed the Domina, a low grumbling of curses following them up the stairs. She'd ordered the Myrmidons to wait outside. They'd be no use here. Each step on the staircase summoned memories she'd rather forget. It had seemed so thrilling at the time. Each day brought a new meal to savour, new jewellery to try on, a fitting for a new dress. Wine was not the only luxury she'd been drunk on. And there was the not inconsequential fact that people deferred to her. She was no longer a starved and pinched common girl with a sickly brother. The courtiers thought her the Silent Queen. It had made her heady, gilding her with a confidence she'd never known. It had seemed like the ultimate defilement to seduce the assassin on Anea's throne. He'd come to her straight from a kill, a murder to frame Lord Dino Erudito.

'Pray Fortuna smiles upon us,' muttered the Domina, one hand raised to knock on the door.

By persuading him?

'By surviving.' The Domina released an uneasy breath. 'I think it best you wait here.'

Eris withdrew to one side of the door, where shadow consumed her. The Domina knocked, the force of her hand doing more than rousing the occupant. The door swung open, revealing a cramped room, the bed made neatly despite the crudeness of the blankets. Eris followed the Domina's gaze up to where it came to rest on the assassin, feet hooked over the rafters. He pulled himself up until he was bent double, hands tucked behind his ears, grunting with the exertion. Stripped to the waist and sweating freely, his blanched skin was covered in a tracery of lines, the scars gold in the candlelight.

'We have need of you,' said the Domina, crossing the threshold.

The assassin ceased his labours, hanging inverted, the lower part of his face covered with a mask. Eris had never discovered what lay under his concealment, despite their coupling. He could have been anyone. It had not mattered; only the simple mindless lust that had overtaken her, sated on the seat of Anea's power.

The assassin shook his head, dismissing them with a wave of a scarred hand.

'But you enjoy killing,' said the Domina, 'so you'll kill for us again.'

The assassin hinged at the waist, one hand going to the rafters, the other pressed to his boot. A blur of motion, and he had flipped down from the ceiling, facing the Domina as he landed, one foot hooking behind her own. One hand clutched at her throat, forcing her off balance, while the other had summoned a knife. The promise of steel was just a finger's width away from the Domina's eyes, now wide with shock. The silver staff clattered to the floor as she held up her hands in surrender. The sound escaping her lips was not a plea but a sob. He answered the sound with one of his own, a hiss.

Eris watched them, assassin and Domina. It was no secret she loathed them both, but of the two she could less afford to lose the Domina, despite her many threats. Eris stepped into the light, meeting the assassin's gaze with reluctance. He did not release the Domina, knife resolute with the promise of death.

It is not her I need you to kill, Marchetti, she signed.

The knife edged closer to the Domina's eyes, eliciting another whimper.

Our Lord Erebus has need of you. Come, we have much to talk about.

32

5

The Herald of War

Medea Contadino had absolved the Silent Queen from being a revenant but the sisters' knives remained unsheathed, hidden beneath scapulars or concealed in voluminous sleeves. The town's streets were quieter than she remembered, if indeed she remembered correctly. They trudged through slush, flakes swirling about them, the sky overhead promising more of the same. They did not take her into the chapel, guiding her to a building she did not recognise. She blinked away tears of frustration, angry that another memory had failed to resurface. Strange that she should forget such an impressive structure.

Columns and colonnettes embellished the building, adding an air of solemnity. The stone steps to the doors were at least thirty feet wide and swept clean of snow. The doors themselves were varnished oak, with a brazier inside, lighting a vestibule. The beneficent gaze of Santa Maria watched over everything, her pale face carved from limestone. Here the saint read from a book, there she cradled an infant, another iteration took a pose of prayer. The procession of women entered the nave, where stained-glass windows with lozenges of red cast bloody light through the interior. Row upon row of dark wood pews stood in orderly lines.

The Silent Queen was led to a bathhouse by the sister's leader.

'I'm Disciple Agostina.' The first hints of crow's feet framed her eyes above her veil, one an icy blue, a match for the head-scarf, scapular and slender cord that encircled her waist. The other eye glinted an earthy green, complimenting her olive skin. 'Canoness Contadino will see you as soon as you're presentable.'

There was an awkward pause. Clouds of steam clung to the columns, and braziers hissed and popped. Warmth crept back into the Silent Queen's fingers; her hunched shoulders relaxed.

'I hope you have more to say to her than you do to me.'

The Silent Queen jabbed a finger toward her mouth.

'You're mute?'

She nodded in response.

'Oh, I'm sorry. I . . .' Disciple Agostina turned away and gestured with an open palm. 'There are clean vestments there. Leave your dirty clothes in the basket. Do you want me to keep that for you?' She pointed at the jug.

The Silent Queen shook her head and clutched her clay vessel tighter.

'As you wish. I'll be waiting outside when you're finished. Would you like a fresh veil?'

Another nod, more emphatic than the last.

Disciple Agostina retired behind the door, but not before glancing back, curiosity in her blue and green eyes. The Silent Queen set down the clay jug and looked about the candlelit chamber, watching steam drift and linger on the air. She disrobed in seconds, shedding the rags of her captivity with fervent need. She removed her veil last but hesitated before discarding it. She scrubbed at the worst of the filth using a coarse wool cloth, rinsing and wringing out the grime in a bucket of tepid water. Fingers scoured and set to scrubbing, the damp cloth excoriating the filth that clogged her pores. Sensation flooded back into her limbs, winter's cold replaced by the warmth of the chamber.

Twice she paused, almost crying with relief. She was free, warm. Better to be in the care of the knife-wielding Sisters than guarded by Myrmidons.

With the worst of the grime gone, the Silent Queen eased her way into a bath, inch by inch. Despite the warm water she feared she might never be clean again, the taint of the oubliette ingrained for all time. The foulness could be remedied, she decided, but her mind would require more than steam and hot water to be cleansed. She feared for the memories that might never return, and not knowing their loss.

The Silent Queen slipped beneath the surface and closed her eyes, holding her breath for as long as she dared. Dino's face appeared, a memory of her apartment, he rumpled with sleep. There had been reptile, a drake? The name was unclear to her. Why had he slept in her armchair? Had she needed a bodyguard, a protector? Had she done something to deserve being cast into the oubliette?

The Silent Queen broke through the surface of the water, scrubbing at her skin. She worked at her flesh as if a sloughing-off might reveal secrets beneath. So intent was she that Disciple Agostina entered and found her unveiled. Each woman stared at the other, shock suspending time, the steam casting the moment in a dreamlike haze.

'Oh' was all the disciple said. The Silent Queen saw the horror in the woman's eyes and remembered why she wore a veil. She pressed her hands to her face, feeling the sharp edges of her deformity, the way her face twisted and warped. No lips to speak, or even a jaw to finish the lower reaches of her face. Mandibles grew from the soft flesh, the space beneath her nose a ragged hole. This was the source of her silence, and her difference. She remained in the water, head bowed, unwilling to meet Agostina's eyes. The sister slipped a hand beneath her sleeve, fingers curling around the hilt of a dagger, no doubt.

'You never said you were underkin.'

A shake of the head, eyes locked on the steaming water.

'You're Orfano?' The words were laced with incredulity.

A single nod, still refusing to meet Agostina's eyes.

'That's impossible. The Orfani are—'

The Silent Queen hissed, a crease of annoyance on her brow.

'You'd best dress and come with me. It's late and Canoness Contadino is waiting.'

The clothes felt strange, but she was grateful for them. Anything to ward off the chill of winter. Her headscarf was a pure white, matching the scapular, while her belt was a fine turquoise rope. The new veil was a blessed relief after witnessing the revulsion she elicited. The jug remained a reassuring weight, clutched to her torso in crossed arms. It was an ungainly talisman but

35

one she was reluctant to part with, a vessel to store her new memories, a reliquary of recall.

They moved through the church, Agostina keen to reach the canoness. Two sisters emerged from a side door, hands lingering in their sleeves, promising a sharp end should anything untoward occur. Other sisters gave furtive glances at their passing, some gesturing to each other. The Silent Queen stopped and stared with rapt attention, watching their fingers and hands speak. Another memory blossomed, this one warm with remembering. The sisters used gestures she and Dino had devised, sketched the same words, made the same symbols. She had spent long winter nights creating the silent language so she might eschew scratching out her words in books of blank parchment. A thrill of recognition surged through her. Disciple Agostina touched her lightly at the elbow, breaking the reverie.

'Canoness Contadino is waiting.'

The balcony looked out over Demesne, all massive scale and intricate detail. Difficult not to be awed by it, even in the chill darkness of a winter night. Rows of arched windows, lead lattices criss-crossing the glass, regiments of shutters, ivy tendrils beyond counting ascending the walls, buttresses holding back an impossible weight of stone.

The Silent Queen dared a glance over her shoulder. Armed sisters waited inside the church, beyond the door that led to the balcony. Agostina remained close enough to intimidate. She had no doubt the disciple would lay her throat open if she gave her cause. Canoness Contadino stood ahead of her, hands resting on the balcony parapet, regarding the sullen city, framed by two slender colonnettes that supported the sloping roof above them. Squat cherubs perched on the walls with contented stony smiles; a brazier shed orange light and meagre warmth.

'Impressive isn't it?' said the canoness without turning. 'All of those corridors and pantries and kitchens made by human hands. All the courtyards and tunnels, the storerooms and cellars. Plans were found recently that showed Demesne was meant to have an eighth floor. The king loved the number eight. They say he was obsessed with spiders. Eight legs. Do you see? Eight floors.'

The Silent Queen nodded.

'And when you turn the number eight on one side it becomes the symbol for eternity. No wonder he lived so long. Perhaps all spiders do.' The canoness retrieved a shawl of heavy wool in charcoal grey from an oak chair. 'You'd best take this. We've only just warmed you up.'

The shawl was a comforting weight on her shoulders, warm from the brazier. The canoness regarded her with an intense scrutiny, unsmiling, unspeaking. Clutching the clay jug tighter, the Silent Queen tried to remember the *Marchesa* Contadino. A moment of clarity: Medea had been a kind woman with a warm singing voice, enchanted by roses, her husband and her children. And yet the woman standing in front of her was a distinctly dangerous stranger with an unfriendly mien that threatened anger at any second.

'There aren't so many people left in Demesne now,' said Medea. 'It's a place of ghosts. Many people have found work on the estates or built cottages near the farms. The truly brave have fled further still.'

Medea's eyes were intent, as if weighing every reaction and gesture her audience might make. The Silent Queen offered nothing.

'Those who remain are jealous of the *cittadini* in the south. They want the same rights and protections Duke Marino affords his people. They can't understand why his sister has chosen such a dark path. And whispers grow, whispers of war between the siblings. They say Duke Marino wants to free the people of Demesne from this mindless tyranny. He always had a penchant for justice, that one.'

The Silent Queen set down the jug at her feet, then held up her hands and tried to make the words, her fingers trembling with the effort of it. She was suddenly aware of her fingernails, jet-black chitin, looking painted to the casual observer. Another tell of her otherness.

Why... was all she managed. She tried again. *Why are you telling me... these things?* she signed.

Medea smiled, a weight of sadness in her eyes that no simple expression of joy could remove. She took a step forward, taking the woman's hands in her own with a gentle care.

'Such clever, pretty fingers.' Her eyes lingered on the chitin nails. 'Such startling green eyes.'

The Silent Queen drew her hands away, folding fingertips into her palms to prevent further study.

'And there's the fact you hold yourself so well. No beggar or fallen woman ever had such an imperious pose. You move with the assurance of one trained by Mistress Corvo, and retain the bearing that comes from standing before a *maestro di spada*.' Medea cast an appraising eye over her from head to toe. 'Seeing you, I'd swear on the lives of my children that the girl on the liar's throne isn't Aranea Oscuro Diaspora after all.'

The Silent Queen staggered as if struck. Agostina dragged the chair closer and the Silent Queen sank into it willingly, tears hot at the corners of her eyes. She was bent double with the shock of hearing her name, lost to her all this time. Medea dropped to her knees and cradled the woman's head.

'Tell me,' she whispered. The Silent Queen raised her eyes and took a shuddering breath.

Oubliette. The word was almost painful to make, her fingers hesitating with the pain of its association. *I do not know who I am. My memories . . .* The act of making the words revealed the awful truth of it. *I do not know who I am.*

'How long were you down there?' asked Medea in a velvet tone.

I cannot remember. Say my name again, please?

'Aranea Oscuro Diaspora,' said Medea, tears of compassion bright in her eyes. 'We called you Anea; you always hated your full name.'

This much was truth. Aranea, named by the king after his love of spiders in all their forms. Another cruel reminder of being different, of being Orfano.

'You poor, poor child,' said Medea, taking Anea's hands in her own, the warmth a comfort. Snow began to fall, much like Anea's tears.

'This secret will stay between the three of us,' said Medea.

38

'No one has to know who you are. You're simply another novice found on the street.'

I feel as if I have ceased to exist. Surely I have missed so much.

Medea stood, gazing at Demesne as if in a trance, as if the recent past were written upon its walls. When she turned to Anea her expression was downcast, her eyes unfocused. 'House Fontein is no more; the guards have all left, replaced by the Queen's – sorry, replaced by the impostor's – Myrmidons. Russo serves the impostor still.'

Russo, the Domina.

The Domina came to me in the oubliette. Confessed her betrayal.

'Then we'll execute her for her treachery,' said Medea with no trace of anger, just a cold intent. Anea regarded the woman anew. The Medea she had known had always had the kindest of hearts, the most diplomatic of souls. She had never made an ally of death.

Why are you a canoness? Why have you abandoned House Contadino?

'Abandoned?' Medea's face paled. 'You really don't remember?'

I do not remember, or I do not know. Is there a difference? The words came to mind more quickly now.

'There is an old custom. Widows are permitted to withdraw to a monastic life.'

Widow?

'They killed him.' Medea lifted her chin, clenched her jaw a moment then continued. 'Lured him to his death. My precious Emilio. I waited years for him, wanted him for more nights than I can recall.' Medea stood, eyes unfocused, as if seeing through time, back to a day when she had lost her love. 'That *sciattona* Salvaza took him from me. She always wanted him. She couldn't stand it that he married me. In the end she made sure no one could have him. Emilio was lured out into the woods with the promise of negotiations, but it was an ambush. Massimo too, and more besides.'

Salvaza would never do such a thing. Open war between the houses?

'Salvaza Prospero did exactly that.' Medea turned her back

39

on Anea, resuming her place at the parapet. 'I ordered Dino to assassinate her, but he lacked the stomach for it.'

Where is Dino now?

'They say he tried to defeat a dozen Myrmidons single-handed.' Medea looked down at the quiet town and sighed. 'All so Stephania Prospero could escape.'

Anea could think of nothing; her mind simply refused to work, refused to accept what she was hearing. The wind gusted harder, bringing yet more flakes of stark white. She trembled and shook, clutching hands across her stomach.

Medea turned back and looked down at the flagstones of the balcony.

'I'm sorry.'

Is anyone left? Anyone that I cared about?

Medea shook her head. 'The coup was thorough. I only survived because I was mad with grief.' Medea wrung her hands. 'No one expected me to recover.'

And Demesne?

'I don't know who this impostor is, but she's set herself against Lucien. The Silent Queen versus Duke Marino. This isn't a war this island can afford, not in lives or coin.'

Hoofbeats on cobbles interrupted Medea's musing. Anea roused herself from the chair, drawing alongside her at the parapet. Agostina joined them.

'Who rides so late at night?' said the disciple.

The rider sat atop a coal-black steed wearing a mottled cloak in a matching hue. A single raven perched on his shoulder, favouring the few souls who traversed the winter streets with a haughty stare. The rider was mud-flecked from the road; snow sat in the folds of his cloak. A steely glint of armour reflected from the weak lantern light. The horse was unhurried, passing at a walk. Anea was unable to take her eyes from the rider as he crossed the piazza, a sword much larger than anything she had seen before slung across his back.

'This will end badly,' said Agostina in a quiet voice, 'May the Saint protect us.' She kissed her fingertips and pressed them to her forehead.

Three stout men emerged from an alley bearing cudgels,

making an obstacle of themselves. The raven called out in a mocking tone.

'House Del Toro,' explained Medea. 'Angry *cittadini* with a rightful axe to grind. They'll have something to say if the rider is part of the impostor's cabal.'

There was a moment of calm in the street, the rider slowing his mount to standing. The men of House Del Toro looked up to the hooded rider; some words passed between the two sides before the bravos departed without recourse to insult or challenge. The rider remained motionless while the raven fussed at the feathers of one wing.

'Even the thugs of House Del Toro are cowed by him,' said Agostina. The rider continued on his way, wending through the streets of the town on his black mount.

He is a herald of war. Anea's hand flickered faster now. *Any chance we had of stopping this conflict died the moment he arrived.*

'I hope you're wrong,' breathed Medea.

I am not. He brings only death.

6

Herald in Black

The Feast of Midwinter was held in the great hall of House Fontein. The floor tiles were a polished slate grey, devoid of artistry and ornamentation. The portraits that hung on the walls showed imperious grim-faced antecedents, variously dripping medals or scorn. The Fontein bloodline had been rich in aquiline noses, high foreheads, deep-set eyes and furrowed brows. The women had been drawn from minor houses to avoid the ghastly consequences of inbreeding.

Why we still call this place House Fontein escapes me, signed Eris, *now that the bloodline is ended*.

'Perhaps,' said the Domina.

Was smiling outlawed? Eris frowned at the portraits.

'There was never much to smile about in House Fontein. They grew more sour with each generation. Perhaps it was that sourness which made the last duchess barren.'

Eris looked over the armada of tables in the great hall, all laden with cutlery and wine glasses. Candelabra stood at intervals like sails of wax and candlelight.

The next Feast of Midwinter will be held in House Erudito.

The Domina raised her eyebrows and pouted but said nothing.

Flags from regiments that had not survived the Verde Guerra loomed in the corners of the great hall. Each was a stark reminder of men lost to madness. The windows were concealed behind vast drapes of scarlet and black, while a fire crackled in the hearth, meagre consolation for the winter chill. A candelabrum hued with verdigris, medals from the war and

42

a ceremonial blade crowded the mantelpiece. Braziers had been dragged in, loaded with coals lest the cold sap the joy from the revellers.

Why not take down these ugly paintings and decorate the entire hall anew?

A slow smile quirked the Domina's lips. 'Because then people would forget House Fontein and its wayward duke.' The Domina stopped before a portrait of a white-haired man staring angrily from the oils. 'They'd forget his constant opposition to the throne.' *And his bitch of a wife*, she added in the silent language.

Is it true he was assassinated? asked Eris. The Domina broke her scrutiny of the portrait, casting a look over her shoulder as the first guests arrived.

'Some say he died abed with a courtesan.'

And yet you accused Lord Dino Erudito of his assassination.

The steward gave a brittle smile and took her seat at the top table. Eris took the seat beside her. 'The great hall of House Fontein remains as it is to serve as a reminder. We want the houses minor and major alike to remember how he opposed the throne. And how he met his end.'

You really think the death of one duke sends a message?

'How many assassination attempts have you survived?'

Eris nodded. Not even the most surly bravo would dare raise a blade to her. Anea had not enjoyed such security during her rule.

Why was he killed?

'Because he was too dangerous to live,' said the Domina in a hushed voice, leaning close.

And the bloodline is truly ended?

'There are rumours,' said the Domina, 'rumours the duke sired a bastard. But I'd not worry yourself with the fate of an illegitimate son. What do you imagine he'd do? Walk in here with a sword and demand vengeance?'

Not in single combat, but through political means. Is that not the way of Landfall?

The Domina paused. 'Perhaps it was once. Now we have the Myrmidons.'

43

'Is everything to your satisfaction, my lady?' Eris looked into the kindly eyes of Viscountess Datini. House Datini had become the de facto caretakers of House Fontein since the disappearance of the duchess.

'You are to be commended, Viscountess,' said the Domina. 'You set a fine table. I'm sure the kitchens have surpassed themselves.'

The eyes of the viscountess lingered on the Domina's lips. Eris supposed the matriarch's hearing was in decline.

'You are too kind, Domina.' The old woman sighed, eyes blinking. 'But I am afraid this is the final feast I will oversee.'

'Oh?'

'I am retiring from life in Demesne. The pace is too fast for such a one as I.'

'It pains me to hear that,' replied the Domina. The viscountess smiled and hobbled away, each step weighted with the six decades she had endured. Time had not been kind.

Will she return to her estate in the north? signed Eris.

'Pardon?' The Domina flushed a moment. 'Yes. Yes, I would expect so.' A servant stepped between them and poured wine for the Domina, leaving the Silent Queen's glass unfilled. This was the part of the deception that Eris despised the most. The Silent Queen had never taken food or drink in public on account of her disfigurement. When required to attend formal dinners Anea participated in conversation, never in the meal itself.

The remaining guests took their seats, smiling and laughing, many far gone with drink. They gossiped and sniped, breaking bread and secrets alike. Servants fussed and pulled chairs or replaced dropped cutlery. Few failed to notice Viscount Datini, who dined with Dottore Allattamento. Viscountess Datini left the great hall without sparing her estranged husband a glance, much less a greeting.

Things are serious between the Datini.

'Political marriages,' said the Domina as if this were explanation enough.

Has there been any word from Marchetti? It's been a full day now — she could be anywhere.

44

'Don't speak of that here,' said the Domina, eyes fixed on the plate in front of her.

The great hall of House Fontein became quiet, conversations dying on the lips of the revellers. Cutlery clattered on plates and all heads turned to the doors. Eris looked across the many tables to see a messenger present himself like a shade risen from nightmare. Mud caked his boots and clogged their buckles. Snow lay in the deep creases of his heavy riding cloak, black and olive green, spattered with mud. The hilt of a great sword was visible over his left shoulder, a promise of death to all, while a raven perched on his right shoulder. The dark bird favoured the room with a baleful glare. Ravens had once been a common sight on the rooftops of Demesne, yet their numbers had dwindled following Lucien Marino's departure. Suspicious souls declared the ravens' departure an omen of Demesne's waning influence. Others said the dire birds would return in the company of Lucien himself. Eris dismissed it all as the speculation of idle fishwives. The appearance of the messenger gave her a reason to reconsider.

Which house does he belong to?

The figure pushed the cloak over his right shoulder with a hand gloved in thick leather, prompting the raven to fly up to the rafters. A copper clasp, fashioned like a cataphract drake biting its tail, adorned the messenger's breast. It was pinned to a tabard of deep brown, featuring seven dashes of turquoise like arrowheads.

'House Vedetta,' whispered the Domina. 'One of Lucien's scouts.'

Could this be the bastard son of House Fontein? signed Eris.

The Domina shook her head and opened her mouth to speak, but certainty abandoned her. 'I can't be sure.'

A dull gleam of mail was visible beneath the tabard; the face remained unseen, obscured by a hood and a painted carnival mask. A dismissive sneer had been carved on its pale lips, while the eyes and cheeks were embellished with turquoise flourishes. A single Myrmidon stepped forward to intercept the uninvited man. The Myrmidon found his sword arm pinned across his

45

body, was taken by the throat and forced headlong into the door frame with a dull clatter of armour.

'What is the meaning of this?' bellowed the Domina. Several of the guests flinched. The cloaked figure slammed the Myrmidon into the door frame once more, then let the soldier slump to the floor. 'Explain yourself.'

'I am *capo* of House Vedetta, successor to Delfino Datini, answerable to Duke Lucien Marino. I am his Herald.' The voice that emerged from behind the mask was raw and ravaged, if not by time then certainly by steel. It was a damaged thing, but not diminished in power. A scroll was produced from a leather tube, unfurled with unhurried reverence. The Herald held it aloft, the dark eyes of the sneering mask fixed upon Eris.

'Duke Lucien Marino can no longer ignore the welfare of the Santa Maria *cittadini*. As a result he proposes a vote of no confidence in Lady Aranea Oscuro Diaspora and her so-called Myrmidon throne. This is a formal declaration that Duke Marino will no longer send a tithe. The few trade agreements that still exist between our towns are at an end.'

'This is treason,' said the Domina. She slammed a hand down on the table, and all eyes in the hall turned to her. 'Duke Marino does not decide how Demesne is run, nor does he dictate terms to Lady Diaspora. I suggest you ride back to—'

The raven heckled and took to wing, closing on the Domina. She cowered back, and the dark bird circled the hall before perching in the rafters once more.

'And I suggest you hold your tongue, Domina,' said the Herald. 'There is more.'

Eris could think of no response, stunned by the palpable aura of violence that emanated from the rider in black as he rolled the parchment and concealed it once more. The sneering mask returned its dark gaze to the top table.

'Duke Marino will only negotiate when two criminals are turned over to his custody.' The Herald took a step forward, causing a handful of diners to shrink back. 'You will surrender the individuals known as Erebus and Marchetti.'

As if summoned, the assassin peeled himself free from a

shadowed corner, approaching the Herald. The guests craned their necks as Marchetti's sword slithered from its scabbard.

Eris began to sign a reply to the demands, but it was Simonetti, seated at the far end of the hall, who spoke first. The archivist stood, looming over assassin and Herald alike.

'No blood shall be spilled at the Feast of Midwinter,' he said holding out calming hands. Marchetti turned to Eris, who shook her head. The assassin stepped back, sheathing his sword with a flourish before folding his arms with an air of petulance. 'And your timing leaves a lot to be desired,' said the archivist. 'We've barely begun our starters.'

'Viscount Simonetti,' said the Domina, 'perhaps you could limit you attention to the library, as is your remit.' Eris grabbed her steward's sleeve then signed, her fingers quick. The Domina had no choice but to translate.

'Tell Lucien Marino he forgets himself. It was I, Lady Aranea Oscuro Diaspora, who ennobled him as duke. The hand that creates can also destroy. There will be no end to his tithe or to our trade agreements. As for his demands, inform him there is no such person as Erebus. While Marchetti is a protector of the Myrmidon throne. I will not simply accede to these demands—'

'Then there will be war,' said the Herald. 'And all of your feasts, your pretty gowns and your great halls will be turned to ash.'

Simonetti was on his feet again before Eris had formed a reply. 'Please,' said the archivist. 'Landfall is not such a large island that we can easily accommodate such violence. Perhaps an arrangement can be made.'

'This is the arrangement,' said the Herald, handing the scroll to the archivist.

'Well, that is, ah, unfortunate.'

'I suggest you commission your headstones now,' said the Herald, addressing the guests. 'Duke Marino will not spare anyone aligned with a traitor queen.'

'Ruggeri?' Simonetti's voice was a whisper. 'Is that you behind the mask?'

The Herald did not reply, face turned toward the top table in silent challenge.

The shock that had bound Eris to inaction fled in that moment. A terrible rage tempered by frustration overtook her. If only she could speak. Her fingers began slashing out symbols on the air. The Domina's eyes widened as she watched Eris sign.

Tell Lucien he is welcome. Let him bring his inbred rabble of fishermen, let him bring his invertito *and his intellectuals to Demesne. Tell him I await his arrival keenly. Tell him his reward will be a quick death on the blades of my Myrmidons.*

The Domina turned to the Herald and opened her mouth to speak.

'No need,' grated the voice from beneath the hood. 'I understand.'

Marchetti slunk forward, slipping behind the cloaked Herald with a ready dagger. The knife hand drew back for the fatal thrust but the raven descended from the rafters, gliding down on silent wings. Talons snagged in the veil, tearing it free. Marchetti turned away, clamping hands to his mouth, dropping the dagger as he did so. The Herald paid the commotion no mind.

'I will convey your words, my lady.' The Herald withdrew, pausing to glance at the assassin before marching away.

'War? You're going to lead us to war with Duke Lucien now?' said Duchess Prospero, dangerously close to shouting. They had departed the feast to meet in an abandoned practice chamber of House Fontein. Simonetti had duly followed them, as had Viscount Datini and Dottore Allattamento. Duchess Prospero had escorted Maestro Fidelio, who did his best to remain invisible. The houses minor were either too stupid or too afraid to make an appearance, for which Eris was grateful. Marchetti slunk in at the back of the room having reattached his veil.

No one arrives unbidden at my Feast of Midwinter and dictates terms. I am the Silent Queen. I dictate the terms. I rule Landfall in case any of you had forgotten.

The Domina repeated the words more from habit than need. It was suspected that all present understood the silent language, although Duchess Prospero made a show of feigning ignorance.

'Dictating terms?' replied Duchess Prospero. 'You just threatened to kill him.'

'No more than he deserves,' added Viscount Datini.

I should have a capo *I can consult.*

'I, ah, believe the position has remained empty since Dino Erudito killed the previous *capo*, my lady,' said Simonetti.

How convenient.

The Domina failed to translate these last words, one hand pressed to her mouth, face pale. The anger drained out of Duchess Prospero. It was no secret the *capo* had been her consort; mention of his death still had the power to silence her. The chamber lapsed into a wordless malaise.

Lucien would not dare bring war to Demesne. Too many people he cares for live here.

'It is because he cares that he's willing to make war,' said the *dottore*, earning him a sour look from Eris.

'There is the simple issue of numbers, my lady,' rumbled Viscount Datini. 'An army needs to outnumber its opponents by three to one for unquestionable victory.'

'Precisely,' said the *dottore*, 'and Lucien would need more again to besiege Demesne.'

'I estimate Duke Marino can equal the number of Myrmidons serving in Demesne,' said Viscount Datini. He exchanged a look with the Domina. 'None of the House Vedetta scouts are as well equipped as the Myrmidons.'

Do not call him Duke, signed Eris. *He is not a duke, he is a traitor.*

'Yes, well, Lucien couldn't begin a campaign until spring at the earliest,' said Simonetti, 'We have months to, ah, prepare, my lady.'

'So it's war then?' said Duchess Prospero. 'No discussion, no negotiation, just war?'

Sometimes the correct answer is the most obvious. The Domina resumed translating.

'And you just happen to have conveniently created this army of underkin,' replied the duchess.

'We call them Myrmidons,' replied the Domina.

Eris pointed one finger at Marchetti, who until that point had been slumped against the wall, arms folded.

Escort me back to my room. I tire of this pointless debate.

Eris threw the door to her apartment wide open, storming into the sitting room to stand alone at the window. The stars looked down from their places, glittering like frost. Below, the town was dark, the few lights showed only unkempt streets and abandoned wagons waiting for horses that would never come. She looked at the dark fields and woodland beyond the town, the stark light of the moon edging them in silver.

Marchetti was a silhouette in the doorway. The assassin entered, hood pushed back, single eye a dark shadow above the veil. Her chamber was bathed in cool light, a conceit of blue glass lanterns hanging from the ceiling. Eris watched Marchetti cross the threshold in the reflection of the window; she'd not the stomach to turn and face him. Just having him so close was torment enough. His footsteps made no sound. For a hopeful second she thought he would retire, but the assassin closed the door, crossing the room until he stood beside her. She watched his fingers in the reflection, a dreamlike lull settling in about her eyes and shoulders, pressing against her temples, making her yearn for sleep.

We have not had a chance to speak since you banished me. I sent letters. You declined to reply.

Eris shook her head. 'I never banished you. I had no say in that decision.' She sighed. 'I asked for you be treated here, to recover from your wounds, but...' Her gaze strayed to his ruined eye. Marchetti looked away.

And the letters?

A hesitation. 'I never received them.'

A creasing of the assassin's brow confirmed his disbelief. *So that night in the Ravenscourt? It meant nothing to you?*

'Just the actions of a young woman drunk on wine and power.'

And tinctura.

She nodded

So I have waited for the last three months in vain?

Eris shrugged. 'It was hardly a great romance.' She looked past his reflection to the bleak countryside beyond. 'I wanted you and I had you. You may as well accept it.'

Marchetti turned away, picking his way across the room. She watched him hesitate at the door, wondering what words to cast in her teeth as he departed. None came. The handle turned.

'There is one more thing,' she said. 'The Herald mustn't return to San Marino. Do you understand?'

She saw the assassin's nod in the reflection of the window. The door opened and he was gone, leaving her alone.

Eris waited by the window, wondering who might interrupt next, but no one came. The shocks and revelations of the day weighed on her mind: the Herald and his promises of war, Simonetti's endless meddling, her reliance on the Domina and the resentment that grew with each day.

'Who are you?' she whispered, searching the streets below for some glimpse of the Herald. 'Ruggeri? Fontein's bastard perhaps? Who are you?'

It would be another hour until she cried, a confused lament for her brother spiked with self-pity. She succumbed to sleep with a promise on her lips.

She would find Anea and she would kill her.

7

The Terminus Inn

It was early enough that the sun had yet to rise above the reach of the trees, leafless branches stark against the lightening sky. Landfall shone, snow-covered fields reflecting the winter light. Smoke coiled from chimneys in the distance as *cittadini* woke to face the day's chores. Snowflakes fluttered down in an eerie calm.

'And here I am, waiting to see if we go to war.'

Delfino Datini stood beneath the porch of the Terminus Inn and filled his pipe with moonleaf. It had not been a restful night's sleep despite the improvements to the inn over the years. Once it had been a run-down farmhouse; the Verde Guerra and increasing traffic to San Marino had ushered in a reverse in fortunes. The mattresses had been mean and thin when he'd first stayed here, now they were packed with clean straw, made up with new sheets and thick blankets. The owners, two brothers, had found wives and hired staff, transforming the gloomy farmstead with the sounds of laughter and industry. The comforting smells of furniture polish and fresh-baked bread filled the air, fires crackled in the hearths. Vases were filled with cut flowers during the summer, but it was not summer and no flowers could provide cheer against the promise of coming violence. The inn was a world away from the misery of Santa Maria just twenty miles to the north, the oppressive bulk of Demesne casting a dire shadow over the tumbledown town.

Delfino's thoughts turned to his own home, far away in San Marino, with its stunning pavilions and concentric streets. It wasn't long until his reverie shifted to the olive skin of his lover, the scent at the nape of her neck, how her voice sounded in the morning. A tap on the shoulder roused him from his introspection. Corvino extended a hand and gestured Delfino to surrender the pipe. The *aiutante* had yet to tie on his veil, three vivid scars running along his cheek in parallel.

'Hand it over.'

'Just one smoke. It's not as if she's here, and I—'

'Promised her you'd stop.'

'I never thought I'd have to worry about you nagging me.'

'Said it makes you taste like a chimney.' The *aiutante* thrust out a hand once more and Delfino acquiesced. 'And the pouch,' pressed Corvino.

'I could easily take on a new *aiutante*, you know. I could retire.'

'No, you couldn't. And no one retires at thirty-six; you'd get bored.'

'I have my painting.'

'Hardly regular pay, is it? Besides your purse is nearly empty.'

'I don't think you're cut out for this *aiutante* business,' said Delfino, scratching his beard. Corvino took the contraband inside.

Delfino's thoughts turned to the upper reaches of Demesne, the pointed spires and the vast dome at their centre. A smile crossed his lips. He didn't miss the place at all.

'If I never set foot in that pile of stones again I'll have done one thing right, at least.'

The *aiutante* emerged a few minutes later with two steaming mugs of coffee.

'This is much more what I had in mind,' said Delfino. 'Fetching, carrying, being useful.' Corvino pressed a mug into his master's hands before shrugging on a riding cloak. The clasp was a cataphract drake in copper, biting its tail. He'd dressed for the road, a sword at each hip, riding gloves to insulate against the chill. Both the scouts wore the half-skirt common to House Vedetta.

'You'd have made a fine soldier in another life,' admitted Delfino.

'Prefer scouting to fighting.' Corvino took his mug of coffee and settled into the opposite corner of the porch.

'I'm fairly sick of waiting,' said Delfino after a few minutes. 'I hate waiting. I'm not a man who waits well. Being unoccupied is like torture.'

Corvino nodded slowly but didn't make eye contact. He sipped from his mug and regarded the sky with a wary expression, as if the clouds themselves were dangerous. Delfino had said the very same thing the day before, and the day before that.

'Remind me why I volunteered for this?' Delfino asked.

Corvino gave a small smile. 'Same reason you promised to give up smoking your pipe.'

'The things we do for love.'

The two men nursed their coffee and half an hour passed with Delfino lost to his daydreams again.

'Wait may be at an end.' Corvino nodded toward Santa Maria, where a speck of darkness showed on the road.

'Is that him?' asked Delfino.

Corvino shrugged, crossing his arms over his chest.

'I wish it would stop snowing. I don't fancy riding all the way home in this.'

'Could be worse,' muttered the *aiutante*. The rider drew closer, becoming more distinct with each passing minute, solidifying. Even at this distance they could tell the horse was galloping, the man's cloak flaring out behind like the wings of a predator.

'Looks like him,' said Delfino. 'Big black horse, big black cloak.'

Corvino turned and headed back inside.

'Where are you going?' called Delfino.

'Saddlebags. We're leaving.'

'It would be nice if I was consulted before the arrangements were decided,' grumbled Delfino. 'At least we can go home now,' he mumbled to himself. 'Assuming we get through the Foresta Vecchia.'

'What?' Corvino shuffled past him, laden with saddlebags.

'Nothing.' Delfino tried to put his pipe between his teeth but found his hand empty.

They spent long minutes grooming their mounts, buckling saddles with care, speaking in restful tones to horses sensing departure.

'Eat up, my beauties.' Delfino patted his horse. 'It's going to be meagre fare once we're on the road.'

'Going to be a long ride home.' From anyone else it would be a note of complaint, but not from Corvino, just acceptance of the task ahead. The horses stamped and whickered, shaking heads that set their reins jingling. Delfino left the stables, hands unconsciously reaching for the pouch he'd handed over to his *aiutante*. He swore under his breath and searched the road for the Herald.

'It's him,' he called over one shoulder, as if it needed saying. Corvino exited the stables and pulled up his veil. Always a quiet man, Corvino was near silent in the presence of the Herald. Hardly surprising given the aura of violence that lingered around the cloaked figure. That they served the same master was small comfort.

The insistent thump of hooves brought the black mount closer, breath steaming on the crisp winter air. The Herald slowed to a trot for a few minutes, then a walk, until he loomed over the men. The steed snorted and stamped.

'It's war.' The words were horrible gravelly sounds. The raven perching on the Herald's shoulder stared back with an angry squint in its beady eye, beak a cruel spike.

'You only arrived last night,' said Delfino, incredulous. 'Was there no attempt at negotiation?'

The cloaked figure on the black steed leaned forward, the hilt of the great sword glinting from behind one shoulder. The raven muttered.

'Do I look to be in the mood for negotiation?'

'At least let me speak with my mother.'

'To what end?' said the Herald. The horse snorted again, kicking at snow and wheeling about before its rider reasserted control.

'Perhaps she can reason with...' The scheme died on Delfino's lips. It was too harsh a winter for such optimism.

'Viscount Datini will refuse any request from his outcast son on principle,' said the Herald.

'Are they still alive?'

'Yes,' said the Herald with a tinge of regret, 'but your father is deeply allied with Anea's new coterie of advisers.'

'And my mother?' Delfino winced as he awaited the response.

'I didn't have time to enquire,' said the Herald. 'Anea's refusal of Lucien's terms was total. She wants war, she welcomes it.'

'Lucien didn't leave much room for compromise,' admitted Delfino.

'Sweetness is for lovers and poets,' replied the Herald. 'There's no deal to be made. Their corruption has lasted long enough. The people are suffering. It's time to bring Anea's rule to an end.'

'And Duchess Prospero?'

'Still alive. For the moment.'

Delfino looked from the Herald to his *aiutante* and cleared his throat.

'We're really going to war on the strength of one message?'

'This was their last chance, Delfino.' The Herald shifted in the saddle. 'Lucien has reached out numerous times, but now his forbearance is at an end, and mine too. Anea made it very clear she was happy to meet us in battle. Let's not disappoint her.'

'No chance of her giving up Marchetti or—'

'None at all. And Marchetti is very much alive.'

The three men stood in the stark winter sun, only the caw of distant birds disturbed the silence. The snow ceased its dizzy descent and the clouds darkened, leaching all hope from the day ahead.

'We'd best ride back to San Marino then,' said Delfino with resignation.

'Don't waste a single day,' said the Herald. 'Change horses when you can.'

'And who will pay for all these horses?'

56

'I will.' The Herald slung a fat purse that jingled as Delfino caught it. The weight was reassuring.

'It'll be more expensive in the long run if we wait for Erebus to invade San Marino come the spring.' The Herald turned his mount, the black steed surging away, keen to be on the move. The raven took to wing, flying ahead of its master.

'I can't help thinking he wants this war as much as Anea does.'

'Can't disagree with that,' said Corvino.

Delfino turned to his *aiutante*. 'You were right, we're leaving.'

The two men said their goodbyes to the innkeepers. The brothers bowed to Delfino and bade him return soon; they embraced Corvino and forced some parcels of food into his hands before he mounted.

'I didn't realise you knew the Terminiellos so well.'

'They took me in after I escaped,' said Corvino, his tone terse. 'They were the first people I wrote to after you taught me to write.' He urged his mount forward, indicating the conversation was at an end. Scout and *aiutante* headed across the white panorama of Landfall, horses kicking up slush. The roads were almost indistinct from the fields, all smothered with snow. Only the trees stood watch, dusted in white. The two men commenced the long journey back to San Marino and the hard decisions that waited there.

8

An Unkindness

Three days had passed since Anea's escape from the oubliette.
She was grateful for the sanctuary of the church. The simple act
of retiring to bed was a luxury, even if her sleep was fragmented
and fitful. She woke sobbing, trying to pick between the illusion
of dark dreams and flashes of a past she struggled to remember.

'It's hardly surprising, given all that you've been through,'
said Medea. 'Give yourself time to recover.'

I have already lost too much time, signed Anea. *There is no
time. War is coming.*

'The *nobili* speak of nothing else,' said Medea, 'The Herald
has seemingly disappeared into thin air. People are wondering
which of the houses minor will remain true to the throne.'

'It won't matter,' said Agostina, 'The Myrmidons are incor-
ruptible.'

Anea learned the silent language anew, shaping the symbols
and gestures with increasing confidence. Never again would
she be without the means to articulate her thoughts. It was as
if she were being reintroduced to an old friend, and with each
gesture she relearned a memory of Dino or a conversation she
had once had.

She occupied her mind with work, studying the houses
minor and their representatives. This much was familiar to
her. Keeping abreast of the court had been her second love after
the sciences that consumed her so. The distractions made her
time in the church more bearable, but in her quieter moments
the cold truth remained – Dino was dead.

Agostina taught her the rudiments of knife fighting but

Anea remained weak from her time in the oubliette. Try as she might, she could not regain her strength, too stricken with grief to eat, spending long hours staring off, remembering a time when Dino had stood guard or shared some vital confidence. That he had died while she had been imprisoned only added to her sense of powerlessness. Dino was far from the only soul she missed.

What of Virmyre?

'Dino said we should expect him,' said Medea that morning, 'but he never arrived. I can only assume the impostor had him killed too.' She nursed a cup of coffee in both hands to ward off the chill, helped in no small part by the shawls and furs draped across her shoulders. 'He might be in the oubliette for all we know. He might have fled to San Marino. I wouldn't blame him.'

They were standing on the balcony, which had become Medea's informal office despite the cruel chill of winter. Medea derived pleasure from watching the *cittadini* go about their business in the streets below.

Virmyre. Anea made the word as if the gesture itself were arcane. Her fingers resumed their signing after a pause. *They used to call me the* strega *princess.*

A shadow of embarrassment crossed Medea's face, confirming she was familiar with the epithet.

I was told witches could cast spells? Is there some conjuration to bring back the professore?

'I wish you would,' said Medea. Anea didn't bother to reply. Hope was fading, dwindling in her heart. Other times her chest was a series of jagged aches, mourning for Dino, but also the betrayal of the Domina.

'Are you still hauling that crude thing about with you?' Medea indicated the stoppered jug.

I pretend to keep my new memories in it. Perhaps I can hold on to these ones.

'And the old ones?'

Anea shrugged. *Some have returned to me, but I fear many remain lost beneath Demesne. There is no reason to it as far as I can determine. It is beyond frustrating. I remember those closest to me best. Virmyre, Dino, Russo. All dead.*

'Russo isn't dead.'

She may as well be. Certainly there is nothing of the person I once knew in the Domina.

Agostina arrived on the balcony. Slush clung to the disciple's boots, the hem of her robe damp.

'There's to be a session of the Ravenscourt, my lady. You'll be allowed entry on condition you remain quiet.'

Medea sneered. 'That's small reason to attend. Still it's important we remain visible, even if our voice is silenced. We need to keep abreast of the situation. I don't want second-hand news.'

I want to go. Anea's fingers had made the words before she'd thought it through, yet she felt a conviction she'd not known since her escape. Medea raised an eyebrow, sharing an incredulous look with Agostina. *I want to attend the Ravenscourt. I want to see it with my own eyes.*

'But if you're discovered?' said Agostina in a quiet voice.

'You'll be dead,' added Medea.

'And us along with you.' The disciple looked away, unwilling to meet Anea's eyes.

'Every Myrmidon in Landfall will be looking for you,' reasoned Medea.

Which is why none of them will expect me at the Ravenscourt. I want to see the pretender for myself.

'We've no way of protecting you,' said Medea.

And if Lucien or Dino were here? Would either of them cower here while people suffer?

'I suppose we should find you a disguise then.' Medea shook her head. 'I can't imagine you'll be dissuaded if you're evoking the names of Lucien and Dino. Stubbornness runs in your blood.'

I prefer to call it determination.

'Come. We don't have long,' said Agostina, ushering the women inside.

Anea walked beneath the triumphal arch of Demesne. In truth the structure was three arches surmounted by a steep roof, the line broken by delicately tapered turrets. Dormer windows had been shuttered against the winter, and decorative shields displayed heraldic colours. The arches led to a man-made chasm between Houses Prospero and Contadino, in turn leading to the gates of the Ravenscourt.

I never thought I would have to spy on my own court.

'It's not really your court any more,' said Medea quietly. Their boots crunched in the snow, flakes spiralling down from maudlin skies.

'This place was called the King's Keep in earlier times,' said Agostina, keen to fill the silence between the two women.

I know, replied Anea. *It was I that renamed it.*

'If anyone asks, indicate you're Medea's handmaiden,' whispered the disciple. Anea nodded, then bowed her head and lowered her eyes.

The gates opened to receive them with a protesting groan of hinges. The three women passed into a broad circuitous corridor, walking directly to where a man in a veil waited. A scar ran through his left eye, neatly dividing his eyebrow. His remaining eye studied the women intently. Anea cast her gaze over his boots and britches, all in battered brown leather, matching the heavy gauntlets. An unadorned scabbard held a short sword with a broad blade.

They entered the long corridor beneath the Ravenscourt itself, passing under the gazes of Myrmidons, faces hidden behind their curving helms. Up they climbed, through the king's library and past the countless tomes, joined by others, nobles and messengers.

Who was that? asked Anea.

'The bravo?' breathed Medea. 'He's called Marchetti. I've not seen him for months.'

Anea searched the faces of the nobles from the corners of her eyes. *What is he?*

'A Myrmidon. He probably serves her in the same way Dino served you.'

Spy?

'Assassin.'

I ordered assassinations?

Medea raised her eyebrows 'Someone killed Duke Fontein,

and it's not so difficult to imagine that Emilio was murdered to redress the balance.'

Surely I would never stoop to such . . . Anea's gestures stalled as Medea had looked away, more concerned with their entrance.

The Ravenscourt was not as Anea recalled, if indeed she remembered it rightly. It had been a place of light and hope with windows set into a vast dome, swathes of white fabric hanging from a balcony. The floor had always been polished, the atmosphere fragrant, the throne modest and carved of oak. The scene that greeted the usurped queen was quite different.

The white drapes had been replaced with turquoise fabric decorated with an ivy leaf motif in gold, the colour of House Diaspora ascendant. From the gallery above the throne hung a vast black curtain, embellished with copper in the shapes of leaves and vines. The windows had been shuttered, the meagre light provided by twisting candelabra in sinuous designs, figures entwined in unseemly poses. Dust occluded the floor in drifts; the scent lingering on the air was faint yet unmistakable – the stench of the oubliette, of sickness, of atrophy, of forgetting.

Anea's stomach knotted as a surge of panic coursed through her, constricting her chest and then her throat. She resisted the urge to run, instead looking at her feet, pressing her hands together, fingers pointing to the dome above.

'What are you praying for?' asked Medea.

I am not praying. I am trying to stop my hands from shaking.

They didn't have the chance to speak further.

'Viscount Simonetti,' Medea said with a smile of gritted teeth, 'blessed archivist of Landfall.'

'Canoness, so good to see you,' rumbled the tall man. Anea recognised his face but nothing more. If the archivist noticed Medea's new handmaiden he paid her no mind.

'Tread carefully, my lady,' said Simonetti. 'Something is afoot, something that has put Lady Diaspora in worse humour than usual. Her pet assassin is never far from—'

Simonetti's eyes darted to the back of the room. Anea turned to see Marchetti enter the Ravenscourt, circling around to the left, passing behind the columns and drapes. His remaining eye searched the crowd, restless.

The canoness and the two sisters approached the throne under the gazes of the nobles. Russo stood to one side of the dais, her garb frayed, the silver staff lacking its former lustre. And at the centre, seated on a collection of artefacts arranged in the parody of a throne, sat the impostor. Anea clenched her fists. Had they really all been duped by such a shallow imitation? Was there anything she shared with this woman aside from gender? True, the impostor possessed a similar build, and the jade eyes above the veil were a striking green. Her hair fell long, a vibrant blonde the colour of summer corn, but that was where the sham reached its end.

Her skirt consisted of black lace over turquoise silk, while her corset was made of calfskin dyed black, matching the elbow-length gloves she wore. Her exposed shoulders and décolletage were divided by a sash of turquoise, littered with obsidian beads. Her make-up gave the illusion of eyes half-awake.

'Welcome back to the Ravenscourt,' intoned the Domina, interpreting the impostor's signing. 'The Sisterhood are ever welcome among the *nobili*, assuming they can behave themselves.'

Medea curtsied and inclined her head.

'If only I could manage a pale imitation of your own behaviour, Lady Diaspora.' The nobles quietened, the Ravenscourt waiting for the next riposte. 'You are an exemplar of conduct to us all.'

Anea swallowed, uncomfortable with the attention Medea was drawing to herself. She had hoped to remain unnoticed. The impostor clapped her hands slowly and then made a few gestures.

'I do so enjoy having you in attendance, Lady Contadino,' translated the Domina. 'It adds a certain flavour to proceedings.'

The canoness inclined her head again and withdrew to the right-hand side of the Ravenscourt.

'A pity the flavour isn't nightshade,' said Medea, loud enough the words reached Anea and Agostina's ears and no one else's.

'And you have a new handmaiden, how charming.' These were the Domina's words. Anea took her spot beside the canoness but refrained from meeting the Domina's eyes. 'This

63

new-found religion is refreshingly quaint, ever a crutch to the commoners.'

The nobles laughed, some forced, others in genuine mirth.

'I'm going to cut out that *puttana*'s tongue one day,' muttered Medea from behind a fan. 'But first I'm going to make sure Duchess Prospero meets a suitably bloody end.' The canoness turned to Anea. 'The impostor is yours to do with as you wish.'

Anea struggled to keep her expression neutral. It was times such as these that only the ashes of Medea remained, burned up by the vengeful canoness.

'Don't look so shocked, little sister. You know it's no more than any of them deserve.'

The Domina's staff slammed against the dais three times, preventing Anea from responding. Marchetti took a spot behind the impostor's right shoulder, his flint-eyed gaze staring from behind the Myrmidon throne. Anea found her eye drawn to him time and time again. The nobles dropped to one knee. Anea did the same, though it grated to do so.

'This session of the Ravenscourt is open,' declared the Domina. 'You may bring your concerns before Lady Aranea Oscuro Diaspora.'

The nobles got to their feet, as did Anea, seething at the use of her name. Simonetti took a few steps forward from where he had been standing beside Maestro Fidelio.

'My lady, once you were a keen advocate of making the written word available to the *cittadini*. You ushered in a new age of knowledge after decades of restrictions by the king. However, the funds needed to staff the libraries have dwindled in recent times. Perhaps I could prevail upon your good nature—'

Someone sniggered loudly, prompting Simonetti to cast a look of annoyance over his shoulder.

'Perhaps I could prevail—'

'I think not.' The Domina lent her voice to the imposter's gestures. 'It was I who declared the common folk were no more, elevating them to *cittadini*. It was I who opened the doors to the libraries and encouraged knowledge to flourish in the town of Santa Maria. However, with so many of the *cittadini* gone I have a hard choice. Books or blades?'

A soft rumble of rumour filled the Ravenscourt, the topic singular – Duke Lucien Marino's Herald of war.

'We can't very well defend ourselves from Duke Marino's army without swords, can we?' said the Domina, no longer translating. Simonetti frowned but said no more.

'Perhaps if you'd been less keen to create your army there'd be some money in the coffers to help the *cittadini*.' As one the Ravenscourt looked around to the source of the voice. Drago Romanucci stood with a hand resting on the hilt of his sword. 'Do you not wonder why a full third of our people have absconded? Do you not see the steady rise of taxes, or the profits the houses major skim from the farmers and craftsmen?'

A voice in the crowd bid Romanucci be quiet. The House Del Toro *dirigente* turned to see Viscount Datini staring back from beneath a deep scowl.

'And if I don't speak out, who will, Viscount? Not you, old man.'

Marchetti stepped down from the dais, eyes fixed on Romanucci.

'And here comes Lady Diaspora's henchman to ensure our obedience,' sneered the Del Toro *dirigente*. The tension in the room, always unpleasant, was now a sickening thing, threatening to spoil into violence.

Was Marchetti responsible for Dino? asked Anea.

'No. Dino was killed by regular Myrmidons. Stop signing. Anyone can—' But Medea got no further. Marchetti had turned, his attention on the Sisters of Santa Maria. Anea felt his single eye upon her, could feel it peeling back the vestments, seeing past the disguise.

'There won't be anyone to rule over unless the throne acts soon.' Duchess Prospero raised her voice over the murmuring of discontent. 'Drago is right to speak his mind.'

Those in attendance waited to see who else would lend their voice to the debate, but Anea wasn't listening. Marchetti approached her, each footstep unhurried. Anea touched Medea's elbow, heart kicking in a staccato beat. The room was stifling, the heat suddenly unbearable. Still the assassin approached, hand on his sword, eye assessing, scrutinising.

And then Medea collapsed. Bystanders gasped with surprise. Anea knelt to attend to the canoness. On the throne, the impostor rolled her eyes and signed something. Agostina fluttered a fan beside Medea's face. Marchetti's advance faltered, wrongfooted by this sudden turn of events.

'Take her away,' said the Domina in a bored voice. 'See she gets some air.'

Anea and Agostina hefted the limp form of the canoness and struggled the length of the Ravenscourt. A tide of whispers swept in around them.

Drago stepped in and took the limp canoness from the two women. 'Let's get her back to the church,' he said, nodding to Agostina.

Anea looked over her shoulder to see Marchetti trailing them at a none-too-discreet distance. She quickened her pace, walking alongside Drago, hoping the *dirigente* would draw the assassin's attention. Medea's eyes flickered open, then a whisper.

'I'm fine, but Marchetti knows.'

Anea nodded that she understood, a chill sweat on her spine.

They pressed on, out of the Central Keep and through the long chasm between the houses, under the triumphal arch, wending a route through the town. If Drago was burdened by Medea he didn't show it, never pausing to adjust her weight, walking with the simple plod of a beast of burden. Medea's arms had snaked around his muscular neck and she held herself close to the man.

Marchetti remained a few score feet behind them, a deep frown above his remaining eye. The gap between pursuer and pursued diminished, the assassin keen to reveal the truth of Anea's disguise. They were almost at the church, steps rising ahead, leading to salvation. Drago didn't hesitate, taking them two at a time. They were at the doors when Anea felt a hand catch hold of her arm, jerking her round to face the scarred and veiled assassin.

Drago pressed on into the church. Agostina reached into her sleeve with a look of sick resignation. To draw a weapon would only hasten their end, but their options were few. Anea was reaching for the knife concealed in her own sleeve when a

Myrmidon pressed one hand to Marchetti's shoulder and shook his head.

'The church is sacrosanct; we don't interfere.'

The assassin stared into the visor of the armoured soldier. Anea guessed he held some rank judging by the crimson symbols on his shoulder. The assassin did not release her. The urge to use the knife strapped to her forearm was a powerful one.

'Let her go,' said the Myrmidon. 'We don't cross the church.'

The assassin declined to reply and Anea stared at his veil, wondering what lay beneath it. Men rarely took the vow of silence in the name of Santa Maria, less so the Myrmidons. Surely he was mute, just like her.

Marchetti went for his blade, but the Myrmidon laid one hand over the assassin's sword arm, pressing himself in close.

'Come now, little brother. Let's not make this worse than it needs to be.' There was something familiar to that voice, a tone from dream or memory. Marchetti's grip on Anea's arm slackened, but the intensity of his gaze did not. He turned to the Myrmidon and shoved him back, stepped in and shoved again.

This was all the distraction Anea needed. The doors of the church boomed shut, sealing the assassin outside. Only then did she slump down in the vestibule, her breathing ragged and quick.

Marchetti knew.

9

The Sisters

Eris shifted on the Myrmidon throne and hissed with frustration.

The Domina turned to face her. 'My lady?'

Eris gestured with the blade of one hand, two quick strokes across her throat. The steward made a sullen pout in reply. The staff boomed against the dais three times, signalling the session ended. The nobles complained and made a show of voicing their dissent. Aides and courtiers filed through the double doors in slow procession, glad to be free of the cloying atmosphere. Eris stood, looking for Marchetti among the lingering nobles. Her attention was drawn to a solitary figure approaching the dais. Viscount Datini hobbled toward them, hands clasped in the small of his back, face flushed scarlet with fury.

'I want a solution to Dirigente Romanucci. Is there no way to disgrace him?'

'The people feel they are represented by the *dirigente*,' replied the Domina. 'Let's not deny them a fiction that makes them happy. It may be the only thing holding back a new wave of riots.'

The viscount dragged his slash of a mouth into something that resembled a smile. 'Perhaps the *dirigente* could run into some thieves the next time he stumbles home from the *taverna*?'

The Domina looked from the old viscount to the Silent Queen for permission. Eris shook her head.

'I'm in agreement with the queen on this, my lord,' said the Domina in a soothing tone.

'Pah! He's a jumped-up teamster's son with dreams of a

republic.' The viscount grimaced. 'He gains influence every time he speaks in the Ravenscourt. You're giving him a platform.'

'We'll reconsider if Romanucci becomes an impediment to our plans.'

Eris narrowed her eyes, then signed, *What plans?*

The Domina looked at the Silent Queen and forced a tight smile. 'I'm afraid I need the room now, Viscount.'

'Is something amiss?'

'Our lady is tired,' said the Domina. The last remaining nobles exited as Simonetti waited in the centre of the Ravenscourt, straining to eavesdrop on the Domina's conversation, no doubt.

'As you wish,' grunted Viscount Datini, performing a wooden bow.

Where is Marchetti? Eris signed. His presence was a near-constant source of irritation that razored her nerves, yet she felt no relief in his absence.

'I thought you tasked him with following Medea back to the church?' said the Domina.

No, I did not.

Eris watched Simonetti greet Viscount Datini at the centre of the Ravenscourt. The old man waved the archivist off and went on his way.

There was no need for Marchetti to be here. He should be out hunting the prisoner. It has been days and he is not likely to find her here. Eris frowned.

'What is it?' said the Domina, taking a step closer.

Marchetti has found her, she signed, but the Domina wasn't looking, instead heading off Simonetti as he approached the dais.

'I'm simply, ah, saying . . .' Simonetti blinked behind his optics. 'If you were to make a few conciliatory gestures people may forgive this rather unpopular army you've created, and, ah . . . Where is she going?'

Eris turned her back on both the archivist and the Domina, using the door behind the throne. She emerged into a corridor where two Myrmidons waited to escort her. The Domina was at her heels, followed by Simonetti. Eris tried to recall the last few moments of the session in her mind. She'd watched the assassin step down from the dais, watched him prowl the dusty court to silence Romanucci. A typical display of bravura so common in men who wielded blades. And yet hadn't the assassin paused as he drew parallel to the canoness? His pace slowed, his direction altered. He'd advanced on the trio of women just as Medea Contadino had fainted.

What do you know about Drago Romanucci?

'He's the second *dirigente* to be voted in,' said Simonetti. 'The Del Toro bloodline died out after the war. He speaks for everyone on that estate and the surrounding villages.'

'Perhaps you can impart something we don't already know?' said the Domina, following Eris deeper into House Contadino.

'He's, ah, popular with those he represents and a firm supporter of Landfall becoming a republic. Houses Schiaparelli, Elemosina and Previdente all convene with him from time to time.'

'And?' pressed the Domina.

'Might I remind you my title is archivist. I specialise in books, not people.'

The Domina stopped, turning to glower. Simonetti wiped his optics clean on his robe and glowered back, the effect undone as he blinked. Eris regarded the pair of them.

Not now. Come on. I have need of you. Both of you.

They found themselves in an old apartment thick with dust, where long-forgotten furniture hid beneath discoloured sheets. The curtains were holed and tired, and they walked on mildewed carpet strewn with the corpses of moths.

'Well, this is cheerful,' muttered Simonetti.

'This was Lucien Marino's apartment,' said the Domina. There was a reverence to her voice, but her eyes showed a wariness bordering on fear. 'He was Lucien Contadino back then, before he became a Fontein.'

Eris crossed to the window and regarded the town. The church stood before them, a wide and solid affair with doors made to resist intruders rather than welcome worshippers.

A deep balcony ran the width of the building; smoke from a brazier curled around the lip of the roof. Bells hung from a stone arch to one side, waiting to call the faithful to prayer.

'Are you thinking about converting?' asked Simonetti, a small smile on his lips.

Medea Contadino was accompanied by a sister of Santa Maria. The sister did not wear the order's customary blue, instead opting for white.

'There is another order of sisters,' said the Domina. 'Might they have their own colours?'

'The sisters in San Marino wear olive green,' supplied Simonetti.

Eris nodded at the archivist, eyes bright and alert.

'And who do you suspect the mystery sister is?' said the archivist. The Domina's eyes widened as she made the connection. She shook her head at the Silent Queen, but Eris turned back to Simonetti and began to gesture.

I have received word that my opponents seek to defeat me. Not by force, but with subterfuge. They plan to replace me with a double. This is why I have employed Marchetti. It is his job to hunt the double before she can kill me and assume my role.

'This sounds, uh, rather far-fetched, my lady,' said Simonetti, glancing at the Domina for reassurance.

I believe Marchetti has found the woman who intends to deceive us.

Eris glanced down at the town just as Drago Romanucci appeared from a side street, carrying the canoness. The other two sisters pressed in close about the man.

'The one in blue is known as the disciple,' said Simonetti. 'Sister Agostina Desideria.'

The sister in white looked back over her shoulder, then ran a few steps to keep up with the *dirigente*. The group turned a corner, heading for the church steps.

'But the church would never become embroiled in a plot to take the throne,' said Simonetti, the note of doubt in his voice belying his conviction.

'I think we should be more concerned with Drago Romanucci,' said the Domina, a scowl on her pale face.

71

'There's Marchetti,' breathed the archivist. Eris nodded. The assassin followed Romanucci and the sisters up the church steps. A Myrmidon intervened just as Marchetti grasped the sister in white. There was a moment of dispute, then the sister hurried into the church, doors booming closed in the assassin's face.

The Domina released a sigh and Eris unclenched aching fists.

'We shan't see her again,' said Simonetti. 'Men aren't permitted in the church except for services, and armed men are forbidden altogether.'

Mention this to no one. Now go and bring me the fastest and most able seamstresses and tailors from House Prospero.

'Well, it's not as if I have anything to do at the library, is it?' Simonetti departed the room, the angry gazes of the Domina and Eris following his every step. The door grated shut before the Domina spoke.

'You're playing a dangerous game, filling his head with talk of impostors.'

Eris shrugged and looked back at the church. *Simonetti is not so wise that I cannot fool him with a simple double bluff.*

The many clocks of Demesne announced the small hours before the vestments were ready. It was still dark when she rose, the handful of hours spent in bed sleepless ones. Eris prepared herself, no need to rouse her maid while Demesne slumbered, and best that Isabella not know of this new deception. Eris selected an old mare from the House Erudito stables and pressed a dozen *denari* into the stable boy's hand. She held a finger to hidden lips, her veil the attire of a sister of the San Marino order. Setting aside the haughty demeanour of Lady Aranea Oscuro Diaspora was a blessing she'd not counted on. The stable boy nodded to her and tucked the coins in his boots.

The mare plodded through empty streets to the very outskirts of the town. Strange to be awake in Santa Maria at such an hour, and without escort. There had been no need to leave Demesne since she'd become the Silent Queen. The title was accompanied by the constant presence of Myrmidons. The sun's golden rays found her alone, surrounded by *cittadini* who hated her. Small mercy the majority were still abed. Eris shivered beneath the vestments, telling herself it was the spiteful winter chill that made her shiver.

The remaining stars faded from view like discarded memories until only one remained, an amethyst eye in the firmament. The old *sanatario* loomed above the townhouses. She took the building as her cue to turn her mount toward the streets. Anyone seeing her would assume she had ridden from the south. The mare's hooves sounded on cobbles, a few *cittadini* turning to stare, going about their chores once curiosity had been satisfied. Her mount carried her to the steps of the church, so much smaller than Demesne yet imposing nonetheless. She dismounted, taking a moment to unbuckle her saddlebags. *Cittadini* nodded to her and bade her good morning and Eris replied, anxious they might question her disguise. Her knock was loud and insistent, the wait long.

'Any time before I freeze to death, Sisters.'

A panel of dark wood slid back, gentle eyes staring out with curiosity.

'Who calls?'

'Sister Dahna, Dahna Esposito,' replied Eris calmly, 'from the San Marino order.' She'd rehearsed this much before the mirror during the long hours it had taken the dressmakers to sew her disguise. 'I've ridden through the night to reach you; please allow me entrance.'

The door opened after several clicks. The sister on the other side curtsied. The vestibule was no less chilly than outside.

'I'm Sister Consolata.' She took the saddlebags while Eris retained a small canvas bag and her bedroll. 'You must be tired. Come, I'll take you to the kitchen.'

They had barely crossed the threshold when Eris was questioned again.

'One moment, Sister.' Eris withered under the scrutiny of the disciple's unnatural eyes. Sister Agostina, so meek in the Ravenscourt, was transformed by sanctified ground, a fearless presence.

'You must be the disciple of Santa Maria,' said Eris. Agostina Desideria nodded, then narrowed her eyes. Eris curtsied a second too late. 'I've heard so much about you.'

73

'What brings you to Santa Maria?' Eris felt as if the disciple could see through Sister Dahna to her very bones. 'And where is your escort?'

'My escort –' Eris took a breath, unprepared for such careful accounting '– were farmers from the Elemosina estate. They saw me through the Foresta Vecchia.'

This appeased Sister Consolata at least. Agostina's green and blue eyes continued to appraise her.

'As for my purpose, I am looking for a cousin. Is it possible you have had any new additions to the order recently?'

'Why yes—' began Sister Consolata.

'We receive many new converts all the time,' intoned Agostina.

'Perhaps I should present myself to the canoness?' said Eris brightly.

'I think that would be proper.'

Eris grinned, more from relief than joy. She'd not considered that Agostina would patrol the church at such an hour. The three sisters walked through the nave, passing between rows of varnished pews.

'Is the canoness recovered from yesterday?' asked Eris, relishing the role of Sister Dahna.

'She is indeed,' said Sister Agostina, who stopped and turned, knife in hand. Eris eyed the wicked length of steel, mouth dry. 'Do tell me how you came to know of the canoness's ill health, despite riding through the night to reach us.'

Sister Consolata reached for her own knife, slowed by confusion.

'Well,' began Eris, 'the farmers...' But she'd been undone by her own cleverness. She threw the canvas bag and bedroll, which unfurled. The disciple stumbled over the bag, knife tumbling from her fingers as she sprawled on the floor. A heavy thump sounded as Sister Consolata dropped the saddlebags.

Eris fled, daring a look over her shoulder as she reached the doors, wrenching them open. Sister Consolata was helping the disciple to her feet. A handful of white- and blue-robed sisters had been roused by the noise, emerging from doorways with knives and questions in equal measure. Eris sprinted down the church steps to the old mare, but a shadow had fallen across the horse. A shadow wearing a mottled riding cloak, a raven perched on one shoulder. Her feet skidded beneath her as she tried to stop. The Herald lunged forward in the lost seconds it took to regain her balance. The raven took to wing in a blur of black feathers.

Eris fled across the piazza, heart beating like an anvil struck, limbs feeling just as heavy. *Cittadini* gawped in surprise. The sight of a sister in full flight was rare indeed, more so when pursued by an armed man. A few brave souls attempted to slow the Herald. A flat hand flashed out from the cloak, knocking aside the inquisitive. Eris cursed the vestments that clung to her legs, then cursed the Herald, surely lifting his great sword at this very moment. On she ran, lungs pricked with seamstresses' needles. The town was fully awake, tradesmen going to their chores as the sun climbed ever higher. Her breath was a ragged thing, painfully drawn, tears streaming from eyes in desperation, heart ready to burst through her ribs.

And then she was alone.

She slowed, turned, stopped. Panic had led her to the triumphal arch. Four Myrmidons emerged from a side street, swords bared. The tramp of boots as other Myrmidons passed behind them, joined by the stark sound of hooves. The Domina stared down from on horseback, a mocking smile on her purple-painted lips.

'Did you honestly think you could just throw on some robes and fool an entire order of sisters?'

'Why not?' replied Eris. 'I do it in the Ravenscourt every day.'

'Apparently the sisters are more vigilant than the *nobili*.' Another smile.

Eris stormed past the Domina, beneath the arch, down the bleak chasm between Houses Contadino and Prospero.

'Do you have any commands?' shouted the Domina, her tone laden with ridicule.

Eris wrenched the veil from her face, casting it to the floor.

'Arrest any *puttana* setting foot outside the church. And when you find the Herald, bring him to me.'

10

On Sacred Ground

Anea had risen early, woken from dreams of the oubliette and the attendant darkness. The church was rich with silence but for the frantic beat of her heart. She could taste the foul waters of her former prison, stagnant with forgetting, provoking the usual fears: how much of her memory had she lost permanently, how much was yet to return, and would the remembering of days unknown bring relief or only sadness?

Sleep was not a friend to her, but company was a balm and she wasted no time seeking it out. Anea lit more candles than was necessary, washing in the basin as if a trace of the oubliette still lingered on her skin. The clay jug was a reassuring presence on her bedside table, the stopper loose, the varnish chipped. It was a strange keepsake but one she had no desire to relinquish. Soon she was attired in the vestments of Santa Maria, so different to the gowns and dresses she had grown up in.

Her boots scuffed on the stone steps of the spiral staircase. The church's reverent silence had given way to a subdued atmosphere. Anea pressed on, a blanket about her shoulders providing a measure of comfort, an addition to the shawl she also wore. All the layers in the world were not insulation enough at this time of year. She shoved against the balcony door with a shoulder, grunting with the effort.

'Still having trouble sleeping?' Medea cradled a small mug in her slender fingers. She stood to one side of the balcony, concealed by shadow. Anea nodded and closed the door behind her. The balcony at the front of the church was frigid, the brazier providing scant comfort. A copper kettle sat atop coals glowing orange, a wisp of steam emerging from the spout.

We should get an extra one of these, signed Anea, pointing to the brazier. Medea looked back to the town, lost in her thoughts. Anea regarded the streets of Santa Maria. *Cittadini* headed to work in the fragile light of early morning; rooftops were made smooth with snow, which fell lightly, drifts collecting in seldom used alleys. All else was a gritty slush, grey streaked with black. The clouds overhead were static, oppressive swathes of grey hanging low in the sky.

'There was a time when it seemed the houses were invulnerable,' said Medea, staring to the horizon. She sipped her coffee. 'No one had been assassinated for more than a decade. Then we lost Stephano – to a staircase, would you believe?

Stephano Prospero was not assassinated, signed Anea, although she wasn't sure how she remembered the fact, or if it were true.

'We'll never truly know the architect of his death. Ten years later and Duke Fontein dies. And then Emilio...'

Anea struggled to remember the latter of these events. Shouldn't she at least have a glimmer of recollection?

'Not that I suppose you mind of course.' Medea smiled coldly. 'You were trying to bring about a republic, were you not?'

Anea's fingers moved slowly in the chill. *Never like this. Through diplomacy, not murder.* The two women looked over the town, much of it derelict. *Why are you in such ill spirits this morning?*

'Someone tried to infiltrate the church,' said Medea. Her eyes drifted across the many windows of Demesne as if trying to decipher some clue or tell from the edifice. She set down her mug and toyed with her prayer beads. 'I think she was here for you.'

Anea retreated to the small library located above the kitchen at the back of the church. It was one of the warmer chambers in the building. The familiar presence of parchment and scrawl stilled her ragged nerves; if the church were to be her prison then so be it. She picked at scraps of food as she read, spiriting them discreetly under the veil. Even the idea she might regain her throne seemed ridiculous. Not that it was her throne any more; that jumble of Myrmidon armour was as foreign to her as the Domina who stood beside it.

'There you are,' said Agostina. 'Good morning, and may the blessings of the Saint be upon you.' The disciple took a seat at the table Anea had commandeered. A bruise on the right side of her face had just started to darken, a blue stain around her eye.

What happened?

'A sister from the San Marino order dropped in.'

Did she disapprove of the incense?

Agostina paused a moment before seeing the humour despite her injury.

'She was asking if we'd had any new converts.' Agostina's blue and green gaze lingered on Anea. 'She claimed she was looking for her cousin, but there were plenty of things about her that didn't ring true.'

They were looking for me. Marchetti could not gain entrance so they sent a woman.

'I have a feeling it was your friend, the impostor.' Agostina forced a smile. 'It seems she's expanding her repertoire.'

She would never come herself, signed Anea, eyes wide with shock. *It is too dangerous.*

'Unless she was overconfident, or arrogant,' said Agostina. 'Perhaps both. I'll wager the latter.'

Anea paused before forming new words, resigned to the telling of them all the same. *I have to leave. Marchetti knows I am here. She knows I am here. I am putting you in danger, all of you.*

Agostina stood, circling the table before kneeling in front of the Silent Queen, one hand alighting gently on her forearm. 'She only suspects you're here, she can't be sure.'

I cannot go back to the oubliette. Anea's green eyes hardened to jade. *I will not.*

'We won't let that happen,' soothed Agostina.

Does it ever bother you? Anea gestured to Agostina's eyes. Startling blue and deep green.

'My eyes?' Agostina shrugged. 'Not so much. But then I don't spend much time at the looking glass.'

Is that why you became a disciple?

'Matters of faith are always more pressing than simple vanity.' Agostina looked uncomfortable for a moment. 'Who knows about...' She gestured to the lower half of her face.

Anea sighed, fingers weaving new gestures. *The Domina, Lucien and my maid, although she has gone to her rest now. I suspect my impostor knows, if the Domina has briefed her properly.* Anea held Agostina's gaze. *And now you. I would prefer to keep it that way.*

'Is that why you never married?'

Matters of duty are always more pressing than those of love.

Agostina smiled at the mimicry. 'I disagree. If not for love then what?'

Men are fickle, cowardly creatures in the main. One look at my face and even the most ardent suitor would—

'Things are worse.' Medea walked into the library, then paused when she saw the women together, Agostina on her knees before Anea. 'Apologies for my...'

Directness, signed Anea. *How are things worse?*

'Best you come to the balcony and see for yourselves.'

And there I was thinking I might remain warm this afternoon.

The balcony of the church was all but overrun with sisters staring down at the piazza and side streets of Santa Maria with forlorn expressions. At least as far as Anea could tell, as many of them had taken the veil. This particular fashion had come about to honour the Silent Queen back when Anea still ruled. The veil was taken to symbolise modesty and the importance of silence over needless chatter.

Why did you bring me up to this pigeon coop you are so enamoured with?

Medea arched an eyebrow. 'Your memories may be incomplete, but your humour is making quite the return.'

'Myrmidons,' said Agostina. This, as it turned out was an understatement. There were not merely a handful, or even a dozen.

How wonderful. Anea shook her head. *Did she send all of them?*

'It does look that way,' said Medea.

'Impossible,' replied Agostina.

How many? And why?

'Two on every street corner,' replied Medea. 'As for why? Retaliation for our poor hospitality this morning.'

Sister Consolata pushed her way through the door, surprised to see so many sisters on the balcony. She clutched a scrap of parchment.

'Who delivered this?' asked Medea, taking the note from her.

'A messenger of House Del Toro,' supplied Sister Consolata. 'We can trust them.'

Agostina nodded at the canoness. 'What does the note say?' Medea dragged in a long breath and Anea decided she would not like what would come next. She was not disappointed.

'It says the Herald of Duke Lucien Marino waits for us in the safe house at the edge of town.' Medea looked up from the note. 'You and I should seek him out before midnight. It says he is wanted by the throne.'

I cannot imagine our new friends will oblige us by letting us leave, signed Anea, nodding to the Myrmidons.

'We'll be arrested the moment we set foot on the steps.'

'They wouldn't dare,' countered Agostina.

I need to speak with this Herald. I need to let Lucien know what has happened. I need to tell him about the impostor.

'It's because of you we're currently under siege,' said Medea. 'You can't go out there.'

Do you honestly think you can convince the Herald that Demesne is ruled by an impostor? It sounds like a work of fiction or a day-dream gone bad.

'I'll be fine,' said Medea. 'I can very persuasive.'

With no proof?

'Fine,' said Medea in a tone that said anything but.

They waited until the sun began its descent, the disc a pearly shimmer edging toward the horizon. The church had its share of tunnels and side doors – who ever had drawn up the plans had been neither short-sighted nor stupid. Anea and the canoness emerged not among Myrmidons, but in a side street with a long-forgotten door set in a darkened archway. The keystone featured Santa Maria, the saint made small, her benevolent gaze staring out over the street.

'They really did think of everything when they built that place,' said Medea.

If I never have to set foot beneath ground again—

'I'll be sure to bury you at sea.' Medea straightened her gown. She had eschewed her vestments and dressed in a manner befitting a *marchesa*.

'This is larger than I remember,' she said, tying her belt a fraction tighter. 'Clearly, religious food is less than filling.'

Anea smoothed down her own clothes, all cast-offs from Medea which had been quickly adjusted.

I cannot believe we are disguising ourselves as nobles.

'Who said anything about disguises?' said Medea. 'I'm dressed as myself.'

Lead the way. We cannot afford to risk the Herald fleeing the safe house before we reach him.

Their boots crunched into snow many inches deep. The fall had turned to grey paste in the main streets, but it was a crisp and chilly traverse through the winding back alleys. The Myrmidons stamped their feet to keep warm and wrapped themselves in dark cloaks. The attention they afforded the two women was cursory at best.

'That's what I like about underkin: they're not weighed down with an abundance of imagination. Or curiosity. They tend to follow orders to the letter.'

There's not a huge difference between Orfani and underkin, you know? Just fortune and title.

'And a suit of armour.' Medea's humour slipped from her face like a mask. 'Emilio died on the blades of underkin, so you'll forgive me if I'm not kindly disposed toward them.'

Anea pushed her hands beneath the fabric of the shawl she wore, willing warmth back into her fingers. Her gaze dipped to the cobbles – so she wouldn't slip, she told herself. She knew the vengeful gaze that occupied Medea's face all too well; she had no need to see it again.

*

The safe house was on the edge of an unremarkable district on the western side of town. The streets were quiet, most houses abandoned, with a few rare slats of yellow light spilling across the snow.

'It's the one with the pale blue door and shutters,' said Medea. They were across the street a few doors down. The sky had darkened to slate, tinged with midnight blue in the east. Clouds stained the heavens, daubed like white paint.

Is that not somewhat obvious? The colour of the door was the blue of the Order of Santa Maria.

'I suppose,' said Medea. 'I expect they were hoping they wouldn't have to use it.'

There does not seem to be anyone there.

'Wait here. I'll see if this mysterious Herald has managed to evade capture.'

But you—

'Once we know it's safe I'll wave to you. If not, well, at least you'll have a few moments grace to evade them.' Medea smiled sadly. 'I wouldn't advise going back to the church.'

Why are you doing this? Risking yourself for me?

Medea looked at her as if she'd recited an obscure joke.

Why not remain anonymous, or go to your children?

'I want justice for Emilio. The only way that will ever happen is by restoring you to the throne. Without you I was biding my time, plotting assassinations I could never hope to see carried out. Now I don't have to.'

Medea turned away, making the short walk across the snow-covered street before Anea could form a response. The town had become a place of shadows. Medea approached the door with cautious steps, her head turning this way and that. Anea felt the tension yawn in her gut and pressed her back against the wall behind her. She willed the next few seconds to pass without incident, almost prayed to the Saint herself.

Medea knocked; the door opened.

Time slowed, seemingly frozen by the bitter winter night. Someone shouted, and Myrmidons emerged from doorways on either side of the house. Most wielded swords, but an equal number shone lanterns. Medea turned to run but received a fist to the stomach, sending her to her knees.

Anea shrank back from the light, slithering along the wall, almost falling through an archway that led to a small yard, empty except for a trio of barrels. She dared to look past the corner into the bright light of the Myrmidons' lanterns. The Domina had joined them from a hiding place, standing over Medea with a smirk. Something passed between the two women but Anea could not determine the words. A crunch of boots on snow, close and quick, as a Myrmidon approached the yard. Anea flinched back into darkness.

'She must be here somewhere.' The Domina's voice, so used to silencing the nobles. Anea squatted down beside the barrels, shivering with cold, shaking with terror. A beam of light penetrated the arch, then spread further, reaching into her meagre hiding place, leaching away darkness and safety. The Myrmidon blocked the entrance to the yard, lantern held up in one fist, a sword clutched in the other. Anea looked into the dim points of light beneath the curving helm, knowing he saw her, feeling his gaze meet hers. How pathetic she must look, kneeling among barrels like a common thief. She, Aranea Oscuro Diaspora, rightful ruler of Landfall, defender of the people, bringer of a republic. The Silent Queen, the *strega* princess, the great reformer. And now she'd be dragged out into the street, slaughtered like a sow.

'Nothing here,' grunted the Myrmidon, lowering the lantern. He turned his back. 'She's long gone.'

Anea almost sobbed with relief, clasping a hand over her veil to stifle the sound.

'The Myrmidons at the church said they saw two women.' The voice of the Domina, no more than a score of feet away.

'Let's widen the search,' replied the Myrmidon. 'She could be heading back there this very moment.'

The light dwindled.

The sound of boots on snow and cobbles faded, and Anea cried hot tears, fearing for Medea's life.

II

Eris Unbound

Eris had not chosen to rise early, yet wakefulness was preferential to dreaming. She lurched upright, hands clasped to her chest, heart racing at an unbearable pace. Tremulous seconds passed as she persuaded herself she no longer ran through the frozen streets of Santa Maria. It mattered not that the doors were locked and bolted; the Herald haunted her. He stood at every corner, crouched on rooftops, stared at her from windows. Everywhere, the carnival mask followed her steps, flashes of gold and turquoise in the gloom of dreaming. This was the fifth time she had been snatched from her rest. It would be the last.

'Nightmares, my lady?' Isabella was in the sitting room. A needle flickering through fabric; mending an old glove split down one seam. A cup of coffee steamed on the table beside the armchair.

Eris crossed her arms over her chest, the soft silk of her nightgown creasing.

'You're here early.' Her words were no warmer than the wind howling around the towers and weathervanes of Demesne.

'I thought you might have need of me after yesterday's ...' It was rare that Isabella made eye contact, she addressed the floor for the most part. 'That is to say, Dottore Allattamento suggest I arrive at dawn.'

'How very thoughtful of him.'

Isabella attended the Domina also. With fewer and fewer people they could trust, there was little choice. Dottore Allattamento had vouched for Isabella's discretion but this had not endeared the woman to Eris.

'Will you require the black gown today, my lady?'

Eris nodded. The maid had wasted no time in learning her mistress's favourites, be they attire or the perfumes that pleased her most. She knew the meals Eris craved when in a low mood and which wine to fetch.

'Shall we plait your hair today, my lady?'

Eris nodded, grateful for someone else to make decisions. 'Time to become the Silent Queen once more.'

Eris looked in the mirror, took in the shape of lips about to be hidden beneath a veil for the long hours until night returned. She would not be sitting here had her eyes been any other shade of green, and yet Fortuna had seen fit to bestow the similarity. A simple peasant girl transmuted to Orfano with a few light touches of foundation, kohl and rouge, plucked eyebrows. These were the hallmarks the deception had been built on. A sleight of hand named Aranea Oscuro Diaspora. The maid began to plait her hair into a corn-blonde rope.

'You're not the first woman to attend the Domina, are you?' said Eris, head bobbing with each tug on her hair.

'No, my lady.' That reluctance again. Eris couldn't blame her. A single word in the wrong place could spell catastrophe. 'There was another before me, my lady.'

'You know her name,' pressed Eris.

'Fiorenza, my lady.' She didn't cease in her task, fingers entwined between tresses.

'And what became of her?'

Isabella glanced at the looking glass, offering a rare meeting of gazes. 'I was told she was killed. I was told it was Lord Dino Erudito.'

'And why was that?'

'They say she was with child. Lord Erudito flew into a rage when she told him.'

'And yet your answers suggest you don't hold with these facts.'

Isabella considered her next words with as much care as she favoured each blonde tress. A slip could reduce the intricate weaving to the most appalling of knots.

'You hear so many things, my lady. I lose track of what is gossip and what is real.'

'A masterful evasion. You'd be the darling of the Ravenscourt.'

Eris noted the girl favoured her right hand, the left wrist thinner, the fingers kinked.

'How long have you worked for me now?'

'Just over two months, my lady.'

'And yet I feel I barely know a thing about you, Isabella.'

'I'm an open book, my lady. Ask whatever you wish.'

'What happened to your wrist?'

Isabella blushed, but Eris couldn't decide if it was embarrassment or anger that lent colour to the maid's cheeks.

'I fell.' She cleared her throat. 'Down a staircase, my lady. Clumsy of me. I should have paid more attention.'

Eris smiled, savouring a morsel of gossip, a morsel with the meat of truth.

'Except the fall wasn't your fault, was it? You fell because Duke Fontein was haranguing you. You fled his apartment and slipped when he followed you into the corridor.'

'My lady is well informed.'

'A broken wrist, and all for, what was it?'

'A glass of red wine. Spilled, my lady.' She continued plaiting, voice leached of tone. 'Spoiled the duke's rug.'

'And yet rugs can be replaced. Your wrist remains—'

'It's of no matter, my lady.'

The women locked eyes in the looking glass.

'Apologies, my lady. I did not mean to interrupt. I forgot myself.' Eris shrugged, then smiled. 'The duke is at his rest and I serve you now. You and the Domina.'

'That's true. Duke Fontein is indeed dead. I heard he was poisoned.'

'I heard it was old age, my lady,' replied Isabella, her response quick.

'A woman's place in Demesne is such a complicated affair.'

Isabella nodded in agreement but remained silent.

'Marriage and duty, intrigue and lust. What are your thoughts?'

'I envy the men,' said Isabella, her voice quiet yet hard. 'They pass through life with barely a thought for the cares of women. Many treat their horses with more respect.'

'Well, take care you don't end up like poor Fiorenza.'

'Pregnant, my lady?'

'Dead, Isabella.' Eris turned on the chair, looking into the maid's eyes. 'Be careful you don't end up dead. And seeing as you have difficulty separating fact from gossip, you might choose to refrain from speaking of such things at all.'

'Yes, my lady. I understand.'

'Certainly you'll never speak of what is said in this apartment, or what you see here, no matter how charming the questioner.'

'Yes, my lady.'

Eris smiled, but there was a note of defiance in the maid's tone.

'I think I rather like you, Isabella. Better you have some spirit than be another mindless drone. Scores of those throng the corridors of Demesne already. And not all of them wear Myrmidon armour.'

'Thank you, my lady.'

'Come,' said Eris, pulling on a pair of leather gloves. Isabella gathered her shawl, but it was anxiety that wrapped her completely, giving pause to her movements and tripping her tongue.

'W-where are we going, my lady?'

'I use to love the Ravenscourt. But no longer. Do you know, the home I grew up in could fit inside it some twenty times over, at least.'

'It's an impressive chamber, my lady.'

'It's a cell.' The maid recoiled at the sudden reversal of mood. Eris held out a hand to indicate she meant no harm. 'It's a cell, Isabella. One where we are shackled by ceremony, chained by the many dictates of the *nobili*, held down by edicts and customs we barely understand. How do you tolerate it? The great and minor houses with their endless wants?'

Isabella opened her mouth to speak, then lowered her gaze.

'They plead poverty as they dine on venison. They bemoan cruel fortune as life gives them fine clothes.' Eris eyed the windows, aware she was as much thinking aloud as speaking for Isabella's sake. 'Not one of them has ever lived without a roof over their head. Not like me, not like Sabatino.'

'Perhaps you should sit. I could bring you tea.'

Eris waved off the suggestion. 'I can't abide them, all milling around the Ravenscourt for any scrap of prestige or power. And behind everything, behind the curtain, listening, waiting...' Eris stared beyond the windows as the sun made a bloody smear of the sky.

'My lady?'

'Never mind.' Eris sighed and fixed the turquoise veil over her face. 'The Ravenscourt is not the only place a woman of influence can do business.'

Eris swept through the corridors of Demesne. Her appearance drew obsequious attention at every turn. She emerged in the House Contadino rose garden, trailed by a dozen dignitaries and messengers. Of the latter, four were sent to summon her private counsel. The former were dismissed, leaving her alone but for four Myrmidons guarding the main doorways.

'Fetch hot wine,' she said quietly.

'As you wish, my lady.' Isabella curtsied, as keen to be free of the inclement weather as the Silent Queen's mercurial spirit.

The winter sun was fully risen, casting a flat light. The wind had no mind to tease the trees, and even the frequent snow declined to fall. The windows that overlooked the gardens were blinded by shutters, flaking scarlet paint, white chevrons stained by rainwater and time.

'How perfectly lethargic,' Eris whispered. Her feet stirred the gravel as she crossed to the statue of Santa Maria, despoiled by the first touches of moss and guano. How many conversations had the stone saint overheard? Certainly a wealth of secrets had alighted on those stony ears. Perhaps the saint had been witness to kisses, those given freely and those stolen. And there was the child, held fast in a carved embrace. Eris's memory of her mother's arms was unclear. She turned away, unseeing eyes falling to flower beds left untended. The many bushes had become an unruly mass, waiting to slash and pierce those lacking a thick skin.

'Not so very different to Demesne,' muttered Eris running a hand down the side of the Saint's face. A shadow fell across her and for one terrible moment she was certain the Herald had returned to finish his work. The assassin she laid eyes on was not the one who wanted her dead, though. Not yet, at least. Eris stood face to face with Marchetti, his hood pulled up against the chill.

Thinking of converting? said his fingers. Eris glowered at the assassin's mockery, then looked around to ensure it was safe to speak.

'I'm not ruling it out.'

I heard your brief career as a sister was unenlightening.

'And I understand you had a religious experience yourself. Turned away on the steps of the church.'

You know why I was there.

'Of course I do. Why do you think I tried to gain entry? Instead I had to deal with this so-called Herald.'

I might have protected you if you had thought to include me in your plans.

'Why haven't you found him yet?'

The town is half empty and Demesne is riddled with hiding places. He could be in a derelict hovel or sleeping in House Contadino itself.

Eris stepped closer, dropping her voice, stomach tight with anger. 'How hard can it be to find a man with a sword across his back and a raven on his shoulder? It's not as if he's inconspicuous.'

Marchetti shrugged and cocked his head to one side. *Most of the* cittadini *think him revenant, or worse.*

'Ridiculous.' Eris pouted, but conviction was wanting. 'Simonetti thinks he might be the old swordmaster, Ruggeri. The Domina suspects the Herald is no more than a simple scout.'

No one else will do this thing for you, continued Marchetti. *Be grateful I am hunting him at all, whoever he is.* Marchetti cast his single-eyed gaze over the rose garden. *Why have you come here?*

'To be alone. There are still a few caretakers in House Contadino but it's largely abandoned. I get petitions every month or so, begging me to ensure the place doesn't fall down.'

Marchetti looked up at the scarlet and white shutters.

'This rose garden was Medea Contadino's stronghold. It was said the *marchesa* tended to the flowers herself, messengers coming and going as she knelt among the blooms with muddied fingers.'

Eris bent forward at the waist, snapping a prickle from a stem, regarding the brown spike between her gloved fingers.

'Medea was an adept politician. How cunning the image she crafted, a *marchesa* among the flowers. The farmers would feel kinship with her, attending the earth and the plants in her care.' Eris discarded the brown spike, lost amid the black soil. 'While the *cittadini* would presume those under Medea's influence would be nurtured.'

I had never thought of it like that. The assassin's fingers paused. *Impressive.*

'I wonder how many of those same House Contadino *cittadini* and farmers feared they may be pruned back if they outgrew their usefulness?'

That was never the Contadino way.

'No. You're right, always nurturing. And yet Medea withered once cut free of Emilio.'

She has grown back. Tenacious and thorny.

'I've a feeling she'll cut the palm that grips too tightly.'

A jut of the assassin's head indicated they were no longer alone. The Domina passed through double doors held open by Myrmidons. Gravel sounded crisply with each stride.

'I had hoped I'd never set foot in this place again.' The Domina looked around with a sneer twisting her purple lips. 'Is there any particular reason you've got us freezing to death in this wretched garden?'

'I'd rather Erebus didn't know every last detail—'

'Of your failure?' The Domina smiled.

'Not all of yesterday's failures fall at my door,' replied Eris.

'You remain empty-handed,' countered the Domina, 'while I have Medea in custody.'

'I don't want Medea Contadino; I want Anea. Dead. Now I've got a canoness I didn't ask for, an assassin who doesn't kill anyone and a Domina who struggles to follow simple orders.'

Allattamento entered the garden, a wary look in his eye as he turned up the collar of his jacket against the cold.

'Oh good,' continued Eris. 'And a *dottore* who can't cure diseases. I'm surrounded by incompetents.'

Allattamento approached, bowed, opened his mouth to speak, then thought better of it. He folded his arms across his chest, frowning against the cold.

'So what now for Demesne?' asked the Domina. 'What next, my lady?'

'What next?' repeated Eris. 'This was never part of the arrangement. I never expected the threat of war.'

'We have Medea,' replied the Domina, attempting a more conciliatory tone.

'That will only incite Lucien to gather his army,' said the *dottore*. 'He'll come on the pretext of rescuing her.'

'How gallant,' intoned Eris.

'The *dottore* is right,' said the Domina. 'House Del Toro will have dispatched a messenger to Duke Marino, asking that he bring forward his plans to intervene.'

Isabella emerged from the doorway, almost losing her grip on a tray bearing six goblets. Viscount Datini shuffled along beside her, a hint of a smile on his face. Eris let slip a silent curse. No more speaking with the viscount present.

Can we use Medea as insurance against war? Eris signed.

'You can't threaten the *marchesa*,' said the *dottore*.

Lucien would not dare put her life at risk, replied Eris. *His compassion will stay his hand. It is his greatest weakness.*

'Some say it's his greatest strength,' said the Domina.

Now is not the time to start admiring our enemies. Eris flashed the Domina an angry glare.

'If you kill Medea there will be total war,' said Allattamento. 'House Del Toro will lead. Schiaparelli and Elemosina will rally to Lucien's houses.'

'The *dottore* is correct,' said Viscount Datini. The old man squinted at them from beneath bushy white eyebrows. 'Such serious faces. Did you take someone captive by mistake?'

'It wasn't a mistake,' replied the Domina through gritted teeth.

You are unusually playful today, Viscount. Have you received good news?

'Not news exactly, but my fortunes are greatly improved.' Eris watched him smile at the *dottore* as Isabella served the wine. Allattamento smiled back, making a comment in the viscount's ear.

'All in good time,' replied the old man. Isabella served Marchetti first, who declined to drink on account of his veil. The Domina took a goblet next, then put it back on the tray and took another.

Do you really think I'd poison you? signed Eris with a scowl. The Domina answered with a shrug.

'If you're prepared to kill Medea then what hope for the rest of us?'

'I think it's safe to say our lady still has need of allies, don't you?' The old viscount smiled. 'Where is Simonetti? Did you not call him?'

He was sent for.

'Can we trust him?' asked the viscount. 'He is close to the Contadini.'

There was a quiet moment of unease as they regarded each other anew, tallying up old scores and former alliances.

'Simonetti was always loyal to the throne,' said the *dottore*. 'He is loyal to our Lady Aranea Oscuro Diaspora. And to the many books he so loves.'

Then where is he?

The *dottore* shrugged. 'I'm not his keeper, my lady.'

'You seem very sure of yourself,' said the Domina.

'House Erudito have always placed knowledge before intrigue,' said the *dottore*. 'Simonetti is no different.'

'*Conoscenza, perseveranza, eccellenza,*' said Viscount Datini as Isabella served the wine. The maid's eyes lingered on the *dottore*; his own gaze was far from proper as she turned to serve Eris, who shook her head.

Take one for yourself. You must be freezing.

'Thank you, my lady.' Isabella returned inside and the *dottore* did his best not to follow her every step with his eyes.

92

I have no intention of killing Medea Contadino, signed Eris; *only to use the threat to keep Lucien from our door.*

'It won't work,' said the viscount. 'And worse still, you risk pushing House Prospero into an alliance with Contadino and Marino.'

Salvaza Prospero would never risk her house, signed Eris. *Besides, Medea wants Salvaza dead.*

'Holding Medea will neither precipitate nor delay the inevitable. War is coming,' said the Domina. 'All we can do is trust to the protection of the Myrmidons.'

I do not believe in inevitability, signed Eris.

'We're all slaves to the will of Erebus now,' added the Domina.

All of the Domina's self-pity, the arch rebukes, her maudlin responses, sharpened to a single point, like a stiletto. Except Eris wasn't armed with a stiletto, only the palm of her hand. The slap echoed around the rose garden, the silence that followed like a deep chasm. Dottore Allattamento and Viscount Datini blinked in surprise.

I belong to no one, signed Eris. *Not to you, and not to Erebus. You can be a slave at a time that suits me. Perhaps if you stopped taking so much* tinctura *you might think straight.*

'Who is Erebus?' said Viscount Datini, but the question went unanswered as Marchetti stepped between the women, a stern cast to his single eye.

Eris met the look and signed, *Find them, or I'll turn you and Medea over to the Herald just to appease Lucien.*

The advisers departed, casting wary looks over their shoulders as the Silent Queen stood seething amid the tangle of near-dead rose bushes.

'Medea Contadino will destroy this entire kingdom,' breathed Eris, 'just to avenge one man.

Outrage and Accusation

Anea spent the night wandering the streets, wedging her slight frame into doorways. She hovered at the edge of consciousness only to wake with the force of her shivering. Her frozen feet led her to House Erudito. A supposedly great house, it had succumbed to a neutrality so apathetic the Myrmidons had ceased posting guards there. The soldiers of House Fontein had at least maintained the pretence of protecting those who served Demesne. The Myrmidons who had replaced them existed only to ensure loyalty to the throne. She passed through the gatehouse with arms crossed over her chest, fingers pushed into armpits, anything to ward off the cold. A side door remained open, this a blessing after the previous three, all locked.

Anea trudged along the corridors, breathing warmth onto her numb fingers. Memories of Maestro Cherubini filtered back to her. The enlightenment and reason of House Erudito had been a welcome ally under Cherubini's guidance. Her abiding memory was of a cheerful, sometimes nervy, avuncular man, his intellect the equal of his appetite. Was he dead? She didn't think so. His fate remained intangible to her, another memory yet to resurface.

She recalled when Virmyre had made a home here, a time when House Erudito had been a place of refuge to a young girl with no words save the ones she scrawled in books. Distant now, a time before she and Dino developed the silent language. These were not bright epiphanies of remembering, rather a gentle swell of knowing, like the sound of rain in the night.

Other memories returned to her in that numbed and sleepless

fugue state. Russo had provided the greater part of her education. She had been *professore* back then, and also a friend. It had made sense to elevate her to Domina. The shivering woman tried to guess at the combination of events. Had she been an unwitting alchemist transmuting loyalty to betrayal? Was Russo punishing her for an ill deed since forgotten? Anea shook her head, frustrated by the gaps in her memory. No trace of Russo existed, she told herself; only the Domina remained. Anea pressed on, glad to be free of the spiteful breeze, aware her breath steamed in the air beyond her veil.

Lost in her musing, she found herself outside Virmyre's apartment. The door had been smashed, the lock rendered useless. She slipped inside to find a dusty interior. Moments spent fumbling in the dark rewarded her with candlelight but a quick inspection revealed the *professore* was long absent. She picked through the man's belongings, gently denying the admission he was gone. Another soul lost to a period of time she struggled to remember, another friend betrayed by the Domina. The search yielded a few useful items. Moments later she was wrapped in a thick blanket, curled up on the couch like a hound, the rise and fall of her chest the only movement. Her exhaustion was total.

'I'm terribly sorry to interrupt your rest, my lady.'

Anea jolted awake. The solitary candle had burned low, flickering with the promise of drowning in wax. The owner of the voice was an indistinct shadow beyond the meagre limit of the candle's nimbus, a tall figure wrapped in robes and gaunt in the dim light. Anea's pulse quickened.

The Majordomo.

She flung the blanket aside, lurched upright, the point of a stiletto leading the strike. The weapon had been Virmyre's once; even now he protected her from beyond the grave. Her attacker collapsed on his knees with a nervous cry.

'Wait, I'm unarmed!'

Hardly the words of the Majordomo. This wasn't the cadaverous haunter of her dreams – how could it be? Hadn't Lucien himself killed the king's steward? Anea stood over the slumped

95

figure, holding the stiletto point to the man's throat. Then the realisation – the last time he'd knelt before her she'd made him viscount. The point of the stiletto lowered. She took a step back, placing the steel on a bookshelf behind her.

Simonetti?

'Yes.' The man stood and rubbed his knee with an anxious glance. 'Ah, do I know you?'

Once perhaps. No longer. What time is it?

'Just before noon. I was passing by and noticed the door ajar. Are you hurt? Do you need a *dottore?*'

She shook her head, noticed him casting an eye over her attire, Medea's clothes.

I should be asking that of you.

'I'm fine,' he said, voice an unconvincing rumble. He continued to rub his knees though clearly his pride had sustained the greater wound.

I apologise. You startled me. I did not hear you enter.

'You look familiar to me,' said the archivist, squinting in the gloom, 'yet I can't place you.' The candlelight made amber ovals of his optics, reflections on a shadowed face.

I am just a maid, turned out of my home last night. I came here in desperation. I meant no intrusion.

Simonetti stared for a moment longer than was polite. She was sure he'd pieced together the deception. Anea fought down a surge of panic.

'Well, I won't tell anyone you're here,' rumbled Simonetti. 'I'm sorry I woke you. I must attend the Ravenscourt; there are grave matters afoot. I'll leave you to your, ah, sleep.'

Anea nodded, watched the man who had archived her library turn his back on her, watched the gentle soul she'd made viscount reach the door. He faltered a moment, then turned.

'I could, well, if you needed it, I could find a craftsman, have the lock repaired.' He looked around the apartment with unhappiness twisting on his lips. 'I've a feeling Virmyre would want you to have the key.'

Thank you, she signed, *but that is not necessary.* She paused. *There is perhaps one thing you can do for me.*

*

The Ravenscourt thronged with protestors from Houses Del Toro, Elemosina and Schiaparelli. Representatives from other houses attended, well aware Demesne had reached a turning point, desperate to hear the fate of Medea Contadino. Those with standing occupied the floor of the Ravenscourt itself; the remainder glowered from the balcony, keeping their distance from the black-curtained enclosure behind the throne.

Duchess Prospero had gathered a selection of supporters. If Medea could succumb to such an ignoble end then Salvaza's future looked equally precarious. The duchess's page lurked by her elbow, the surly look on his face almost concealing his worry. Representatives from Houses Martello and Acquarone stood with her, bolstered by a handful of bravos from House Schiavone. The bravos flouted etiquette, duelling blades hanging from their hips for all to see, preening beneath the deep scarlet of their attire. Usually allied with House Fontein, they had seen fit to find patronage with House Prospero.

The many *professori* and scholars of House Erudito lurked at the back of the Ravenscourt, studiously neutral. They blinked and muttered, yawned and complained, akin to a colony of bats in their black robes.

By far the greatest number of people present were the Sisters of Santa Maria, who had all but invaded the vast chamber. They stood in clusters of fours and fives, some on the balcony, some on the black and white tiles of the court itself. Others crowded the staircases, craning their necks to see. They were armed with hard stares, and bore lanterns that turned back the ever-present gloom of the Ravenscourt.

Drago Romanucci stood beside Disciple Agostina, thumbs tucked into a wide leather belt, scabbard hanging at his hip. His message was clear: no one would touch the disciple without paying a high price. Romanucci's presence was emphasised by the contrast with Agostina, olive-skinned to her paleness, broad-shouldered compared to her slight frame, a hint of challenge in his pose while the disciple stood with bowed head.

Anea regarded the Ravenscourt from the balcony, from amid the crush of bodies. None spared the stranger much attention, although few women served as messengers in Demesne, fewer still for House Erudito. She shunned the light, her three-cornered hat pulled low, throwing deeper shadow over her veiled face. The britches, tabard and hat had been supplied by a reluctant Simonetti. She hadn't specified why she needed them; he had declined to ask her.

The archivist entered, as if summoned by her thought. Simonetti escorted Dottore Allattamento, while Viscount Datini followed in their wake, a sour fury in his deep-set eyes. Simonetti looked to the balcony, eyes alighting on the messenger he had outfitted. A small nod of recognition passed between them. She was positive the archivist knew her identity, yet they'd both left that particular truth unsaid. Better he prove the evidence of his suspicions for himself. Wasn't that the way of academics?

Simonetti and Allattamento took positions near the dais, taking care to put distance between themselves and Duchess Prospero, declining to stand alongside Agostina. Anea wondered what it must be like to be the only supporters of a hated ruler. Viscount Datini shouldered his way between them, standing in front of both, the jut of his chin a challenge.

The Domina emerged from behind the Myrmidon throne, her silver staff shining in the light of scores of lanterns. Anea thought the woman looked pale, strangely youthful yet exhausted.

Medea was brought forth, escorted by four Myrmidons. The *marchesa*'s fine gown had been torn, the hem stained with filth from her cell, a ragged dirty shawl about her shoulders. Her gaze was downcast, chestnut hair awry about her delicate face. Always a petite woman, she had been further diminished by incarceration. Ten more Myrmidons entered through the main doors, advancing in pairs, taking up positions by the columns. The room stirred, a susurrus of uneasy whispering.

Marchetti appeared on the dais in battered leather armour and stood to one side of the Myrmidon throne, hand resting on the hilt of his blade. His single eye sought Drago Romanucci, yet if the *dirigente* was concerned he made no show of it. Anea thought she detected the hint of a mocking smile on the man's lips.

The Domina's staff slammed against the dais three times and

98

the audience dropped to one knee as the Silent Queen entered, taking her place on the throne. Anea had always been seated to see her subjects file into the room, made it her custom, yet the Domina and imposter arrived late. Anea wondered just how prepared they truly were.

'This session of the Ravenscourt is open.' The chamber rose to its feet, still silent. 'Lady Aranea Oscuro Diaspora wishes it to be known that Marchesa Medea Contadino is guilty of sheltering an enemy of Landfall.'

A commotion of dissent, muttered insults.

'SILENCE!' The silver staff boomed down, and then once more the room settled. Drago Romanucci stepped forward, raising his hand as casually as one might greet a friend. The Domina failed to hide her annoyance.

'Romanucci,' she grunted.

'That's Dirigente Romanucci.' The big man winked. A rash of giggles broke out on the balcony. Romanucci looked at those behind him, making sure he had the full attention of the Ravenscourt.

'My lady.' He nodded to whoever sat on the throne. 'Perhaps you might share with us who it is you think the *marchesa* is concealing.'

The impostor flickered out a few words. Anea noticed she mangled the last gesture.

'An escaped prisoner from the oubliette,' said the Domina.

'Was her crime to exist without a name?' Drago smiled again.

'No one said the prisoner was a she,' replied the Domina.

'And yet I have my sources,' replied the *dirigente*.

'Medea Contadino is hereby stripped of her title,' said the Domina warily, 'and will remain in custody until she provides word of the prisoner's location. Treason will not be tolerated.'

The Ravenscourt erupted in outrage. For once, all the houses were united, if only in contempt. Anea felt a surge of anxiety. The fate of Landfall rested not on the proverbial knife edge, but a stiletto point. The slightest pressure would see the nation run through, fatally wounded.

'At least grant her permission to speak.' The crowd parted, drawing back from Duchess Prospero, who had drawn herself

99

up to her full height. 'I'm not sure what sham trial this is before me, but I believe it customary for the accused to speak in their defence.'

Anea, so long the political opposite of the duchess, wanted to applaud. Quite how Salvaza loaded each word with such seething disgust was a bravura performance.

The Domina looked at the imposter, a frozen moment of panic passing between them. Anea guessed they hadn't foreseen this. Perhaps they'd thought to cow the room with the Myrmidons. Perhaps they'd imagined the nobles would acquiesce without question. Perhaps they hoped Medea had been written off as a zealot, maddened by her husband's death. Eris shook her head. Medea opened her mouth, only to find a thick gauntlet silencing her.

'Let her speak,' began the cry, becoming a chorus from houses major and minor alike. The Domina leant close to the impostor queen and whispered. The Myrmidon restraining Medea removed his hand. Anea couldn't breathe such was the power of her anticipation.

'The woman sat on the throne is not Aranea Oscuro Diaspora –' Medea's voice carried easily '– nor has she been for many months.'

The imposter looked aghast, while the Domina paled with shock.

'We have been duped by a charlatan with an unclear agen—' Medea got no further. Another Myrmidon clamped thick fingers clad in leather over her mouth.

'So it seems the unnamed prisoner has a name after all,' said Romanucci. 'Or have you murdered Anea?'

'No one has murdered anyone.' The Domina forced a smile. 'You want to believe a woman gone mad with grief? As you wish, but these accusations are unfounded.'

'It makes a certain sense,' added Salvaza Prospero. 'Anea would never have never outfitted an army, not when she could spend good money establishing her republic.'

Shouts and catcalls sounded from across the Ravenscourt, gradually becoming a chant, a single word: 'Betrayer. Betrayer. Betrayer.'

The Domina fled, disappearing behind the Myrmidon throne as the assembled nobles continued their chant. Eris followed her lead, not daring to meet the eyes of the angry crowd. More Myrmidons filed in from behind the throne, forming a cordon of brown-armoured figures at the edge of the dais. The crowd surged forward to be met by fists. Swords were drawn, deterring everyone but Romanucci, shouting at the top of his lungs for the release of Medea. The nobles recoiled. A lone voice screamed on the far side of the Ravenscourt, a cry to escape. The nobles needed no encouragement.

Simonetti looked to Anea, his brow creased in confusion. A Myrmidon on the dais behind him raised his head to follow his gaze, looking directly at the false messenger. Anea couldn't be sure what the Myrmidon saw but decided she had lingered too long.

The crowd jostled and shoved as Anea shouldered her way through, almost losing her hat. A brief glance behind confirmed what she feared most. The Myrmidon had stepped down from the dais and was pushing through the crowd toward the stairs. One hand pressed to the hilt of the short sword she had stolen from Virmyre's apartment, Anea pushed past a surly member of House Del Toro and through the doors of the Ravenscourt.

Moments later she emerged into the corridor that ran the circumference of the Central Keep, losing herself amid the crowd. Rumour and speculation sounded on the air in a fevered drone. Anea's relief was short-lived. The Myrmidon trailing her had gained ground, an armoured hand forcing those too slow or unwilling to move from his path. Anea looked for a way out but the nearest exit was the gatehouse leading to House Contadino. She took it, glancing over her shoulder, past *professori* and several sisters, and casting furtive looks at the Myrmidons on guard; none moved to intercept. She pressed on, breaking into a run, turning a corner. A look snatched over her shoulder revealed the first Myrmidon had been joined by a second, trailing him by a score of feet.

Anea hissed.

Onwards, finding stairs, climbing them two at a time, her boots slipping on stone, scabbard slapping the wall. Heavier boots sounded on the steps below her. She turned another of Demesne's seemingly endless corners, into yet another unlit corridor. She ran as fast she dared in the half-light, expecting to trip at any second. A clatter of armour from behind confirmed her pursuer was not giving up. He took a moment to steady himself after colliding with the wall. The slit in the curved helmet levelled and she knew he had seen her again.

She ran. On and on until her lungs felt they might split, her calves hot lead, thighs dull stone. A staircase down, a locked door and a moment of breathless panic. On into the rose garden, over gravel that slipped under sliding feet, past the statue of Santa Maria and to the doors on the opposite side. She pulled at the handles and hissed again.

Locked.

Anea turned, the Myrmidon emerging into the pale afternoon light. There was no need to rush – he'd cornered her after all – drawing his sword with deliberate slowness. She drew her own blade in response, a feeble weapon against such heavy armour. Anea blinked back her tears.

The Myrmidon came closer.

13

O My Beautiful Liar

This is not what I was promised, signed Eris as she retreated from the Ravenscourt. *I was promised safety.*

Twice they crossed paths with nobles, clusters of the disenchanted, the angry. Twice the Myrmidons pushed through, threatening with naked steel when resistance escalated from shouted protests.

'I did warn you not to parade Medea in front of the Ravenscourt,' countered the Domina, 'She's a person, not a battle standard.'

The Myrmidon was under strict instructions not to let her speak.

Using the silent language was a further impediment to her rage. Simonetti followed with Viscount Datini. Their belief that she was the true Silent Queen would shatter the moment a single word fell from her lips.

'I suggest we find the Myrmidon responsible,' said Allattamento, walking beside her.

'They all look the same to me,' grunted Viscount Datini.

'It was one of the senior Myrmidons,' added Simonetti behind them, his voice so quiet as to be missed altogether.

Isabella had prepared hot wine for their arrival at Eris's apartment. The fire roiled and burned in the hearth. Eris crossed to the window, framed by the winter light, shaking with anger. Viscount Datini took the offered wine and claimed an armchair. Simonetti mumbled his thanks.

'Hardly the display of power we needed,' said Viscount

Datini. 'The relationship with the *cittadini* and the *nobili* is the worst it's been since you swept to power.'

Eris laced her fingers, an angry scowl her only response.

'Thank you for your insight, Viscount Datini,' said the Domina with a tight smile. 'We're all perfectly aware how the political landscape looks after today's fiasco.'

Isabella offered wine to the Domina only to be waved off.

'My lady, when will you denounce this accusation?' Allattamento sounded convincing despite his complicity. It had been he who had coached Eris in the silent language after all. The *dottore* had also procured and refined the chemicals to stain Eris's hair the same corn blonde as Anea's.

'We'll say this is the desperate action of a widow broken by grief,' said the Domina. This suggestion earned her a sour glance from Eris, but she continued unabashed. 'We'll say she'd go to any lengths to seek revenge. Medea is well known for her hatred of the Myrmidons.'

As if on cue the door opened and Marchetti entered.

And here is the prince of the Myrmidons himself, signed Eris. *Neither use nor ornament.*

Marchetti nodded to the assembled nobles but did not raise his eyes.

'Is there any word of the Herald?' said Viscount Datini, twisting round in his chair. The assassin shook his head. The mere mention of the cloaked figure was enough to silence the room.

Simonetti stood by the fireplace, cradling his wine in one hand while the other fussed with the cord that belted his robes. The wine remained untouched, the look in his eye distant. His jaw was home to stubble many days old and his optics were smeary. Eris jutted her head at the archivist, the Domina taking her lead.

'Does something trouble you, Viscount Simonetti?'

All eyes turned to the archivist.

'It was Anea who made me viscount,' he rumbled in a distracted tone.

'You mean Lady Diaspora,' chided the Domina. 'We haven't discarded formality just because we're behind closed doors.'

104

'Ah, forgive me, my lady.' Simonetti shot an apologetic look at Eris but avoided her eyes. 'I am unwell and not myself.' He handed his wine back to Isabella. 'Excuse me.' A short bow to the Silent Queen, nods to the others, and the archivist was gone.

Eris turned her back on the room. Simonetti was all that remained of the coterie that had been close to Anea. Russo had turned, Virmyre was missing, Dino dead. Only Simonetti provided a link to the original Silent Queen. Eris had precious few supporters. The cost would be high indeed if Simonetti was beginning to suspect.

'Is there any way I can be of service?' said Viscount Datini, breaking Eris's chain of thought.

The Domina interjected before she could conjure any words on her fingers. 'You have spies, my lord?'

The old viscount nodded. 'Of course.'

'Have Simonetti watched,' said the Domina. Eris wasn't the only one to glower at her; Allattamento's displeasure was written clearly on his face.

'He seems troubled by the day's events,' continued the Domina as if this were reason enough. 'We can ill afford to lose him at a time like this.'

Viscount Datini sipped his wine and rubbed his forehead with the fingertips of one hand. 'I took the precaution of assigning a few men to the archivist after our discussion in the rose garden.'

Is that so? signed Eris.

'All houses spy on each other, my lady,' said the viscount. 'It is merely a matter of survival. To refrain is to invite catastrophe.'

'It's done now.' The Domina waved a weary hand. 'Keep us apprised if anything untoward should occur.'

Viscount Datini stood and drained his wine glass before bowing to the ladies and taking his leave.

If you have no further use for me I will let you continue running Demesne, signed Eris.

'One of us should,' replied the Domina. A second of shock crossed her face, not quite believing the words had slipped out.

Eris's anger eclipsed her desire to keep up the pretence. 'Get out of my apartment.' The Domina nodded and left. 'You are dismissed, Isabella.' The maid followed, unable to keep the look of relief from her face. Eris, Marchetti and Allattamento remained, the silence taut.

'I made a mistake,' said Eris finally. Allattamento nodded but said nothing. Marchetti made no move. 'Everyone seems convinced I want to kill Medea when it's the Domina I'd rather execute. Maybe I should kill them both?'

Allattamento's eyes widened, and he opened his mouth to speak.

'Many a truth said in jest,' added Eris before he could form the words.

'Why don't you sleep on it?' said the *dottore* drawing close. 'Think on it anew in the morning. I can give you a preparation if you wish?'

'All the drugs in Landfall won't prepare me for tomorrow.'

'A preparation is—'

'I know what a preparation is. Must you be so literal?' Curiosity creased her brow. 'Why are you still here, Dottore?'

'I need to speak to you with regard to a delicate manner.' Allattamento shot a glance at Marchetti, who remained by the door, hands never far from his weapons. Eris gave a brittle laugh. She'd no desire to spend time alone with the *dottore*.

'There's very little Marchetti doesn't know. You can speak your mind here.'

'I'm not sure that's wise.' The *dottore* set down his glass and clasped his hands in the small of his back, much like Viscount Datini.

'I've made mistakes enough for one day,' she replied. 'One more won't hurt.'

'As you wish, my lady.' The tone of Allattamento's voice was a stark contradiction to his words. 'I have a confession of sorts.'

Eris held out a hand, stilling the words that would come next. 'Marchetti, could you wait outside and see we're not interrupted, please? By anyone.'

The veiled assassin bowed and slipped through the door, closing it silently behind him as he went.

'This had better be important. I've yet to forgive you for the loss of my brother.'

'Precisely. Which is why I need you to listen.' The *dottore* took her hands in his and led her to the couch. They sat, heads bowed close like lovers. Or conspirators. 'The roots of your brother's death did not grow from my failure.' Eris made to stand. He rested a hand on her arm, a plea in his eyes. 'Wait. Hear me out. That's all I ask.' She remained seated, spine as straight as any sword, eyes glittering coldly. 'I needed a specific medicine to cure your brother, one I could have made with access to the king's machines.'

Eris nodded. It was well known the king had hoarded vast amounts of knowledge, some stored in dusty tomes, yet more on thick sheets of obsidian that spoke in old dialects. Others revealed incomprehensible diagrams sketched in ghostly light.

'I tried. I tried for months, but no one knows more about the king's machines than Anea. I asked Erebus to let me see her, to interview her, but he refused. Three times I asked him. Three times he declined.'

'Erebus would never let harm come to my brother,' countered Eris. 'My service was conditional on his safekeeping.'

The *dottore* shook his head, a deep sadness in his eyes.

'You're lying.' Her words were tainted with desperation. She needed to believe he was lying; the possibility of this truth would tear down her everything.

'Erebus wants you alone,' said the *dottore*. 'He wants you lonely. He wants you weak and dependent.' Eris frowned, throat constricted with emotion, breath shallow. 'Dependent on *him*. As long as Sabatino lived you had an agenda. Now he's gone . . .'

The only sounds in the room were the crackle of burning wood in the hearth and the ragged drawing of breath as she struggled with the shock. Medea's outburst in the Ravenscourt had been bad enough, but the *dottore*'s revelation rendered Eris dumb. Long seconds dragged by as she marshalled her thoughts, as unruly as the nobles of the Ravenscourt. The noise in her head was deafening.

'Dependent on him,' she said at last. 'Just as the Domina depends on him for *tinctura*.'

'Precisely. It was Erebus who sealed your brother's fate. I'm

107

tired of you throwing his death in my face. It's long overdue you knew the truth of it.'

'And the Domina?'

'She set up the meetings with Erebus. I had hoped she might help me persuade him.' The *dottore*'s eyes held hers. 'She knows everything.'

Eris felt the familiar heat of her anger, a welcome reprieve from the sadness that had threatened to overtake her just seconds before.

'Why are you telling me this?' she intoned. 'Why now?'

'It's only a matter of time until the people turn against you, then Erebus will install another marionette in your place.'

'I'm not his puppet.'

The *dottore* shrugged. 'It's him or you, I'm afraid. You have to do what's necessary.'

'What do you mean?'

The *dottore* took a stiletto from inside his jacket and offered the hilt to her. She looked down as if a poisonous snake had appeared in her cold hand.

'I can't do that,' she replied, placing one hand on his. It was a poor imitation of the gesture he'd used to calm her just moments before. 'And certainly not alone. I need allies,' she breathed. 'I need a friend.' She flashed a glance intended to be alluring, but all she managed was uncertainty. 'I need you.'

'I'll help you but only in ways that do not expose me. I'm not sure poison would even work on Erebus.'

'We could both be killed for this.'

'Precisely, so you need to consider your next actions with the utmost care.'

She looked at the blade. The hilt was wrapped in soft calf-skin dyed crimson and black. The blade had a triangular cross section, words in gilt along each side. **TEMPO. VELOCITA. MISURA.** Her hands began to shake.

'Sabatino,' was all she said.

'Yes. I tried. I really did. It's part of the oath we swear. I would never have let something happen to him if . . .' The words tailed off as Eris held out one hand, not wanting to hear any more.

'*Tempo. Velocita. Misura.*' She read the words aloud from the blade. 'House Fontein's motto.'

'You'll escape suspicion. The Domina will assume it was Fontein assassins, retaliation for the duke and duchess. Payback from his rumoured bastard.'

Eris nodded. 'A disbanded house is the perfect culprit.'

'Is there anything else you need?' said the *dottore*.

Eris regarded the man, sure of his words yet unsure of his motives.

'And what of you when this is over? The next *maestro* of House Erudito?'

'Nothing like that.'

'Is the Domina next on your list? Do you covet the crimson robes and the silver staff?'

'There is no list,' said the *dottore*. 'I simply want to walk away from all this madness, all this sickness. I'll head south. Perhaps the Previdente have need of my services.'

'And what then?' asked Eris. She'd never considered leaving Demesne until now.

'I'll marry. There's someone I'm close to.' Paolo Allattamento forced a tight smile, and Eris though he'd given away more than he'd wanted to.

'Who is she?'

'No one among the *nobili*.' Eris detected a loathing in his words. This at least was something they had in common. 'And you'll be able to rule as I wish. I dare say you'll be more popular without Erebus pulling your strings. You may even be able to avert the war.'

'I thought you wanted an assassination, not a miracle.'

'Why not both? But Erebus must be removed first.' The *dottore* stood, knocking over an empty wine glass before performing a wooden bow. 'We'll speak again' was all he said before he slipped from the room. Eris followed him to the door and watched him stride away over the gleaming flagstones of the corridor.

Marchetti leaned against the far wall, eyeing the retreating figure of the *dottore*. She crooked a finger and gestured him in.

Unwise to appear without the veil, he signed when the door was closed.

'I want to look forward to a time when I don't have to wear this. I want to look forward to a time when I don't have to be her any more, a time when I don't have to use the silent language. I grew up in a woodcutter's hut on the edge of the Foresta di Ragno. The woodcutter had died and no one wanted the place on account of the thatch falling in.'

Marchetti frowned, then gestured that she should continue.

'My mother died the first winter we stayed there, and after that it was just me, looking after my brother. We never had anything like this —' she gestured to the room and all its finery '— never had food like this, or wine. We barely had clothes.' Eris had drifted to a window and was staring over the town, its rooftops blanketed in snow. 'And we never had deception or corruption.' She turned to Marchetti. 'We never had assassination.'

What are you suggesting?

'I need you to do something for me.' It only made sense as she said it, a reckless gamble. 'Something well suited to your repertoire. I need you to avenge my brother's killer.'

Marchetti shook his head and paused a moment. *You want me to kill Allattamento at a time like this?*

'No.' A shake of her head, a sudden tightening of her gut. 'I need you to kill Erebus. He killed my brother. I want him dead tonight.'

Marchetti took a step back, as if the very act of hearing the words made him complicit.

Erebus. Even the way he formed the word with his fingers was filled with reverence, even after his brief exile. *I cannot do this,* he signed. *You know I cannot do this.*

'He cast you aside the moment you failed him.' She watched the assassin's brow crease as he accepted the truth of it. 'You owe him nothing.'

True enough, but when he dies you will do the same. I am not so stupid as to think you sought me willingly. The order had to have come from him.

'Name your price.' The words were blunt, almost accusatory.

You know what I want, he signed, taking a step closer.

Eris shuddered. It had been many months since her drunken indiscretion in the Ravenscourt, yet the memory of that night remained like a sour taste, a source of shame that lingered.

Strange to think I have never seen your face until now. He took another step closer, his good eye intent. *I had always assumed you were underkin, but you are actually fully human.*

She nodded. 'Does it matter?'

A single shake of his head. *People place too much importance on birth.*

'And you want –' Eris swallowed, unable to draw her gaze away from his ruined eye '– us to be together?'

Erebus crafted me to be no more than a sharp tool, something to remove his opponents. I want to be more than just a killer, just as you desire to be more than an imitation of Anea.

The assassin drew close, fingers tracing the curvature of her hips, the small of her back. The smell of leather and oiled weapons was overwhelming. It was as if Marchetti barely existed, just a form made to fulfil duty. Should he not smell of blood or the grave? Where was the charnel stench of death so often a companion of assassins? She fought a tremor of disgust – disgust for herself, not for the underkin who pawed at her with such reverence. Eris steeled herself.

Surely you feel the lack of allies, of friends? I could be . . . His hands faltered, not knowing what word to sign next.

'I'm not in any sort of mind to decide who I should give my heart to.' Eris couldn't meet his eyes as she said it. 'Despite everything that's happened there's one simple truth.'

What truth?

'I barely know you.' The assassin withdrew, a frown above his ruined eye. She saw herself mirrored in his remaining eye, arms folded, clutching at herself. 'But I know we have things in common.' Marchetti nodded. 'I know we've both been used by Erebus, and I know we can both survive this.'

So we will be together?

'I need you to avenge my brother,' she whispered. The assassin pressed his body to hers, veiled face pushed into the hollow of her neck, drawing down lungfuls of her scent.

'Say you'll do it.'

Say we will be together.

Deceit, always her closest ally, abandoned her. The lie would not form in the face of Marchetti's single-minded hunger.

'I can't,' she whispered

A stunned moment, incredulity hardening to anger. Eris held her breath, not knowing if she had just signed her own death warrant.

Would I not protect you? Provide for you? Adore you above all others?

'I'm sorry.' Eris forced a smile. 'There's nothing wrong with you...'

The assassin stepped back, pressing a hand to his veil. He turned away just enough his ruined eye was hidden from her. A pause.

'Marchetti, I'm sorry.'

I suggest you kill him yourself, said his fingers. He refused to look at her. *Maybe you will kill each other and I will be free of you both.*

Eris watched the assassin leave, eying the stiletto where it lay on the couch, glinting gold with the promise of death. But whose?

14

The Purge Protocol

Anea stood in the House Contadino rose garden, back pressed to the stout timber of double doors that should have lead to freedom. She tugged at them in earnest, yet they remained resolutely locked. The blade she held was perhaps two and a half feet, a broad, flat blade in fashion with the bravos, so different to the longer, lighter blades she'd trained with. A cross in the Maltese style decorated the juncture of hilt and blade. The balance of the weapon hinted at the work of a master craftsman, but this was small compensation against the armoured figure bearing down on her, sword held in a low guard, body turned sideways on, curved helm betraying neither fear nor mercy. Anea could barely see her assailant's eyes. She watched his footwork, waiting for a tell.

A second Myrmidon entered the rose garden, running as best he could, weighted down by breastplate, helm and bracers. The crimson chevrons on his armour marked his seniority. Would they even deign to bury her, or leave her corpse as fodder for the roses? The senior Myrmidon pulled a stiletto free rather than the customary sword. The first Myrmidon was almost upon her, raising his blade to strike, flat light of the winter sun shining from the blade. She prepared to parry, gripping the hilt in both hands, as Ruggeri had taught her so long ago. She'd step aside if she could, perhaps scoring a strike to his knee, immobilising him as she passed.

A collision of bodies.

The senior Myrmidon had thrown an arm around the first and was attempting to thrust the stiletto into the gap between breastplate and helm. The Myrmidon jerked back, the point meeting breastplate instead of throat, sliding from armour. Anea stared in confusion. More wrestling. The first Myrmidon tried shrugging off the lethal embrace. The stiletto stabbed toward his throat again, but the blade skittered from the helm's faceplate, scoring it from eye to jaw. The Myrmidon slammed an arm back, armoured elbow crashing into the helm of his superior. He turned and raised the sword, swinging down with a grunt, but the blow was parried on the forte of the stiletto.

Anea lunged, blade describing a wide arc that struck across the thighs of the Myrmidon. The strike elicited an anguished cry, muffled by his helmet. The Myrmidon collapsed to the ground, hamstrings severed. His opponent stamped a foot down on the sword arm of the fallen, then knelt on his chest. His left hand clamped down on the fallen Myrmidon's helm, holding it fast. His right thrust the stiletto under the jaw into the soft palate. A desperate, ragged sound emerged, pitiful and ugly. Blood jetted, viscous crimson. The Myrmidon twitched and shook and his superior pressed the stiletto point deeper. The body stilled, the air souring as bowels voided. Anea held out her sword, point hovering in the air near the helm of the victor. The senior Myrmidon set the stiletto down on the chalk-white gravel, now slick with gore, holding out his hands to prove he meant no harm. Anea nodded. Hands rose to the helm, lifting it free of his head.

Virmyre looked at her, brow creased with curiosity, a single question on his lips.

'Anea?'

She nodded, a fierce tremor running up her arm and coursing through her body – the grief she had denied herself and a surge of relief. Virmyre embraced her, awkward in the armour. None of that mattered. He was alive. Her greatest confidant and ally was alive, and somehow younger than she remembered.

'Shall we go, Highness?'

He wasted no time, taking up his helm, keen to resume his disguise. A moment later and he was smashing a window, circumventing the locked doors that had thwarted her escape. He shouldered his way through, taking care to hammer shards of stubborn glass from the frame with an armoured fist. Where was the mild *professore* of her childhood? The Virmyre she had known was a calming presence, measured, precise.

A trio of Myrmidons appeared on the on far side of the rose garden, pausing as they spotted the lone messenger beside the shattered window. Anea clambered over the sill, uncaring of any remaining glass. An angry grunt confirmed the Myrmidons had seen their slain kin. Virmyre grasped Anea's hand, urging her to flee.

They ran through House Contadino, Anea stunned by the lonely corridors. Contadino had always been a place of cheerful industry and toil. She knew Emilio's death had marked a downturn in the fortunes of the house, but this was too much to bear. It was not the great house she remembered.

Virmyre marched along unlit corridors, no time to spend on stealth or caution. Sword in one hand, his other not releasing Anea's even for a second. From behind them came the sounds of armoured soldiers stamping over flagstones, checking rooms. Anea's heart beat hard in her ears, breath a jagged saw.

'The whole place is in uproar,' whispered Virmyre as they stood at the junction of two corridors. 'The Houses will be out for blood after Medea's revelation. Major and minor alike.'

And on into the lonely depths of unused kitchens, pantries empty but for memories and echoes. Lucien had played here once, lingering close to Camelia. A frantic moment and a bolt sliding loud in the dark, then daylight. Footsteps behind them, impossible to tell how close. Virmyre pulled her through the doorway.

Anea stood on the porch of House Contadino, staring at the wooden granaries on the far side of the courtyard. Their doors were variously open or smashed. Barrels lay strewn in disarray, yawning open or splintered apart. Virmyre lifted the crossbar from the gate and dropped it to the cobblestones with a dull smack. Anea moved toward the gate, reluctant to leave Demesne. This had been her home, the source of her power; now it promised only violence.

'Look out!' said Virmyre, too late. Anea was wrenched back, a gloved hand around her mouth. She was lifted onto the tips of her feet, boots scrabbling for purchase.

'Wait!' Virmyre reached out with one hand, placating.

'What's going on here?' The Myrmidon's voice was laced with uncertainty. That Virmyre wore the armour of a senior Myrmidon gave them an edge. Anea's hand sought the stiletto she'd threatened Simonetti with just hours ago.

'You're holding the queen,' said Virmyre in a calm voice. 'She's in disguise so I can escort her from Demesne, away from the *nobili*. She's already survived one attempt on her life today.'

'But the queen is in her apartment.'

'That is a decoy,' soothed Virmyre. 'This is the real queen.'

The Myrmidon's grip slackened; Anea was lowered.

'Apologies,' grunted the Myrmidon. He fell back with a wordless shout as Anea plunged the stiletto into his thigh, collapsing, hands curling around the hilt. Virmyre surged over and smashed the pommel of his sword against the wounded man's helm. The Myrmidon's head bounced from the cobbles before his body went limp.

You realise you were telling him the truth? signed Anea. *I am the queen.*

'Good point. Just not the queen he thought you were.'

Anea shook her head and retrieved the stiletto.

'I never was any good at lying,' intoned Virmyre.

Through the streets of Santa Maria and out to the edges of town, Virmyre led them away from Demesne, scurrying from its ranks of arched windows. Twice they hid in doorways. Clusters of Myrmidons trooped past, feet stamping the snow-slicked streets in lockstep.

'Almost there,' said Virmyre, the words stifled by his helm. Anea could do nothing but follow. *Cittadini* in the streets stared after them, wariness and distrust on their faces.

The lower three floors of the old *sanatorio* were still lined with shelves, still crowded with books of all dimensions. No need to doubt the veracity of her memory, this place at least remained sacrosanct. The building itself was still illuminated by stained-glass windows. The only divergence from memory was the covering of dust obscuring the rosewood floor. Turquoise carpets ran like trails between shelves and desks, less vibrant than she recalled. Stepladders kept vigil over shelves, their formerly gleaming brass handrails dull.

'They closed the library first,' explained Virmyre, leading her deeper into the building. 'They worried the *cittadini* would start getting ideas above their station.' He led her to the far side, pausing to draw back a thick tapestry concealing a door. 'Which made my life easier. Now I'm the sole resident here.' Virmyre produced two keys on a length of cord around his neck, then used them in strict order. 'Even Simonetti barely visits – so much for being archivist.'

Into darkness they climbed, ascending a spiral staircase, stone smooth beneath their boots. Only the smell of damp greeted them. Up they went, emerging on the fourth floor. No polished rosewood timbers here, no verdant carpets or brass railings. There had been little change from when the cells had once housed the insane. A lantern turned down low, shedding silvery light, sat atop a barrel.

Anea tugged at Virmyre's hand, slowing him. He removed the helm and she drew in a startled breath, the sight of him no less shocking the second time. Pale blue eyes under fine arched eyebrows, black hair and a goatee run to full beard.

I spoke with Simonetti earlier without revealing my identity, she signed.

'You spoke to him? How?'

Anea recounted her stumbling to Virmyre's old apartment, the shock of being woken, Simonetti outfitting her with a disguise.

He will be confused, especially after Medea's outburst. He may even be convinced.

'True enough, but Simonetti is close to the impostor. I don't trust him.' Virmyre lifted the lantern. 'Come on.'

Virmyre's room was a barren place on the top floor, his only companion a mannequin.

'For the armour,' he explained, rapping his knuckles on the breastplate. Once the room had been two cells. 'It was quick work with a sledgehammer,' rumbled Virmyre by way of explanation. A single unmade bed was pressed into the corner, a worn armchair beside it. The other furniture consisted of a square chest with iron bands, a rickety chair, a solid desk strewn with clutter, raven quills and ink, a stiletto, a spare lantern and a specimen jar holding a preserved cataphract drake in solution. The wall above the desk was covered in sheets of overlapping parchment, a great map of Demesne penned in black. Red ink denoted rarely used stairs or corridors. Thin lines ran between different sections of the castle.

Secret passages?

'Not so secret any more,' said Virmyre. 'I used to scold Lucien for sneaking about and eavesdropping. Now my very survival depends upon it.'

What happened to us? Her fingers formed the words hesitantly, fearing the reply. Virmyre unbuckled his breastplate and grunted with relief, then sat down on the bed and started fussing with other clasps.

'We became addicts.' He sighed. 'Addicted to work, to discovery, and then to *tinctura*.' It was rare for Virmyre to sully his face with expression, yet he frowned at the memory. 'We thought we were being so clever.'

What is tinctura? *What does it do?*

'You of all people should know that . . .' he said, then raised his chin, understanding brightening his eyes. 'Ah, they kept you in the oubliette. That's why the Domina insisted on female Myrmidons to guard the place. She couldn't trust the male ones.'

Anea nodded, feeling not despair for her lost memories but anger at her incarceration.

'That's why I couldn't find you. And you drank the water?'

A single nod.

'Lethe.'

They took my memories from me. I cannot remember how they abducted me, or if I was conscious when it happened. She looked away, then her fingers resumed gesturing. *Tell me what happened, all of it.*

'*Tinctura* has certain regenerative qualities,' said Virmyre. 'However there is a deadening of empathy. The need to socialise diminishes.' He discarded a bracer to the armchair. 'We became lost in our research, not noticing the Domina was being

118

manipulated, not aware Dino was struggling to maintain your rule. We became isolated from those outside, even from each other.'

Dino. Her fingers sketched out his name slowly, each gesture with a gentle care. *Is he really...*

'I can take you to his grave. The Domina saw to it he was given a proper burial. It seems she had empathy enough for that, at least.' Virmyre rubbed his forehead and cleared his throat.

The Domina is an addict too?

Virmyre nodded. 'It's how Erebus bought her favours, that and ever-reliable money.'

Who is Erebus?

'An unseen conspirator. He wrote to the Domina as an ally, a concerned *cittadino*, but the deeper she fell into his pocket the more he demanded of her.'

And you stayed?

The old *professore* nodded. 'I hid the majority of our findings, but Erebus already knew the secret of distilling *tinctura* and a few other concoctions besides. He seized a number of the king's machines and he's become very adept at using them.'

Using them for what?

'He's breeding Myrmidons now, refining the bloodline – more of the strengths, fewer deformities. It'll still take time, generations, but imagine – an army with Golia's strength, Lucien's agility, Dino's ability, your intelligence.'

Anea swallowed. She had buried the painful truth of her birth beneath duty and hard work. The Orfani were the result of glorified experiments, the underkin by contrast were the failures.

I had hoped the Orfani would be the last twisted creations in Landfall, she signed.

'There are many worse than Myrmidons,' intoned Virmyre, 'Myrmidons might be persuaded to follow you.'

If only that were true. She hesitated. *What do you mean, 'worse'?*

'I've read his entries, the king's own insane records. He mentions "Huntsmen" without really describing what they are. They remain asleep, waiting to cull the population in case of revolt.'

The same creatures we fought in the Verde Guerra?

'Perhaps,' Virmyre said. 'They need to be woken with a ritual. Of course, the king failed to detail what that ritual is.'

You do remember he was completely insane?

'Good point.'

Does he mention anything about the ritual?

'He refers to it as the Purge Protocol. It was something to be used as a last resort, if the people turned against him.'

Anea turned back to the great map of Demesne. The first and second floors had been drawn in meticulous detail, House Fontein and the Ravenscourt illustrated with masterful precision. She reached forward and lifted the sheets. Beneath were the lower levels, the plans less distinct, with fewer annotations, then the sewers and cisterns. A surge of dread squeezed the air from her lungs. She turned to Virmyre, trying to still the trembling of her hands as she signed.

I know where your monsters are sleeping.

'The Huntsmen? Here in Demesne?'

There are more machines, larger than a man, beneath House Prospero. I saw them as I escaped from the oubliette. Dozens of them, perhaps a hundred. Each like a sarcophagus stood on its end.

Virmyre removed his other bracer and looked up. 'Go on.'

There was something . . . inside them. I think I woke one.

'Doubtful.' Virmyre ran a thumb over his bottom lip. 'The ritual I mentioned requires an artefact. Without that the ritual can't be completed.'

What artefact?

'I was hoping you could tell me. We spoke of it before you were taken. You mentioned an object that didn't resemble any of the other devices or machines we'd uncovered. Do you remember?'

Anea shook her head. The actions the *professore* described might as well have been another person's. Anea felt a swell of frustration. She hissed.

'Perhaps it will come back to you in time?'

And if not?

'Then the Huntsmen will remain asleep. No bad thing, I assure you.' Virmyre removed the rest of his armour and changed into nondescript britches. A cloak and wide-brimmed hat completed his attire.

Where are you going? she signed.

'To buy you a horse and saddle. You'll never make the journey to the coast on foot.'

San Marino?

'Of course.' Virmyre took a step closer. 'You have to explain what's happened to Lucien. We can't take back the castle without an army.'

I am not going to San Marino. You know how dangerous the Foresta Vecchia is.

'And what do you intend to do in the meantime?' said Virmyre, an edge to his voice she didn't care for. 'I've been sneaking around for months, wearing that armour, eavesdropping on the Domina or Viscount Datini when I can. I wanted to send a message south, but the Domina keeps a keen eye on the Myrmidons. More than once I've nearly been discovered.'

How does this relate to me going to Santa Maria?

'Because I know all of this, and I can't think of a single way to take back the throne. I'd hoped letting Medea speak today would be enough.'

Anea shook her head.

'People are leaving the town in droves,' said Virmyre in a quiet voice. 'The taxes are pushing the *cittadini* to the brink of starvation. Some have risked crossing the *foresta* without an escort. That's how much they fear this "Silent Queen". I thought you'd want to set that right. I thought you'd want to reclaim your kingdom, your title, your reputation.'

Of course. I want all of those things but not if it means war.

'It's your name she's destroying.'

That is a given, but no reason Lucien's men have to die reclaiming a throne I lost.

'Assassination then. Demesne has a long history of it.'

Anea frowned at Virmyre's suggestion. He had been a teacher of science, a stony-faced widower, a voice of reason in the Ravenscourt; he had never been a killer. She shook her head.

The Domina, Viscount Datini, Simonetti, Paolo Allattamento, so many. The roots of this run deep, so deep we may bring down the very walls of Demesne. It's hopeless. We have to wait, we have to be cautious.

'*You* may have lost hope,' said Virmyre with the beginnings of a sneer on his lips, 'but some of us are still fighting.' The *professore* turned on his heel and left, his boots drumming an angry beat in the emptiness of the old *sanatorio*.

15

Denial and Disparagements

Eris stood before the gateway. A dozen more steps would take her from House Fontein into the central keep. She'd attired herself in black, a lightweight damask with matching gloves and veil. That the gown's cost was sufficient to feed a family for a month was a fact she overlooked. Her hair was swept up in a plait encircling her head, forming a halo of blonde around her anxious face. In essence she was dressed for a funeral – one that could not come soon enough. She'd forgone shoes, making an ally of silence, padding along Demesne's corridors in stockinged feet. Her toes would be chilled for hours to come.

A brazier stacked with peat lent the corridor a ruddy light. The Myrmidons on watch were hellish statues, armour the colour of dried blood. The air was a rich fug, earthy yet cloying. The Myrmidons saluted. Would one of them notice the lack of jewellery? Or the absence of kohl, so neatly applied to her jade-green eyes? She suppressed a hiss of annoyance, her entire existence subterfuge, her previous life barely remembered.

'My lady?' said the nearest of them. Eris nodded in response. She couldn't use the silent language, not when her right hand carried the steel and gilt of assassination. She thrust out her chin and squared her shoulders; she had no need to explain why she was abroad at such an hour.

'Do you require an escort?'

She shook her head, hoping they wouldn't insist, grateful they had asked. So often the Myrmidons fell into step behind her without asking. They turned back to the light of the brazier, continuing their conversation in low voices. Eris released a breath of relief.

Onward, under the gaze of armoured watchers. None expected the stiletto, lying against the inside of her forearm. She passed unchallenged, the steel point pressed against her elbow. Her fingers ached from clutching the hilt. **VELOCITA.** The word winked to her in the darkness, molten gold in the brazier light.

The longcase clocks of Demesne called out in sombre chimes, muted peals announcing the threshold of a new day. And yet the small hours were so fraught with danger, she reasoned. One could see in midnight, yet fail to greet the rising sun. Death was a constant companion in Demesne.

The Domina emerged from the white doors leading to the Ravenscourt, startling Eris from her introspection. The red-robed woman was just visible around the curving walls of the corridor, diminished by her lack of headgear and the silver staff of office. Eris hated it here. The walls were reinforced with rib-like buttresses, as if she were alive inside a vast, petrified snake. Oak doors some twelve feet high closed with a solemn resonance, a despairing rattle of chains followed. The doors had been painted white at Anea's insistence, but a thousand grubby fingerprints from greedy nobles had left their mark.

Eris held her breath, clutching the stiletto tighter. The Domina paused, casting her eyes to the ceiling as if communing with the Saint. One hand rose above her head, clasping a sliver of glass, a vial with a tiny nozzle. Seconds passed. Eris had intimate knowledge of the ritual, was well acquainted with the substance that dripped into the Domina's eyes. Beneath her disgust lay the familiar pang of need. The Domina drew a shuddering breath as the drug began to uncoil. First would come a rush of sensitivity: the simple act of breathing a sensuous luxury, fingertips charmed by texture, sound an enchantment, silence begetting awe. The drug would delve deeper, all tiredness ebbing, sweeping her away on a wave of elation and confidence. And then icy self-assurance. Eris knew every nuance of *tinctura*, had experienced each change herself, both subtle and profound. The Domina cleared her throat, blinking her eyes as the solution ran down her cheeks like spent tears.

Eris fought the urge to flee. Turning away now might prevent discovery, yet the same motion might betray her. The Domina took a moment to screw the cap on the vial before turning away, red robes swallowed by the darkness. Eris could only wonder what required the Domina's attention at such a late hour; her apartment lay in House Fontein yet her feet led elsewhere. Did she seek a lover or conspirator? Eris released a captive breath, the grip of the stiletto slick with sweat, a tremor in the fingers clutching the hilt. The corridor swallowed her down, bringing her close to the white doors. She pulled a two-pronged key from her bodice, slotting it into the blackened metal of the lock. The doors shuddered, the oppressive weight of silence giving way to the sound of chains behind wood. Counterweights and cogs did their work, meticulous and heavy. The doors yawned inward, revealing a deeper darkness in the gloom.

The king's library lay on the floor beneath the Ravenscourt. This was Simonetti's realm, his place of refuge since the main library had ceased opening its doors. The king himself had pawed through these very volumes in his more lucid moments, or so the archivist said, who never missed an opportunity to embroider the importance of his charges. The books that lived in the old *sanatorio* were but copies, scribed over countless hours. Numberless cloth- and leather-bound tomes rested on shelves of mahogany, titles gleaming bronze and gold in the meagre light of oil lamps turned down low. Neat slips of parchment declared each section in a scholarly hand. Ladders provided access to subjects unguessable. Even House Erudito's brightest struggled to decipher the secrets within. Eris passed them all without a flicker of interest. The room was a conduit. She had no use of knowledge, only action.

By night the Ravenscourt was a vast mausoleum possessed of a similar darkness. Candles had been snuffed out, the smoke from those tongues of flame a faded memory. A solitary lantern on the gallery above the dais hinted that those who rested here were not dead, merely asleep. The stained glass of the lantern's sides shed a purple nimbus. Eris took the stairs, head bowed, eyes fixed on the amethyst light. She pressed her arm into the small of her back, the steel of the blade blood-warm in the bitter cold of night. Sweat beaded her brow despite the chill. She edged around the curving path of the gallery, the floor of the Ravenscourt below vast and black and white. The curtain stood before her, bronze leaves made lavender by the strange light, as if tarnished through association.

Eris lifted the heavy fabric weighted at the hem with chain. She tried to swallow, throat dry as grave dust. The sickly tang of the unwell invaded her senses, the veil she wore no protection from the stench. She ducked beneath the fabric's edge, steadying herself as the curtain slumped to the floor. It had been many weeks since she'd ventured here, sparing herself the hidden parody of the Ravenscourt. The scene made her gag, a vignette of corruption; only her innate stubbornness prevented her from emptying her guts.

The floor was littered with misshapen bodies pale from lack of sun, grey at their extremities. Most had wraps of crude cloth tied around their waist, but that was the limit of their dignity. Deformity was rife. A few had arms ending in blunt stubs; others featured vestigial limbs sprouting from chests. Spines extended from forearms and shoulders, chitin fingernails beetle black and midnight blue. No two were the same, but they were not completely adrift of commonality. These were the wretched. Not human or underkin in any real sense, but a species apart, bred for a specific purpose. Twelve of them slumbered on thick rugs, clutching at bulbous stomachs ripe with the unborn. It was the otherness of their visages that unnerved Eris the most. None had discernible eyes; their noses were dull stubs or ragged holes; mandibles lay beneath, twitching in their sleep. Eris looked over the straining skin of their torsos, wondering at progeny to come. More recruits for the Myrmidons.

And presiding over the scene, the greatest and most warped Myrmidon of all, a refugee from the Nine Hells, Erebus slumbered above the tableau of knotted bodies, suspended on six legs of jagged chitin, each limb longer than a man. His chest was a mottled shell, while a bulbous segmented thorax replaced human legs. A Myrmidon helm had been crammed onto his head, modified with curving blades jutting forward, mandibles in steel. He had not always looked this way; once he had worn the shape of a man, borne the title of Majordomo. He had been the greatest and longest-serving instrument of the king, and his most insidious betrayer.

Eris stepped through the bodies of the wretched, hoping they slept deeply enough that she would not rouse them. The stiletto had doubled in weight; there could be no other explanation why her arm ached with such weariness. Another step, her foot alighting on a spent vial of *tinctura*. The glass cracked but did not break. The vial glittered like a star, reminding her of another time, another night, another moment standing on the dais of the Ravenscourt.

She'd charged Marchetti with killing a serving maid, the blame to be attributed to Lord Dino Erudito, a pretext for arresting him. Rumours had been started to support the fiction, whispers and confidences at court. The scheme had been suggested by Erebus and Eris had been all too keen to execute his orders, eager the plans came to fruition. She'd not cared at the time for the life of one innocent. She was barely herself, not content with playing impostor; another subtle change had occurred. *Tinctura* sang softly in the deep sinews of her body, deadening remorse and empathy in equal measure. And there was the heady reassurance of power, even if it were only a power she pretended to. How Eris marvelled at the new life Erebus had given her. Gowns intricate and beautiful beyond imagining, no scarcity of food, drinking wine instead of water. And greater than all these, Sabatino safe, attended by Dottore Allattamento no less. All these things in return for pretending to be Anea. She could have anything she wanted as the Silent Queen. Apartments, jewellery, furniture, staff... Why not Marchetti?

The assassin had appeared in the Ravenscourt to confirm the killing, as obedient as he was silent. He'd been unscarred back then, the eyes above the veil hard but beautiful in their way. With a slow gesture, languorous as any courtesan, she ushered him onto the throne with the promise of sex. He'd followed, hands trembling with the shock of intent, wanting her more than she realised. Legs parted, astride the throne, certainly there could be no greater statement of power, a subversion of everything the prim and regal Anea stood for. Marchetti knelt before her, fumbling at his britches. Had he lain with a woman before? What opportunities would an underkin have? Had he sampled only the quick satisfaction of whores?

And far above, in the dome of the ceiling, a pale face looked down through a window. A haunted stare she didn't recognise, shocked at her carnal desecration. She hadn't cared at the time. Only when she learned that Sabatino had died as she seduced Marchetti did she feel the pangs of revulsion, appalled by the callous act, a mindless coupling that served only to defile Anea's seat of power. Certainly there was no pleasure in it. The oak chair had become a constant reminder of that night, the night Sabatino had died while she sampled the intoxication of power. She'd had the oak chair burned a week later, the Myrmidon throne a pleasing replacement.

'You come to me late, little ghost.'

Eris flinched, almost dropping the stiletto. How long had she remained captive to remembering that shameful episode? How long rendered immobile with regret? She hadn't considered Erebus might be awake, had been hoping to strike in his sleep. Any bluff or pretext for her visit was unprepared. The reason lay along the length of her forearm, recompense in steel.

'You're still making gifts of *tinctura* to the Domina?' She prodded the spent vial on the floor with a toe, a disapproving frown above the veil.

The armoured head of the colossal aberration nodded once. 'I have one vial left from the current batch,' droned Erebus. 'It is yours if you wish it.'

For a single dream-like moment her left hand floated up from her side, the palm held open to receive. Then a single thought stabbed into her brain, colder and sharper than any steel.

Sabatino.

Eris clasped her hand into a fist, then drew it back to her breast, pressing her knuckles against her sternum. She closed her eyes and saw only Marchetti, thrusting rudely against her on the throne.

'What other potions have you uncovered?' she said. 'What variations have you distilled?'

'Nothing fit for you, little ghost.' The whisper he spoke in was a poor fit for the vast creature he had become.

'Nothing you could have given my brother?'

'Ah, Sabatino.'

'Don't say his name.' The words came from between clenched teeth. She'd not allowed herself the luxury of that word since his death.

'There was nothing we could do to save your brother, little ghost.'

'You lie. Allattamento told me everything. How he wanted to find a cure, some medicine stored in the king's machines, but you denied him.'

'It is the *dottore* who lies, little ghost. I promised you I'd make Sabatino the *capo*, did I not?'

'Why would Allattamento lie to me?'

'Only you know that. Perhaps he tired of the blame he so richly deserves. Did he go on to ask something of you, grant some dispensation? Was it the first step of a lengthy seduction? Or did he ask you to perform an act he lacked the courage for after he spread his lies?'

Eris swallowed, feeling her stomach shrivel, a dull ache beneath her leaden lungs.

'And you, so racked with guilt.' The whisper became a drone, filling her senses like a hangover, like a migraine. 'All too keen to believe.'

She flinched as if struck, took a hesitant step back. Erebus could not have known she was lost to *tinctura* when Sabatino had died. Her master had remained in the oubliette back then.

'You're lying,' she repeated, the words an angry hiss. Had spies learned of the night with Marchetti as Sabatino succumbed to consumption?

'You are lonely, my little ghost.' The words so tender, at odds with the grotesque creature towering above her. She nodded with the truth of it. 'You require a consort, no?'

Eris had no answer, the stiletto in her grip as useless as the handful of scattered replies she dared not make. She had never been close to anyone in Demesne, too busy playing the role of Anea to even consider such a thing. The thought was a cruel one – that she was neither desired nor desired anyone in return.

'Perhaps the time is ripe for a royal wedding? It would take people's minds from their many woes.'

This was not the outcome she had foreseen. Words hung from her lips, coiled about her tongue, denials and disparagements.

'A wedding this summer,' continued Erebus. 'Your courtship should begin soon, no? You may have any man in Landfall. Any man as long as he is a Myrmidon.'

'I can't.' The words slipped free so quietly she doubted Erebus heard them over his droning voice. 'I said I don't need a consort.' A wretch at her feet writhed a moment, then hauled herself upright, waddling away to a spot behind Erebus.

'Very well, little ghost. But it seems to me you are in need of something, if only to stop you listening to the *dottore*.'

'I'll retire now.' Eris backed away from her master, stumbling in the gloom. Wretches woke and clambered away from her, ungainly and slow, distended stomachs painfully swollen.

'Little ghost?'

Eris had lifted the curtain, ready to exit, so close to escaping into the Ravenscourt proper, yet she could not deny her master's voice.

'Yes, my lord?'

'If you ever come before me with a weapon again I will kill you myself.' One vast leg tapped the floor like a scythe blade eight feet long.

Eris looked down at her hand, the evidence clear. **MISURA.** The word, filigreed in gold, so clear, the blade flashing in the amethyst light. She'd been so keen to leave she'd failed to conceal the very reason she'd visited.

'The castle is unsafe,' she said by way of excuse, but her voice wavered and the response came too late.

'Yes. Very unsafe,' droned Erebus. 'No telling who will be found dead, or when.'

16

The Albero Estate

House Albero perched atop a swell in the land overlooking the broad expanse of dark trees beyond. The Foresta Vecchia was lush with silence, the deep green pines hidden beneath fresh snow. Passage through the forest was a safer ordeal since the Verde Guerra, but few could say they enjoyed spending time underneath the canopy, least of all the veterans who had served in the war. Veterans like Delfino and Corvino.

House Albero had flourished despite the forest's inhabitants. Dwellings clustered inside walls that described a loose hexagon. Slender *campanili* towered over the houses where the walls formed corners. The collection of buildings was something more than a village, the crowded streets and alleys not quite a town.

'Every so often I wonder how my life could have turned out better,' muttered Delfino, 'then I'm grateful I don't live here.'

'They had their reasons,' said Corvino.

'Hardly.'

'Gambling debts, a fist fight and that business with the tavern keeper's daughter.'

'It was she who sought me.'

Corvino shrugged.

The *campanili* were lit with torches and braziers, beacons in the midnight darkness. No other estate in Landfall boasted such defences, only Demesne offered any comparison.

'Remind me why we're doing this?' said Delfino, stifling a yawn behind a fist, eyelids heavy, dull aches in his backside and the small of his back.

'Same reason you gave up your pipe,' said Corvino.

'And you really left the moonleaf back at the Terminus Inn?'
Corvino nodded.

'That pouch might have fetched a good price.'

'You'll thank me one day,' replied the *aiutante*.

'The things we do for love,' muttered Delfino. He was dog-tired and twice as filthy. They'd changed horses at every opportunity along the route, pressing their mounts hard and paying a small ransom to maintain their pace. More than once they'd ridden through the night, snatching the odd hour of sleep here and there.

'This saddle is going to disintegrate, I'm sure of it.'

Corvino had no reply, instead whispering kindnesses to his horse as it trudged onward obediently.

'I'm going to bathe every day for a week when we get back to San Marino.'

Still Corvino said nothing, squinting at the gatehouse, where Albero pennants hung limp from poles, warm brown and rich purple in the flickering light of torches.

'Horrible combination of colours,' said Delfino. 'I'm glad we don't have to wear them.'

Corvino shrugged. 'Got bigger problems than offending your taste.'

'Being an arbiter of good taste is a weighty responsibility,' replied Delfino with a wry smile. They urged their horses up the gentle slope to the gatehouse, waving at the men behind the battlements. None waved back.

'I hope they're not expecting bribes,' muttered Delfino. The gates did not open, black iron studs lending emphasis to the lack of welcome. The riders reached the heavy pitted wood and wheeled their horses, craning their necks to see if anyone looked down.

'Wake up, you idle bastards!' shouted Delfino.

'The diplomatic approach,' said Corvino.

'I'm tired, my arse hurts, I want a bath, and we've still got to get through the forest, which isn't my favourite place, as well you know.'

'Hoy there!' A voice from above.

'At last,' grunted Delfino. 'Open the gates! We're freezing our teats off down here.'

'And who might you be, with your frozen teats an' all?'

'I'm Delfino Datini, scout for Duke Marino. We're on a—'

'It's him!' said another voice from behind the battlements. Delfino closed his eyes and waited for the inevitable discussion. 'It's Denari Datini. His father kicked him out for being a wastrel.'

'I heard he was caught—'

'Didn't he spend all his money on—'

'That's why they calls him Denari, you idiot.' The voices quietened but continued their dissection of the past.

'Ten years,' growled Delfino to Corvino. 'Ten years. You'd think there'd be a limit to how long gossip stays in circulation. Wouldn't you? I mean you'd think?'

'Try not to,' replied the *aiutante*.

'Try not to what?'

'I try not to think,' explained Corvino.

'Will you let us in?!' bellowed Delfino at the battlements.

'Not tonight,' came the reply.

'Who are you?'

'Sergente Idle Bastard, at your service, my lord.' Sneering laughter followed.

'I'm sorry for my opening remarks, Sergente.' Delfino forced a tight smile, his tone indicating anything but apology. 'If you could just see fit to—'

'It's after curfew. Too dangerous to open the gates, my lord.'

'What?' seethed Delfino. 'I'm on business for Duke Marino.'

'And we serve Viscount Albero, you stuck-up jackass.'

'Let us in. We can't stay out here all night; it's too cold.'

'You're not bringing your pet *strega* in here, Lord Denari.'

Delfino flashed a look at Corvino. The *aiutante* took a deep breath but said nothing.

'Please. We've ridden a long way. We're exhausted, and it's cold. I'll explain in full to Viscount Albero if you're concerned for the—'

'Fuck off, Denari. Take your witchling elsewhere.' Raucous laughter followed.

'It's times like this I can understand why the Herald is so keen to go to war,' said Delfino.

'These cretins are on our side,' said Corvino.

'Depressing, isn't it?' Delfino clucked at his horse and shook the reins. They had passed a small copse of trees perhaps half a mile back. That would have to provide shelter for the hours until dawn.

'Wait,' whispered Corvino. There was the sound of scraping wood – someone lifting the crossbar of the gates. Metal bolts grated as they slid back.

'Hoy! What's going on down there?' The urgent stamp of booted feet could be heard as one of the pitted doors swung inward.

Corvino touched his heels to his horse's flanks and trotted beneath the arch of the gatehouse, hooves ringing on slick cobbles. Delfino followed, dreading the inevitable officiousness of the guards when they reached the far side.

'You must be Sergente Idle Bastard,' Delfino said brightly. Three guards lurched to a standstill at the base of a stone staircase between the wall and a townhouse. As one they went for their swords. Corvino slid from his mount with steel in both hands before Delfino could open his mouth to speak.

'Hold on there!' But the guards were keen to save face. Delfino swore and dismounted with a grunt, then pulled his own sword free of its sheath

'S'pose you used your *strega* to slip through the walls,' spat the *sergente*. He was a hatchet-faced man, nose and chin competing with each other for length.

'Stand down,' said a voice in the darkness. The guards squinted at the source of the command; Delfino turned to follow their gaze. Only Corvino remained still, eyes locked on his tormentors, swords held low. A bead of light glowed orange in the gloom; a trace of moonleaf smoke drifted on the air. Delfino felt the irresistible urge to buy a new pipe. Nardo Moretti stepped into the light, took a long drag and blew out a plume of smoke. Just months ago he'd been the senior messenger of House Contadino, sad witness to the changing fortunes and the tragedy of its *margravio* and *marchesa*.

'And who might you be?' asked the *sergente*, squinting in the gloom.

'Huh. Reckon I'm the *capo* of House Albero,' said Nardo, 'so what say you fuck off back up the wall?'

'My lord, I apologise,' replied the *sergente*, trying to bow, turn and mount the steps all at once. 'I didn't recognise you in the dark.' The guards flashed sullen glances at Corvino before resuming their posts. Delfino sheathed his sword and gave a merry wave.

'Thanks for your hospitality,' he called after them. 'See you again some time.'

The hatchet-faced *sergente* turned and flicked fingers from beneath his chin.

'You always did know how to make an entrance, Delfino,' said Nardo. 'Not so good at making friends.'

'I always preferred the company of women; they tend to carry fewer weapons and take offence less easily.'

'Huh.' Nardo toked on the pipe. 'Your heart's always been in the right place but your brain is in your britches.'

'Probably why I'm such a good scout.' Delfino grinned and pressed a palm into Nardo's. 'No women to distract me.'

'I was talking about your arse, not your cock.'

'Ah.' Delfino scratched his beard and tried to ignore the smoke teasing his senses.

'How you keeping, Corvino?'

'Same as ever.' The *aiutante* sheathed his swords and shook hands with the *capo*. 'Keeping this one out of trouble.'

'Not doing such a great job tonight.'

Corvino shrugged. 'Getting to be more work than I can handle.'

'Let's get inside,' said Nardo. 'Reckon I'm too old to be stood outside in this weather.'

The kitchen of House Albero was a cosy affair, with brass pans and wooden utensils hanging from neat hooks. The walls were whitewashed plaster and the hearth was wide, crackling with a fierce fire. It was some time before the bath tubs were ready and the servants wore looks of barely restrained mutiny. Nardo flashed the odd frown at them while cleaning his fingernails with a knife.

'Won't hurt them to do a bit of work,' he growled under his breath as they sat at the kitchen table. 'Fools don't know how good they have it down here. Huh. We worked for a living in Demesne.'

Delfino said nothing, imagining a life spent in the unsmiling service of Nardo. He'd never been the happiest of souls when his master Margravio Contadino had been alive, much less after. Corvino pulled aside his veil but turned away to keep his scarred face in shadow. Some dark bread had been sawn into thick slices; a good ham and a hard cheese lay on a wide chopping board. Delfino devoured what was offered, making free with the hot wine.

'I think I could kiss you,' said Delfino. Nardo's frown made it clear how keen he was on that. 'For the food. If you were a woman of course.'

'Huh.' Nardo nodded, and Delfino gave up on any vestige of humour or levity.

'So it's war then?' It was barely a question, but Nardo asked all the same. Delfino nodded, mouth too full to give a proper answer.

'Anea's not giving up Marchetti,' said Corvino, picking at crumbs of cheese. 'Or Erebus.'

'Spoiling for a fight by the sound of it,' added Delfino.

'I've known her since she was this tall.' Nardo gestured with a hand held at the level of his stool seat. He shook his head. 'You never really know anyone, do you?'

Delfino and Corvino resumed eating, neither having an answer for the messenger. The last year had aged him terribly: a few years younger than Delfino, he looked to be in his early forties. Rigid discipline kept his spine straight and shoulders from slumping, while the suit he wore was a sombre black, red and white sashes tied at his waist. Small wonder the servants failed to warm to him when he paraded his old loyalties so obviously.

'So it's a bleak winter and a summer of bloodshed to look forward to,' said Nardo, 'as if we haven't had a gut full of that.'

'No, we'll need to march straight away,' said Delfino.

'Things are critical,' added Corvino.

'Reckon the council will have something to say.' Nardo set

down a knife and laced his fingers. 'Marching foot soldiers through the winter is no option at all. You of all people should know this from the Verde Guerra.'

'We've got our orders,' said Delfino, remembering how implacable the Herald had been on the issue. 'I didn't really feel like discussing it.'

'Huh.' Nardo looked away to the fire. 'The weather will wear at the men as much as the enemy. It's a bad business.'

'There's no doubt of that,' said Delfino, cradling his wine, 'but Anea's left us no choice. *Cittadini* are starving to death; taxes creep up; Lucien is under pressure to save the sisters in Santa Maria. House Fontein is finished, Contadino in exile—'

'You don't need to tell me how it played out.' Nardo's hands curled into fists. 'I was there.'

'Sorry, Nardo. I meant no disrespect.'

A silence smothered the kitchen, only the crackle and pop of firewood intruding on the hush. Delfino was as tired as he had ever known, resisting the urge to slump over the table and sleep where he sat.

'San Marino will be left undefended if the council agree to send troops,' said Nardo a few moments later. 'That's not going to be a popular option. You know how hard life has been on the coast.'

'We've got our orders,' said Delfino. 'And Lucien won't abandon the *cittadini*, even if he has to ride to Demesne on his own. I'd like to retake Demesne while my mother is still alive. I owe her that much.'

A servant appeared through a door, tousle-haired, eyes bleary with the hour.

'Your baths are ready, my lords.'

Delfino and Corvino pushed themselves to their feet.

'You never really know anyone, do you?' said Nardo, still staring into the fire. 'All those years we stood by Anea, stood by Russo. Hell of a thing.'

'We'll make this right,' said Delfino softly, laying a hand on the *capo*'s shoulder.

'No.' Nardo shook his head. 'You won't. No one can. It's only going to get worse.'

17

A Kind of Darkness

A week had passed since Virmyre had brought Anea to his chamber. In essence they were strangers to each other. Too much had occurred in the time spent apart. Too many things forgotten, by Anea at least. Her memories of Virmyre bore little relation to the man in the Myrmidon armour. Their new friendship took root slowly, the matter of Demesne itself left unsaid, lest it salt the earth between them completely. She'd traded the darkness of the oubliette for the gloom of the *sanatorio*. The meagre light that crept through the slender windows faded all too soon. She cursed every short winter day, insisting on lanterns, making free with lamp oil, anything to be spared the oppressive pitch-black of her confinement.

'What was it like?' he asked her one night, late. Virmyre's plate held a few crumbs of cheese, the bread gone, salami the same, nothing wasted. Only dregs of wine remained. He'd conjured a tablecloth and candelabrum since she'd arrived, stolen from House Erudito. Cutlery appeared in greater quantity, then glasses. They never ate together, Anea's disfigurement put paid to that. They enacted the charade of dining only as a chance to bridge the gap of their estrangement. Anea didn't answer, fingers toying with a fork, eyes intent on the tines.

'What was it like being down there for so long?' pressed Virmyre, rich baritone disturbing the velvet quiet. No other sound intruded, the town sleeping behind shuttered windows and locked doors.

It is difficult to remember. Her fingers hesitated. *A kind of darkness, I suppose. Not of the more obvious sort, although there was plenty of that. The only light I saw was provided by the Myr-midons bringing me food.* She bowed her head. *It was the* . . . Tears appeared in the corners of her eyes, suspended by lashes. She dashed them aside with the back of her hand, her brow a crease of indignation.

It was the uncertainty. And the loneliness. I could not even speak to myself. She gestured to the veil as if this were explanation enough. *My entire existence was darkness with only the sound of dripping water to break the monotony. I could not even rely on my memories for company. I wondered what my voice would sound like, if it would provide any comfort. Is that foolish?*

'It would have been more foolish had you not wondered, I think.'

And you?

'I made a prisoner of myself long before they did.' Virmyre sat back in his chair and released a sigh. 'Absorbed by work and sleep and work again. I looked for you one day, and you were gone.' He shrugged. 'Just gone. They told me you had taken ill.' He gave a slow shrug and shook his head. 'I was so numb with *tinctura* I didn't think to look for you.'

When was that?

'The middle of *Augusto* . . . I don't know for sure. But I stopped taking *tinctura* completely at that point. I sought out Dino, spoke to him. That's when they snatched me. The *capo* and a handful of his cronies.' His hand strayed to his beard, thumb and forefinger tracing his chin. 'It was the day before the impostor announced the Myrmidons' formation. I watched the riots from my cell window. That was a long night I'd rather forget.'

But you escaped?

Virmyre shook his head. 'No. Dino released me two days later. I've been living in a kind of darkness myself since then. Alone, prowling Demesne disguised as one of them.'

When did you realise that they had replaced me?

'I'd hoped to speak to you, but the Domina was never far away. The doors to your apartment were always guarded by four Myrmidons.' Virmyre picked up the wine bottle and shook it, frowning at the empty vessel. 'It's a good thing I didn't gain entry—'

Because it was not me in the apartment.

'And I'd have been captured again, with no Dino to come to my aid.'

She retreated then, bedded down, clutching pillows, squeezing her eyes shut for the tears that came all too readily. Dino's loss was the one pain that had yet to diminish, as bright and sharp as any blade.

'I'm sorry,' whispered Virmyre from the door of her cell. 'I miss him too.' The candlelight faded and Anea drifted into the arms of sleep.

Winter ushered in more snow under the cover of star-flecked night. Anea woke to a town ankle-deep in fresh white. She stood by a window, a blanket clutched about her. Her sleep had not been restful, her dreams mired in the sediment of the oubliette. Startled moments of wakefulness had left her rank with fear, both of capture and of death at the hands of Marchetti. Any of the Myrmidons might spell her end, but it was the scar-ravaged assassin she feared the most.

'There you are.' There was more than a hint of relief in Virmyre's baritone. Anea turned and nodded, lacking the desire to communicate. 'It's beautiful at this time of day.' The *professore* nodded to the town. 'It's a shame when all those footprints stamp the snow into slush.'

Virmyre was dressed in horseman's boots and thick britches, a tabard of simple brown over a leather jacket.

Going somewhere?

'Yes, if you'll join me.'

Where? Will it be safe?

'I didn't smuggle you out of Demesne just to hand you back a week later.'

Where are we going?

'That I can't tell you. Not far.'

Anea shrugged. Keen to sample the sharp light of a winter's day even as she feared capture.

Are you sure this is wise?

'You've remained unseen for a week. You could be halfway to San Marino by now. Come on. Being cooped up in here is doing you no good at all. And there's something you need to do.'

What?

Virmyre flashed a rare smile, but his eyes held only sadness.

The ponies were not young, good-tempered or particularly obedient.

'But they were cheap,' rumbled Virmyre. 'We should be grateful they haven't been boiled down for soup.'

That is disgusting.

'People are eating far worse.'

They took the east road from Santa Maria, almost blinded by the glare of sun on snow. Everything about the journey was too much for Anea's dulled senses. The sky too bright, the air too cold, the road uneven, her mount too stubborn and slow. She drew a disgruntled silence about her, but it did little to fend off the chill.

'Well, this is perfectly dreadful,' said Virmyre, 'but I suppose it could be snowing.'

Anea said nothing. The rising sun had begun its subtle work on the fields, shoots of green showing beneath the melting white. Trees sloughed off their dusting, muffled thumps of snow falling to the ground beneath. She had given up on the wary anxiety of looking over her shoulder.

'No one will follow us,' said Virmyre. 'They've abandoned the pretence of caring where the *cittadini* live. It's as if they want the entire population to move south.'

She lost herself to the plod of the pony, regarding the countryside anew. The snows would cease come the spring, and the land would awaken. Plants would rouse themselves and open leaves and petals to the sun; animals would emerge from hibernation to fill the forests with the sound of life, legs scurrying, wings flapping, birdsong on the air. The thought of it cheered her. Perhaps she would build a cottage beside the Foresta di Ragno and live in obscurity.

'Almost there,' said Virmyre. Anea blinked away her

thoughts. They had arrived at the cemetery. Thick ribbons of crisp white decorated the top of the wall; every headstone and angel wore a coat of the same. A deep stillness prevailed, the trees looming in silence. Even the attending ravens held their coarse tongues.

The ravens came back.

'Yes. This Herald seems to have quite a following. The *cittadini* speak of little else. They say it's an omen Lucien will return and free them from the mad queen.'

He slid from his mount with care, then tied the reins to a piton hammered into the cemetery wall.

Why have you brought me here?

'Come down from the saddle and I'll show you.'

Anea hesitated, a suspicion of what Virmyre had planned stilling her.

Can we return home? I have enjoyed the ride but I am very tired.

'This will only take a moment.' He held up a hand and she took it on instinct. Soon they were passing between the black wrought-iron gates, rusted open with yellowed bindweed choking the hinges. The snow was perfect and untouched, collected in drifts in the cemetery's corners.

The last time I was here was . . . Anea frowned. Funerals were an all-too-common event in Demesne, yet her memory slipped and slid beneath the grasp of her recollection.

Who was it? Who died?

'Angelicola perhaps?' offered Virmyre. 'He died of a heart attack when the underkin first attacked. Of course, we didn't know they were underkin back then, nor did we realise they lived beneath Demesne on the edge of starvation.'

And then Erebus persuaded the Domina to create the Myrmidons, an army of the lost, of the outcast.

They had crossed the greater part of the cemetery and were near the back, where the mausoleums of the great houses rose above more modest markers for the dead.

I would really rather return now. I am very tired.

'Just humour me a moment longer.'

The Erudito mausoleum bore Doric columns at each corner,

two more flanking the entrance. Dolorous cherubs decorated corbels, water stained and green.

Do you not find it strange that this is larger than some of the hovels in town?

'There's much that I find strange about Landfall. That we look after the dead better than we care for the living is no great surprise.'

Anea entered the darkness of the mausoleum, a tightness close to panic beneath her breast, hands endlessly wringing the corner of her shawl. The sarcophagus wasn't far from the entrance. Virmyre busied himself with flint, Anea shivering in the cold as the lantern light finally etched the interior with an amber glow.

'This is where he sleeps,' said Virmyre. He kissed his finger-tips before laying a hand atop the cold stone. Anea might have kept a rein on her feelings if not for the catch in the man's voice. It was the tiny break of one who had lost loved ones before and knew he would do so again. The sound was the finest fracture, Anea's heart fracturing with it.

The white marble sarcophagus bore a carved sword on the lid, the hilt at its head. A beautiful carving of a slumbering cataphract drake curled about itself at the foot. Anea's tears ran freely, shoulders shaking with the evidence of what she had heard but wished to be otherwise.

'I think they gilded the lily by adding the drake.' Virmyre pointed to the marble reptile, a frown creasing his brow. 'I've reason to believe Stephania took Achilles to San Marino. Shame she couldn't have taken Dino there too.'

I failed him.

'No.' Virmyre shook his head. 'We failed him together. He came to you. Perhaps you don't remember, but he came to you one night late. I interrupted, of course. We were close to perfecting *tinctura*. I should have left you to your conversation, but we were so close to discovery. Who knows how that night would have fared had I possessed the good sense to let a brother confide in his sister?'

I could have said no. I should have said no.

'You remember?'

Anea bowed her head, wrapping arms about herself as the night remembered itself to her in vivid detail.

He was trying to tell me something, something about being different.

'He fell in love with Massimo,' said Virmyre, 'which after Cherubini's expulsion must have been torture.'

Dino was invertito?

'Makes a certain amount of sense with hindsight, doesn't it? All those years serving Landfall and not once did he ...' Virmyre shrugged.

Seek the comfort of a woman?

'Yes.' Virmyre cleared his throat.

I wish I had given him the time he needed. I abandoned him when he needed me the most.

Virmyre took her in his arms, holding her close and letting her cry herself out against his chest. They stood in the quiet of the mausoleum for many minutes, each lost to the sadness of unfulfilled responsibilities.

Anea turned away and laid one hand on the stone, eyes shut tight as if conferring a benediction. She released a fragile sigh and turned to Virmyre.

'This is why I want you to retake the throne. We can't let Dino die in vain.'

Anea took a step back, her gaze hardening beneath a furrowed brow. *You brought me here to blackmail me?*

'Anea—'

Do you really mean to use Dino's death as a means to motivate me?

'Don't you agree that—'

He died so Stephania Prospero could escape to San Marino. Yet where is she? Has she returned to avenge him? Has she returned at the head of a conquering army?

'Anea, I simply thought you should have the chance to pay your respects.'

You have never lied to me before; why start today?

'Very well, I'm a liar.' Virmyre glowered at her. 'And you're a coward. Stephania Prospero isn't here to avenge Dino, but you are. He was your brother! And you mope around the *sanatorio* without any desire for justice? For retribution? The Anea I knew killed anyone who raised a fist to her kin.'

I had a hairpin given to me by Dino, a silver one as thick as my finger. I stabbed a bravo in the jugular with it. There was a far-away cast to her eyes that spoke of a memory long undisturbed being dusted off.

'Yes. The night Duke Fontein's assassins came for you.'

Anea turned and slipped through the door. Virmyre had to run to catch up with her.

'And where are you going?'

Anea turned. The maudlin slump of her shoulders was gone, the dipped chin and downcast gaze vanished. A measure of jade shone from her green eyes in the winter sunlight. The ravens called out from the trees, filling the air with a hateful din.

I am going to find a way to get my hairpin back.

18

A Reluctant Pawn

Eris had lost days to melancholic introspection since her failed assassination of Erebus. She filled the hours reading when her concentration would permit. Isabella was sent to fetch new books from the library with increasing frequency. Wardrobes were reordered, unworn gowns donated to hungry *cittadini*, uncomfortable shoes discarded. Hours were lost contemplating Santa Maria through windows opaque with condensation. She ate alone, the wine bottles sent to her rooms returned empty without exception. She didn't care for the vintages, only that the taste salve her isolation. The bath tub was a refuge. She wallowed for hours, the water descending down the scale of scalding, hot, warm, tepid, then finally frigid. And in the background, a constant presence in a life lived in miniature, was the stiletto she'd taken to the Ravenscourt. It took pride of place on the mantelpiece, an ornament of failure.

She had meant to avenge her brother.

She had meant to free herself.

A knock sounded from the apartment door. Eris roused herself on the couch, tied on a veil, pulling her shawl about her, black satin nightgown beneath. She hadn't bothered to dress in more than a week. A Myrmidon entered, one of the female ones, no longer required to serve in the oubliette.

'It's the archivist, my lady,' said the Myrmidon in a quiet voice. Eris nodded, gesturing for him to enter. The Myrmidon stiffened, a moment of confusion. Expectation demanded the Silent Queen send the man away. Hadn't she done the very same to every caller for the last seven days?

The Myrmidon returned to the corridor, muttering disbelief. Simonetti ducked beneath the lintel of the door frame, regarding the woman on the couch with eyes full of questions. Was there a hint of concern? And was it concern for himself or, the unthinkable, concern for the Silent Queen? Suspicion was the more likely answer. The gaunt archivist bowed, hands folding around a green cloth-bound book.

'My lady.' He forced a smile.

You have grown a beard. Her fingers teased out the words slowly.

'Ah, well. Yes. I'm still trying to decide if it suits me.'

Eris shrugged. The archivist concealed his disappointment by removing his optics and cleaning them on a sleeve of his robes.

Are you busy?

'I, ah, well, not really. The only people who send for books with any regularity are yourself and Dottore Allattamento.'

You have something for me?

'Ah, yes.' Simonetti held out a book, delivering it to her outstretched hand with a wary look. 'One of the last meetings you held was in the rose garden.'

I remember. You missed it.

'That's correct. I ran into problems at House Erudito.

Problems?

'Oh, nothing important. You know...' Simonetti gestured vaguely but didn't elaborate.

Eris sat up straighter, wondering what the archivist was holding back. He sensed her suspicion and plunged on, gesturing to the gift.

'I took the opportunity to locate this book on plants and insects and so on.'

Eris nodded, setting the book on the couch beside her, paying it no attention. Simonetti failed to cover his disappointment.

So I am to be the new gardener?

'No, not at all, but the garden brought Medea a lot of pleasure. I wondered if you might enjoy it too.'

Medea. Eris sighed. *I suppose the Domina insists that we keep her chained up?*

'I'm afraid so, my lady.' The archivist laced his fingers. 'Is there no chance you might be persuaded to release Marchesa Contadino?'

Eris shrugged. *I think the majority of my advisers would rather I kept her prisoner.*

'A pity. But you are the queen.' Simonetti folded his tall frame into an armchair and leaned forward, one hand straying to his new beard, the other twisting the cord at his waist. 'You are, ah, missed at the Ravenscourt, my lady. This spat with the Domina has lingered for much too long. When will you return to us?'

I choose . . . Eris stared at the flames as they danced in the fireplace beneath the mantelpiece, beneath the stiletto. For a single moment she was on the gallery of the Ravenscourt, behind the dark curtain and its bronze leaves, in the presence of Erebus.

I choose never.

Simonetti opened his mouth, closed it, then cleared his throat. He rubbed his forehead, blinking behind the optics. 'I—' He got no further, silenced by one outstretched hand.

I am sick of it. Absolutely sick of it. She signed slowly, eyes unfocused, as if staring through the flames in the fireplace itself. *I have sat here and tried to think of ways to make it work. As if Demesne were some great device, all cogs and counterweights, like so many longcase clocks. I have tried to manage the expectations, the obligations, the duties. How to satisfy the Domina and the wants of the* nobili. *And I realised I no longer care. I just want it to stop.*

Simonetti blinked a few times, optics flashing in the firelight. 'If I might make a, ah, suggestion, my lady?'

Eris shrugged and picked up the green book. It would take a legion of gardeners to tame Medea's neglected roses.

'I have spent most of my life in Demesne, but my family own an estate with a few farms in the surrounding countryside.' The archivist lowered his voice. 'It's not, ah, unimaginable to think a noble woman might retire there in relative obscurity.'

Eris was already shaking her head.

'A cottage will never be a castle,' continued the archivist, 'but it may offer some insulation from your troubles.'

You would have to sail me away from Landfall itself in order to save me.

'Well, the, ah, offer remains, should you change your mind.'

The Domina would hunt me down if I fled. And you too, for helping me.

'Only if she knew where to find you. You could take a new name.'

It would never work, kind as the thought is. Viscount Datini has spies watching you. The archivist blinked and sat up straighter. *And I suspect they are watching me too.*

'I see. I, ah, had no idea.'

Eris nodded, bleakness settling in, maudlin as any drunk.

'Forgive me for saying so, but you haven't seemed yourself these last few months. Is anything amiss?'

Besides inadvertently imprisoning Medea Contadino and Lucien Marino threatening war?

'You were unhappy a long time before those, ah, events.'

Cherubini's expulsion and Duke Fontein's assassination were hardly cause for celebration.

'And the business with Dino perhaps? He was your brother, after all.'

Eris nodded emphatically, cursing herself for forgetting such an obvious turning point in Anea's life. Of her pretended life.

'If you needed to, ah, confide in someone. Someone less combative than the Domina . . .'

I have nothing to tell you, Simonetti, but thank you all the same.

The archivist stood and made to depart, reaching the door before sparing her one last glance. 'Did you ever find the woman attempting to replace you?'

Simonetti? Her fingers danced over the syllables of his name.

'Yes?' he replied, a note of hope making the word bright in the quiet.

Lose the beard.

'Yes, my lady,' said the archivist, bowing.

Simonetti's small act of kindness was like a seed that refused to die no matter how rocky the soil. Eris washed and dressed, combed her hair, filling the chamber with expletives as she

149

teased apart matted locks. Her hair, like her thoughts, had become a tangle of vines. For a time she contented herself with Simonetti's book of plants and insects, but her restless mind asserted itself once more, recalling the archivist's words.

The only people who send for books with any regularity are yourself and Dottore Allattamento.

Allattamento's murderous errand was the sole reason she remained sequestered away. He'd in turn remained distant, not calling or so much as sending word since that hateful night.

Eris threw the windows open; she'd suffocated in the apartment enough. Below, the town went about its sleepy business, smoke from coal and wood and peat fires lingering over the town like an oppressive shadow. It was a mercy she didn't have to live among them, scratching out an existence in the snowy streets, huddling for warmth beside the desperate and unclean.

The Silent Queen's walk through the castle prompted stifled gasps, but she refused to stop for greetings or small talk. The Myrmidons that loomed at her shoulder deterred those keen to petition her. Eris did not have far to go; Allattamento's apartment was close by. Her knuckles sounded loud on his door, then again a second later, insistent and impatient.

The *dottore* cracked open the door, peering out, eyes widening in surprise. A stammer, a sideways glance before recovering himself.

'Apologies, my lady. I wasn't expecting you. One moment.' The door closed, and Eris clenched her fists, glancing at the Myrmidons, their blank-faced helms betraying nothing.

The door swung open. Allattamento ushered her inside while the Myrmidons remained in the corridor. The *dottore*'s sitting room was a concoction of scrolls, old books and glass vials sporting slivers of parchment describing their contents. A cataphract drake basked in the hearth, turning heavy-lidded eyes toward the Silent Queen. Eris approached the desk, on which a sand timer sat beside quill and ink.

I am interrupting something?

'Not at all.' Allattamento offered a nervy smile. 'I was awake much of the night with Viscount Datini. He was unwell and called for me. You caught me napping, my lady.'

A useful man to be allied with, signed Eris.

The *dottore* forced a smile. 'I don't approve of everything he says, or the opinions he keeps, but he pays well and the work is adequate to my talents.'

Are we overheard? signed Eris. The *dottore* shook his head.

'Only the Myrmidons outside, if you can trust them?'

'Do you?' said Eris, glad not to have to sign her every word.

'A thorough inspection of the Myrmidons was carried out following Medea's revelation in the Ravenscourt. We never found out who was responsible. It might have been a mere accident.'

'Unlikely.'

The *dottore* shrugged. 'You didn't come here to ask me if we can trust the soldiers.'

'No. I didn't.' Eris undid the veil at one side of her face, letting it fall aside. 'I came to return this.' She reached under her dress and retrieved the stiletto from a sheath at her calf.

'What?' Allattamento frowned, refusing to take it from her grasp.

'I tried. But I'm an impostor, not a killer.'

'But your brother?'

'Sabatino was never going to live to old age.' The justification was weak, as hard to say as to admit it might be true. 'Fortune never made him to last.' She picked up the sand timer, holding it on its side, watching the grains slide along the glass. 'All the blessings of Santa Maria would never sustain him.'

'But I could have—'

'No, you couldn't. And you've no way of proving it, or that Erebus prevented such a thing.'

She continued to grasp the stiletto, holding it by the blade, hilt proffered to him, **TEMPO** flashing from the blade.

'I could have saved him had I acquired the correct medicines, but—'

'You'll speak no more of it. Take the stiletto.' She thrust out the weapon again, gold letters spelling **MISURA**.

'You must do it, Eris.' Allattamento's eyes flicked toward his bedroom door. 'We must be rid of him.'

'Then you do it. Cut the cancer out of Demesne.'

'You know I can't get close enough. Only you can speak to him.'

'I failed.' She threw the stiletto down, blade puncturing the rug, piercing the wood beneath. 'I stood before him and tried with the very weapon you gave me.'

Allattamento blanched. He swallowed and said nothing.

'He threatened to marry me off to one of his Myrmidons – so I can have a gaggle of misshapen bastards, no doubt.'

They stood in silence, the *dottore* shocked at the news of Eris's failure, she in turn shocked by her confession.

'What will you do?' said the *dottore*.

'I don't know, but I had better think of something soon. Time is a luxury I don't have.' She placed the sand timer on the desk, watched the sand falling, falling into the empty chamber below. 'If I could just find someone to kill Erebus for me.'

19

San Marino

'I never tire of setting eyes on this place,' said Delfino Datini with a smile. Corvino nodded. They had left the forest that morning but their wariness remained. The horses were coated in mud as far as the knee and fit to drop. Delfino had long decided on a new travel cloak, even if it cost him his last coin.

San Marino waited before them, three pavilions of gleaming curves the colour of seashells and coffee brown, traces of cyan and silver glittering in the sun. Each was a mile wide, seeming to hover above the town, shielding its districts from rain and snow alike. Only the wind hounded the *cittadini*, and never more so than in the winter. Wooden walkways carried people over streams that babbled to the cliffs beyond.

'Too bad we won't have a chance to stay,' muttered Delfino.

'Unless the vote goes against us,' replied Corvino.

Delfino opened his mouth to speak, falling silent as the tower loomed from the mist. It transcended architecture, not merely a building but a presence, a shocking vertical at odds with the gentle vastness of the domes, yet constructed of the same glimmering cream, whorls of iridescent cerulean beneath its skin. How long it had stood none knew, and Delfino suspected the tower was keen to retain its mystery. Some fifteen storeys tall, it was an imposing edifice that unsettled him even now after a decade of familiarity. Being party to what the building contained made Delfino no less uncomfortable. The tower twisted, a slight skewing of flying buttresses that plunged into the earth like burrowing worms. The tower tapered at its apex, separating into four blunt points, sloping angles piercing the

153

winter sky. Delfino's fingers strayed to the drake clasp at his breast.

'Over there.' Corvino pointed toward a tiny figure waving a hand of greeting from the top of the nearest dome. Delfino waved back with a broad smile.

'I hope they have some wine ready.'

The edges of the pavilions boasted banner poles bearing rectangles of turquoise, brown, grey, black and white: Duke Marino's houses.

'The vote will be close,' said Corvino.

'Scolari will do as Lucien wishes. Terreno too. Salvaggia is Rafaela's sister after all.'

'The church?'

'I expect so.' Delfino shrugged. 'But Ricco only leads House Artigiano for profit; he's never been unduly worried by ethics.'

San Marino edged closer. Delfino sighed with relief as their horses carried them beneath the pavilion's edge. Townhouses nestled alongside each other in neat rows, brightly coloured shutters contrasting with pastel-hued walls. Taverns occupied the corners of curving streets, handfuls of revellers braving the cold to sit outside watching the foot traffic. Corvino waved to a pair of stable lads who lounged on a barrel smoking moonleaf.

'Friends of yours?'

Corvino nodded.

'I'm not sure I pay you to have friends,' said Delfino, squinting at the stable lads.

'Barely pay me at all.'

'There is that.' Delfino sought the once-familiar pouch at his belt but found nothing.

'I'll be making sure you don't resupply,' said Corvino.

'Always looking out for my best interests,' replied Delfino with a sour look. They rode on toward their destination, hooves ringing on cobbles, their horses providing a vantage point over the milling pedestrians. Clusters of shops displayed wares for every pocket; proud shopkeepers served eager patrons.

'It's a far cry from Santa Maria,' said Delfino in a quiet voice.

'Santa Maria is a far cry from Santa Maria,' replied Corvino.

*

In time they found themselves at the Main Assembly, divested of their horses, spirited away to stables for the comforts of washing and brushing and food. Delfino envied them, desperate to spend as long in the tub as he could manage. The centre of the pavilion was a clearing reached by a profusion of archways and alleys, watched over by storefronts and cafés. A vast platform dominated the centre, its focal point an open-centred circular stone table. High-backed chairs of intimidating design waited to seat the influential.

'I always hated council meetings,' muttered Delfino.

'Tried to make me attend in your stead on more than one occasion,' replied Corvino.

'Another reason I should fire you. You never did obey me.'

The *aiutante* shrugged and pulled down his hood, leaving the veil in place.

The council were waiting, just as Delfino had hoped, though seeing them didn't fill him with joy. It was a closed meeting, with only the most senior present. Lucien broke free of the cluster of councillors, greeting the scout with a firm handshake and a clap on the shoulder.

'You brought the weather with you then.' The black hair remained an artfully ragged length, better to cover his missing ears. He'd dressed for the road, riding boots and britches, a tailored jacket of dark brown with turquoise embroidery on the cuffs and lapels, a half-skirt in a matching hue. Lucien was at once the figurehead of House Marino yet retained an echo of the clothes worn by House Vedetta's scouts, the copper clasp of a cataphract drake worn proudly on his chest. Perhaps it was an unconscious choice, but Delfino doubted it.

'I'd hoped it would be sunshine and warm breezes by the time we got through the forest,' replied Delfino, 'but it's still very much winter.'

Corvino made to bow but Lucien thrust a hand forward and shook his instead.

'We can dispense with the formalities.'

'It *is* a council meeting, my lord.'

'Oh. You're right.' A hint of a frown crossed the duke's face.

'Did you have any trouble in the forest?' he asked, voice quiet. Delfino nodded and waggled a hand.

'More than I would have liked. Not enough to stop us getting through.'

Lucien sighed and chewed his lip before flashing a glance toward the council. His hand drifted to his sword, and Delfino knew the man was lost to memories of the Verde Guerra.

'Are you ready for this rabble?' he said after a pause.

'I'm not sure I was ever ready.' Delfino searched the faces of the councillors. 'None was terribly keen when you made me *capo*, and all were still less keen when I stepped down.'

'Your talent for disappointing people is a refreshing constant.' Delfino knew that Lucien was joking, but it smarted all the same. 'Come on,' said the duke. 'They're waiting.'

Each representative sat at the great table of the Main Assembly, a secretary to hand, scrawling notes in ledgers of stiff parchment. Standing behind each high-backed chair were an *aiutante* and a messenger, all possessing grim-faced gravitas or affecting self-importance.

'The *nobili* never really change, do they?' muttered Delfino. 'And I say that as one of them.'

'At least the sisters manage to keep their feet on the ground.' Corvino nodded toward the Sisterhood's representative, Sister Fabiola Azzuro. She was a woman of some fifty years with a hardness born of self-imposed austerity. A younger sister sat beside her with inkwell and quill. Two more crowded behind, veiled and silent, wrists draped with rosewood beads. Sister Azzuro nodded at Delfino, who forced a smile in response.

'She knows what's coming,' said Corvino.

'I've long thought the sisters had their own network of spies,' agreed Delfino.

Sat beside the Sisters of Santa Maria was Anastagio Ricco, feigning a doze. One age-spotted hand rested on the other, both propped on the curving handle of his polished walking cane. His son sat beside him, resplendent in a pale grey frock coat, the embroidery dark brown, the colours of House Artigiano.

Just thirty, Ricco the Younger was every bit as ruthless as his father and twice as keen.

'Mind that one,' said Delfino as the council took their seats. 'He'd pull your teeth from your head and sell them back to you as buttons.'

'It's why I became a scout,' said Corvino. 'Feels like a honest living.'

Next along the table's gentle curve was Sebastiano Bassani. A thick winter cloak added to his impressive bulk, a dark-scaled cataphract drake nesting in the fur about his neck. Bassani's thick moustache was almost matched by the brows that crowded above his heavy-lidded eyes. The cart drivers' representative folded his arms and lifted his chin as Delfino flicked a lazy salute.

'Still popular with House Prospero's lackeys,' muttered Corvino. Delfino failed to hide his smile, provoking Bassani's anger further.

Cherubini was a significantly more friendly proposition. He drew up his chair and flashed Delfino a happy wave. There was colour in his cheeks and a cheerful energy about the *maestro*, so different to the man who'd arrived in disgrace months ago.

'Making him *maestro* of House Scolari was one of Lucien's better ideas,' said Delfino. Corvino nodded and looked away.

Lucien favoured Delfino with a smile before taking his seat. He'd taken to the role of duke well, even if he were less keen on the title itself.

Duchess Rafaela Marino sat beside her duke in a turquoise gown and deep-brown stole. A drake perched on each shoulder, the infant reptiles just a few months old, slumbering coils of scales. Olive-skinned and lovely, Rafaela was the darling of the *cittadini*, a commoner married to her figurative prince. Rafaela searched the faces of the council, then remembered herself and flashed a smile at Delfino.

Rafaela's sister sat beside House Marino as *dirigente* of House Terreno. Salvaggia consulted with her secretary and neither cared or noted who else was present. Delfino was glad. The less he interacted with the woman the better; even eye contact was more than he cared for.

'Odd choice,' said Corvino.

'Best to keep her busy,' said Delfino, struggling to keep the bitterness from his voice, 'else she cause even more trouble.'

The last member of the council sat alone, eschewing house colours, aides and sycophants alike. Ruggeri had been a *maestro di spada* once, but Anea's formation of the Myrmidons had forced his defection. None had expected him to venture this far south, and fewer guessed Lucien might offer him an influential position. Ruggeri nodded to Delfino, one soldier to another.

'Taking their time,' muttered Corvino with a shiver. The extraordinary dome did much to protect the *cittadini* from the elements, but the winter chill remained. The councillors had brought braziers to light beside their seats. The two scouts had only their cloaks.

'Well, cough it up then.' Ricco scowled, blinking.

'I think what the councillor means –' Lucien flashed a warning glare along the table '– is that we're grateful you undertook a hazardous journey in such miserable conditions and are keen to hear your report. Can someone get these men a drink?'

Delfino laid out the Herald's request for soldiers, such as it was.

'And that's all he said?' asked Rafaela.

'He wasn't in the best of moods, but that was the core of it. Anea—' Delfino swallowed as Bassani cleared his throat. 'Lady Diaspora rejected the terms, declining to hand over Marchetti, who serves her. She welcomed the coming violence. It seems whoever is advising her actively wants war in Landfall.'

'And it has to be now?'

'The longer we leave it the worse things will be for the *cittadini* of Santa Maria,' replied Delfino. 'And the Myrmidons will have more time to train.'

A hush settled over the table as the councillors reflected on the developments in the north. Only the arrival of a page, offering two mugs of hot wine to the road-stained scouts, broke the stillness.

'Marching soldiers in winter will bring nothing but misery,' said Ruggeri, sat forward in his seat, elbows propped on the table. 'Making camp on the road is slow and hard, with this much snow harder still.'

'People are starving to death because of the rising taxes in Santa Maria,' replied Delfino, keeping his tone level.

'And we'll strain the hospitality of our allies along the route,' continued Ruggeri. 'Houses Albero, Schiavone, Allattamento and Elemosina all suffered during the drought. None has much food to spare.'

'That's not a good enough reason not to go,' said Lucien. 'There's plenty that's strained during wartime, food the least of it.'

'Tell that to hungry soldiers,' said Bassani with a smirk.

'Could we speed the journey using wagons?' asked Lucien, favouring the cart drivers' representative with a frown. Bassani blinked a few times and rubbed his moustache a moment. Ricco the Younger offered a handful of whispered words before the large man nodded.

'It's a quiet time of year for the many cart drivers I represent.' He cleared his throat and looked around the table. 'I would expect them to charge the same rates for passage as at any other time of year.'

'And I'd expect a little patriotism,' said Lucien from gritted teeth.

Bassani shrugged and sipped his wine, adding nothing further, his position clear.

'Taking men across country by mule and cart is no faster than walking, my lord,' suggested Ruggeri, before turning a hard look on Bassani.

'It's true,' replied Bassani, 'but the journey will be much less pleasant if the troops have to carry their own gear.'

'The church will gladly contribute toward the costs,' said Sister Azzuro in an imperious tone, 'if it will ensure the safety of our sisters in the north. Let us not forget the cost of human life before we tally the profits.'

If Bassani had any shame he'd clearly left it at home. Far from being chastened his smile deepened.

'Let the cart drivers wait it out,' said Salvaggia, addressing her sister, 'Our farmers have plenty of wagons and will gladly make the sacrifice if we ask them.' Lucien brightened, turning to Cherubini for further reinforcement. The *maestro* winced

159

and wrung his hands, opening his mouth to speak twice before finally giving voice to his thoughts.

'Historically speaking –' the *maestro* looked to Ruggeri for support '– we know that the greater losses of the Verde Guerra were suffered during the winter. We'd be doing our soldiers a disservice by sending them to war at this time of year.'

'They're scouts,' added Ruggeri. 'We don't have soldiers, we have scouts. Certainly not soldiers in plate armour like the Myrmidons. We're skirmishers at best.'

'I think it best we wait until spring,' said Ricco at the urging of his son. 'We'll wait until spring, then send word to the estates. Duke Marino's charisma will soon have them joining our banner.' Delfino couldn't be sure if the old man was being insincere. Lucien kept his countenance neutral and let the comment pass.

'The poor and the vulnerable can't leave Demesne,' said Delfino, impatience a hard edge in a tone struggling to remain polite.

Ricco continued as if he'd not heard. 'There's no telling what we could do with the taxes from the houses minor.' Ricco the Younger sat back in his chair, folding his arms with an air of satisfaction. 'Demesne would dwindle, strangled by a failing economy.'

'And the population of Santa Maria would dwindle along with it,' said Lucien.

'I'm not sure Anea cares about the economy any more.' Delfino sneered at the Riccos. 'Myrmidons will garrison the estates the moment Del Toro, Elemosina or Schiaparelli declare for Duke Marino.'

'They can't dispatch troops everywhere at once,' countered Lucien.

'And neither can we,' said Ruggeri. 'Any men we send to Demesne weaken us here, at home.'

The council sat back in their chairs and Delfino flashed a glance over his shoulder. Corvino shook his head, then turned his back on the council.

'We vote then,' said Rafaela impatiently.

'Those for sending scouts to Demesne immediately,' said Lucien, eyes fixed on Ruggeri. The duke raised his hand. Salvaggia and Sister Azzuro did likewise.

'Three.' Lucien glanced at Rafaela, who couldn't hide her disappointment. 'And against?'

Ruggeri, Ricco and Cherubini raised their hands.

'Bassani?' asked Lucien.

'I am undecided.' He paused to smooth down his moustache. 'I abstain until a later time.'

Lucien clenched his jaw and rested a hand atop Rafaela's. She whispered to him, and the council shared an uneasy moment. They were all aware of Lucien's temper.

'Then we are adjourned.' Lucien stood up. 'We will not send scouts to Demesne at this time.' He flashed an angry glance down the table at the Riccos. 'And may we all think long and hard about the many *cittadini* who won't be alive by the time we marshal our forces, or our convictions.' Duke Marino strode toward the nearest steps, leaving the councillors and aides to mill about. Few had anything of consequence to add. Rafaela extricated herself from the gathering and approached the two scouts.

'What does this mean?' she asked.

'Means we're fucked,' grunted Corvino. Delfino flashed an angry glare. 'Apologies, my lady,' said the *aiutante*.

'The Herald was very clear,' said Delfino. 'Time is of the essence.'

'Well –' Rafaela looked over her shoulder '– we'd best find a way to become unfucked then.'

Corvino coughed a laugh into his fist and Delfino smirked. A few of the councillors looked up from their conversations, and Rafaela met their stares with a hard smile.

'What do you suggest, my lady?'

'I don't know,' admitted Rafaela. The drakes, who had spent the meeting asleep, woke and scurried from one shoulder to the other, staring about with flinty gazes. 'But my husband didn't kill the king just to let another maniac rule in his place.'

'No, he killed the king for you, Rafaela.'

'I'd never thought of it quite like that,' she admitted.

'The things we do for love,' said Delfino.

'Something like that,' replied Rafaela. 'Let's get you two cleaned up and think on our options. How are your contacts with the local horse traders, Delfino?'

20

Market Day

Anea worked during the day, lost amid long tables bearing scores of the king's machines, searching for some edge or advantage. Many of the larger constructs had died. She'd never decipher their uses, the tiny purple eyes glassy and black. Smaller machines disguised as books reeled off transcripts of theories in a stilted, antiquated version of the old tongue. And there were slabs of black obsidian, ghostly pages of instruction and direction, whole volumes on biology and chemistry, untold chapters on the realm of physics, schematics for devices beyond imagining.

'Have you found your hairpin yet?' said Virmyre.

Not yet.

Was it a trick of her mind that he was more like himself? she wondered. Certainly his mood had softened in the two weeks since the cemetery. His frustrations had lessened, perhaps eased by her renewed interest in the king's machines.

'Did you discover anything of note?'

Nothing. Not a single mention of the Purge Protocol or any arte-fact. Not a word on the Huntsmen. The chamber of sarcophagi beneath Demesne was never far from her thoughts.

They used to call me the strega *princess. Would that I could cast spells.*

'Lightning?' said Virmyre. 'Flames from your fingertips perhaps?'

I would put the whole castle to sleep and walk in unopposed.

'Much more subtle. I approve.'

She stood slowly, stretching her arms and pressing fingers to the base of her spine.

'Why don't you step out with me? We'll buy supplies, replenish our wine stocks.'

Anea rolled her eyes. *With all of Demesne searching for me?*

'Things have changed.' Virmyre shook his head. 'The patrols have been relaxed. The Myrmidons rarely stray beyond the walls, worried House Del Toro will attempt to rescue Medea, no doubt.'

Or protecting their impostor.

'Unlikely,' replied Virmyre. 'She's barely been seen since Medea's revelation. The Domina has been managing the day-to-day running of Demesne.'

Much as it ever was. Anea felt a pang of guilt. If only she'd spent as much time ruling as she had amid the mysteries of the king's machines. Virmyre nodded and inclined his head, a tiny acknowledgement of shared neglect.

'What are you looking for –' he gestured to the many machines '– in all of this?'

Something, anything, to help us. At first I thought there might be a way to get a message to Lucien.

'But he'd need to see you in the flesh to confirm you were really you.'

Anea nodded. 'And then I wondered if there was some way of freeing the creatures from the sarcophagi. Some way of controlling them.'

'You'd have a small army at your disposal, and no need to endanger the lives of Lucien's scouts.'

This almost feels like old times, working here with you.

'And look where that led us. Come on. It'll be good for you to get some fresh air.' He snatched a glance out of the nearest window. 'And for me to venture outside without armour on.' Virmyre ventured into Demesne every few days, now wary of relying on the disguise since he'd rescued her.

Fine. Anea looked around the cell with narrowed eyes. *Although I insist you wear a blade.*

'Granted, Your Highness. I will arm myself to the teeth.'

Are you mocking me, Virmyre?

'You wound me with the implication.' His eyes twinkled with mischief but he managed to keep the smirk from his lips.

She dressed in clothes he'd bought from the market for a fictional daughter. A long skirt, cream blouse, black bodice and matching cap to hide her corn-blonde hair. Her shawl was somewhat mangy but was pressed into service all the same. The veil was problematic, but it was not unknown for devout *cittadini* to take the oath of Santa Maria. Virmyre was dressed as a merchant, his attire fine but not gauche, certainly not expensive enough to attract attention. He'd even bothered to shave.

Are you sure this is strictly for my benefit?

'I never said any such thing. If you think I've given up on the fantasy of leading a normal life you're quite insane.'

We are in the sanatorio, *you know.*

'Good point.'

They descended the stairs, he opening the door to the library, pushing past the tapestry. 'All those years I spent teaching brats in House Erudito, now I spend my days here. It seems I swapped one madhouse for another.'

I see your sense of humour is returning.

'Humour is all we have left.'

They walked the streets, and if the *cittadini* paid them any mind it was cursory. The impostor's rule had discouraged curiosity, people's priority to avoid the attention of the Myrmidons.

Everyone looks so pinched and ragged.

'The food shortages of the summer have been compounded with a steady rise in taxes. A *denaro* for this, two *denari* for that, a tax on livestock, another for bedrooms. The list is as long as it is ridiculous.'

And so my cittadini *have moved away.*

The evidence was impossible to ignore. Those few people who remained resembled the revenants of childhood stories, quiet shades tramping the snow-slicked streets. Too many windows were unlit, too many doors boarded up, abandoned carts and piles of refuse. Santa Maria was suffering a slow death.

You wanted me to see this. You want this to spur me into action.

'Ah, my transparency is showing.' Virmyre shrugged. 'Quite the contradiction.'

So you admit it?

'Anything is better than interrogating half-dead machines for secrets as obscure as they are useless.'

I told you I was looking for an advantage. Anea glowered at the *professore* but quickly stopped before they drew attention to themselves. They walked on.

'Come on, it's market day,' said Virmyre. 'Let's see if we can find something good to eat.'

The market, such as it was, huddled for warmth in the centre of the piazza, close to the church. This, Anea decided, was no accident. The sisters provided much custom for the traders. Men and women accosted passers-by from their stalls, stamping their feet in the cold. They called out from under brightly coloured awnings. Braziers sizzled, columns of smoke diffusing into the flat grey sky. Children sucked pork grease from fingers and chomped on stale bread. A rotund man in furs offered wine from a barrel, a battered wooden cup in each meaty fist. The rosiness of his cheeks confirmed where the greater part of his profits went. His cart was piled high with barrels – empty, Anea guessed, more an advertisement for his trade than a store for his goods. The horse that stood near the wine merchant was no better than a nag. Anea remembered a time when stalls crowded the piazza, when the storefronts and shops threw open their doors even on the coldest of days. Santa Maria could not lay claim to be even a shadow of itself.

Virmyre pressed a dozen *denari* into her chilled fingers. 'This won't stretch far, so get what you can.'

She dared not ask where he got the money from. She suspected the answer would be as unsavoury as the produce on sale. Virmyre strolled toward the wine merchant.

No sooner had the *professore* turned his back than Marchetti appeared, stumbling from the door of a tavern. Anea couldn't tell if he were still drunk from the previous night or had made an early start. Perhaps he'd sought to fortify himself from the cold. A ripple of anxiety passed through the crowd. Many of the sisters betrayed their alarm, hands straying to loose sleeves, where sharpened steel waited to be drawn. Marchetti stumbled toward a sister, turning suddenly and wrenching the veil from her face. She called out and pushed the assassin away, shock giving way to indignation. Anea felt a pang of jealousy: the woman's face was whole. The veil was a symbol of piety, not a tool of concealment.

Marchetti continued his stagger across the piazza, accosting another sister, who was caught unaware. Again he dragged off the veil, again he was pushed back. The next sister he intercepted had no mind to suffer the fate of those before her. A knife glittered in the sunlight. The sister stepped forward, slashing a diagonal of bright steel. Marchetti, for all his drunkenness, stepped beyond the limit of her reach. His hands flashed out, grasping her wrist. A pivot of his body and she was wrenched off balance. Then a twist of an arm, dragging a cry from the sister's lips. The knife clattered to the cobbles followed by her veil, torn from her face in a fury.

The piazza, previously a sullen churn of downcast *cittadini*, was now emptying. None of the townsfolk could guess why Marchetti acted so or what he sought in the faces of the sisterhood, but they scurried away, fear polluting the air like smoke. Stallholders were forced to choose between protecting their stock or reaching safety.

Anea pressed a hand to her veil and turned away, circling the cluster of stalls away from the eyes of the assassin. Virmyre remained lost from view. She wondered if he had fled. Surely he wouldn't leave her? Another sister cried out in anguish nearby, a trio of *cittadini* women helped her regain her feet. Anea pressed on, her unveiling a death sentence.

Marchetti was preoccupied with no less than four sisters fleeing together, desperate to reach the gates of the church. The women lifted the hems of their robes, taking the steps two at a time. The doors to the church boomed shut after they passed through. The sound of bolts sliding into place could be heard, the grunt of wood on wood as heavy timbers slotted into place. The assassin threw a dagger in disgust, the blade tumbling hilt over tip before lodging in the wood. It was then Marchetti turned on his heel, his eye settling on the simple merchant's daughter and the veil she wore. Anea cursed herself for not fleeing back to the old *sanatorio* at the first sign of trouble. She turned and began to walk away; to run would draw his further attention. The desire to glance over her shoulder was almost impossible to deny. Had he decided to follow? Was he trailing her? Her feet, sodden with snow, carried her over cobbles, past the stalls and their wares.

No sound reached her: no footfalls, boots scuffing on stone, the urgent percussion of running. Nothing. Silence followed in her wake and with it the strangling anxiety of discovery. Her curiosity demanded she glance over her shoulder. Nothing. Only when she hurried onward did Marchetti appear in front of her like a conjuration, the white scar through his eye vivid. A knife slipped free of its sheath, the set of his shoulders making it clear there would be no escape.

Anea's hands clenched into fists, her right hand still clutching Virmyre's gift. She flung the handful of coins in Marchetti's face and lurched to the side, her feet already skidding on the cobbles. The assassin fell back and she was free, for a few seconds at least. His hand clamped around her wrist, yanking her round to meet his glare, bloodshot and furious. The knife rose, the weak sunlight making the steel a dirty white. Anea twisted but could not get free.

A clamour of wood.

Barrels from the wine merchant's cart tumbled down, some bouncing on the cobbles, others rolling; one came apart like cheap furniture. Marchetti was knocked down, struck once, twice, three times by the barrels. Anea leaped backward, turning without hesitation, sprinting for the church steps. She slammed into the doors, fist beating an urgent plea. A glance over her shoulder revealed the supine form of the assassin amid the barrels and Virmyre affecting a limp as he trudged away from the cart. Anea felt a mixture of admiration but also pique. Had she been bait?

The doors opened and Sister Agostina ushered her in wordlessly.

*

It was strange to be on the balcony of the church again, stranger still to be there without Medea. Anea felt a wash of unhappiness as she remembered the canoness, along with a strong undercurrent of guilt. She hugged herself and waited, the chill of the balcony as pervasive as the isolation she felt. Agostina presented herself but made no pretence of etiquette or courtesy.

'Three weeks she's been in there. Three weeks.'

I am well aware how long Medea has been captive.

'Is there really nothing you can do?'

Would you like to come and fight the Myrmidons with me? If we corner them one by one we could retake Demesne by – she waggled a hand in estimation – *next winter?*

'She went with you to meet this so-called Herald.'

It was a trap. How were any of us to know?

'So it's your responsibility to get her back, to free her.'

Perhaps it escaped your notice, but I am trying to find a way to free Demesne before war breaks out.

'Well, don't let me stop you.' Agostina retired from the balcony, leaving Anea to watch the stallholders return. A score of children arrived, a ragtag regiment, pausing only to pour scorn on the battered Myrmidon. They gestured with raised fists, calling out curses.

'*Strega.*'

'*Figlio di puttana.*'

'*Buco del culo.*'

And so on.

Marchetti got to his feet and took a moment to collect his wits. He leaned on a barrel, one hand clasped to the back of his head. The pack of children moved off, realising the underkin would not rise to the bait. Marchetti pulled his hood up, further proof the insults fell on deaf ears.

The door behind Anea creaked open; she greeted the newcomer with stiletto in hand.

'Can't say I blame you.' Virmyre regarded the weapon, expression grave. 'Next time I suggest we take the air you can slit my throat first.'

Anea sheathed the stiletto then began to sign. *The last thing I need is a corpse. You are more useful alive. For now.*

'I bow to your greater wisdom, Highness. Agostina is in fine humour.'

I am surprised the sisters even let you in.

'I promised to take you with me when I left – that got their attention.'

He joined her at the parapet, following the direction of her gaze to where Marchetti was taking his first tentative steps. A trio of women emerged from the tavern, tousle-haired, last night's make-up smudged and smeared. They moved with a sultry cat-like languor, provocative in their dishevelment. The assassin moved toward Demesne, footsteps slow, head bowed.

I doubt there is anyone more miserable in Landfall, signed Anea.

'Surely you can't feel any sympathy for him.'

They watched Marchetti draw level with the women. One approached and drew an index finger along the span of his shoulder, then danced around him, ending in a clumsy pirouette.

Look at him.

Marchetti took a step toward the woman who had made an invitation of herself. She fled behind her friends, her mocking laughter sounding over the piazza.

What are they doing?

'The whores don't sleep with Myrmidons,' said Virmyre, his voice empty of contempt or endorsement. 'And Marchetti, more than anyone, is a Myrmidon to his bones.'

He lives at the heart of Demesne, within Santa Maria itself, yet he can turn to no one. She watched the assassin pass from sight, away from the women who taunted him, their cruel barbs marking him long after he'd passed.

Even prostitutes look down on him.

'Come, we should return to the *sanatorio*,' said Virmyre in a quiet voice. 'I've a feeling these streets will see plenty more Myrmidons before the day is done.'

21

The Winter of Suspicion

Eris swapped the confines of her apartment for the darkened maze of Simonetti's library for a time, yet her restlessness remained. Books came and went from her possession without care, but she clung to Simonetti's gift like a talisman. The words of the green cloth-bound book took root in her mind. An idea blossomed.

The House Contadino rose garden was the very mirror of her tangled thoughts. The frosty light of a winter's day was poor exchange for a dimly lit corridor, but here they were, beneath the dim disc of the cloud-occluded sun. The Myrmidons at the door had escorted her. They maintained a respectful distance, leaving her to wander the paths.

A circuit of the overgrown gardens led to a singular discovery: Medea's gardening tools remained beneath a bench, still rimed with the morning's frost. Eris set about the task with rusted shears and a trowel crusted with dark earth. Soon she was stained to the elbow with soil, knees muddy, gown ruined. An appraising eye confirmed the task might take all week, perhaps even two. The thought gave her a sense of serenity not known for months. She earned a score of shallow wounds for her troubles, the many prickles of the roses defying her best efforts. She hissed in complaint. But while her hands laboured, her mind had time to tug at other deeply rooted problems, many just as thorny. How to dispose of Erebus? What of Allattamento's agenda and the motives behind it? How to control Viscount Datini or at least elude the man's spies. Beneath this tangle of questions came an agenda of her own that surprised her: how to keep Simonetti safe through the winter of suspicion?

Hours passed before an obstacle appeared in the garden, as red as the flowers that would bloom there come springtime. Each footstep in the gravel provoked Eris's disdain; she only looked up from the soil when to do otherwise would have been ridiculous.

The Domina stood before her, silver staff polished to a gleam, robes immaculate, eyes wide open with an alertness bordering on mania. Eris guessed the steward had dosed herself with *tinctura*, alchemical courage for the conversation at hand.

'So this is where you've been hiding,' said the Domina, casting an eye over the flower beds.

Eris made no reply, her fingers continuing to seek out the weeds growing among the roses. Each unwanted plant pulled from the ground rewarded her with a feeling of deep satisfaction.

'Erebus is keen to see you resume the throne. He...' The gravel beneath the Domina's feet complained as she shifted her weight. 'He is concerned that Dottore Allattamento poisoned you against what we are trying to achieve.'

Eris stopped working, forming words with soiled fingers. *I have been reading, you know.* Eris looked at the Domina. *Books. Lots of them.*

The Domina hesitated, confused by Eris's reluctance to address her remarks, then continued unabashed. 'Lord Erebus made it clear to me that he tried everything he could to save your brother.'

I read about many subjects. Dipping into various subjects here and there. Eris glanced at the trowel that lay discarded by her knees, noted the pointed blade. Not so different to a stiletto.

The Domina opened her mouth but forgot what she had to say. A few seconds passed before she said, 'Lord Erebus also asked that I sound you out regarding the postponement of the marriage he suggested.'

And by chance I was reading about flowers. Roses in fact. The stems promise a multitude of cuts to the unwary. So many thorns. Eris looked up at the Domina, who seemed defeated by the

171

evasions of the muddy woman kneeling before her. *The book cited the biggest threats to cultivated roses as insects, arachnids and fungal diseases.*

Eris rose from her spot at the side of a bed, clutching the trowel in a dirty hand. The Domina took a half-step back, her eye slipping down to the simple tool, as if aware of Eris's dark intention. The blunt tool would offer a painful death if it manage to piece the soft flesh of her stomach, a death of many hours, bleeding out, rich soil infecting the wound. The Domina paled. Eris dropped the trowel, which fell point first into the dark earth.

Insects and arachnids, she signed.

'Well, I can see you're busy,' said the Domina, the mania of her eyes surrendering to a sickened panic. Eris was enjoying the silent language, perhaps for the first time ever. There was a measure to it, a rhythm, the satisfaction of controlling the tempo of the conversation.

A few hours' gardening has not made me an expert any more than reading a few chapters of that book – Eris drew herself up to her full height – *but I think I am starting to recognise a pest when I see one.*

The Domina fell back another hesitant step. 'Perhaps we should continue this conversation later, when you've had more time to think on what I've said.'

The steward exited the garden, staff stabbing through the gravel, the winter breeze clutching her crimson robes as she returned to the warmth of Demesne. Eris dismissed the Myrmidons with a single gesture; theirs was a thoughtful hesitation before nodding their assent. A handful of seconds passed before Eris departed the rose garden by the opposite door.

The walk through the town had not been planned. It was as if she had abandoned reason completely; her last excursion had almost spelled her execution. A shawl rescued from the chaos of House Contadino provided some measure of comfort. She wore it atop her own, a mangy disguise. The shawl, together with her mud-slicked gown and dirtied fingers, made a commoner of the impostor queen. There had been other rewards for haunting the corridors and empty apartments of House Contadino. Roses in red and white, crafted from silk, had survived the months of abandonment. It had been roses that had decided her course.

The muddy commoner was unmolested, only her gnawing hunger providing company. Strange to be hungry again after the abundance of luxury. There had been times before she'd become Eris when she'd begged for the most miserly scraps. The greatest of these had always gone to her brother; better he keep up his strength to resist the many racking coughs he suffered each winter.

Sabatino – the reason she'd forgone the safety of Demesne. The roses were an ill-fitting tribute, too romantic, lilies more traditional by far. The cemetery was visible down the gentle incline of the road, wrought-iron gates rusted open like welcoming arms. The walls were upholstered in ivy, now withered under the cruel gaze of winter.

Sabatino. Yes, they'd been hungry, and yes, he'd needed medicine she could never dream of buying. Oftentimes they barely made enough money to buy shelter, he remaining resolute and without complaint. And then the strange proposition from Allattamento, an offer of reprieve from a hidden master. Had there ever been any question she would agree? How could there be?

Sabatino. She'd done it for him. That's what she told herself. She'd become the Silent Queen for him, endured hours of lessons, learned to walk a certain way, imitated gestures and mannerisms. All had been done for Sabatino so they might have warm clothes and a place to live. Who cared if she needed to displace Demesne's rightful ruler? Anea's medicines were the finest one could buy, assuming you could afford them.

'Nobles.' Eris let the word fall from her lips like a curse. 'A self-serving, self-indulgent mob of entitled inbreds.' She fell silent upon realising her own behaviour had not been so dissimilar in recent months.

The graveyard was not so different from the rose garden. They shared gravel paths and a wilful neglect. The grasses that grew in the cemetery had overtaken the paths' edges, reaching as high as the knee. Headstones peered out from yellowing

173

vegetation, names and dates obscured by nature's gentle insistence. Angels with pale stone faces kept vigil over the fallen with water-stained gazes, white wings now verdant with touches of moss.

It took her longer than she would have liked to find Sabatino's grave, more moments that she'd care to admit. How had her brother's resting place been so easily forgotten? Was the geography of his death such a small matter? Another grave lay beside her brother's, newly dug and awaiting an occupant. A shovel rested atop a mound of rich loam, a temporary marker for the burial to come. Eris clutched the silk roses and regarded the plot of earth, the headstone hinting at the boy who lay beneath the soil.

I am so sorry, she signed. Making confession in the silent language made the telling of it more profound. If asked, she could not say why, only that spoken words seemed crude and banal. Better she trust to the solemnity of silence.

I was not there when you needed me most. At the end. I was... Her mind strayed to Marchetti. *I thought I was being so clever. I thought I could be whatever they wanted and have whatever I wanted. I though I could keep you safe, but I realise now I lost my way.*

Sabatino said nothing, never having counted loquaciousness among his sins.

The dottore *came to me a few weeks ago, filled my head with secrets or fictions. No way to tell them apart. Maybe he fed me a mixture of both.*

The weather turned. For a second a spectral wail drifted on the wind, the many weathervanes of Demesne infamous for their unholy song. Eris shivered and cursed.

I cannot help but believe him. A dottore *will lie about many things, but they are sworn to protect life. He would not lie about that, would he?*

Sabatino said nothing, never having counted contradiction among his sins either.

I will have Erebus killed for you, I swear it. The silence of the cemetery was absolute. *I will see him dead and the Domina too for her complicity.*

It was in that moment that the raven alighted on the head-stone of her brother's grave. There was nothing petite or mean about the dark bird, the blackness of its feathers matched by its stern gaze. Its beak was long and sharp, so like the stiletto she'd returned to Allattamento. Eris stepped back from the dire visitor, looking for a hiding place among the dead. The raven stretched its wings, and the wind rose with it, whipping grit into the air. Eris threw a hand up to protect her face and stumbled away, blinking, blind. Her eyes watered and stung, her ears filling with the sound of hooves. They approached at speed along the road she had walked so willingly, as if led by enchantment. Her eyes watered, carrying away the irritation but revealing what she feared the most.

A mumble of yellowing grasses, faded earth from the road, the grey of vine-choked cemetery walls, an off-white sky; all indistinct, all waiting to remember colour come the spring. Standing amid the washed-out tableau was the absolute dark-ness of the Herald. He held out one hand, palm up, and for a second Eris dared hope for a reprieve. The gesture was not meant for her. The raven took wing, alighting on the Herald's shoulder. She imagined a hint of cruel amusement in the set of the mask's mouth.

There was nowhere to run, no place of safety. She had come seeking the counsel of her dead brother; now she would join him. The Herald's cloak rippled in the wind, the raven calling out in a strident tone, answered in kind by kin hidden among the trees.

Why do you wish me dead? To speak would reveal the decep-tion; she'd be killed where she stood. Better to cling to the fiction she was Anea.

'You betrayed everything.' The words emerged in a rasp from behind the mask, an element of gravel to the delivery, as if the small stones under their feet lent him their voice. 'The promise of elections, of a republic, the welfare of the *cittadini*. Everything.'

My hand was forced. This much was true; she'd issued few edicts on her own initiative. *If you could just get me away from this place, away from Demesne, away from Erebus.*

'Don't play the reluctant pawn. You've not merely broken faith, you've shattered it. Completely.' The Herald paused. A change in the set of his shoulders, his head lowered. 'The roses?' He gestured at the silk flowers she clutched in the crook of her arm. 'From the Contadino gardens?'

Eris nodded, unsure what to say. The Herald paused a moment.

'And you refuse to give up Marchetti and Erebus?'

I cannot. She began to sign her desire to be free of Erebus, but the raven launched into the grey sky, the commotion of feathers drawing her attention from the Herald. And also his right hand. A stunning strike, mute shock, the familiar sting she'd tried to forget. Her knees buckled, gravel biting through the fabric of her gown. She blinked away flashes of brightness, her face burning from impact and abrasion. A steely scrape confirmed the inevitable. The Herald stood over her, great sword held in both hands, cloak thrown back.

'Pray to Santa Maria if you wish,' said the Herald, 'but she never granted me any peace.'

Eris watched the Herald raise the blade above his head, a wordless terror rose in her chest. Death was just a heartbeat away.

22

Erebus Revealed

'Where are we going?' said Virmyre with more than hint of complaint. Anea didn't have time to sign, her left hand held his, the leather of his gauntlet rough on her fingers. She all but dragged him along the corridors of the *sanatorio*. 'At least tell me if we're in danger.'

She led him through the secret door, down the spiral staircases of the library, pausing only to pick up an unlit lantern and a pouch of matches.

'I have to say,' grumbled Virmyre, 'I'm a touch bemused by this newfound fascination for going outside. It's not as if we enjoyed much success this morning, is it?'

All true, of course, but even the threat of Marchetti couldn't deter Anea.

'And you threw most of our money at the assassin, so we're hardly in a position to buy more food.'

Anea silenced him with a look.

They pushed through the doors of the *sanatorio*, rushing down the outside steps. Gargoyles looked down with pained expressions, watching them stalk the empty street. Marchetti's drunken assault had seen off the few *cittadini*. No one wanted to be present should he return. His retribution would be stern at best. The market stalls had packed up early; only stray dogs and inquisitive cats greeted them.

'I'm not really an advocate of blind faith, Anea. At least tell me why you're marching us into the teeth of the enemy.'

She'd insisted Virmyre wear the Myrmidon armour; it was no great deduction to assume they were heading back to Demesne.

'I can't kill every Myrmidon between here and the Ravens-court.'

Anea didn't pause to reply. They were in the small courtyard by the chapel of Santa Maria, the winter sky disgorging flecks of sleet. She pushed the lantern into his hands and began to sign.

She has gone to the cemetery. I saw her leave House Contadino from the window.

'Your impostor?'

Anea gave an emphatic nod. *And it looks as if the Herald did too. Perhaps now is the time to retake the throne.*

'And did you think what will happen if she comes back?'

Anea squared up to him. *You have been sulking because I would not do anything for the last three weeks. Now I am doing something.*

'Good point.' Virmyre looked around to be certain they remained unseen. 'We'd best get on with it. But where are you taking me?'

There are other ways in than through the front door.

'This is how you escaped from the oubliette?'

Anea nodded. *There must be other doors, other passages that lead up into House Fontein.*

No one had bothered to board up the entrance to the tunnel beneath House Prospero. It gazed at them like a dark eye. Anea spent long moments trying to light the lantern, her shaking hands an impediment.

'Let me try.'

Cold was all she signed after giving over the flint and steel. Virmyre nodded, playing along with the fiction. They both knew she was filled with dread. The prospect of returning to Demesne's underworld would make the bravest of hearts falter. Virmyre lit the lantern and held it aloft. He enclosed her fingers with his free hand.

'That should warm you up.' And for a second there was the ghost of a smile beneath those pale blue eyes.

The tunnel was not dry, but nor was it ankle deep in filth as it had been when she escaped. Her destruction of the boards at the tunnel mouth had drained the worst of it, making their passage easier. The smell remained, the stench a reminder of her worst anxieties, imprisonment and forgetfulness. She squeezed Virmyre's hand, causing him to turn, armour outlined in the light. He pulled her close, arm wrapping about her shoulders.

'I'm not going to let anything happen to you.' His voice was loud in the quiet, a challenge to her fears. 'I've already failed you one time too many.'

The old man kissed her gently on the forehead, the coarse hair of his beard tickling. Anea felt a bloom of warmth in her chest, and hope.

The sarcophagus chamber was just as she remembered. They spent some time looking for the machine she had stumbled against.

'I can't see inside any of them,' rumbled Virmyre, 'and I'm fairly grateful for that.' He lied of course, for her benefit or his own. Beings could be seen beyond the smoky glass, alien and grotesque. Here was something resembling a dark snout, there a glint of an unclosed eye. Each sarcophagus was identical to those around it, no clue indicating where Anea had woken the sleeper within. Each machine and the occupant it contained remained inactive, perhaps lulled to torpor by the basso drone that resonated through the chamber.

Anea tugged on the old man's arm, pointing at the floor. At the centre of the room was a disc of metal. Dust obscured most of it, but the lantern light glinted on two pairs of footprints. One of the walkers had clearly been wounded, feet dragging through the dust as he passed. Virmyre knelt and brushed at the limit of the disc, blowing the dust away gently. There were concentric grooves but no inscriptions.

'Extraordinary. It must be seven feet across or thereabouts.'

Anea held the lantern and watched him work. She pointed a single index finger toward the centre.

'I see it.'

An aperture. Virmyre duly stretched toward the hole. Anea lunged forward, pulling him back by the shoulder, but it was too late. Two fingers slipped into the centre of the disc. Anea almost dropped the lantern, eyes fixed on the small yet ominous opening.

Nothing happened.

Virmyre stood and wiggled his fingers at her with a raised eyebrow.

'All safe and sound. I'll wager that's where your artefact goes, some amulet or charm on a gold chain, I expect.'

They pressed on to the far end of the chamber, eyes of amethyst light tracking their every move.

'Over here.' Virmyre took the lantern from her. 'The sink hole you escaped through.'

A nod. *I do not remember that doorway, but it was dark and I may have missed it in my haste.* A moment later and they were scaling steps, back to levels of Demesne more familiar to them.

'Where now?'

I cannot be seen attending the Ravenscourt in this. She plucked at the humble skirt she wore. *I need to show people the Silent Queen. The real Silent Queen.*

'The impostor moved her apartment to House Fontein,' said Virmyre. 'Closer to the protection of the Myrmidons – they have their barracks there. She made a show of moving all of your furniture,' he explained, 'but left the wardrobes. I thought it strange at the time, but now it makes sense.'

Anea guessed the impostor was not quite the same size. Copies of her outfits would have been created for the deception by House Prospero tailors and seamstresses employed by the Domina.

The pretend Myrmidon and the Silent Queen had used more than one of the many secret passages to get this far. Slipping out of House Fontein had been tricky enough. Now Virmyre turned the key in the lock of Anea's apartment, forgotten amid the silence of House Contadino.

'I always like to keep old keys handy,' he explained. 'You never know where you might end up.'

Virmyre entered, drawing back the curtains to banish the half-light. Anea stood in the doorway blinking. Her apartment was hollowed out, stripped bare of all the possessions she'd held dear. She couldn't recall what was missing but felt the loss all the same; the phantom theft of unremembered gifts. She'd hoped that here she might regain some glimmer of herself, summoning memory through the trivia of her existence. Given time Erebus might erase the very idea of Anea, not just from the minds of the *cittadini*, but from herself.

The wardrobes were a bastion against the desolation, the many moths of the castle unable to destroy their contents. There was a thrill of recognition as she opened the doors. Scent drifted out, invigorating her senses. Her perfume she realised. Fingers traced rich fabrics; simply touching them was intoxicating.

'They say clothes do not make the man, or woman in this case,' said Virmyre, 'but I've a feeling that proverb is about to meet an untimely end.'

Anea looked over her shoulder at the *professore* and gave a satisfied nod. She needed something to grab the attention of the nobles, something bold, stark even. A move away from the dark colours her impostor loved so dearly.

'Do you know what you're doing?' said Virmyre, voice low. He had crossed to the window, a reassuring outline in the armour, helmet beneath one arm.

I know precisely. Things are about to become very chaotic.

'Try and leave the roof attached. I'm not sure the treasury can afford the pantiles.'

I promise nothing. Now look away and let a lady dress.

The Ravenscourt had been in session for perhaps half an hour when the doors opened, groaning on their hinges. The Myrmidons were caught unaware, at first rushing forward to intercept the latecomer. Steps faltered; the soldiers could only stare at the vision in white beneath the pointed arch of the door. A whisper surged through the room, leaping from mouth to ear and mouth again, turning the heads of all. Representatives of the houses minor gasped, messengers blinked in surprise. And at the far end of the chamber, presiding from the dais, was the Domina. A frown crowded her features, her mouth opened to issue a challenge, but none came.

Anea was dressed in a white gown featuring a stiff corset.

The sleeves flared at the wrists, neckline straight along her collarbones, folded over, leaving her shoulders bare. She'd painted her nails a platinum white in order to cover the black chitin. This was not a gown of the court, nor was it in any way traditional. It was by turns fitted and loose, embroidered with faint geometric patterns. Crowning the audacious attire was a headpiece of radiant silver, a fan shape sweeping back from her head. Argent tassels framed her face. This at least was an echo of something Anea had worn when she still ruled.

Virmyre marched behind her, holding the lantern close to her head, creating a nimbus to those who parted in front. It was as outrageously theatrical an entrance as there had ever been. She needed their attention, and courtiers were drawn to spectacle like merchants to money.

Simonetti pushed his way through the crowd, meeting Anea in the exact centre of the chamber. The nobles withdrew with looks of astonishment, many wary of the escorting Myrmidon.

'I'm so glad you had a change of heart following our talk, my lady.' The archivist smiled and bowed.

I am afraid you have me confused with someone else. Excuse me a moment.

Anea swept past the archivist, who stared after her with with a question frozen on his lips. The Silent Queen approached the dais, the Domina stepping down to make a show of her respect. A short bow, not nearly deep enough. Anea's fingers spelled out two simple words.

May I?

She held out her hand for the silver staff of office. The Domina narrowed her eyes in confusion, but Anea simply extended her hand again. The Domina relinquished her symbol of office, reluctant and confused. Anea turned to the Ravenscourt and inspected it. There was a stirring of memory, like a name on the tip of her tongue, tantalising yet elusive. No time for that now. Anea turned and swung the staff with both hands. The Domina gave an agonised yelp and collapsed as the length of silver smashed the backs of her knees. She curled into a fetal ball and shuddered. The Ravenscourt gasped in shock. None of the Myrmidons moved. The silver staff, aglow by the light of Virmyre's lantern, rose again, then fell, striking the Domina across the shoulders. And again.

Anea threw the staff down in disgust and stepped onto the dais, turning to face Virmyre. She tapped two fingers to her veil. Virmyre nodded and removed his helm, eliciting yet more astonishment from the Ravenscourt

'You have all been duped,' announced Virmyre, reading the movements of Anea's clever fingers. 'It is exactly as Marchesa Contadino told you.'

Duchess Prospero stepped forward but said nothing, the court falling silent once more as Virmyre raised his hand for silence.

'I am Aranea Oscuro Diaspora. They cast me into the oubliette and I forgot my name, forgot who I was, forgot what I stood for and the promises I had yet to keep.' Anea paused, seeing only shocked faces. There were so few of the people she had come to rely on. Dino, Cherubini, Stephania Prospero, Massimo, Emilio Contadino – all gone. Her fingers continued spelling out her words and Virmyre lent his voice to the gestures.

'This creature –' Anea gestured at the Domina '– my trusted servant, my treacherous friend, supplanted me with an impostor, ruining Landfall, saddling us with an army we have no use for, goading us into war.'

The Myrmidons edged closer, the full import of Virmyre's words rousing them to action. The woman in white who commanded the dais continued signing. An order was barked, and the armoured soldiers crowded past the nobles, but their way was blocked. Drago Romanucci placed himself before the dais, sword in hand. Other bravos from House Del Toro were squaring up to the soldiers. The threat of violence settled across the Ravenscourt. Anea knew she had lost their attention.

'This wasn't my work alone,' whispered the Domina, dragging herself to her feet. She held one arm across her chest, face racked with agony. 'I never chose war. I never chose this.'

The Myrmidons resorted to more direct methods to reach the dais, drawing steel on the bravos who had made obstacles of themselves. The unarmed were cut down where they stood if they proved too slow. The crowd swept and roiled about them in a storm of outrage and horror. Virmyre seized Anea, attempting to lead her back to the main doors, through the very centre of the Ravenscourt. Anea couldn't decide if the screaming was worse than the smell of blood. A man staggered past holding the stump of one wrist, ashen, mouth hung open in shock. The doors of the chamber boomed shut, four Myrmidons forming a barrier before them.

Do they mean to kill everyone?

'Come on,' shouted Virmyre, leading her back to the dais, past a fight that saw two nobles slashed chest to hip. Three bravos dragged a Myrmidon to the floor, and stilettos made bloody arcs in the air, the points finding gaps in the armour.

'Up you go,' said Virmyre simply. The drapes at the chamber's sides had been Anea's idea; she had never imagined they might be used to escape the Ravenscourt. Up she went, hand over hand, digging her heels in for traction. A messenger in Prospero livery on the balcony reached over, helping her up. Virmyre followed.

The Ravenscourt was a crush of fear and fury. Some sought to protect those they loved, others were eager to defeat the Myrmidons. The majority sought only escape, but the doors held fast.

'Highness?'

Anea reached over and grabbed Virmyre's wrists, hauling and heaving with every ounce of her being.

'So good of you to help,' he grunted, pulling himself level with the handrail and over the top. 'Remind me never to climb in armour again.'

What do you think they are hiding behind the curtain? signed Anea.

'Let's find out.' Virmyre grasped at the heavy fabric, hands seizing the bronze leaves. Anea joined him, straining with all her strength. Others joined them, hands clawing at the heavy wool, seizing the veil that had been drawn across the Ravenscourt. Wooden supports surrendered with a groan, the curtain fell to the dais below, a patch of night sky littered with leaves.

The Ravenscourt forgot their struggles, consumed with revulsion.

'What in Nine Hells is that?' said Virmyre, horrified at the grotesque vision looming above the throne. Erebus shifted, six pinion-like legs lifting with arthritic motions, the Myrmidon Lord, a god to the insects made massive through ego and science. Wretches stirred and cowered beneath him, shrieking as they hobbled away, a congregation of the strange.

Erebus, signed Anea. Virmyre nodded, mute with appalled fascination.

The Domina watched the stripping-away of the deception, tear-stained and afraid, all her carefully constructed lies unravelling. Her biretta tumbled off, hair spooling loose, auburn over crimson robes, as the last of the black curtain slipped over the edge of the gallery. The fabric tangled about three vast insect legs, dragging Erebus toward the edge. He was drawn inexorably to the dais below by the weight of cloth and bronze. All fighting ceased; all mouths forgot their cries. Slowly the aberration toppled forward, legs scrabbling for purchase.

Virmyre growled a curse and lunged forward, slashing at Erebus, steel gleaming brightly. The creature raised a scythe-like leg to fend off the strike, parrying Virmyre's blade. It was enough: dragged by dark fabric and off balance, Erebus fell to the dais in a thrash of limbs. The sickening impact silenced those still fighting. The Ravenscourt could only stare as Erebus righted himself, twice the height of a man, larger than a pair of oxen. The forelegs twitched with fury.

'This way,' came a shout from the main doors. Anea's eye fell on scarlet robes. The Domina was pointing toward the way out. People hurried through to safety, to the remainder of their upturned lives.

'She's helping them escape,' said Virmyre, 'after everything she's done.'

The Domina ushered the people out before feeling Anea's eyes upon her. A look of regret haunted her features. Her one good hand danced over the fingers of her lame arm, forming crippled words in the silent language: *I am sorry*.

Anea stared down at her from the balcony as the people fled from the monstrosity.

Erebus lurched from the dais, slamming one foreleg into a bravo, breaking ribs with ease.

Anea's fingers formed a reply: *Yes, you are.*

Erebus advanced, a wordless fury sounding from beneath the Myrmidon helm. Courtiers were run down, pages caught beneath chitinous legs.

'Come on, Highness.' Virmyre helped Anea to the roof though a hatch meant for maintenance work. Breathless, they set out across Demesne's rooftop landscape, stunned by what they had seen. The full impact of Erebus registered more deeply with each second.

'He was so –' Virmyre blinked '– huge.'

Anea nodded, and minutes passed before either of them could form any sort of question.

'What will Russo do now?' asked Virmyre.

I am unsure. Anea looked away, unfocused, feeling outside of herself. *Erebus will kill her, most likely.*

'And us? What do we do now?'

Find Medea Contadino. Before Erebus finds a reason to kill her too.

23

A Raven, a Revenant

The wind whipped about Eris's shoulders, her tresses dancing in the wind as the Herald raised the great sword in both hands. The awful moment captured his every detail: worn boots with a profusion of buckles, scuffed with gravel and spattered with loam; the cloak, so easy to dismiss as black, a subdued motley of dark green, charcoal grey and midnight blue; a surcoat of darkest brown accented with turquoise, a copper brooch in the shape of a cataphract drake biting its tail at his breast. And within the darkness of the hood a smirking carnival mask.

Instinct insisted she look away, eyes coming to rest on the simple headstone of her brother. Her promise to avenge him was just minutes old and already doomed to failure. Gravel found its way into her hands, silk roses forgotten. The Herald's great sword reached its apex, death a second away. He'd split her from collarbone to navel. Her hands raked up, flinging gravel into the dark space beneath the hood. Eris's reward was a shocked grunt. Whatever the Herald may or may not be, he at least had eyes. He stumbled back, the sword captured by gravity, its tip snagging in the long grass beside the path. A gloved hand reached beneath the hood. A stifled curse. Eris needed no further invitation. Lurching to her feet, she sprinted past the Herald, lashing out with both hands, sending the apparition sprawling. And then the earth swallowed him, a creature returned to hell. There was a dull thump, and then another. The first belonged to the Herald, the second his great sword, both falling to the bottom of the open grave alongside Sabatino's. Eris didn't expect him to remain there for long.

She ran. And not the wind nor bruised knees nor muddied skirts could slow her. She reached the gates, lungs a ragged jumble, heart a-flutter in her chest. She would not join her brother in death. Not today. A glance over her shoulder confirmed what she had feared with every panicked step. A hand in thick leather rose from the grave and clawed at the sodden earth; the mud-spattered mask emerged after it, surging over the edge. He was the very image of a revenant, the vengeful undead of dark tales told in Landfall. The risen spirit whispered of by parents to scare disobedient children.

Eris struggled to mount the Herald's horse, foot slipping from the stirrup. She pulled herself onto the creature's back with aching arms. The mount tolerated her presence, making no move despite her insistent shaking of the reins. The raven circled above her head, turning an eye on her before swooping down. Its talons gouged her scalp, tangled in her hair, wings a confusion of dark feathers. Eris cried out, her voice drowned by the harangue and vehemence of the raven. She flailed at the bird, one hand striking her attacker, the other twisted in the reins. The talons remained, the raven struggling to stay aloft.

A look snatched at the cemetery confirmed the Herald had emerged from the grave, slick with mud, favouring one leg as he stalked toward her. The fall had cost him. That he could be injured at all brought some consolation.

Eris kicked hatefully at the horse, heels drumming against its sleek black flanks. She whipped an arm at the raven, which broke free of the entanglement, talons leaving her blonde tresses stained with blood. The Herald was close, sword trailing behind him, point scoring a groove in the gravel, the sound a maddening scrape. She wanted to scream.

The horse finally bolted so hard Eris slid from the saddle. The reins bit into her hand, holding her in place on the black steed's broad back. Eris bounced, slammed and buffeted against the horse as the gallop became a charge. The iron tang of blood filled her mouth as her teeth bit her tongue. Both hands now clutched the reins, legs clamping. A fall at this speed would mean a quick death, if she were fortunate. The other option was too awful to consider: lying in the road, broken yet breathing, unable to move, waiting for the Herald to finish her. She talked to the horse, at first cursing, then in gentle supplication. Coaxing, begging.

By the time they reached the town the steed had slowed to a merciful trot. Eris whispered her thanks over and over, feeling as grateful as she'd ever known. The familiar sight of the Myrmidons was equal parts pleasing and surprising. Four of them lurked by the gates of House Contadino. Why security was so strong at the abandoned house was a mystery. The Herald's horse slowed as they approached, raising its head. The mount and Herald were well matched in bravura if nothing else.

Eris slipped from the saddle, legs threatening to collapse, knees all but buckling. Her hands betrayed the full extent of her distress by their nerveless shaking. She pressed tremulous fingers to her scalp. The wounds inflicted by the raven stung. Hot tears of shock brimmed in her eyes, making a shimmering place of the world.

Let me in.

The Myrmidons remained unmoving, no sign to acknowledge her presence. She took a step closer and signed again.

I would like to come in.

All four Myrmidons turned to face her, curving blank helms revealing nothing but insectile indifference. She felt, rather than saw, suspicious eyes.

I am Aranea Oscuro Diaspora.

'You and everyone else,' replied the nearest of them.

What do you mean?

'We had a Silent Queen in here this afternoon,' explained the Myrmidon standing nearest.

'In a white dress,' supplied another of the faceless guards.

I have just returned from the cemetery.

'She does look as if she came back from the dead,' muttered another. There was a cruel snigger, but the Myrmidons made no move. Hands drifted to the hilts of swords.

Please. Eris glanced over her shoulder. *There is someone trying to kill me. Just send for the Domina. She will know who I am.*

'It was the Domina who gave the order. No one enters and

189

no one leaves.' This from a Myrmidon at the back, a senior judging by the red chevrons on his armour.

It is the Domina I need to see most.

Silence.

Eris looked back over her shoulder. The road to the cemetery was obscured by the many buildings of Santa Maria. She imagined the Herald limping along, great sword dragging in the dirt, implacable. The Domina had locked her out. Except the Domina hadn't known she'd left the castle. Her actions weren't hostile, merely inconvenient. An inconvenience that could spell her death.

Eris took the reins of the black steed and proceeded no further than two steps. She turned an angry glare on the horse to receive an aggressive snort. The creature stamped a hoof to make its position absolute.

'Fine. Stay here then.' She flashed a look at the Myrmidons. 'They'll probably eat you alive,' she whispered by the horse's ear. 'It will serve you right. You nearly killed me you were galloping so fast.'

The horse raised its tail, releasing several clods of dung that landed on the cobbles and steamed in the chilly afternoon. Eris cursed and walked away. Before she had wanted to scream in terror; now she only wanted to scream in frustration.

The sun slipped below the horizon, along with any hope of gaining entry to Demesne. A second knot of Myrmidons refused entry to the Central Keep, with more talk of a Silent Queen in white.

'But you know me,' she whispered, lifting the veil as if this were proof enough. The Myrmidon leaned forward to inspect her.

'You humans all look the same to me.'

The Myrmidons laughed, making coarse comments as she departed for the lonely streets of Santa Maria, edging toward lanterns, all too few in the oppressive gloom. The sparse lighting showed a gentle fall of sleet, appearing from the darkness like weak stars falling in their millions. The sleet slicked the cobbles, shiny and black in the night. And then at last, on frozen feet, she stumbled across a trio of women.

'I'm so pleased I found you. I need shelter.' But her words were breathless and quiet, made inaudible by shivering.

'Ooh, fancy dress. Shame you're all covered in mud.' The first of the women was in her late thirties perhaps, hair lank and long. 'And a veil? Suppose you're one of those zealous types? Come to tell us to fix our sinful ways, have you?'

The lines in her face had been etched by starvation and worry in equal measure. It was a harsh tithe, made more so by the many men who had claimed a part of her with each transaction. Eris knew that life all too well; she had been on the periphery of it, almost succumbing at one point. Courtesans, elegant, cultured and alluring, were a work of fiction in Landfall. Whores catered to the rough needs of *cittadini* and *nobili* alike.

Eris removed the veil.

'No lessons from me today,' she said, a rueful smile playing on her lips. Even as the words spilled from her mouth she knew she had made a mistake. Her tone, the very way she pronounced each syllable, was as different to the way the women spoke as her attire was to theirs.

'Ah, what's a nice *nobile* girl like you doing out here?'

'And unescorted?' provided another.

'Come courting with your love, only to find yourself walking home after he'd had his way?'

They regarded her muddied gown, the soil on her fingers, the blood in her hair.

'You wouldn't be the first.'

'They're all the same.'

'Pigs.'

'Worse than pigs.'

And so on. The whores chided and teased, scathing about men.

'Can you give me shelter? Do you have a place I could stay?' Eris struggled to make herself heard.

The three whores fell silent. A dangerous edge slipped through the winter night, sharp as any dagger.

'Place to stay?' said the oldest, all traces of humour, caustic or otherwise evaporating from her face. 'Do you think we'd be selling ourselves if we had a place to stay? Do you think we'd be out here in the depths of winter if we had a score of *denari* to our name.' She took a step closer. Eris struggled to stand her ground, the scorn spilling from the woman a physical force.

'You go back to your pretty castle. Go back to your Silent Queen and the endless list of taxes.' An index finger extended like a stiletto, stabbing Eris in the chest. 'You tell her what you've seen.' Another stab of the dirty finger. 'And if she's a shred of compassion in her black heart then she'll stop gouging the poor for every coin we got.'

Eris stumbled back and glowered at the woman. 'She will hear every word as if she were here herself.'

The *taverna* was not far from where the whores had their pitch. Eris contemplated her revenge during the short walk. She would have them thrown in the oubliette – once she had managed to get inside the castle. She luxuriated in the planning of her retribution, impatient to see the looks on their haggard faces as the Myrmidons arrested them. She imagined setting the iron grille in place as they screamed for mercy.

The *taverna* shed golden light from latticed windows. Eris knocked at the door with numb fingers, wincing at the pain. The door opened onto a gruff face. Grey stubble and creases were drawn into a frown. The man's main attribute was an overlarge nose featuring a slew of broken blood vessels. This was a face well acquainted with late-night drinking and all the regrets that accompanied it.

'You're not covered in shit, are you?' Eris looked at her muddied clothes. 'Because it smells bad enough in here as it is.' He gestured back over his shoulder with a hand like a shovel.

'Ah, let her in, before she catches her death,' shouted another voice from inside.

The sleet had thickened to snow, falling with greater intensity, promising a miserable journey home for the revellers.

'You'd best come in,' he grunted. Eris stepped over the threshold, clutching her shawls about herself, shaking a flurry of white from the fabric.

'Close the door against the draught, Peppino!'

'Ah, look! She's like a drowned kitten,' said a female voice much slurred with drink.

Eris couldn't disguise the revulsion she felt. The man behind the bar was broad shouldered with a neck as wide as the blunt dome of his skull. He wore a singlet beneath a greasy leather apron, arms maps in flesh, pale scars tracing every route to pain and hardship. She'd been here before. This was the *taverna* where Marchetti had stayed.

'Come in, dearest, come in.' A woman in her fifties grinned. There was a great deal lacking in her smile — of teeth and humour. 'We're drinking to the end of the world. Can't be long now, dearest, can it?'

The *cittadini* were every bit as disgusting as the wretches attending Erebus. They were scarcely human, shambling things awaiting an unnamed apocalypse, too lazy or stupid to escape. A dozen of them took succour from tumblers, fussing at dice or cards. The smell of cooking lingered on the air, its rank fumes diminishing any appetite Eris had.

'Here! Look, there's someone else.' Peppino wrested a cudgel from a place of concealment. 'Bravo in a cloak with a black bird on his shoulder.'

Eris turned so hard she stumbled, silencing the ragged assortment of patrons. Peppino fixed her with a look, then locked the door. Furtive glances were directed at the windows, the glass smeared and misted with condensation. None could mistake the shadow that fell across the panes, deeper darkness in the winter night.

'He's not coming in here,' said Peppino, 'not while I'm standing.' The drunk drew himself up to his full height, made ridiculous by the vast gut that hung over his belt.

Tap. Tap, tap.

Peppino's bravura was undone by the nervous glance he exchanged with the barman. No one spoke, every eye turning to Eris, unkind and accusing.

'It's her he wants.' The words were just a whisper but impossible to miss.

'There he is,' said a blonde woman, descending into a

coughing fit. The Herald loomed at another window, rapping a single knuckle against the glass. *Tap. Tap, tap.*

Eris shivered, wanting to scream with frustration.

Tap. Tap, tap.

'We could always ask him what he wants,' said Peppino, his bravado reduced to wheedling.

'No.' Eris surprised herself with the strength of her voice, loud in the anxious silence. 'He's dangerous, very dangerous. He won't stop with killing me once he's started.' The tapping stopped. Wary smiles were exchanged and the patrons breathed easier.

'Ah, don't worry yourself with it.' This from the crone with the missing teeth. 'He's gone now. Lovers' tiff, I expect.' Raucous laughter, but hollow and forced. The crone flashed another grin.

The soft mumble of voices resumed their banal conversations. More drinks were ordered. Eris did not sit down. She would not move from her spot in the centre of the room, could not take her eyes from the door. Peppino remained on guard, cudgel clutched in meaty fist.

Tap. Tap, tap.

The patrons leaped from their chairs, and the crone made a show of clutching her chest.

'We're all doomed, I tell you,' she squawked. Flashes of metal in the lantern light, daggers drawn from concealment. The blonde woman succumbed to her affliction, face purple from coughing. And underneath the commotion the insistent sound once again.

Tap. Tap, tap.

'Right you.' The barman pointed a thick finger at Eris. 'Out you go.'

'No, wait! Please? You can't. You mustn't. He means to kill me.'

The man gestured to Peppino, who discarded the cudgel to take Eris by the shoulders, forcing her toward the *taverna*'s back door.

'No, please. Don't send me away. You can't send me away. You don't understand.'

He dragged her through the storeroom behind the bar, past wine racks and casks. Her fingers clawed at Peppino's tunic, wrenched at his sleeves, but the man was too strong. The barman fussed at the lock before giving Peppino a curt nod. All the time Eris berated them both, souring the air with curses.

The door was thrown open, Peppino thrusting her out into the snowy street, the white crunching underfoot. She slipped and stumbled. The door slammed shut and locks clicked into place as she flicked her fingers at them from beneath her chin. The dark street was empty in both directions, each corner quiet and lonely. A multitude of snowflakes emerged from the darkness above, fluttering down.

'Fuck' was all she said before dashing away into the freezing night.

24

Various Methods of Escape

Anea and Virmyre found themselves in strange company following their flight from the Ravenscourt. While most nobles had escaped through the main doors some others and the lower orders had exited via the balconies. Scores of dead remained, hacked apart by Myrmidon blades. The hatches provided for workmen to maintain the roof had granted many a refuge, leading to a landscape of sloping angles and rusting weathervanes, surreal and bleak in the falling snow.

'I'd still rather be up here than down there,' said Virmyre to himself. Anea couldn't help but agree. Sobbing and subdued muttering surrounded them. Anea felt ridiculous in her white dress, which offered no protection from the wind and cold.

'What *was* that creature?' said someone behind them. The question needed an answer, yet all were stunned with incomprehension.

Was that really Erebus? signed Anea after the question had driven her to distraction.

'Undoubtedly.' Virmyre shook his head in disbelief. 'I've seen mention of sciences that can alter bodies, of machines that grow new flesh and graft it to a host.' He swallowed. 'But that?'

The sight of the six-limbed aberration stalking across the Ravenscourt was etched inside Anea's eyelids. It waited every time she blinked, bringing memories of screaming and the smell of blood. Erebus had sloughed off the fragile flesh of men along with any vestiges of humanity. For a moment her mind drifted to the chamber beneath House Fontein with its ranks of sarcophagi.

Could the creatures below House Fontein be his design?

Virmyre inclined his head, thoughtful. 'Difficult to know. It would seem pointless to create an army of Myrmidons if one had a hundred or more such creatures.'

Could such a creature be slain? Assuming we could get past the Myrmidons.

'Who would fight him? An old man and a displaced queen?' Virmyre sighed. 'We need a champion. We'd need a score of champions.'

The refugees separated into clusters of threes and fours, seeking doors and stairwells back to their homes. A few idled in the shadows of forgotten towers, too scared to descend from Demesne's rooftops to the horrors below.

Any idea how we escape this insanity?

'No.' Virmyre rubbed his chin with a thumb. 'No one in Demesne is safe. Erebus wants to supplant humans with underkin.'

There must be somewhere we can go?

'I noticed Salvaza was keen to hear what you had to say. We could try House Prospero.'

Anea turned to the few nobles who lingered, gesturing for them to follow. To her surprise they did just that.

'Naturally we sealed the gatehouse to the Central Keep as soon as my people were safe,' explained Salvaza Prospero when Anea and Virmyre presented themselves. The duchess stood in the centre of House Prospero's great hall, now an infirmary. Servants and pages of all persuasions were tending to the many wounded. Erebus and his Myrmidons had inflicted grievous casualties on the nobles. The room was filled with the tortured cries of those still suffering. Others merely wept, inconsolable for the lost. Salvaza's page regarded Virmyre and Anea with a look of awe. To be so young in such momentous times, thought Anea. She'd been that young once, though it seemed an eternity ago.

'Send messengers to House Erudito and make sure they return with a dozen *dottori*.' Anea found herself admiring Salvaza Prospero – the duchess was impressive in a crisis. Her page followed in her wake, close to tears. 'I don't care how they get there just as long as we have *dottori.*'

An ashen-faced messenger with a ripped tabard stepped forward. 'But the doors are sealed and the way is dangerous, my lady.'

'I know a way,' said Virmyre, still clad in Myrmidon armour, the helm lost fleeing the Ravenscourt. The duchess turned to them, then blinked, her eyes moving from one to the other.

'I honestly thought you were dead.' There was a look of amusement in her eyes.

'There have been times where being dead might have been preferable,' rumbled Virmyre. 'But I'm committed to seeing Anea realise her dreams of a republic.' He glanced at Anea. 'And seeing that she rules once the republic is founded.'

'Well, it's good to know we still disagree on the things that matter.' The duchess smiled.

'I'll find you a *dottore* if I can.' Virmyre bowed and departed with the messenger.

'Some men really do improve with age, don't they?' said Salvaza, but Anea didn't think the words were meant for her. Porters and aides moved around them, tending to the wounded, covering the dead. The duchess turned to the Silent Queen, resplendent in dirty white, an angel in Pandemonium.

'They threw you in the oubliette.'

Anea nodded.

'It makes a certain kind of sense. I've always disliked your policies, but the Myrmidons?' Salvaza shrugged and shook her head. 'I told everyone that was most unlike you. It seems I was right, it wasn't you at all.'

Anea let the duchess revel in her self-congratulation. There was no question the woman opposed the republic, but it seemed she had developed a taste for fair play.

'And you drank the water?'

Another nod from the Silent Queen, green eyes unfriendly. She'd not needed reminding of her eroded memory.

'I see,' said Salvaza.

These people would be better off at the church, signed Anea, keen to change the subject. *The sisters are most adept at the care of the wounded.*

'And give up House Prospero?' Now it was Salvaza who flashed a hostile glare. 'Just relinquish everything my family have worked so hard for? I think not.'

Do you think Erebus cares about the previous generations of your family, for tradition? Do you think he will decide to spare your house, your servants, your allies?

Salvaza looked pensive before casting her gaze across the hall and the people in the service of House Prospero, people loyal and gifted. And there were the missing, most certainly killed, their only crime seeing Erebus unveiled. Salvaza's page shuffled his feet, looking profoundly uncomfortable at the mention of Erebus.

'You probably don't know,' said Salvaza in a quiet voice. 'That is, very few people know, but Erebus threatened to kill Stephania.' She sipped from a wine glass. 'He used her as leverage. Do you remember Stephania, my daughter?'

Anea nodded. A spirited girl, the image of her mother but with a kinder heart. Then something else, another unremembered fact.

She was due to be engaged to Lucien.

'That's right, before he fell in love with that commoner.'

'That commoner' is now Duchess Marino. You might want to bear that in mind.

'Perhaps it's time I joined Stephania at the coast?'

I think that wise. Landfall will need leaders when this settles down. Stephania will need your counsel.

'And will it?' Salvaza turned to face her, an edge of steel in her voice. 'Will it settle down?'

I will deal with this. Anea signed the words calmly. *And if I do not, your worries regarding the election will be resolved.*

'You'll stand down?'

I will be dead.

Salvaza's eyes widened in both shock and understanding.

'So you're staying here?'

Yes. You and your house must help Lucien retake Demesne.

The duchess sighed, massaging her brow. 'I'll give the order to evacuate House Prospero. We have carts and wagons in the outer courtyard.'

Anea watched as House Prospero began the task of dismantling itself. The wounded were delivered to the church, into the arms of the sisters. Families packed up their lives as the remaining bravos and a few retired soldiers guarded the gatehouses. Few spoke, the minutes that passed taut, painfully so.

Virmyre had yet to return.

The great hall was empty now, House Prospero a churn of quiet panic, people hurrying under heavy loads. Anea did her best to stay out of the way, waiting in the inner courtyard, crowded with workshops and tanneries. The cobbles here were flecked with sawdust, slick with all manner of oils and unguents. The people Anea encountered regarded her with wary expressions on tired faces, trying to separate the impostor and the Silent Queen. Anea sighed and clutched herself tighter. It was not her memory that had sustained the greatest wound, but her reputation. There would always be a measure of suspicion. Trust had been broken. The impostor had left an indelible stain, the mark of Erebus.

Anea searched the faces of the people, feeling as lost as she had ever been. A face emerged through the crowd of evacuating *cittadini*, familiar yet not the face of Virmyre. This face wore a veil just as she did, its brow bisected by a cruel scar, the left eye like white marble shattered.

Marchetti approached, knife in hand.

Anea looked about and saw only innocents. All the armed men were at the gatehouses or escorting wagons to the church. There was no one to protect her. The doors at the opposite end of the courtyard beckoned, offering hiding places in abundance. She fled past scores of wooden workshops, awnings in colours dull with age. People parted, reverently or otherwise.

Into the darkness of House Prospero she ran, past storage rooms and pantries, kitchens and offices. She could almost feel the tip of his knife slipping under her skin, sliding between muscles, between ribs. She ran, the white dress flapping about her legs, slowing every desperate step. Left and then right, scattering *cittadini* before her, upending cases and sacks of possessions as she stumbled. A glance over her shoulder confirmed Marchetti was entangled in the chaos she left in her wake. He slammed a fist into the face of a man who dared challenge him. The crowd dissolved.

Into the night of the outer courtyard, bursting through double doors. The last vestiges of day had dwindled into twilight, just as the bright hope of survival dimmed in her heart. It was here that the greater part of House Prospero readied themselves, heading back to estates with which they shared ties of blood or marriage.

Anea ran, hands grasping her dress, lest she trip on the hem, leaving her supine for Marchetti's eager blade. Breathless, out through the gatehouse past the astonished onlookers, into the quiet streets of Santa Maria. A mistake, she decided. Someone would come to her aid had she remained within Demesne. Or perhaps not. An alley promised deeper darkness, welcome refuge from Marchetti's restless eye. But darkness did not welcome her, instead concealing shattered wood. She tripped and slammed against the freezing cobbles, bruising her knees and drawing a pained hiss from behind the veil. Anea knew he was behind her before she'd regained her feet.

Marchetti blocked the end of the alley, dagger in one hand, the other occupied with a sword. His chest rose and fell, rhythmic, steady. His one good eye remained unseen, a pool of deeper darkness in a face comprised of shadows and hard lines.

What now? she signed when he made no move. He sheathed the sword and took a step closer. The knife disappeared also, until only the promise of words remained in his murderous hands.

What happens now? she repeated.

What usually happens when an assassin corners his mark?

Anea felt a pang of incredulity tinged with fear.

You can stop all of this. She gestured to Demesne. *Put an end to being despised by all who set eyes on you.*

Another step closer. His breathing showed no sign of slowing. *I am despised by everyone in Landfall.*

201

It does not have to be so. She noticed her hands shook as she signed.

It is not something that is undone so easily. He stepped closer. The moon emerged from behind the clouds at that moment, and Anea could think only of tales of revenants and unkind spirits.

Without me you are nothing, she signed, desperately hoping it was true.

Is that so? There was a playful challenge to the way he formed the words, twisting his hands just so, italics in his gestures. *Explain. It will make little difference, but explain if it pleases you.*

Anea stepped toward him. *I define you. You were only returned from exile because of me. What happens when you complete your task?*

He shrugged. *There is always someone else to kill.*

True, but there is no shortage of killers. She raised her head, looked him in his one remaining eye. *Are you really so indispensable to Erebus? He does not strike me as the sentimental type.*

Marchetti shook his head. *The Domina will take me on as retainer once I kill you.*

The Domina cares for no one. I am proof of that. You are more pathetic than I thought, if you believe otherwise.

And then his hands were on her throat, her knees buckling both from the force of his grasp and the weight behind it. She reached up past his strangling hands, her fingers making yet more words.

I know what it is to be alone.

For a second she wasn't sure if he'd bothered to read her signs. She formed the words again as the edges of her vision grew dark. He released her, unable to finish the task and reply at the same time. Evidently his need to respond outweighed his desire to kill.

You know nothing of loneliness.

He stood over her, gaunt in the moonlight, breath a ragged saw in his throat, veil fluttering with the force of it.

I survived the oubliette. Her fingers were almost numb with cold, but she pressed on. *I have lost brothers to deception, been betrayed by the Domina. I know full well what it is to be alone.*

I am not alone. But even as he made the gestures his shoulders slumped. It was in that moment she knew she had him, but it would take more, require something that joined them without pause or debate.

I have watched you, she signed: *outcast by Erebus, turned away by whores, reviled by the people in the street, feared in the Ravenscourt.*

Marchetti's remaining eye became flinty with anger. *I think I will start by cutting your fingers off.*

I know what it is like to be reviled.

Reviled? Marchetti shook his head. *The people loved you.*

Anea's hands hands shook, remembering the time Lucien had seen her asleep, the expression on Agostina's face in the baths. She thought of all the times she'd ordered servants to remove the mirrors from her rooms and the many long years she'd kept her greatest shame hidden from sight. She removed the veil to show the source of her silence. There was no jaw, a few tiny teeth emerging from gums beneath the place where her top lip should have been. Insect-like mandibles unfolded in the chill air. Warped and ravaged, the lower half of her face made her a creature of nightmare. Flesh hardening to chitin.

I know what it is like to live among people and not be one of them. Orfani, underkin. The first were made to rule, the second to suffer.

Marchetti looked at her and blinked, then dragged in a gasp as if he had forgotten to breathe. He slumped to his knees before her. A hand came up, and for second Anea wondered if he might strangle her again. He traced the line of a mandible with a gentle finger. It was the first time anyone had touched her deformity, she could barely manage it herself.

Marchetti paused, squeezing his one eye shut as if in great pain, clutching and finally tearing his own veil aside. Anea gasped. They might have been twins, terribly misshapen twins. His remaining eye brimmed, a single tear tracking down his cheek to become lost in the unkind geography of his face. Anea reached an arm around his shoulders, the other hand smoothing back the hair from his brow, feeling him weep and shake. She knew what he was feeling. Shock, relief, an undercurrent of fear that would not abate for some time. The Silent Queen held the assassin in the darkness of the alley, hugging him tight amid the detritus of the derelict town. Long moments passed, the cold stars above their only witness. Marchetti slid from her embrace, but made no gesture.

Help me return Demesne to the light, signed Anea.

It cannot be done, he replied.

Help me kill Erebus, for what he has done to you, to us.

A shake of the head. *It is impossible.*

If not for politics then at least to prevent him spawning more twisted children. Children like us. Please?

The assassin looked away to the stars, breathing deep and calm. The sounds of House Prospero *cittadini* departing drifted on the breeze.

Come the republic, we will all be equal. We can all have a new beginning.

Assassins do not get new beginnings, signed Marchetti.

'Anea!' Virmyre's voice in the night.

Silent Queen and assassin alike tied on their veils, Marchetti helped her to her feet. They stood close, hand in trembling hand. Anea feared the fragile spell that bound them would unravel as he broke contact.

'Anea?' Virmyre, closer now.

My only companion has been death. Marchetti's hands moved slowly, each word considered. *My entire life all I have known is death. I will follow you into the Nine Hells if you can show me something else. I will gladly help build your republic.*

I can show you something else, she signed, *but more death is inevitable.*

'Anea?' Virmyre turned the corner of the alley and stared. This would take some explaining.

25

Tip of the Blade

Eris fled through the streets of Santa Maria, keen to escape
the *taverna*, fresh snow falling as she hurried. Lights shone
from upstairs windows, casting pale yellow rectangles across the
snow. Something was happening at House Prospero, a flurry of
activity. She paid it no mind, her fear of the Herald strangling
any curiosity. She ran in the shadows, beneath the overhang
of upper floors, where the snow was less thick and the footing
less treacherous. A glance over her shoulder confirmed she was
alone. She wanted to cry with relief but remained far from
safety. Her pace slowed until she slumped against the corner
of a townhouse, her breath too loud in the quiet. Perhaps the
Herald remained at the *taverna*, watching the front door from
the street, biding his time. She doubted the Herald would be
troubled by such a thing as cold.

A sign above her head creaked in the wind, demanding her
attention. A board advertising the services of a *dottore*. Eris
opened her mouth in horror. Perched on the board was the
sleek bulk of the raven, regarding her with a furious eye. A
coarse exclamation broke the silence of the night, a strident caw.
The sound was like a blade taken to her flesh. She wanted to
scream, if only to drown out the sound of the bird. The raven
flapped its wings and continued to stare.

Eris ran.

She didn't know, couldn't know where her feet led her. She'd
not grown up in Demesne; the streets of Santa Maria were an
unfamiliar tangle. Anea would know the town like it were a
part of her. The Silent Queen had encouraged people to build

here after all, the derelict splendour of the town a reminder of those good intentions undone. Eris cast the thought aside and concentrated on running, forcing tired legs to carry her on. It had been many hours since she'd eaten, her stomach a cruel snarl she tried to ignore. Strength abandoned her, forcing her to stop and catch her breath.

Eris leaned against a well, sheltering beneath its tiled roof. The courtyard was smaller than the one at House Contadino, barely an eighth of the size. The chapel of Santa Maria stood nearby, a stout building, fortified and safe. The promise of sanctuary was intoxicating. The sisters would be compelled to give her shelter.

She slammed a numb fist on the door. If the Herald didn't kill her she'd die of cold by dawn. The door remained closed, no light appearing at the windows. There was a darkness about the place that spelled abandonment.

'The church,' she whispered, keen to turn back the tide of silence that washed in around her. 'I'll go to the church.' She breathed deep and tried to still her shaking hands, folding them across her chest. The church of Santa Maria was but a short walk through the slumbering town. The Herald couldn't be everywhere at once. She could survive this journey if she were cautious and clever.

The raven alighted on the small roof over the well, calling to its master. Eris all but fell to her knees with the force of the sound, startled and exhausted. She cursed the bird, wanted to break its neck and stamp on its wings. Wanted to feel fine bones break beneath her boot. In the end she satisfied herself with throwing a snowball, which sailed past her target. The raven replied with greater volume and Eris ran, but not before seeing a flicker of darkness in the crisp white courtyard.

'I'm going to die,' she whispered between ragged breaths drawn into aching lungs. A circle of darkness beckoned her, promising seclusion. She fled to it gladly. Inside, the stonework stretched away beyond sight, an old sewer from Demesne. She stumbled in, the passage longer than she'd dared hope for. A pause, turning to see the Herald's outline at the tunnel's mouth. She could go no further, unable to discern her own hands, probing the pitch darkness. The raven's call changed her mind, amplified by the tunnel's curving walls. Her feet jolted into action, hands held out in front, waiting for the moment her fingers met a barrier, revealing the dead end that would see her cornered. But the tunnel stretched on, taking her beneath House Fontein and whatever waited there.

Eris blinked, confused by amethyst light emanating from above her head. Not one light. Dozens. Dozens of bright purple eyes gleamed amid deep shadows. She stared in wonder at the chamber, orderly rows of coffins stacked on their ends, at least a hundred, she supposed. Fingertips brushed the nearest of them, finding not wood but stone. Sarcophagi, but who would bury the dead standing up? What strange tradition was this? A deep sound permeated the dark, a heavy vibration in the air. It was a mindless drone, the sound taking a knife to nerves long past frayed. Eris picked her way through the ranks and columns, curiosity diminished by the Herald's pursuit. She crouched low and turned aside, making her way to one side of the chamber. The sound of raven's wings sent her to her knees. She pressed herself flat against one of the sarcophagi. The sleek stone was smooth, so strange, unlike anything she knew.

A shadow passed through the purple gloaming, feet kicking up tiny dust phantoms in the underworld. The raven perched atop his shoulder and stared into the gloom. Eris shivered. Here, more than ever, the Herald looked like something from nightmare, a wraith among the dead. She turned, taking care not to scuff her feet and betray her hiding place. The Herald continued his relentless search. Eris peeked around one side of the sarcophagus. Her breathing slowed, heart the same.

How long she waited she couldn't say. Time was a pitiful crawl with only scores of dead and the pervasive drone of the chamber for company. She edged from one sarcophagus to the next, finding her way back to the centre. Footprints in the dust, and not all of them belonging to the Herald. Different-sized feet for one thing, and different directions of travel. Some headed into the castle, others back the way she had come. And beneath all the dust and the stories it told, a circle of metal set into the floor. Perhaps it had once been a dais. She was torn with indecision. To wait in the darkness or flee back through the tunnel? Had the Herald departed, or did he remain hidden among the obsidian slabs? She listened intently; only the chamber's ominous drone reached her ears, the distant drip of water. She knelt down and began to crawl toward the exit, crossing the broad metallic disc as she went.

Tap. Tap, tap.

'Don't bother standing.'

The Herald stood but a score of feet away, blade drawn, but not the great sword he'd wielded earlier. The raven cawed. Eris imagined there was a note of triumph to the sound.

The Herald paused.

'You're not her, are you?'

Eris shook her head.

'Anea would never remove her veil. Never.'

Eris had removed the veil to appease the whores but not thought to reattach it. She had no reply for the Herald, her deception unmasked.

'Even I don't know what lies beneath that scrap of secrecy.' The words were still the gravel-scoured sounds she'd heard earlier, but there was a new timbre to them. One she knew all too well. Sadness.

'At first I was told I would be a decoy.' She'd been rehearsing this lie for some time, the words strained now she was forced to use them. The Herald made no move, left a silence for her to fill. 'Paolo Allattamento, he promised to keep my brother safe if I agreed to impersonate the Silent Queen. In time I realised I wasn't just a decoy, but a replacement for her.'

A flicker of hope. There was just enough truth woven into the lie that it might hold fast, might make strong the slender cord that her life dangled from.

'And where is your brother now?' The mangled voice had regained some of its subdued anger.

'Dead. He fell ill. It was he I visited in the cemetery.'

'And you didn't think to tell me you were an impostor back there?'

'I didn't think you'd spare me, impostor or not.' This at least was true. She had spent so much time being the Silent Queen she didn't know how to be herself any more.

'You committed treason,' stated the Herald. 'You could have written to Duke Marino at any time, warned us of the deception. You could have freed yourself into the bargain. Why didn't you?'

Eris swallowed. There were no stones to throw here, no open grave to shove him toward. There would be no desperate escape, no horse waiting to spirit her away.

'The Domina.' Eris didn't know what lie would come next, but why not implicate her greatest rival?

'What of the Domina?' said the Herald, taking a step closer. The raven flapped a wing and made a guttural sound.

'She reviews everything I write, to stop me passing edicts without the approval of Lord Erebus. All the messengers are in on it. I can't even write a poem without scrutiny.'

The hood dipped a few times, and Eris realised the Herald understood. Far from being a creature from nightmare, the Herald was undoubtedly a man, someone who knew the ruling elite of Demesne.

'Can I go? Will you let me go free? Please? If I promise never to return?' She could hear the rising desperation of her voice. Heard the same question asked twice, the pleading. The Herald rapped the floor with the tip of his blade.

Tap. Tap, tap.

She followed the line of the weapon, noting the pommel took an unusual form. A gryphon's head perhaps, difficult to tell in the darkness.

'What happened to Anea?' The words were quiet, barely heard over the basso thrum in the sarcophagus chamber. Eris shivered with fear, still kneeling on the broad disc of silvery metal. What would she say next? Would it be lies or truth that sustained her? The raven cawed again, skewering her with accusation. Perhaps now was the time to resort to truths without the embroidery of fiction.

'Erebus cast her into the oubliette many months ago.'

Another nod from the Herald.

'She wasn't herself, so far gone with *tinctura*, so immersed in

209

her work. Erebus abducted her with the help of the Domina and the Myrmidons.'

'And she died down there?'

'She escaped four weeks ago. Erebus ordered Marchetti to hunt her down.'

The Herald remained immobile, amethyst light washing over every contour of the cloak and his carnival mask, making a phantom of him in the darkness. The mindless drone of the chamber filled the space between them. Eris nursed warmth into her cold fingers, nurturing a flicker of hope that might see her live one more day.

Tap. Tap, tap.

The restless sword hit the floor, and with each percussion Eris's optimism faded. She would die in a forgotten chamber of Demesne, left to rot without even the comfort of knowing she might be laid to rest beside her brother.

'I need to see Erebus,' said the Herald.

'What?'

'I need to see Erebus. You're going to take me to him.'

'I can't.' Eris swallowed. 'I mean, he's in the Ravenscourt. He hides on the gallery above the dais, obscured by a curtain, surrounded by wretches.'

'Then that's where you'll take me.'

'He's heavily guarded,' she warned. 'Even the finest swordsman in Landfall couldn't defeat so many.'

'The finest swordsman in Landfall is dead, and it was Erebus who had a hand in his death.'

'Facing him would be suicide. He's unnatural, massive and powerful.'

The Herald, so implacable in pursuit, so resolute in purpose, turned to one side. The tip of the blade hit the floor once more.

'This much is true,' he admitted.

Tap. Tap, tap. The Herald's frustration and violence were almost tangible in the stale air.

'And Anea?' asked the Herald. 'Where did she end up after she escaped?'

'She was hiding in the church,' said Eris, 'but after Medea

was taken she fled. We … I mean the Domina doesn't know where she is hiding. Marchetti has been unable to find her.'

The Herald turned aside one moment, lost in thought. Eris glanced back toward the entrance, wondering if she might outrun him. Or might it be better to flee further into the castle, losing him in the labyrinthine corridors of Demesne? Might she too become lost, forced to wander in dark places until starvation claimed her?

'I can't trust you,' said the Herald, taking a step closer. His fingers stretched, flexing around the hilt of the sword. 'Give me one reason to spare your life.'

Eris looked into the dark eyes of the carnival mask, remembering her dead brother, how she'd likely join him unless she proved herself to the Herald.

'One reason?' Her chin came up, tone defiant. 'I can give you three.'

'Do so then.'

'I can help you rescue Medea Contadino.'

'What else?'

'We want the same thing – Erebus, dead.'

'A good reason,' said the Herald hefting his sword, 'but I count only two.'

Eris had succumbed to her usual failing, promising more than she was capable of. She'd promised Erebus she could be the impostor he needed. She'd promised Sabatino to keep him safe. Now she had promised three reasons, without a thought to what the third might be. The Herald's sword glittered in the amethyst light, a killer with two swords and a raven on his shoulder. He was close, so close she could smell the mud of his boots and the oil on his mail. So close she could hear his breathing, even over the dull drone of the chamber.

'You're wasting my time.' The sword was raised, the hilt held in both hands, promising a strike that would remove her head neatly.

Eris gasped as inspiration kindled.

'I can be the Silent Queen you need to command the Myrmidons. I can turn the Domina and Marchetti over to you, preventing the war with Duke Marino.'

211

'Impressive.' The sword found its sheath and the Herald held out a hand. 'You'd best get on your feet. We've much to do. And if you try to escape, if you call out for help, if you raise a hand to me, know this.'

'Know what?'

The Herald pressed closer until the darkness of his cloak almost swallowed her, the glint of the raven's unfriendly eye the only hint of light.

'Know what?' she breathed.

'You'll die before I do.'

26

Medea Unchained

'This isn't going to work.' Virmyre had repeated this senti-ment no less than three times during the journey from the old *sanatorio* to House Fontein. He'd forgone the Myrmidon armour for a leather gambeson in black, with a sword belted at the waist. Sturdy boots and gloves completed his attire. Anea turned to glare at him. It wasn't the plan but their accomplice that was bothering Virmyre. Marchetti walked ahead, pausing only to turn and hold a finger up to his veiled mouth. The slender assassin was made bulky by two lengths of rope coiled over his shoulder.

'I'm simply stating a fact,' continued Virmyre. 'We don't know for sure where they're holding her.'

They are keeping her in a practice chamber, countered Mar-chetti. *This much I do know.*

'She could be in the oubliette by now.'

Marchetti ignored him and peered into the darkness, check-ing no Myrmidons patrolled the rooftops.

We are going to the practice chambers, signed Anea.

'She could be dead.'

Anea folded her arms and glowered, but Virmyre was not deterred. 'How many training chambers are there? Four? Five? Six? We could be searching for her all night.'

The assassin turned to Anea and began to sign. *I do not understand why you brought him. He is slow and he is old. Only the Domina complains more.*

'I can read the silent language, you know,' hissed Virmyre.

Most of the day had been spent like this, the two men pacing the gloomy laboratory above the library, rarely within twenty feet of each other. Anea's hopes they might set aside their differences evaporated each time the men occupied the same room. Virmyre was disbelieving on many counts, primarily about Marchetti's loyalty, but also that they needed him at all.

'Drago Romanucci would help us in a heartbeat.' Virmyre had returned to this point time and again when alone with Anea. 'We don't need this Myrmidon scum. We could request help from other, more loyal men.'

True enough, but he has a score to settle.

'We've all got scores to settle, Highness.'

He has a score to settle with Erebus, she continued. *We can use that to our advantage.*

'I'm just saying Drago Romanucci and the bravos of House Del Toro are a safer option.'

But they do not know their way around House Fontein. Marchetti does. We need him.

The irony of escaping death at the hands of Marchetti only to find herself allied with him was not lost on Anea. She hoped it was worth the price Virmyre was extracting from her in objections.

'He'll turn on us the moment it suits him.'

They say you should keep your friends close and your enemies closer.

Virmyre massaged his brow with one hand. 'Things must be desperate if you're reaching for clichés.'

Anea fixed him with a stern look. *He and I have more in common than you think. At least have some faith in me if you can not trust him.*

The plan, such as it was, was direct. 'Simple' had been Virmyre's cutting assessment, but Anea had listened to Marchetti's suggestion without prejudice. They would climb the walls and gain entrance to House Fontein via a window. Once inside they would seek out Medea and free her, then climb out again. Lucien and Dino had spent many years scaling the walls on some foolish errand or another; now it seemed Anea was destined to do the same.

'There must be a better way,' said Virmyre. He'd spent the

day scheming and consulting his great map, but inspiration had failed him. Erebus controlled Houses Contadino and Fontein entirely, while the *cittadini* of Houses Prospero and Erudito were engaged in the solemn business of packing up their lives.

Erebus has no reason to keep Medea alive now that he is revealed, remonstrated Anea. *Do you really want to risk delaying any longer?*

Virmyre cleared his throat, shaking his head with reluctance. Marchetti had already climbed twenty feet, surging up the stone walls clinging to the ivy.

'He climbs like Dino,' remarked Virmyre. 'It seems all the Orfani and underkin are adept. It must be in your blood.'

Not mine, replied Anea, but Virmyre didn't notice her gestures, entranced by the assassin's ascent. Virmyre turned his eyes to Anea as Marchetti disappeared through a window on the fourth floor.

'He could be gathering more Myrmidons this very second, preparing to arrest us. What makes you think we can trust him?'

Anea shrugged.

'I was hoping for reassurance, Highness.'

We are long past trust. Her fingers sketched the symbols on the chilly air. *Erebus has turned all of us against each other. All we can do is make new alliances and hope they hold.*

'Risky.' Virmyre's distaste was obvious.

Leadership is risk; anything else is maintenance.

Anea flinched as two ropes slapped down the wall.

'Your carriage awaits, Highness.'

They began the ascent. No sooner had Anea climbed the first dozen feet than a terrible premonition overtook her. The room above would be wreathed in flames, billowing curtains of orange and yellow. Tongues of fire would speak the language of destruction, every book on every shelf becoming ash. The apartment would be consumed by an impossible heat, wood splitting and groaning. She froze, muscles taut with fear. She could taste the smoke, feel the roughness of it in her throat. A glance above confirmed darkness, not flames. Not a premonition after all, but a memory lost to the oubliette's rank waters. Then it blazed back to life, shocking and brightly remembered, a night years before when she'd escaped her own burning apartment on a rope of bed sheets, hastily tied.

'Come on. Not much further.' Virmyre regarded her with a look of concern. She shook her head, then glanced down, wondering if there was another way in.

'If not for yourself then at least for Medea.'

The thought of the *marchesa* being executed dragged Anea back to the present. She began to climb again, feet slipping on the stones, hands aching as she hauled herself up. A gloved hand appeared, grasping her wrist, pulling her over the edge of the sill. The sitting room was thick with gloom and shadow. A second later and Virmyre joined them, his grunts of exertion breaking the silence.

Moonlight edged through the curtains, revealing a Myrmidon in the centre of the room, face down on the floor with a pool of darkest crimson spreading from his neck. Anea turned to Virmyre with an arched eyebrow. Marchetti slipped out of the door, leaving them with the corpse.

'Fine. I was wrong. We can trust him after all.'

Apparently so.

Their progress through House Fontein was a cautious affair. Anea's concern for Medea increased with each minute. Marchetti would roam ahead, gesturing them onward through the brightly lit corridors. They slunk up staircases toward the sixth floor, but every door they opened revealed only emptiness. No sign of Medea Contadino, no trace of Myrmidons.

'Where are they?'

Guarding the gatehouses on the lower levels most likely, signed Marchetti.

I thought they would be all over the castle. Anea was perplexed.

The Myrmidons are far fewer in number than Erebus would have you believe, replied the assassin.

'Hence his desire to breed more, and breed them quickly,' added Virmyre.

They kept moving, taking a staircase to avoid a trio of Myrmidons who watched over a junction of corridors.

'This isn't working,' complained Virmyre once they had arrived on the seventh floor. Anea held up a finger to her veiled mouth, then turned to follow Marchetti, who was already moving ahead. It was dark here, lanterns turned low, corridors languishing in shadow. The soft scuff of their footfalls was interrupted by a low murmur. Marchetti gestured for silence, then pressed an ear against the nearest door.

'A training chamber,' whispered Virmyre. 'This door leads to the observation gallery.'

Anea knew precisely what he meant. Suddenly she was swept up in memories of creeping into practice sessions, keen to watch Dino and Lucien. It was here she'd seen the cruelty of House Fontein first hand. Glimpses of shorn hair, flashing scissors and brutal punishments. The *superiore* had made Lucien's life a misery, yet his name remained lost to memory.

Marchetti turned the handle and opened the door, pushing his head into the gallery beyond. He turned back to them and nodded. They entered on hands and knees, shrouded in the balcony's gloom. Light washed up the stone walls from the chamber beneath, failing to illuminate the dome above. The Domina's voice could be heard, a miserable drone amid shuffling feet and the jangle of armour. Anea sneaked to the balcony's edge, hiding behind the panels supporting the handrail.

'You will be tireless, alert, without remorse. Demesne will be ours completely.'

Anea snatched a glance below, entranced by the scene. The Myrmidons queued with helmets removed. The uniformity of their armour contrasted with the varied otherness of their faces, which were not merely unique, as one person to another, but ranged from merely unusual to terribly deformed. For every Myrmidon with a merely striking face there was another with multiple eyes. Some were afflicted with insectile mandibles, much like Marchetti and herself. Here was an atrophied nose, there a woman lacking ears. The most fearsome would barely be recognised as human; a few proclaimed their otherness in more subtle ways.

The Domina stood before them, distributing *tinctura* with an expert hand. The Myrmidons took a moment to orient themselves once dosed. They stood with eyes closed as the drug coursed through them, then replaced their helms, heading to the door in groups of three.

We should go, signed Marchetti. Anea nodded and followed, eager to escape a difficult truth. These were her enemies, and yet she had more in common with the Myrmidons than the *cittadini* she sought to protect. The door to the gallery closed. Anea stood slowly, sickened to her core.

They are like me. Her fingers formed the words, but they were not directed toward anyone. *They are like me.* Part realisation, part confession.

'Underkin are not the same as Orfani,' said Virmyre, earning himself a look of reproach from Marchetti.

Of course they are. The distinction is one of elitism. Any one of them might be another Lucien or Dino. Any one of them could be me. I should be rallying those soldiers to my side; they should be obeying my orders.

'But they won't.'

No, they will not, signed Marchetti. Virmyre blinked, surprised to find the assassin agreeing with him.

They follow Erebus absolutely. He has had a decade to indoctrinate them with the rhetoric of hate. They yearn to kill humans because it is all they know; they have been conditioned for it completely.

But if we could just reason with them . . . signed Anea, but Marchetti shook his head.

Erebus does not use words alone to poison their minds. For a time he used a drug, sottomesso.

'I've read of *sottomesso.*' Virmyre frowned. 'Given like *tinctura*, it instils obedience.'

The underkin were under Erebus's influence in more ways than one from the very beginning.

'So why don't you follow him?' asked Virmyre, curiosity rather than accusation.

Because he cast me out. Marchetti's fingers faltered a moment. *I was exiled for failing to kill Dino. For years Erebus told me I was like a son to him.* The assassin paused. Anea realised she was holding her breath. Virmyre was no different, attention rapt. *No father I ever saw discarded his own so quickly*, signed Marchetti. *We are disposable to him, interchangeable. Who cares if a Myrmidon dies? Who mourns? Erebus has never shown a shred of regret for the lives he has spent ensuring his rise to power.*

Virmyre nodded in sympathy or agreement.

We need to find Medea, signed Anea after a pensive moment.

The remaining doors of House Fontein did not relinquish their secrets so easily. Virmyre tinkered with skeleton keys, picked locks with small lengths of blackened metal. Doors opened onto darkened chambers holding only dust and echoes.

'We'll have to search the oubliette if she's not here,' said Virmyre as he knelt before yet another keyhole. Anea's pulse quickened in response. She couldn't go back to the oubliette, not even to aid the *marchesa*. She frowned, angry at her cowardice. The lock clicked open and Virmyre turned the handle. A sliver of light crept past the door as it swung ajar. Marchetti blew out the lantern in the corridor lest it attract attention. Another balcony, another practice chamber. The scarlet and black banners of House Fontein slumped against the wall like tired soldiers, fabric mildewed. The air was a musty fume, weak light emanating from the chamber below.

Marchesa Medea Contadino sat on a dais, knees drawn up to her chest, head resting against the cold stone wall. Her clothes were filthy, a blanket wrapped about her shoulders. A Myrmidon stood by a door on the opposite side of the chamber. Another leaned against the wall beneath the balcony.

Marchetti communicated with Virmyre, fingers flickering with lethal intent. The *professore* nodded, then man and underkin alike drew their swords silently. Unarmed, Anea could only watch, heart kicking a furious beat. Finding the *marchesa* was fortune enough; escape would require further miracles.

The assassin moved to the far right of the balcony and slid over the edge, hanging from the rail just long enough to slow his descent. He landed on the balls of his feet, rolling onto his side then his back, all in one fluid motion. He was already sprinting toward the Myrmidon by the door when Virmyre lunged over the side. His descent was markedly less graceful, falling on the Myrmidon beneath the balcony.

Anea followed him over the edge, keen not to be left behind, dropping the remaining distance to the granite flagstones. Her feet complained from the jarring impact.

Virmyre, straddling his chest, had his blade across the Myrmidon's throat and was forcing the helm back from his head. Steel bit through flesh. There was a drumming of heels, a frenzied clawing of gloved hands, but the conclusion was inevitable.

Not so on the far side.

The remaining Myrmidon threw a knife. Marchetti's sword swiped the air, attempting to bat away the barely seen weapon. Anea watched in shock as the knife embedded itself in the assassin's abdomen, staggering him. The Myrmidon wrenched open the door and fled.

Anea ran to the assassin, who had slumped to his knees, a hand pressed to the wound. The thrown knife, already pulled out, occupied his other hand, stained with blood.

'Virmyre, is that you?' This from Medea, hope kindling in her eyes. Virmyre crossed to the dais, helping the *marchesa* to her feet. She hugged him and wept.

'No time for that now,' said the *professore*. 'We need to leave. And quickly.'

Marchetti stood, a hiss escaping from behind his veil. Anea reached out on instinct, but the assassin stepped out of reach.

The wound is not deep. His fingers moved slowly, forming each word with difficulty. *My armour took most of the force.* He pressed his hand back to the wound, just above his hip.

You lie, she signed.

We need to go.

Anea ran to the door and thrust her head through the opening. A trio of Myrmidons approached, but there was a glimmer of hope. A key hung from a leather cord on a hook beside the door frame. Anea snatched it, jerking back inside the room. The sound of footfalls grew louder. She slammed the door shut, forcing the key into the lock. A sharp turn of the key, and the hammering on wood began, the Myrmidons grunting with effort on the other side.

'We need an axe!' one of them shouted.

'Back up to the balcony,' hissed Virmyre.

The door rattled on its hinges as the wood split.

This will not hold long. Quickly now, signed Anea, but no one read the gestures she made. Virmyre, Marchetti and Medea had their eyes fixed on the rectangle of light growing on the balcony above them. Anea knew with certainty who would appear from behind the door.

The Domina gazed down, a look of sadness in her glassy, unfocused eyes. She gripped the silver staff, clinging to it with one hand, the other in a sling, a reminder of Anea's violence. Four Myrmidons entered behind her, taking up positions at the balcony's edge.

There would be no climb from the training chamber floor. They would not escape from the balcony. Wood splintered from the door behind them, a cacophony of angry voices in the corridor beyond. Anea looked to the *professore*, eyes frantic.

You did warn me it was a rather simple plan.

'It would be nice to be wrong, just occasionally, Highness,' replied Virmyre.

'You may have given up,' said Medea, 'but I haven't. *Avanti!*'

27

On Reflection

The House Fontein kitchens were pristine, every utensil accounted for, each knife in its place, the many saucepans stored away. Shelves were crowded with jars of spices presented in neat ranks, the stoves polished until they shone. Copper lanterns shed gentle light, and only the soft squeak of mice could be heard amid Demesne's silence. Simonetti entered the room and cleared his throat. Isabella sat alone, staring into the middle distance, head cocked to one side as if listening. Her confidant was a bottle of wine, its cork picked apart by restless fingers, the glass beside it nearly empty.

'Isabella? Are you unwell?'

She shrugged and mumbled, made to rest her face on one hand. Her elbow missed the table top, causing her to fall forward before she caught herself. She grunted.

'Enjoying a drink, are we?' Simonetti lifted the bottle and read the label. Isabella nodded, knocking the glass over as she reached for it. Wine spread over the table like a bloodstain.

'How long have you been down here, Isabella?'

'Not long,' mumbled the maid.

'And why this?' Simonetti set the bottle, two thirds empty, down on the counter.

'Eris, Anea, whatever you call her. She's gone. I have no employment. The Domina will kill me because of the things I know. Just like Fiorenza.'

'Who is Eris?'

'You know. She's the ... the girl Erebus brought in.'

'Ah,' said Simonetti with resignation. 'There was a girl

in Virmyre's apartment, and there was something about her, something that reminded me of Anea before Dino died. And Lady Diaspora – this Eris presumably – filled my head with the notion Lucien was trying to install an imposter to do his will. An admirable double-bluff.'

'I used to arrange her hair and apply her make-up,' said Isabella, slurring.

'And so there is an impostor, just not how I imagined.'

'I'm afraid so.' The words came from behind, sounding anything but apologetic. Simonetti and Isabella peered through the darkness to where a woman with jade-green eyes stood in the doorway. She lacked a veil but looked familiar despite her muddied gown. Streaks of blood lent dark accents to her tangle of blonde hair.

'My lady?' said Simonetti on instinct.

'Not really,' replied Eris, entering the kitchen. The Herald followed her, raven perched on one shoulder. The lanterns flickered, shadows crawling the walls like troublesome dreams.

'Oh dear.' Simonetti took a step back, a wary eye on the Herald's great sword.

'Santa Maria save us,' whispered Isabella. She all but slipped from her stool, undone by wine and fear.

'Don't worry yourself,' said Eris, gesturing over her shoulder. 'He's on our side.'

'And what side is *that* exactly?' said Simonetti.

'The side that's going to rescue Medea Contadino,' replied Eris, crossing the kitchen. 'The side that's going to stop Landfall descending into war.'

'We'll need more than Medea Contadino and goodwill to undo the damage that's been done.' The Herald's every syllable was a subtle pain.

'I, ah, have a feeling you're right,' agreed Simonetti. He turned to Eris. 'Saving Medea won't rid us of Erebus.'

'But I will,' said the Herald. 'But only after Medea is safe.'

'Why are you here, Simonetti?' Eris frowned with curiosity.

'Well, I ah, I was asked to meet the Domina. After Anea – the real Anea – tore down the curtain.'

'What?'

223

'Yes. Everyone knows about Erebus now. It was quite a shock.'

'So why did you come back?' pressed Eris. 'If you know who it is that you truly serve.'

'I hoped to persuade the Domina to release Medea. Russo and I have known each other for, ah, some time. I've no doubt Erebus is a corrupting influence.'

'Something we agree on,' said the Herald. He pushed his cloak to one side, revealing a sword on his hip and a cataphract drake brooch glittering on his chest.

'I have a feeling that you're not so, ah, keen to see the Domina escape.'

'Very astute.' The cloaked figured stalked from the kitchen accompanied by the jingle of armour and buckles, pale yellow light reflecting from the crosspiece of the sword hanging on his back.

'You shouldn't, ah, stay here, Isabella.'

'Go and wait in my chambers,' said Eris, 'and lock the door.'

The maid nodded, eyes unfocused, rising to her feet before exiting to the courtyard, unsteady and unsure.

Simonetti turned to the woman in the muddy gown. 'So you're an impostor?'

Eris nodded.

'We don't have time for this.' The Herald had not gone far, lurking at a doorway that led deeper into House Fontein. Simonetti and Eris nodded. Explanations would have to wait.

Up darkened staircases they climbed, over stone worn down during three centuries. Or so the scholars said. The Herald led the way, Simonetti at the back. Eris gazed at each corner and doorway, wondering what would happen when they encountered resistance.

'Where are the Myrmidons?' said the Herald. Eris shrugged and looked toward Simonetti.

'I don't know,' said the archivist, expression grave. 'They have control of the Ravenscourt and Houses Fontein and Contadino. No one enters and no one leaves. Messages were delivered to Houses Erudito and Prospero. They have until midnight to clear out.'

224

'Erebus is forcing out the remaining houses?' Eris couldn't mask her shock.

'Yes,' said the archivist. 'Out of Demesne. The exodus has begun.'

'And anyone foolish enough to remain will forfeit their lives,' said the Herald before ascending more steps.

Eris all but ran to keep up with him. Then she heard a noise. At first she wasn't sure what the sound was, but with each passing moment her certainty became absolute. Wood being chopped. Someone hacking through a door nearby. A dull boom, the collapse of something heavy. Other sounds echoed down corridors, the unmistakable din of combat. Not the soft percussion of fists on faces and stomachs, this was the ringing clang of steel on steel, lethal strikes turned aside by parries, weapons battering armour. The Herald broke into a run, cloak flaring about him, reaching the next level.

'This can't be good,' said Eris. The Herald's raven cawed and flapped, unwilling to spread its wings in the narrow corridors.

The noises grew louder. Anxiety hastened Eris's every footfall, dread snagged in her every jagged breath. Her promise to the Herald would remain unfulfilled if Medea died. On they ran, Simonetti wheezing behind as the sounds of fighting increased. Was the *marchesa* already dead? And who was fighting who?

'Where are they?' called Eris, but the Herald ignored her, pressing on, straining to follow the terrible sound. 'She's going to die!'

'No,' replied the Herald, drawing the shorter of his swords. 'She's not.'

Eris realised it was a drake, not a gryphon, that decorated the pommel. The tangible aura of violence had returned, emanating from the Herald in waves, fury waiting to be unleashed.

Unaware of them, two Myrmidons occupied the corridor ahead, running toward the fight, their boots stamping a percussion on the stone floor. Eris felt her lack of a weapon keenly. The Herald increased his speed, lunging forward, blade slashing. There was a shocked yelp of pain, followed by a crash of metal. The Herald paused, stamping down with one boot.

225

The tip of his sword plunged beneath the breastplate, piercing the Myrmidon's vitals. The fallen man shivered and moaned. It would not be a quick death, but it was one opponent less in the moments that followed.

Eris stooped for the Myrmidon's sword, struggling to find a comfortable grip. The other Myrmidon turned to discover his dying comrade. The Herald did not hesitate, cleaving down, his opponent's helmet caving in under the blow. Blood dribbled through the eye slit as the Myrmidon staggered back, too stunned to parry. A second later, and his leg had been severed at the knee. Eris gagged, seeing the stump jetting hot blood over the corridor.

'I'm not sure we should, ah, be here, my lady,' said Simonetti.

'Care to suggest somewhere else?'

'I, ah, well ...'

'Exactly,' replied Eris, hefting the unfamiliar sword. The Herald disappeared from view, turning a corner, cloak trailing after. Eris and Simonetti followed in his wake, almost running into him as they entered the practice chamber. The raven called out, a shocking cry that seized the attention of all. The creature took to the air in a commotion of wings, and weapons ceased their rise and fall. An incredulous moment enfolded the chamber, breathless and unreal.

Eris saw the Domina first, standing on the balcony flanked by four Myrmidons. She resembled a wounded general directing the flow of battle, arm held in a sling. Four more Myrmidons crowded Virmyre and Marchetti on the training-chamber floor, preparing to finish them. The nearest of them was a score of feet away. The *marchesa* and the Silent Queen were huddled together on a dais at the far side of the chamber, struggling with a locked door.

The Domina's eyes widened in disbelief as she saw Eris alongside the Herald. Confusion and fury clouded her features for a dreamlike moment, which stretched on, time suspended. All were unsure what would come next.

Marchetti broke the spell, hacking an arm from an opponent, the limb hitting the flagstones with a wet sound. A terrible shriek echoed around the chamber, followed by the clang of steel as the Myrmidon dropped his sword. The soldier fell to his knees with a hand pressed to the stump

'ARREST EVERYONE!' bellowed the Domina, slamming her staff against the balcony floor three times as if attempting to regain order in the Ravenscourt.

'What the fuck is going on?' whispered Eris.

'A very reasonable question,' replied Simonetti.

The Herald sprang forward, slashing at the nearest Myrmidon, who turned to face the new threat. The soldier executed a parry and sparks flared as their blades met. The Myrmidon punched with his left hand. This was avoided easily by the Herald, weaving away with ease.

Virmyre and Marchetti continued to trade blows with their opponents, parrying when they could, dodging when left with no other choice. Virmyre may have kept age at bay with *tinctura*, but his fighting days were long past. Marchetti by contrast was the match of any Myrmidon who drew steel. Eris was confused why he should fight so cautiously.

Simonetti skirted the edge of the chamber, and Eris followed, holding the sword out in front of her as if the steel might provide a deterrent.

'I really wish I'd received some training for this sort of thing,' said Eris, frowning.

'I really wish I was somewhere else entirely,' replied Simonetti. They reached the dais, and the archivist bowed to Anea. Eris looked away, eyes intent on the fighting. Simonetti turned to Medea with an anxious smile on his lips.

'We're here to rescue you,' he said brightly.

'You and everyone else,' muttered Medea. 'I've been stuck in here for three weeks, and now two rescue parties arrive at once.' She flashed a sour look at Anea, who was more interested in events on the balcony. The raven had set about harassing the Myrmidons above as they began to climb down.

Eris gasped as Marchetti dodged a fatal blow, sidestepping his opponent. The assassin stuck one leg out as his attacker circled past. There was a grunt and the Myrmidon hit the flagstones with a crash. Eris couldn't understand why the assassin didn't finish his fallen opponent until she saw the hand held fast to his gut. Rich crimson stained his glove.

The sight of Marchetti's wound broke the spell of her own inaction. Eris swore and rushed forward, the unfamiliar blade rising, arms straining with the motion, then slicing down. Her arm jarred as the steel slammed into the back of the Myrmidon engaging Virmyre. A second's pause, and the Myrmidon's knees buckled. Virmyre's strike relieved him of his head, the helmet spinning away in a torrent of gore.

'Thank you,' said the *professore* from behind gritted teeth.

'We're here to rescue Medea,' said Eris, breathless and shaking.

'I didn't think you were here for the dancing,' intoned Virmyre.

'STOP THEM!' shouted the Domina, eyes fixed on the Silent Queen, who was spiriting the *marchesa* through the ruined door. Marchetti stumbled past Eris, pausing only to give her a quizzical look.

'This is insanity,' rumbled Virmyre, then he too fled the chamber.

The Myrmidon that Marchetti had tripped pulled himself to his feet as the Herald backed out of the chamber. A flurry of parries provided an adequate deterrent. More Myrmidons entered through the door on the balcony. Those climbing down were hindered by their armour yet reluctant to lose their quarry in the circular corridors of House Fontein.

'Run,' said the Herald, 'or I'll cut you down myself.' Eris obeyed.

The Silent Queen had not waited, running hand in hand with the *marchesa*. Virmyre slipped one arm beneath Marchetti's free hand, aiding him down corridors alive with the sounds of movement. Eris looked over her shoulder to see the Herald and Simonetti close by. She had no idea where the Silent Queen was leading them, or even if her life would be spared once they reached their destination. All she could do was run.

One floor down, every level of House Fontein was alive with the enemy, like a hive kicked by unruly children. Two hulking Myrmidons slammed into Medea and Anea from a side corridor. Anea lifted one Myrmidon's helm, thrusting her fingers into his eyes. The soldier crashed into the wall. But the other slung Medea over an armoured shoulder, holding her fast in thick leather gauntlets. The Myrmidon fled, his route blocked by more of his kin. The *marchesa* screamed in frustration, reaching out to Anea.

Eris ducked beneath a wild swing from a Myrmidon who had sneaked up behind, her blade ringing from his breastplate with a clang. Virmyre stepped in, smashing the weapon from the Myrmidon's hands. More Myrmidons filled the junction, the sound of soldiers coming from every direction, blocking the way on every side. The Herald kicked down a door, wood coming apart in a shower of dust. A disused apartment lay before them.

'This way,' he shouted. Eris followed, knowing the Herald offered her best chance of survival.

They almost tumbled over one another in their haste, fleeing the corridor, which was now swarming with their pursuers. The Herald and Simonetti pulled down a massive bookcase to block the doorway, a makeshift barricade. Anea, Marchetti and Virmyre fled from the sitting room to the bedroom. Eris seized her chance to be rid of them, crossing to the window.

The bookcase shuddered as the first of many blows fell upon it.

'They took Medea!' Eris sobbed.

'A war with the south will be unavoidable if Erebus executes her,' said Simonetti.

'We can't help her now,' replied the Herald.

'Everything is lost,' wailed Simonetti, blinking behind his optics.

'You'll be lost too if you stand around crying,' said the Herald. Simonetti nodded. Eris opened the window, slamming the shutter back, feet slipping as she mounted the sill. A glance up confirmed the Silent Queen and her party were climbing for the safety of the rooftops, but much too slowly, calling out encouragement to one another. Eris cast her gaze down to the streets below, shrouded in darkness.

'Head to the rooftops,' said the archivist. 'Follow Anea.'

'I can't. It's too dangerous. I'm not strong enough.' Eris scrambled across the broad face of House Fontein, stepping from window sill to window sill. The wind whipped about her, drowning out the sounds of fighting within the apartment. Eris drew level with a window, the apartment inside dark. The stolen sword proved an effective tool to gain entry. She swung and stabbed and swung again. Glass shattered, soft lead bending. Eris squeezed in, falling to her knees in the darkness behind a couch. She clutched the blade between trembling hands. Her breathing was loud, second only to the sounds of destruction coming from the apartment next door. The Myrmidons were shunting the barricade aside.

'They'll kill Medea for this, and the Herald will hunt me down,' she whispered to herself. Shouts sounded in the night, running footsteps and muttered curses. Her teeth chattered with cold. Simonetti entered through the shattered window. The archivist hunkered down beside her, patting her shoulder with a shaking hand.

'Where is the Herald?'

Simonetti shrugged and opened his mouth to speak but formed no words. He removed his optics and polished them on his robes, releasing a bitter sigh.

'What do we do now?' pressed Eris.

'We, ah, wait. And hope the Myrmidons don't find us.'

28

Spiralling Down

Anea stood on the rooftops of House Fontein, shivering from the cold and the shock of Medea's capture. Everything had happened so quickly, one moment rushing down a corridor filled with shouting and panic, the next Medea gone, snatched from before her eyes. The *marchesa* had reached out with imploring hands, her eyes at once frustrated and afraid. There would be no escape now, no second chance. Anea had failed.

Marchetti collapsed as he crested the edge of the roof. Anea shook him, but the assassin did not respond. Virmyre pressed two fingers to his neck, hoping for a pulse.

'Just unconscious.'

Anea took a knife to her underskirts and fashioned a crude bandage while Virmyre struggled to remove Marchetti's armour. They worked quickly, not knowing if a handful of Myrmidons would stumble across them, finishing what they had started with the assassin's wound.

'That should help,' said Virmyre, 'at least until we can get some proper dressings.'

We have to go back. We have to find Medea, she signed, but Virmyre was busy lifting Marchetti. He struggled a moment before sliding the assassin's body over one shoulder, a cruel echo of how the Myrmidon had stolen Medea.

'He weighs as much as Cherubini,' said Virmyre. 'What do they make assassins out of these days? Granite?' The *professore* set off, traversing the uneven landscape of the rooftops. 'Anea! *Avanti!*'

She followed, picking her way across the sloping roofs,

cracked tiles loose beneath her feet. The wind was a bitter cold and wailed around them.

If Erebus executes Medea then Lucien will declare war to avenge her.

'You don't know that,' said Virmyre. 'Just be grateful they didn't capture you. We'd be in a larger mess if that had happened.'

But after everything she did for me...

'I know. But we were outnumbered. We tried, Anea. We did what we could. And we almost lost you in the process.'

A look over her shoulder confirmed they were alone. Had Simonetti really been there? Had she imagined the Herald fighting the Myrmidons? The girl could only be the impostor, but why seek the freedom of a woman she had imprisoned?

Why was the impostor there? Why was she trying to free Medea?

'Perhaps she's not the willing usurper we assume she is.'

And the Herald?

'Who knows? Come on,' urged Virmyre. He was heading toward a slender spire, a door frame on one side obscured by water stains and guano. It would lead down into the vast corpse of Demesne, the stairwell a throat waiting to swallow them. Beyond Demesne the streets were stained with people, blurry smudges of colour on the dark roads. It was as if the very building were being bled, spilling its life force over the surrounding town, leaving only Myrmidons in the lungs and arteries of that colossal beast. Myrmidons. Insects. Parasites. And wasn't she one of them? A parasite with a pretty title. Being Orfano was an accident of privilege, a roll of the dice from being underkin. That she concealed her otherness behind a veil made her no less repellent than the Myrmidons, who hid behind armour.

'Come on, Anea!' urged Virmyre. His tone was gentle, but the strain was showing. He had set Marchetti down, who remained silent and was doing his best to remain standing, one hand clamped to his abdomen.

They entered the doorway and headed down, following steps that spiralled, like her thoughts, down into self-pity. Questions and accusations tumbled over one another. Anea almost lost her footing, only regaining her balance through good fortune.

She stopped to sit, pushing her face into her hands, feeling the hotness of tears tumble down her cheeks, race across her palms, down her wrists. Tiny rapids of regret.

'They say *tinctura* reduces empathy.' Virmyre stood a few steps below, Marchetti slumped against him, head hanging. 'And the king, in his great wisdom, never documented its long-term effects.'

Is this going somewhere, Anea signed, *because I cannot conceive of a worse time for a lecture on chemistry?*

'The reason I mention it,' explained Virmyre, 'is that I was concerned the effect may be permanent, or that some vestige of dispassion remains.'

Anea wiped her eyes with the back of her hand. *And?*

'Congratulations. You're clearly very much recovered.'

We just lost Medea.

'Yes, we did, and I understand you're taking a moment to mourn her, but I would suggest we get the hell out of Demesne first, Highness.'

Sarcasm is not something one should aspire to, Virmyre.

'Good point. Can we go now? This assassin isn't getting any lighter.'

How is he?

'Bleeding would be the obvious answer.'

House Prospero was all but abandoned. Only possessions remained, items discarded, victims of necessity, each an artefact of a life uprooted, holding memories. The mundane scattered alongside the precious: silver coins resembled constellations on the drab flagstones; here the ring of a great-grandmother fondly remembered; there a jacket borrowed from a friend and never returned. Anea followed Virmyre, her every thought bent to ascribing meaning to the items underfoot. It mattered not that they were merely stories of her own making she told herself, only that each possession have importance somehow. No time to pause or stoop, these were not her things to retrieve; she simply hoped they remained undisturbed. The *cittadini* might return one day. A glimmer of hope persisted that objects both practical and sentimental would be rediscovered by their owners, with all the attendant memories they held.

The streets were strewn with wagons and mules, horses and carts, and a shocking contrast to the endless gloom of Demesne. Lanterns had been hung in profusion, lighting the way for all who left. The *cittadini* displayed a wide range of emotions. Anger and impatience, tears of dismay, blank gazes of shock or stern expressions. And underneath the panic of flight, another feeling remained irresistible and raw. It was not fear of the Myrmidons but a subtle pain that no amount of denial or comfort could assuage.

The *cittadini* were bereft.

Demesne had been the beating heart of their lives, of all lives in Landfall. The roads that led to it were fault lines of law and consequence, fortune and disaster. Only the darkness of the winter night remained. There would be no going back to the unspeakable madness of Erebus lurking in the Ravenscourt.

'The *marchesa* isn't with you.' Anea almost flinched, the words dragging her back from maudlin introspection. She looked up to find Salvaza Prospero standing on a wagon, directing a handful of staff, ordering her troops. Her page lingered nearby, clutching a satchel stuffed with parchment, a smudge of soot on his cherubic face.

'I'd heard some attempt to free Medea was afoot,' continued the duchess. Her page looked hopeful.

Anea shook her head.

'That's ... regrettable.' The duchess looked at her page, who was close to tears but frowning hard to keep them at bay. 'I'll be sure to stop at House Albero and tell the children.'

How do you know the children are there?

'I have my spies.' The duchess gave a small shrug. 'Perhaps I'll persuade them to come with us to San Marino. They can live with me should circumstances dictate. Perhaps I'll be a better mother in my middle years than I was in earlier times.'

I suspect that would be for the best.

Anea cursed that she was unable to remember the names of Medea's son and daughter. The last of Duchess Prospero's porters loaded a crate onto the wagon, cursing under its weight. Those who had horses mounted without fuss, some saluting

Anea, others flashing incredulous looks. Virmyre disappeared into the crowd, carrying Marchetti in the direction of the old *sanatorio*. The duchess stepped down from the wagon, drawing close to the Silent Queen.

'Is there anything I can do, my lady?'

Anea shook her head, but her hands were already moving. *I have wanted a republic for Landfall ever since I knew what the word meant.*

Duchess Prospero nodded. 'You've no need to tell me.' A wry smile creased her lips; the tiredness in her eyes remained.

And you have opposed me every step of the way.

The duchess nodded again, a sigh of resignation. 'Wholeheartedly.'

I would give up all my hopes for a republic, walk away from my dreams, just for the promise of Medea Contadino's life.

'I know you would, my lady,' said Salvaza. 'That's why I respect you. That's why I'll always respect you.'

All she ever desired was to be a good wife and a loving mother.

Salvaza looked down at the cobbles and clasped her hands together, her lips a thin line of frustration.

She was a voice of reason amid the politics and ego of the Ravenscourt.

'You speak of her of her in the past tense. She's not dead yet.'

Anea nodded, but neither of them believed Medea could be saved. The two women regarded each other amid the desperation of *cittadini* keen to be away from the deepening chaos.

'I need to lead my people south.'

Yes, you do.

Salvaza took her place on the wagon and looked back at Anea. 'Is there anything you'd like me to pass on to Duke Marino?' she asked, tenderness replaced by duty once more.

Anea shrugged. *Tell him that I am sorry for making such a mess of things. Tell him I am sorry –* her hands paused – *for everything.*

'Goodbye, Lady Aranea Oscuro Diaspora.'

Goodbye, Duchess.

The wagon moved off, and Salvaza Prospero did not look away until she was spirited from sight, obscured from view by the busy streets of Santa Maria.

It wasn't until Anea caught up with Virmyre that she realised he was not heading to the old *sanatorio* as she had thought.

They will not let you in. They will not let him in either. Not after what he did.

'I thought this Saint of yours enshrined forgiveness.'

I never claimed I was a believer. She is not my Saint.

'Perhaps now is the time to find some faith,' said Virmyre. 'I'm no *dottore,* but I think this one needs a miracle.'

I think we could all use a miracle, signed Anea, but Virmyre didn't see, intent on crossing the piazza, alive with people making ready to leave. They ascended the steps of the church, Virmyre hammering the door with a fist. Anea looked behind them; they had not been followed.

'I won't let you in with him!' whispered Sister Consolatta through the sliding panel set in the door.

'He's half dead, hardly dangerous in this condition,' replied Virmyre. 'Do open the door.'

'He's an assassin! And he works for the impostor.'

'He's a had a recent change of loyalty, and if you don't open the door his longevity will change too. Drastically.'

'But he's a killer!'

'Which means the gifts of your tolerance and hospitality will be so much more profound.'

Anea pushed in front. *I am the rightful ruler of Demesne and I command you to open this door or I will burn the entire building to the ground as punishment for your treason.*

The door opened.

'And there I was thinking I could use reason,' muttered Virmyre as he carried Marchetti over the threshold.

The sisters went about their work without further pause or complaint. Marchetti was taken away on a stretcher. Virmyre followed; he'd picked up a few wounds of his own, though none as serious as the pale assassin's. There was a calming hush in the vestibule of the church, so different to the hustle of the streets and the many distressed voices. Anea watched the procession of sisters and wounded men as it headed further into the nave, swallowed one by one by an arched doorway.

The church was brightly lit, candles warding off the night. It was not warm but the wind had no claim. The smells of incense and polish settled Anea's nerves. For a time she simply stood, basking in the sacred quiet. Silence, so long a torment in her speechless life, was a balm in this place. All remaining resolve departed, and she sat, grasping the pew in front, forehead resting against her hands.

'Praying for your assassin?' Agostina was Santa Maria's disciple in Landfall, an exemplar of mercy, but even she couldn't keep the note of disdain from her voice.

Medea actually. And I was not praying, not really. Just hoping there was some way she might yet live.

'Can't someone rescue her?'

We tried. That is why Marchetti is wounded. He was helping me.

Agostina shook her head. 'I thought—'

I persuaded him that Erebus and the Domina are not the allies he thinks.

'He really put himself in danger for Medea?'

He fought and killed his own for Medea, but in the end it was not enough. They still have her.

Anea spent the night by Marchetti's bedside. The assassin remained in a feverish torpor, stripped of all but his small clothes, body a motley of bruises in lurid yellow and savage purple. The sisters had treated the wound and dosed him with a preparation to ward off infection. Another mixture had been administered to aid his sleep. Anea found herself envious of his dreamless slumber. Marchetti's unfocused eye looked into the middle distance when it opened, only to close moments later. His fingers made no sign or symbol.

Anea soaked a cloth in warm water and wiped his brow, wondering who had slashed his face. Had he killed them for taking his eye and leaving such a mark? Anea frowned, releasing an uneasy breath before removing his veil so she could tend him more thoroughly. She wiped gently, moving the cloth down his face to his jaw, careful not to snare the fabric on his mandibles. The deformity appeared no less disturbing for the soft candlelight. Her investigations of herself had been short-lived; her otherness was more than she could tolerate. Mirrors had been banned from her chambers. She'd not needed daily reminders; her veil and the silence beneath it were evidence enough.

A small figurine of Santa Maria stood on the bedside table, the Saint clutching her infant child, a look of benevolence carved on her tiny face. How Anea envied the kindly smile, her perfect lips giving form to vowels, the tongue creating consonants. The simple joy of a kiss would remain for ever foreign to the Silent Queen. And the Saint had clearly known love – how else to explain the child she held?

Anea swabbed the dried blood from the assassin's hands, turning away from her cold disappointment. How many times had the assassin returned to Erebus, drenched to his elbows in the blood of the fallen? She continued to clean his fingers, thoughts of possible victims surfacing in her mind like restless shades. Marchetti may have killed Dino for all she knew, perhaps Margravio Contadino too.

The figurine of Santa Maria watched Anea stand, damp cloth falling from bloodied fingers. For a moment it looked as if the woman might scream with frustration, but no sound broke the stillness of the humble cell. Growing disgust forced her from the room. The figurine continued its vigil long after Anea had left, watching over the assassin with a gentle smile.

Anea ventured to the library first, finding it empty except for a deep darkness and a deeper silence. Her exhaustion was profound, but her restlessness was greater, urging her on to the balcony. Fingers curled about the door handle as her mind seized on the painful truth: Medea would not be waiting for her on the other side. There would be no words of solace or friendship, one less ally against Erebus. Anea spent long minutes crying in the darkness, pressing a sleeve to red-rimmed eyes. The door opened, startling her.

'Ah, I thought I heard...' Virmyre shrugged, his face solemn in the light of the brazier.

I did not expect you to be awake. I thought...

238

'Something woke me, a sound from outside.' Virmyre pointed a finger toward the triumphal arch. From this height they could see over the roofs of some buildings, yet the darkness conspired with taller townhouses to conceal the source of the sound. 'It's the Myrmidons.'

Attacking the cittadini? *Sacking the town?*

'No. Nothing like that.' Virmyre stroked his beard, pressing a thumb against his chin. 'I thought I could hear the sawing of wood.'

Anea looked down into the piazza. The people had dispersed, taken to the muddy roads for windswept journeys, harried by sleet and driving rain.

At least people have escaped, she signed, but it was meagre consolation. Virmyre was rapt with the mystery beyond their sight. The Myrmidons had strung lanterns from poles, but the light made their purpose no clearer. A wagon arrived with a long length of wood, a full score of the soldiers joining together to hoist it upright.

'I think we should go back inside,' said Virmyre, his voice quiet.

No. We need to stay and discover what they are making.

'We're both very tired.' This much was undeniable, Virmyre looked more drawn and pale than she could remember. 'It'll be dawn soon. Let's wait until the sun rises,' he continued, but she sensed a ruse.

What is it the Myrmidons are so keen to build in the middle of the night?

Virmyre shook his head. 'I don't know – I mean, I can't be certain. Let's get some sleep.'

You know what they are making, she pressed

'We should go inside. You'll see what it is soon enough.'

Virmyre. Her eyes flashed with anger.

He shrugged and chewed his lip in a way that reminded her of Lucien. 'They are building a gallows,' he said, the words no more than a whisper. 'They mean to hang her.'

239

29

The Impostor's New Clothes

House Fontein was situated north-west of the Central Keep. The sun, when it dared to shine on the windows, did so only as it slunk toward the horizon. The house was gloomy even at the height of summer, no art to decorate the walls, the architecture lacking ornament. House Fontein's construction did not tolerate the baroque, too much a distraction from function.

Fontein, more than any other house, had grown at the dictates of vanity over purpose. The dukes of Fontein, trusted with the king's safety, had argued for a share of the taxes in order to expand the training chambers and barracks. They petitioned the Majordomo, wielding an influence the other houses envied. Nobles and *cittadini* alike wondered if Fontein exerted leverage. There could be no other reason the most martial of houses had grown beyond reason. It was a vast maze of routinely empty apartments, trackless corridors and disused training chambers. Eris hated it.

And yet House Fontein was where she woke following the disastrous attempt to rescue Medea Contadino. It had seemed natural to return to her apartment; there had been nowhere else to go. Eris shivered, pulled herself to her feet, blanket wrapped about her like a shroud. She'd slept on the couch, the embers of the fire a dull jumble of orange and grey in the hearth. Fumbling at the mantelpiece with numb fingers provided some illumination. A lantern flickered, the tongue of flame small at first. Simonetti remained sprawled in an armchair, long limbs extended from the limit of the blanket she'd provided. The light failed to rouse him, his eyes stayed closed, optics held in loose fingers, a few days' stubble on the planes of cheeks and chin.

Isabella occupied the opposite chair, also lost to the arms of sleep, curled up like a cat. None had wanted the bed in the adjoining room, none wishing to be alone during the long hours of the desperate night. Better to sleep near the hearth, the warmth a soporific, the company a reassurance even in slumber.

A scrape sounded at the door.

'Simonetti!' Eris crossed to the slumbering archivist, shook his arm.

'Not the cheese!' he shouted, then blinked several times. He shook himself and cleared his throat. 'What? Where am I? Where are are my optics?'

'In my apartment. We came here last night, do you remember?'

'Oh, ah, yes.'

'Your optics are in your hand.'

'Ah, so they are. Thank you.'

Isabella had woken too, regarding them both with a wary gaze.

'If I never drink red wine again—'

The scrape at the door silenced her. Simonetti sat up in his armchair, turning toward the source of the sound.

'I don't suppose by any chance that might be, ah, a rat?'

Demesne was host to any number of creaking floors, slammed doors and distant rumbles. Tales abounded of ghosts; maids and pages doomed to an eternity of servitude. The ghosts of Demesne did many things, so it was said, but Eris had never heard of them scraping at doors.

'It does sound like a, ah, fairly large rat,' said Simonetti. 'Perhaps we should ignore it.'

The women glowered at him.

'Ah, sorry.'

Eris took the poker from the fireplace, the black iron a reassuring weight in her hand.

'From Silent Queen to rat catcher,' she mumbled before unlocking the door. The scraping was louder, urgent, unsettling.

'I'm armed,' she shouted, 'so think carefully.' And with that she flung the door open. Her shriek was broken by the dull clang of the poker as it hit the floor. Simonetti sprang forward, pulling Eris back from the horror in the doorway. Isabella a took a turn at screaming, her hysteria piercing but brief.

What waited at the open door was not intimidating for its height, nor was it physically threatening. It was as warped as it was pathetic, as diminutive as it was grotesque. At a glance it resembled some overly large spider, but closer inspection revealed the body itself was no body at all, rather a human head that served as the bulk of the corpus. Eight spindly legs, like unnaturally long fingers, supported the creature. It regarded them with bright eyes of sky blue, the mouth clamped on a square of parchment bearing a purple wax seal.

'It's a messenger,' said Simonetti, his tone almost reverent. He stooped to take the note from the grotesque, which scuttled away the moment it could.

'You have been summoned to the Ravenscourt,' said Simonetti, his optics now on his nose. He held the parchment out to her, the scrawl on it undoubtedly the Domina's handwriting.

'I don't want to read it,' replied Eris.

'You can't possibly attend,' replied Simonetti.

'The Domina will kill you,' said Isabella.

'Perhaps,' replied Eris. She crossed to a dresser, pulling open a drawer. 'But if the Domina wanted me dead she would have sent Myrmidons. Perhaps Erebus wishes to talk.'

'But why?' asked Isabella.

'I can't guess at what they want.' She looked up from the contents of the dresser drawer, casting a glance over her shoulder. 'But I can at least try and negotiate for you two.' Eris took two stilettos from the drawer, handing one to Isabella.

The maid blinked; Simonetti cleared his throat. It was evident neither had thought Eris might foster some warm regard for them.

'I've a feeling Sabatino would have liked you, both of you.' She flashed a look at Simonetti, who shuffled his feet. 'And there's no reason we all have to go to an early grave, is there?'

She entered the bedroom and changed into a black dress, an

iron-grey shawl completing her attire. Isabella spent wordless moments applying kohl to Eris's eyes, a hint of blusher, rouge on lips taut with anxiety.

'What are you, ah, doing?'

'There's no point having finery if I can't at least die in it.' Eris smiled, but the archivist and maid had no words of consolation.

'I'll get word to you if I can.'

'Must you go so soon?' said Simonetti.

'You can't stall the inevitable.' Eris sighed. 'And Erebus dislikes being kept waiting. Something we have in common.' She opened the door of the apartment, the dark corridors of Demesne beckoning.

The Ravenscourt was much changed. Only the Myrmidons watching at each pillar were familiar. Those at the doors neither saluted nor seized her. A hush lay over the broad chamber like a pall of smoke. The black curtain concealing the usurper of Landfall had been discarded. Eris pressed chilly fingertips to her face. Erebus wasn't the only one appearing unveiled. She smiled and lifted her chin, refreshing to set aside the pretence. The trappings of the Silent Queen had been a prison, all thoughtfully provided by Erebus.

'And I entered it willingly,' she breathed as she crossed the chamber. 'All to keep Sabatino alive and nurture my own terrible selfishness.' Her footsteps echoed. Only as she reached the centre of the room did she discern the change that had befallen Landfall's seat of power. The nobles, fled to the countryside, had been replaced. Not every underkin could adopt the armour of the Myrmidons. Some were too weak, others too hunched and misshapen, bloodlines desecrated by fell manipulation. Broken creatures huddled together on the dais, grateful to be granted audience with Erebus. Underkin courtiers had acquired garments from abandoned apartments. Gowns and doublets had been stolen with no thought to taste or fashion. Eris recognised some of the clothes, struggling to recall who had worn them in better times. The effect was chilling.

And there were the children, nightmares in miniature. They sneered at Eris, lips twisting beneath hungry gazes, those few that had lips to sneer with. Many were dressed as pages and scullions, as disobedient a mob as ever existed. Erebus presided over the multitude of twisted flesh and discarded finery. His spindly bulk formed the focal point of the dais, a terrible sculpture. Impossible to tell if he were awake beneath the Myrmidon helm. Eris picked her way through the Ravenscourt – the Undercourt, she amended.

Dottore Allattamento stood to one side. Before him was a chaise longue where the Domina drowsed, lost in the ecstasy of *tinctura* most likely. Her biretta had been cast aside, hair falling to her shoulders, an unruly wave of auburn in the darkness. Allattamento stepped down from the dais, ashen and tremulous.

'Quite the army of impostors you've assembled.' Eris eyed the underkin, then smiled at the *dottore*. He looked pale and worn, the creases at his eyes deeper than she remembered.

'None of this is my doing.'

'Really?' Eris smiled again. 'And yet it was you who trained me, the first of the impostors. Looks like I'm much in fashion.'

'You can't possibly blame me for this.' Allattamento had tears in eyes.

'You're too successful for your own good.'

The *dottore* opened his mouth to speak but was interrupted by a wail from the dais. The Domina blinked in confusion, mouth opening and closing, too confused to speak. Allattamento hurried back to the dais, helping her stand.

'My staff,' rasped the Domina. Allattamento duly fetched the length of silver. She waved off a trio of stunted children, attired in the rich crimson of her robes.

'I see you've wasted no time recruiting apprentices,' Eris said.

'You tried to free Marchesa Contadino,' said the Domina, her words incredulous and uneven.

'I did,' replied Eris, 'at the urging of the Herald. He threatened to kill me if I refused to help.' She took a breath. Telling the truth was not unlike wearing a new gown. She was enjoying how good it felt, how light the fabric was, the way the cut of the garment suited her.

Erebus nodded, light reflecting from the blades that resembled mandibles.

'Very well,' replied the Domina, her tone declaring she was anything but satisfied. The *dottore* leaned forward to offer counsel, but the Domina waved him away, her attention never leaving Eris. 'And where is the Herald now?'

'You mean the Myrmidons didn't kill him?'

'We assumed he was with you,' said Allattamento. The Domina silenced him with an excoriating gaze.

'And Marchetti?' said the Domina, her voice leached of intonation. 'How did you persuade him to turn against Lord Erebus?'

'Marchetti's change of loyalty was not my work. I suspect Anea won him over.'

'You can't really believe—' spluttered the *dottore*.

'He's a broken creature,' replied Eris, 'unstable, unreliable. He failed us before; he's failed us again.'

Eris snatched a glance at Erebus. Had he ever fostered ambitions for the assassin? No defence was offered of the once-favoured Marchetti; Erebus simply nodded his agreement.

'Lord Erebus tells me you came before him,' the Domina smiled, 'with a blade.'

Eris nodded, no point clinging to denial when her fate looked predetermined. They'd accuse and accuse until she was found wanting.

'That you came to him in the middle night.' The Domina forced a cruel smile, her eyes glassy and unfocused. 'Is it true you were seeking our lord's death?'

Eris nodded again, her eyes drifting to Allattamento. He shook his head and frowned, knowing what must come next.

'Dottore Allattamento revealed to me that he tried to manufacture a cure for my brother, Sabatino. The *dottore* claimed he was denied access to the king's machines. He laid the blame for my brother's death at the feet of Lord Erebus.'

'Lies! Clearly we can't trust her,' said Allattamento, his words hurried and quick. The *dottore* waited for the Domina's response, a sickened look on his aristocratic features.

'I agree,' said the Domina. She gestured to the nearest Myrmidons. 'Take her to the oubliette. No. Execute her right now.'

Eris struggled to remain standing, light-headed and breathless. The new gown she had been so impressed with had turned to rags. For a moment she had thought truth might grant her a reprieve, keep her warm from death's icy touch. The Myrmidons closed in as the underkin looked on.

'Wait.' The word was like a chord, dismal and minor. Erebus lifted his armoured head, addressing the court. 'She speaks the truth, a truth only three people knew.'

The Domina looked up at the vast bulk of Erebus, her face made spectral by fear.

'Naturally the Domina would never seek to move against me.' Erebus let the words hang in the air. The threat and innuendo of the statement was not diminished by the hateful drone of his voice.

Chastened, the Domina dropped her chin, breathing ragged, her grip on the silver staff tight.

Erebus broke the silence once more. 'So the conspirator had to be the *dottore*.'

Allattamento cried out his innocence over and over. Each iteration more desperate, more pained.

'Take him to the oubliette,' said Erebus, his flat drone bored, as if he were ordering dinner.

'My lord,' said the Domina, 'this is most irregular.'

'Please, my lord.' Allattamento was weeping. 'She lies! She lies!'

The Myrmidons dragged the *dottore* across the centre of the Ravenscourt, heading toward the doors in implacable lockstep. The Domina looked from *dottore* to Erebus with a look of incomprehension. Eris closed her eyes, tried to shut out Allattamento's ragged howls, wanting to press the heels of her hands to her ears.

'My Lord Erebus,' Eris raised her chin, lending the full force of her voice to each word, 'I apologise for coming before you with a blade. I was manipulated by the *dottore*, who fed on the pain of my grief. It's no secret I miss my brother keenly.' More honesty, though Eris tired with the telling of it. Both truth and lies were exhausting in their own way.

The Domina turned her attention to her master. 'My lord, surely you can't think to absolve the girl of her betrayal? She has turned Simonetti against us too.'

'What care have I for libraries,' replied Erebus, 'much less an archivist who has always been a staunch supporter of Anea?'

'We must kill him, my lord,' pressed the Domina.

'He may go. I care not,' said Erebus. 'He is of no consequence.'

'I will tell him at once, my lord,' said Eris, glad of the opportunity to absent herself. She curtsied as the underkin hissed.

'My lord!' The Domina's anger finally broke through the apathy of *tinctura*. 'I demand we arrest her, she is dangerous.'

'I'm an impostor with no one to impersonate,' said Eris. 'How dangerous can I be?' She turned her back on them, the complaints of the underkin and the Domina trailing her to the vast doors.

All measure of resolve and control fled Eris the moment she was free of the Ravenscourt. She ran down the steps to the floor below, racing past shelves lined with countless books. Other footsteps followed, fast of pace. She pressed on, down more stairs to the circuitous corridor of the Central Keep. Her senses were filled with flight: the sound of frantic breathing, the beat of her heart in her chest, eyes searching the darkness. And everywhere the dank unsettling tang of putrefaction.

She was almost wrenched from her feet when something snagged her arm. Not something, someone. The Domina spun her round, alabaster face flushed with rage, eyes bloodshot, pupils dilated. She shook with fury, the depth of her rage rendering her mute. Eris pulled away but the Domina's grip was absolute.

'Get off me, you mad old bitch!'

Still she said nothing, her hands reaching to Eris's throat, fingers like crooked claws.

'*Via al diavolo*,' hissed Eris. A stiletto flashed in the gloom of the lantern light as the Domina slammed her against the wall. The women remained pressed together, a rigid embrace, neither daring to let go lest the world see the damage of their collision. Eris could feel blood flowing over her hand.

'Oh, no,' mumbled the Domina.

'I only wanted to escape.' The words had the timbre of apology.

'What have you done?'

Eris stepped back from the Domina, eyes drawn to the hilt extending from beneath the woman's breastbone. The handle was wrapped in black velvet, a contrast to the crimson robes that grew darker with each faltering beat of the Domina's heart. The silver staff clattered to the floor.

'Everything about you is a lie,' whispered the Domina, sinking to her knees.

Eris nodded. 'Until today, yes.'

'A liar for a liar's throne.'

Eris walked away, bloodied hand held out lest it stain her finery.

30

A Study in Crimson

Virmyre collapsed as he headed back into the church from the balcony, a bitter wind chasing them through the door. *Tinctura* had not bestowed a second blush of youth, and he had pushed himself harder than anyone should. The attempt to rescue Medea and the subsequent escape required an accounting, and the price was steep. The man Anea helped to bed looked every one of his fifty-nine years, the corners of his eyes deeply lined, his black hair shot through with grey. She pulled the blankets up around his chin, smoothing them with a gentle hand.

'Is he dying?' Agostina regarded the man from the corridor, wary of crossing the cell's threshold, as if old age itself were contagious.

I hope not, Anea signed, *but he was relying on* tinctura *for so long. It seems it is finally leaving his system.*

'He looks terrible.'

He is wounded, he is tired, and he is nearly sixty.

'And you?'

I cannot deny that I am tired. Her fingers stopped signing and she looked away, a tautness in her shoulders. *I was just thinking: so strange that we come to care for the ones who cared for us in our infancy.*

Anea held his hand, noticing the skin, dry with abundant wrinkles.

'I never realised you were close to Virmyre.'

Not at first. Anea cocked her head to one side as if listening; instead she was kindling memories that came to life like embers stirred into flame.

I was always drawn to Russo. She was something of an older sister to me. And a teacher and a friend. Then the king died, and all those secrets found their way into the light of day. Suddenly I had brothers, half-brothers at least, Lucien and Dino. For the first time I had relationships with men who cared about me. I had been so wary of them until then because of... She gestured to her face.

'And Virmyre?'

Anea took the armchair beside the bed. It was old but comfortable. She sank into it willingly.

He loved Lucien and Dino like sons, so I suppose it was natural for him to take me into his care. We are called Orfani for a reason, and Virmyre was keen to make sure we never felt alone. I suppose the Domina, I mean Russo, must have felt increasingly pushed to the margins.

For a time the only sound in the chamber was gentle breathing, Virmyre taking his rest. Anea watched him sleep; Agostina lingered at the door, caught up in curiosity. Anea indulged it, glad to have someone to tell.

As the years went by it was Virmyre I turned to. He was my research partner and my confidant. Not that I had much to confide, and even then I turned to Dino. Russo must have felt I had turned from her completely. She dragged down a shuddering breath. *Small wonder she betrayed me.* Anea turned tear-strewn eyes to the disciple. *I have failed him. I feel as if I have failed everyone.*

'You mustn't say that,' said Agostina, her voice a warm hush. She entered the room at last, going to her knees and taking Anea's hands in her own, fingers soft, warm. 'Try to get some sleep. We can talk about departing Santa Maria once the sun has risen.'

I cannot leave. We have until spring before war breaks out. I may not have been able to save Medea but there must be something I can do.

'Possibly, but you'll achieve nothing without sleep.'

Anea nodded, drowsing in the armchair for a time before exhaustion overtook her.

Anea returned to her cell just before dawn, barely awake, disoriented from deep slumber, senses muffled with sleep. The edge of the narrow bed provided little comfort as she sat, lifting her veil to pour water into the ragged opening of her mouth. The glass was finely cut and clean, the water within clear and cool. The process of remembering herself had begun with this simple act, she realised. The drinking of water. Clean water. The vision of a hundred sinister sarcophagi filled her mind, each with an angry amethyst eye glowing in the dark. Anea set the glass down with an uncertain hand, eyes unfocused. The glass tumbled to the floor, shattering apart in a rain of silvery fragments. She flinched to full wakefulness, an accusatory glance at the bedside table. The clay jug she had been given in the oubliette stood beside a figurine of the Saint and her nameless infant. Anea eyed the broken glass and white stone figurine with growing indignation.

Was it too much to expect Medea to be rescued? she signed.

Santa Maria smiled but said nothing.

Where is your mercy for her children? Is it not enough they have lost their father? Not sufficiently unkind that they are forced to live far away, refugees from their own home?

Anea was on her feet now, blood seething in her veins, stomach shrunk with anger, hands balled into fists. There was no need for the silent language now; she simply cast her thoughts at the effigy.

Didn't I always try and live within the spirit of your teachings? I may not have been an open worshipper, but I heeded your values and sought to bring them to Landfall.

She towered over the tiny stone figure.

I gave the people hope, gave them education, gave them medicine. I protected the young and the weak, I faced down the privileged and the spoilt. And I get this? A gallows death for Medea, a brother killed by armoured thugs, a castle ruled by a monster, my name despoiled.

She hefted the clay jug and threw it at the wall with all her strength. The noise from the impact was shocking, louder still as the pieces hit the floor. Shards of clay nestled among pieces of glass, terracotta red and translucence.

Well you can go to the Nine Hells if you think I'm fleeing to the coast, thought Anea. I'll die before I give up Demesne you smug-looking *puttana*.

And still the figurine of Santa Maria did not respond.

Anea paused long enough to splash water on her face before departing for the old *sanatorio*.

Simonetti was turning the key in the lock to his apartment when he felt the tap on his shoulder. He turned with hands held out in surrender, then a curious expression creased his face.

'I've seen many Myrmidons of late, yet none so, ah, diminutive shall we say.'

She gestured he should enter the apartment; he complied without complaint. It was no great surprise that books adorned every flat surface, small piles of them flourishing on the floor like rectangular fungus.

'Is it possible you're not, ah, fully grown?' said Simonetti as he closed the door. The armour was an unwelcome weight and not a natural fit, but it served well, protecting her not from attack but discovery. She was grateful for her modest bust. The breastplate, while large, was not accommodating.

'Perhaps you're not a Myrmidon at all.'

Anea cast the helmet aside and removed the much-too-large gloves. Her hair was bound up in a tight plait, her mouth covered by a white veil.

'I'm really rather baffled that such a flimsy disguise got you past the Myrmidons at the gates,' continued the archivist.

You are quite the critic for someone who failed to notice the ruler of Landfall had been replaced by an impostor.

'Ah,' said the archivist, 'I suppose I deserved that.' He squinted, blue eyes scrunched up behind the optics. 'How do I know you're really you?'

I made you a viscount in year 317, barely a year after you started building the library in the old sanatorio.

Simonetti nodded. 'Well, that is widely known.'

Your favourite book is by an author from San Marino. I cannot remember the name of it, but there are poems about cormorants. It has illustrations too. You insist on wearing robes because you think your legs are too thin and do not suit britches and hose.

Simonetti cleared his throat. 'Well, ah, now that we all know who we are, why don't we sit down with some tea?'

The Silent Queen and archivist spent a time establishing just what, if anything, she had been truly responsible for. They perched on the edge of couch and armchair, two strangers gathering fragments of a shattered friendship. The edges of those fragments were sharp, but Simonetti cared not for the keen edge of blame, only the neat ordering of facts.

I cannot determine why you would continue to serve me – I mean her – when she was so obviously corrupt and cruel.

'Well, I had hoped to act as some measure of conscience, my lady.'

Why stay? Why remain here trying to negotiate?

'The change took place very suddenly. Demesne was thrown from crisis to, ah, scandal and back again. The attacks from the underkin, Cherubini's exile, the increasing hostility from Duke Fontein.'

It was a terrible time, worse than terrible.

'Yes, it was, and well, frankly, you could be forgiven for becoming a mite cantankerous in the light of all that, ah, happened.'

But it was not me that issued these cantankerous orders.

'No, it wasn't. But you, ah, did leave us to attend to your research. And you left us in the care of the Domina.'

I lost myself in my work, and became lost to myself and those I loved.

'We all, ah, get lost from time to time.' Simonetti cleared his throat and placed his optics back on his nose. 'Some of us need help to find our way back. That's why I stayed. And that's why you've come to me now, to make sure we don't lose Medea.'

Anea nodded. *Can you help me? Please?*

'Only the Domina can grant that wish, and only when she has been separated from the influence of Erebus. Not an easy thing. She, ah, practically sleeps in the Ravenscourt.'

Can we go to her, or find some way to lure her outside?

'Well, possibly. But she has been locked in session with Eris all morning. It would seem your impostor is on trial for attempting to free Medea. A strange parallel certainly.' Simonetti sat forward, lacing his fingers. His eyes held hers and a look of deep concern crossed his face.

253

'What is it you can offer that makes you think the Domina will free Medea Contadino?'

Anea shrugged, then formed two words with her clever fingers.

An apology.

The walk through House Erudito was brisk. Simonetti followed the Myrmidon, who marched with an awkward gait. The archivist held up a lantern to light hurried footsteps. The candles had diminished in the small hours, lanterns burned up their oil. It was as if the whole of Demesne were subsiding into an abyss, foundations descending into night. They encountered no one.

'I suppose the Myrmidons are guarding the outer gates,' whispered Simonetti as if reading her thoughts. 'Erebus will have a score attending him in the Ravenscourt, of course.'

She nodded in response, hand never far from the blade on her hip, the other balled into a fist of impatience. The gate that separated House Erudito from the Central Keep lay ahead. Two Myrmidons stood close to a brazier, the low grumble of their conversation just audible.

'Oh dear,' said Simonetti. Anea didn't reply, marching toward them without pause. The Myrmidons saluted and she returned the gesture without breaking step, Simonetti walking apace with her.

'I feel as if I am somehow cheating death every time I cross paths with a Myrmidon,' said Simonetti, snatching a glance over his shoulder. 'I'm fairly certain I should be dead many times over.'

Nothing like tempting fortune, is there?

'I, ah, yes. I think I'll be quiet now.'

They were in the circular corridor of the keep, following the sweeping curve toward the great doors that led to the Ravenscourt above.

'What shall we do if . . .' Simonetti's words sputtered out like a flame. The vast white doors to the Ravenscourt were wide open, some impediment preventing them from swinging closed.

The Domina sat with her back to the white-painted wood.

The smear of crimson to one side of her shoulder told Anea everything she needed to know. There was much that was crimson in that moment. The Domina's robes, the tracery of broken blood vessels about her eyes, the trickle at the corner of her mouth. More of that deep red leaked from the channels between fingers pressed to the wound.

Anea removed her helmet, setting it down on the floor as she knelt before her old teacher.

Who did this?

'Why, you did.' The Domina managed a rueful smile. 'Or someone that looked like you.'

Anea turned to Simonetti, *Fetch a* dottore. *Anyone. Quickly.*

'Don't waste your time,' said the Domina, far beyond pale. Her eyes were dull, their motion sluggish. 'None of it was worth it, Anea. Not the money or the power. Not the *tinctura*. Nothing.'

Anea held the Domina's free hand, startled by how cold it was.

'At first I simply wanted to make you proud,' said the Domina, 'but then I resented you for spending so much time with those machines. With Virmyre. With Dino.'

I wanted to make you proud as well, signed Anea. *Remember when we spoke long into the night? We spoke of philosophy and politics. Republic and feudalism. Fears and sometimes hopes.*

'Sometimes the dream of an ideal is preferable to the ideal itself.'

The Domina's eyes were bright with tears now. The blood had pooled around her. 'Take the staff. You gave it to me long ago, before we put you in the oubliette . . .'

Echoes assailed them from within Demesne, distant yet terrible with the promise of approach. Anea sneaked a glance at the length of silver where it lay nearby. She frowned, unsure why she would need such a thing.

I have come for Medea. Is there any chance at all she might be saved?

The Domina shook her head. 'Hers will be the death that forces Lucien to war.

'No one has ever openly executed a member of the great houses,' muttered Simonetti. 'Not even the king.'

'Even now more Myrmidons march from the Datini estate, reinforcements for those we've lost in the recent months.'

More? Anea was aghast. *The Datini estate?*

'Go now, Aranea Oscuro Diaspora. Never forget who you are and what you have achieved. What you will achieve again.' The Domina dragged in a stuttering breath, forced a blood-rimed smile.

If we could just get you to a dottore.

'No.' Her eyes closed. 'Take the staff; you'll need it for the...'

Anea pressed her fingers into Russo's hand, but the warmth was long gone.

'We must go, my lady,' urged Simonetti in a soft voice. His hand rested on her shoulder, yet Anea could not feel it. The Myrmidon armour insulated her from recognition, from harm, from the gentle touch of a friend. It did not insulate her from grief, but that she would hide beneath the helm. She placed it on her head and picked up the silver staff.

Russo sat before her. Professore Russo, once the Domina of Landfall, betrayer of the Silent Queen.

'I'm afraid we really must go, my lady.' The agitation in Simonetti's voice was plain. They turned and unbarred the main gates to the Central Keep, taking many fearful moments to open the various locks. The sound of booted feet on flagstones edged closer. Light appeared, slipping into the corridor and falling on Russo, now a study in crimson, stark against the white wood of the interior doors.

Anea slipped outside, Simonetti waving her away.

'Go!' said the archivist.

She shook her head.

'I'll lock the gates and cause a distraction,' he whispered. The doors closed with a grating sound, shutting Anea off from the fate that awaited the archivist. She wondered what the Myrmidons would do when they found him beside the murdered Domina.

Russo. Russo had died, and the last vestiges of hope for Medea had died with her. Anea marched to the church, hearing the rain patter from the Myrmidon armour. She'd been holding on to another hope, more impossible than she could dare wish for. Perhaps she had disguised it, or else attired it in denial. More likely the hope had hidden among the many others she clung to, just a face in the crowd. The cold rain that fell on Santa Maria sluiced away her naivety. She had hoped to rid herself of the Domina yet somehow retain Russo. Erebus had taken them both from her, and Dino and Medea and her throne. Worse yet that she had no way to avenge herself on the usurper.

The silver staff in her hand was one more burden she didn't need.

31

Indignities of the Past

Eris left the scene of her crime, unable to speak or cry. Even the act of drawing breath had become a chore. The shock of the attack was a tight bodice constricting her lungs.

'I must get away from this place,' she whispered, voice cracked and fragile.

The entrances to the houses were closed. She drifted along the circular corridor from Prospero to Fontein, on to Erudito. Heavy oak doors with iron fittings and thick studs, all barred from the other side. Only House Contadino welcomed her, the gatehouse abandoned, doors ajar. She slipped through, expecting Myrmidons to accost her, but only deep shadows waited. The Domina's blood stained her hand like a velvet glove. The more she tried to wipe away the evidence the more obvious it became. Now both hands were slick with the Domina's murder.

'It wasn't murder,' she said, stumbling through the abandoned corridors of House Contadino. 'It wasn't.' On and on she wandered, an echo, a ghost, putting distance between herself and the dying woman. Another door opened before her, bloody fingertips smearing the wood. She blinked in the daylight, eyes aching after the oppressive gloom of Demesne. Footsteps sounded on gravel, breaking her dazed enchantment before she fell to her knees, bloodied hands held before her face.

'It wasn't murder,' she repeated, kneeling before the statue of Santa Maria at the centre of the rose garden. 'I only sought to defend myself. I never thought I'd use the stiletto. I never dreamed she'd attack me directly.'

The Saint kept her judgements to herself but Eris felt the accusation in the silence.

'I can't believe she came after me...' Eris looked away, keen to be spared the kindly gaze, stone eyes at once dead and all-seeing. The usual tangle of rose bushes threatened to spill from flower beds, over paths and up the walls. Perhaps in time the roses would infiltrate the building, consuming Demesne's every dark corner, shackling the terrors that lived here in thorns. It would be no bad thing if Demesne was lost from view for ever, hidden from the world by blooms of red and white.

'I meant to pull up the weeds, trim back the bushes.'

The Saint listened to her confession with a placid smile, the infant safe in her embrace.

'I'd hoped to return these gardens to their former glory.' Eris heard her voice, heard the babble of nonsense, continuing in spite of it. 'I suppose I hoped if I could get the rose gardens under control I might master some small part of Demesne.' She snorted a cynical laugh. 'As if anyone masters anything in this place.'

'I disagree.'

The voice came from behind, making Eris twist round before she'd gained her feet. She tripped, fell back, clutching the statue for support.

'I didn't hear you approach.' Her tone was accusatory. Viscount Datini shrugged. He stood with hands clasped in the small of his back, as ever. His doublet, britches and hose were a sombre grey accented with deep red. A fencing sword hung from one hip, an ornament and reminder of a prowess long departed.

'Just because I'm old doesn't mean I can't sneak up on a young woman confessing her sins.'

'Hardly the action of a gentleman.' Eris relinquished her hold on the statue, drawing herself up to her full height, frowning down her nose at the surly noble.

'Gentleman? Pah! I gave up the pretence of being a gentleman decades ago. I simply seek to survive as best I can.' The viscount eyed her bloodstained hands. 'Not unlike yourself, I see.'

'Was there something you wanted?' The words were at odds with the sneer on her lips. She needed to inform Simonetti and Isabella they could depart, free from retribution.

'I come here sometimes to think,' the viscount said by way of explanation. 'This isn't an ambush, child.'

Eris felt the lack of a weapon all the same.

'I need to be on my way. I need to find Simonetti.' She passed the stunted noble, feeling his dark eyes on her, the crisp grinding of gravel underfoot.

'You did a very good job of duping us,' he commended, 'all of us.'

She paused, turning to the old man with clenched and bloodied fists.

'You were the pretty face of the devil himself,' he continued. 'I wouldn't have been so keen to do anything I've done had I seen Erebus with my own eyes.'

'That's something we have in common at least.' Eris regarded her fingers, the way the blood stained the recesses of each nail, etched her knuckles in crimson. 'I was recruited by the Domina, trained by Dottore Allattamento.' She looked away, chagrin making a frown of her features. 'I was committed to the task before I knew who Erebus was. Or what he was.' She pulled the grey shawl tighter, bloodstains marring the perfect silk. Did anything of value remain unsullied in Demesne? 'They promised me my brother would be safe,' she said in a small voice. Eris looked past the viscount, back to the Saint clutching her newborn. 'They told me I'd be rich.'

'And yet here you are with barely a *denaro* to your name,' said Viscount Datini. 'What will you do now, child?'

Spots of rain fell among the roses, the skies a haze of smudged white.

'There's nothing I can do,' Eris replied. 'I must leave, and quickly. Erebus has released me once. He won't release me for this.' She held out her bloodstained hands as if this were explanation enough.

'The Domina? Or Allattamento?'

Eris said nothing.

'Come, child. You can tell me.'

She shook her head. Viscount Datini sniffed, piqued by her refusal. He brushed fluff from his doublet.

'And you'll flee to the countryside with only the clothes on your back,' he said after a pause. 'No family, little money, no friends.'

Eris nodded.

'That doesn't sound like much of a life, child.'

'It's not so different to the life I had before, and it's better than no life at all.'

The rain spotted down, unwilling to commit to either shower or deluge.

'Perhaps you'd like me to escort you into town?' The dark-eyed viscount held out a hand. It was as if he were no more than asking to dance at *La Festa*. 'I can assure you safe passage.' He took a step closer.

'You don't have any control over the Myrmidons,' countered Eris, suddenly weary of the conversation.

'I think you'll find I'm the new *capo*, child. One hundred Myrmidons are marching from my estate in the north to re-inforce Demesne even as we speak.'

'One hundred?'

Viscount Datini nodded, an infuriating smugness in the weathered lines of his face. 'Say what you like about the under-kin, but they breed not like the proverbial rabbit, but rather a hive of insects. I turned the Datini estate over to the Domina some years ago.'

'Small wonder the viscountess left you.'

Viscount Datini clasped his hands in the small of his back again and raised his chin, his lips thinning.

'I kept it from her for years, but she was always going to find out. Said I was a callous, beastly little man. She wanted to give the estate to her eldest son.'

'You mean your eldest son; he's yours too.'

'Perhaps.'

'And what did you receive in return for your estate?' asked Eris.

'Why this.' Viscount Datini gestured to the rose garden. 'House Contadino will be mine, renamed after my family. I will die with some vestige of success, some modicum of standing. Datini will no longer be a house minor.'

Eris struggled to comprehend the depth of the man's

261

ambition. Even now in his dotage it was a fierce undercurrent, a rip tide that might drown all of Landfall.

'I'd like you to escort me into the town now, please. Promise me you'll get word to Simonetti.'

'Very well.' Viscount Datini curled his mouth in a smile, but if it reached the sunken pits of his eyes Eris could not tell. 'There's just one thing I want in exchange.' Eris pulled her shawl about her more tightly, fearing the next words to fall from the viscount's sour lips. 'It would please me greatly if you'd accompany me to the hanging.'

The viscount required more than just an escort to the grim spectacle of Medea Contadino's death. He insisted they stop in the great hall of Contadino, where underkin servants waited on them. Eris was brought hot wine; her absent hunger was met with a meagre repast. She forced down mouthfuls, unsure when she might eat again. The viscount laid out his plans for the hall and the entire house: how he'd redecorate, the many staff he'd hire. His talent for monologue was given free rein, her sustained lack of interest scarcely abrading his enthusiasm. He rose from the table and offered an arm, leaving the room with faltering steps.

'The indignities of the past will be salved by the future.'

'Don't you think hanging Medea Contadino is one indignity too many?'

'Pah! Why should I?' The viscount blinked and gave a small shrug.

'She has children.'

'As do I, yet I'd wager no one would shed tears if I were to pass away.'

'Is it not enough her husband was murdered?'

The viscount stopped. They were in a hall leading to the far courtyard, gusting wind the only sound.

'My youngest sons were killed in the Verde Guerra. My wife has left me to join my eldest son in the south.' The viscount scowled. 'Did you know they let men lie with men in that place? A whole city of mindless fucking – artists, whores and so-called intellectuals. Is this the kingdom my sons gave their lives for? Is it? Is this what these bloody Orfani plan for us?'

The walk to the gallows was a silent one following the viscount's bitter rhetoric. Eris kept the detail of Sabatino's preferences to herself.

The gallows had not been constructed well. The timber was rough, the workmanship shoddy, made more so by the spectacle of the triumphal arch behind it.

'Of course, this isn't the original arch,' said the viscount, unable to resist lecturing Eris about Demesne. 'The old arch was far more decorative. Anea tore it down, saying it "bore too many stern, patriarchal faces" and that "people needed to see the Ravenscourt was open to all".' Eris wasn't sure if the viscount was speaking for her benefit or not. He seemed content to ramble. 'And so we ended up with this.'

She regarded the structure: not one, but in fact three lofty arches. Corbel turrets tapered to fine points, sitting either side of a steep roof, a wedge pointed at the sky. A profusion of dormer windows looked out, outnumbered by decorative shields in the varied colours of houses minor and major.

'She gave the stone away to the *cittadini*,' continued the viscount. 'Told them to build the foundations of new homes with it.'

Eris struggled not to roll her eyes. 'That sounds precisely like Anea Diaspora,' she replied, 'charitable and symbolic in one move.'

The wide chasm between Houses Prospero and Contadino had always been a thoroughfare of especial importance, terminating as it did at the doors to the King's Keep. They edged open, a sliver of darkness yawning wide.

'She wasted no time insisting we refer to it as the Central Keep after the king had passed.' The old man was recollecting darker times with a misplaced nostalgia.

'You miss the king,' said Eris. The viscount nodded, but did not meet her eye.

A dozen Myrmidons emerged from the Central Keep, the figure in their midst just a fleck of a person, a woman crushed, stripped of dignity.

'You can stop this,' said Eris to the viscount. 'You can be the man who stopped the war. They'll listen to you – you're the *capo*.'

'Do you really think Medea's survival will prevent Erebus from claiming dominion of Landfall? This is just the pretext; Medea's death is all the permission Duke Lucien will need. The council in San Marino will be outraged anyone could execute a member of the great houses so brazenly. Never mind Duke Fontein was assassinated, never mind Emilio Contadino lured into an ambush. Medea Contadino though, she'll rouse the fury of every *cittadino* and *nobile* who draws breath.'

'But why? Why seek war?'

'Erebus was Orfano once; I don't even begin to understand what he is now. Or his motives.'

'So you've allied yourself with a madman?'

'Only for as long as he lives.'

Medea walked the length of the road, passing through the shadow beneath the arch. Eris clasped her bloodstained hands together. The woman who stepped onto the platform could have been anyone: fisherman's wife, seamstress, *dottore*, lover, *professore*, friend, sister. Any one of them would have been reduced by the grime and hopelessness heaped on Medea Contadino. The Myrmidons had bound her hands, as if even the dream of escape still lingered. The noose swayed in the wind, timbers protesting in lieu of any *cittadino* now fled to the countryside.

'You're presiding over the murder of someone's mother.'

'Her children are welcome to come and avenge her.' He patted the blade that hung from his hip. Eris cast her gaze at the cobbles near her feet. She wanted to clamp her hands to her ears, but there was no need. Medea Contadino seemed determined to pass from the world without protest or pleading. She would not give them the satisfaction, this at least was something she still controlled. Eris couldn't bear to watch, eyes shut tight, the words on her lips ones of prayer.

'May Santa Maria watch over your soul and—' Her concentration was broken by the heavy footsteps of a Myrmidon presenting himself to the viscount. She glanced up and saw Medea swinging from the rope, then closed her eyes, knowing the sight of it with be with her always.

'Thank you,' said the viscount, taking the offered parchment. Eris watched the Myrmidon salute and march away. The note was discarded to the air, fetched away by the wind.

'The Domina is dead, Allattamento is in the oubliette.' The viscount looked at her for the first time since they'd left House Contadino. 'Have you no one to go to?'

'I had hoped to be reunited with Simonetti.'

'Ah, that is unfortunate.' The words were marred with insincerity. She'd played into his hands by uttering the archivist's name.

'Simonetti is suspected of helping Anea escape from Demesne. We are keeping him confined until we have had sufficient opportunity to establish his innocence.'

The viscount looked about the derelict town. Smoke drifted from a lone chimney, product of an unattended fire forgotten in the exodus. The corpse of Medea Contadino swung in the breeze, the gallows wood creaking.

'And, in my role as *capo*, I think it much too dangerous for a woman to be abroad on her own.' He gestured to the Myrmidons standing around the gallows. Four approached. 'These Myrmidons will escort you back – for your own safety, you understand.'

'There's really no need,' said Eris, struggling to conceal her panic.

'Pah. There's every need.' The viscount smiled. 'Lord Erebus is not finished with you.'

Eris wept during the long walk to her apartment in House Fontein, her endurance drained as surely as her determination. Her best guesses and second guesses exhausted her. Erebus remained one move ahead in a game perceived dimly, if at all. Her only remaining companions were frustration and regret, following her back to House Fontein like taunting shades.

The four Myrmidons escorting her said nothing. As the Silent Queen she had ignored the soldiers as a matter of principle. Easier not to speak to those who unnerve you, she admitted to herself. These Myrmidons were not threatening, no more than men in armour carrying weapons tended to be.

They walked at a respectful distance yet close enough to protect her if needed. The longer she walked the less she felt like a prisoner. She struggled with the many stairs, the events of the recent week weighing on her, a catechism of weariness. She felt the responses in every sinew and tendon. Eris approached her apartment. Two Myrmidons took up positions at each end of the corridor, the remaining two stood either side of the door. The relief she felt proved short-lived as the door swung open.

It was not Simonetti and Isabella who waited but three underkin, kneeling on the floor. The low table in front of the couch had been pressed into service as a workbench of sorts, currently lost beneath a bolt of crimson cloth. They nodded as she entered, furtive smiles. The first possessed mismatched eyes and chitin fingernails. Another was hunched and bulky beneath shapeless grey robes; that the smallest finger from each hand was missing did not impair her sewing. The last was afflicted with mandibles and two sets of eyes, one pair above the other. He sat on the floor with the stumps of legs splayed out before him. The underkin had banked the fire, and a kettle sat in the hearth, teapot issuing a thin wisp of steam.

'Hello,' said Eris, her voice shaky. For the first time that she could remember she felt something other than fear. Was this safety?

'Not long now. Your vestments will be finished before midnight.'

'Vestments?' It was then Eris saw it: a tailor's dummy in the corner draped in the robes of the Domina. The dark stain at the sternum was a bloody shadow on the fabric. Eris looked from the dummy dressed in the Domina's robes to the bolt of crimson fabric on the table.

'Erebus has made me the new Domina,' Eris said with cruel certainty.

'Why, yes,' said the hunchback with a smile.

Eris was much too hot, sickness uncoiling in her gut. She could not escape, she would not escape, not while Erebus toyed with her future. The edges of her vision went dark as panic overwhelmed her. Her legs would not respond. Darkness took her before she collapsed to the floor.

32

San Marino

Giovanni Terminiello opened the door of the Terminus Inn and looked up into the familiar if thoroughly concealed face of Durante Corvino. Both rider and horse were in equally poor condition, not far from exhausted.

'Back so soon?'

'Seems that way,' said Corvino, pulling back his hood. He narrowed his eyes and stared the twenty miles to Demesne. Not much had changed besides the melting of snow. 'Any trouble?'

'Heard of plenty, but can't be sure any of it's true.' Giovanni flashed an anxious look toward the town. 'Why don't you come in out of the cold?' He smiled and opened the door a little wider.

'Need to stable the horses,' said Corvino as he dismounted, but Giovanni wasn't listening.

'Make up a bed,' the innkeeper shouted over one shoulder. 'Durante's home.'

'We'll need more than just one,' said another voice from beyond the door.

'Ah, my lord.' Giovanni bowed. 'Apologies, I didn't see you.'

Delfino's mount swished her tail and snorted with impatience.

'*Porca miseria*, don't start with the titles.' Delfino dismounted and pressed his hands to the small of his back. 'I'm not sure I'll ever be able to sit down again. My arse!'

'I wanted to thank you for that generous gift of moonleaf you left us last time you were here,' said Giovanni, clearly hopeful there might be a repeat of the same generosity.

'My pleasure,' replied Delfino through gritted teeth. He flashed a sour look at his *aiutante*, who removed his veil, revealing the deep scars beneath. 'I'm trying to give it up, on the orders of my beloved.'

'Ah,' Giovanni smiled, 'the things we do—'

'For love. Quite.' Delfino threw his cloak over one shoulder, staring back down the road they had taken. It was a misty day and Landfall's rolling terrain conspired to keep what he hoped to see concealed.

'So the two beds, is it?' asked Giovanni.

'Best make up all of them,' said Corvino leading his mount away to the stables. Delfino followed.

'Giovanni seems to think this is your home.'

'Was. For nine months.' Corvino crossed to the other side of his mount, putting the horse between himself and his master. He resumed brushing the dappled grey, whispering soothing words with each stroke. Delfino followed, a crease of curiosity at his brow, unable to form the question he was desperate to ask. The stable was dimly lit, the smell of fresh straw competing with old leather and the scent of horse.

'You know what the *cittadini* call people from the oubliette?' asked Corvino when it was clear Delfino had no intention of abandoning the subject.

Delfino shook his head.

'Not the ones thrown there, but the ones born there.'

'I don't know what they're called,' said Delfino. His voice was quiet in the confines of the stable, anxious of breaching some unspoken taboo.

'They call them underkin. The Majordomo's cast-offs, the king's mistakes.' Corvino kept brushing the horse, not meeting Delfino's eyes. 'No one knows how many lived down there or how they survived. And those that have lived down there—'

'Can't remember,' said Delfino.

'Because of the waters.' Corvino nodded, then resumed brushing his horse.

'And now Erebus has forged them into an army.'

'Seems likely,' admitted Corvino.

'How did you escape?'

Corvino set down the brush and crossed the stables to an empty trough, perching on one corner. He pulled his sword from the sheath and a whetstone appeared in his right hand. The scrape of stone on steel provided a chilling backdrop for hard words told unwillingly.

'Was the night they threw Lucien down there. Dino rescued him, of course. Anea too. Lucien had a knife on him. Things might have gone very differently if not for that small fact. They left without a second thought and left the rope for all who dared to use it. I was the second of the underkin to climb up.'

'And the first?'

'Didn't know his name back then,' said Corvino, tracing the scars along his cheek, 'but I do now. Marchetti.'

'And that was when you came here?'

'Not at first.' Corvino swallowed and focused his attention on the sword, continuing to work the edge with the whetstone. A glimmer of guilt crossed his features, but also anger. 'Stumbled across the Majordomo, all cut to ribbons and missing hands and legs. Thought he was dead. Anyone would. He persuaded us to help him, begged Marchetti to take him to the oubliette. I helped at first. Santa Maria forgive me.' Corvino sighed. 'But I wasn't going back down there, back to the darkness. I ran. I ran for my life. It was all chaos that night, fighting and screaming. I didn't stop running until the sun came up and collapsed the first place I found shelter. I woke the next day in this very stable, and it was Giovanni who gave me a square meal. I could barely speak. Couldn't use a fork much less a knife. They taught me to be a human, Giovanni and Rocco and their grandfather. They taught me to be a child. That's what it is to be an underkin. You're not even human down there. No one is. They helped me choose a name, and it was good for a time. But I was rash and young—'

'You're still young,' said Delfino.

'Younger. I ran away. Then you come along. Was you that taught me to read and to fight, taught me to be a man.'

'I've always known you were different since I first met you,' said Delfino, awed by the sudden confession. 'I never thought twice about it, not really, but I never imagined you had escaped from the oubliette.'

'Born there.' Corvino ceased dragging the stone across the blade and looked to the stable doors. 'Some underkin roam the countryside, maybe even have children in the forests. I suppose they all serve the Majordomo now.' He shrugged. 'Erebus, or whatever name he's picked this year.'

'Why are you telling me now?' asked Delfino.

'Not sure,' said Corvino sadly. 'Just wanted someone to know the whole of it. Just in case we die when we retake the castle. I always tried to do right – by you, by Lucien, Rafaela too.' Corvino pulled off his gloves and regarded the black chitin nails. 'You always treated me as a human. Not many folks do that. Thank you.'

'The things we do for love,' replied Delfino with a broad grin, trying to lift the maudlin tone. 'Anyone would have done the—'

'No. That's where you're wrong.' Corvino slipped his gloves back on. 'People don't always do things for love. Most times they do them for anger or fear or to make themselves feel a bit superior. A lot of folk rarely do anything for love. That's why I followed you all these years.'

Delfino struggled for a response, shocked at the pain that laced each word falling from Corvino's lips.

'So when you say "the things we do for love", well, that means something. Even the times you say it in jest it means something.' Corvino stood and sheathed the sword. The conversation, much like the blade, was put away. 'Let's see what's for lunch.'

Delfino nodded and followed his *aiutante* through the stable doors. 'In the whole nine years I've known you I've never heard you say more than a score of words at a time.'

'Hell of a thing,' replied Corvino.

'Now you sound like Nardo.' Delfino snorted a laugh.

'Well, don't tell him. There he is.' True enough, emerging from the mist on horseback was the gruff *capo* of House Albero. And he was not alone. Several riders followed, wraith-like in travelling cloaks and the mist's embrace.

'Delfino. Corvino.' Nardo nodded to both of them and rolled the stiffness from his shoulders. 'Came up to make sure you do right by Duke Lucien. I worry you can't find your arse with both hands.'

'That's why I have Corvino,' admitted Delfino. Nardo frowned. 'That didn't sound the way I imagined it would.' The scout cleared his throat. 'How many?' He nodded past Nardo to the column of cavalry.

'Huh. Seventy, give or take.'

'It's a start,' said Corvino.

'I thought you said things were only going to get worse,' said Delfino.

'That I did,' said Nardo, 'worse for Erebus, I reckon.'

The sun was setting when Lucien appeared on the muddy road. He had the look of the wolf about him, sly and watchful. His cloak was spattered with gore at one corner, and his black hair was loose about his face.

'I was beginning to worry you'd become lost, my lord,' said Delfino.

'It's always a pressing concern for a damn fool duke. Fortunately I have about a hundred scouts with me. They gave me a few pointers.'

Few at first, then in greater and greater numbers, men on horseback emerged from the mist. The soft percussion of hoofbeats sounded all around them.

'A hundred scouts?' said Delfino. 'But that must be all of them?'

Lucien slid from his horse and landed lightly, throwing back the cloak to reveal the copper drake clasp at his breast and the sword at his hip. His grin was full of braggadocio, and Delfino couldn't fault him for it.

'Ruggeri must have been spitting blood,' said Corvino, clasping Lucien's hand.

'Not exactly.' Duke Marino looked over his shoulder. 'He bought ten horses for the men who didn't own them. Said he didn't agree with what we were doing but appreciated why we had to come. I'm not sure there's a single horse left in the whole damn town. I picked up a few along the route, from Elemosina mainly.'

'So much for marching soldiers on foot,' said Delfino with a smile.

'Light cavalry versus heavy infantry ... I don't know,' said Corvino. Lucien favoured him with a dark look.

'He has a point,' said Delfino. 'We've never fought such a battle before.'

Nardo made his way through the press of bodies, and Lucien caught him in a rough hug.

'Good to see you, boy.'

'It's been a while since anyone called me that.' Lucien grinned. 'Let's get inside. We need to plan this thing if it's to have a chance in hell of working.'

'Reckon it needs more than a plan,' said Nardo.

'It'll need wine,' said Delfino, 'and plenty of it.'

The night saw riders arrive from Schiavone, Allattamento and Del Toro.

'I knew we could do it,' said Lucien, topping up his wine.

'Fewer numbers but welcome all the same,' added Nardo.

'We still don't know how to draw them out,' said Corvino. He leaned against the wall with arms folded, veil tied across his face. An old barn had been requisitioned for the council of war; iron braziers had been loaded up with wood, and an old door had been pressed into service as a table.

'Planning skirmishes on old timber,' grunted Nardo.

'Better than sketching our plans in the mud,' said Lucien. The two men formed the core of the council, being the most senior according to rank and experience. Delfino made suggestions where he could and Corvino added a dash of cold reality when Lucien's optimism threatened to make things fantastic.

Nardo began stuffing a pipe with moonleaf.

Delfino squeezed his eyes shut and clenched his hands into fists. 'Is there any chance you could smoke that outside?'

'Huh.' Nardo finished tamping down the moonleaf. 'Getting a bit precious in your old age, eh Delfino?'

The scout forced a smile and gnawed on a heel of brown

bread. Nardo crossed to the door and paused, pipe in hand. 'I'll check on the men and make sure the fires aren't too big.'

Lucien nodded and gave thanks.

'Going to be a struggle without lances,' added Corvino.

'That's one thing I have in hand.' Lucien smiled, happy to have a counter to Corvino's repeated dourness. 'The men have been going out in small parties to search for wood. Even if we can't find all we need we'll still have the advantage of fighting from the saddle.'

'Won't be much use if they're inside Demesne.'

Lucien circled the table and stood before Corvino. 'Perhaps you might make some suggestions that are worth a shit, instead of pouring cold water on anything that offers a glimmer of hope.'

'Just saying—'

'Well don't!' shouted Lucien.

Corvino shrugged, then turned to Delfino. 'I'll check on the horses.'

'I think that would be good. Help Nardo if you see him.'

The scout slipped through the door with barely a sound. Lucien circled the table and stared at the patchwork map of parchment they had cobbled together. He rested both hands on the table and let his head slump forward.

'I don't remember your *aiutante* being such a miserable *figlio di puttana*,' said Lucien without looking up. 'When did he turn into such a pain in the arse?'

'He's doing what I pay him for,' replied Delfino.

'Sapping morale?'

'Keeping us grounded.' Delfino poured some wine for the duke and then himself. 'If we can't draw them out then we have a siege. In winter. And I've a feeling we'll starve before they do.'

Lucien sighed and took the battered mug, casting his gaze around. 'I think Dino stayed here when he first joined Margravio Contadino for the Verde Guerra. He said, even at that young age, that he was struck how no one seemed to have the faintest clue what they were doing.'

'That sounds exactly like the Verde Guerra,' admitted Delfino.

'What should I do?'

Delfino opened empty hands, gave a shrug.

The door creaked open and Nardo entered, a grim look on his grizzled face. Another man entered behind, Corvino following.

'Dirigente Romanucci.' Lucien smiled. 'Come to join the war effort?'

'More of a messenger, I'm afraid.' The large man took a breath before speaking, and Delfino knew the tidings were grave.

'We've had word Myrmidons were seen marching down from an estate in the north.'

'Marco?' said Delfino, none could miss the desperation in his voice.

Romanucci shook his head. 'I'm afraid they came from your father's estate.'

'How many Myrmidons?' asked Lucien.

'A hundred,' said Romanucci. 'All armed with halberds. They'll be hard work for cavalry.'

Lucien sat down and released a slow sigh. 'A hundred,' he repeated with a bitter laugh. 'What in Nine Hells do I do now?'

'There's something else,' said Drago Romanucci. He lowered his gaze with an expression between anger and sorrow on his broad face.

'What's happened?' said Delfino. The *dirigente* was rarely subdued, but all swagger was gone from the man.

'It's Medea. She was caught helping Anea trying to retake the throne.'

'Anea was trying to what?' Lucien stood up.

'This whole time we've been played by an impostor,' said Romanucci.

'Drago.' Delfino laid a gentle hand on the man's shoulder. 'What happened?'

'They executed her. Medea that is. They hanged her outside the triumphal arch.'

Delfino stared at Lucien and watched the duke's face contort, from shock to anger and on to curiosity.

'What of Anea?'

'I don't know, my lord. Rumours are she tried to rescue Medea.'

'She might have been caught during the attempt,' said Delfino.

'And Anea was usurped?' Lucien shook his head.

'For months, they say, since before I brought Dino to you.'

'We have to go. We can't spare a moment.' Lucien was almost out the door when Delfino called to him.

'We don't have enough men, my lord.'

'Men?' Lucien's eyes glittered in the brazier light. 'Men? They're going to kill my sister? I'm going to slaughter every fucker I lay my hands on.'

33

With a Trail of Footprints

The Sisters of Santa Maria refused to open the doors to a Myrmidon. Only Disciple Agostina's curiosity overcame her reluctance. A Myrmidon carrying the Domina's silver staff was a strange sight indeed.

'I hardly think one Myrmidon is a threat,' said Agostina. Once through the vestibule the Myrmidon found herself greeted by two dozen sisters bearing knives. The doors of the church boomed closed, a puddle of rainwater collecting at the Myrmidon's feet. She knelt down, setting the silver staff on the floor with reverent care; the helm followed. The sisters whispered in surprise at this unmasking, but Agostina simply nodded.

'I was unaware you had left the safety of the church.'

When Anea signed she did so with head bowed, remaining on her knees. Perhaps the sisters thought she did so out of piety, but in truth it was exhaustion that kept her so.

I went to beg the Domina to release Medea.

Agostina took a step closer; a gesture saw twenty-four knives vanish into sleeves.

'What did the Domina say?' asked the disciple.

The Domina did not say anything. Anea sighed. *The Domina is dead.*

Anea looked up into the faces of the sisters, the veiled and unveiled, those who cherished hope and those who merely prayed for it.

There is nothing I can do. Erebus means to kill Medea to precipitate war with Lucien.

'There must be something we can do.' Agostina turned to her sisters, all silent with weary resignation.

I failed to rescue her from imprisonment, and I was too late seeking the Domina's help. Medea would never have been captured if I had not been lured out to meet the Herald.

Anea released the clasps on the breastplate, which clattered to the floor by her knees. The sisters flinched as the sound echoed through the church. The armour had been an encumbrance Anea could bear for a small period of time; the sisters' disappointment would prove a much greater burden. She rose to her feet, head down, tired to her very bones. The press of bodies parted before her. Only when she had reached the baths did she let herself cry.

The church, always a bastion of serenity, was undone as surely as if sappers had dug beneath the foundations. There was no chamber that had not subsided with the news of Medea's fate; no alcove that didn't shudder with the dread; collapse threatened every doorway. The kitchens were consumed with the low murmur of consolation, the nave filled with silent prayers.

Anea did her best to avoid the sisters. Sleep would not come to her, the simple act of curling up in bed offered no rest, despite the weariness of her limbs. After a fitful hour she sat up on the narrow cot, sharpening a knife and thinking of the many ways she would kill both Erebus and the impostor. Anea suspected she would need a larger weapon to end the horror in Ravenscourt. Could he even be killed? she wondered. Had his biology elevated him from the finite? Had longevity excluded him from mortality?

Anea ran a whetstone across the knife, remembering a time when he had been but a tall man in decrepit robes, an absence of colour, of tone, of personality. As the Majordomo he had become not just the voice of their ruler, but his representative. Now the Majordomo bore the name of a god and demonstrated similar power.

How can anyone rescue us from this darkness? The Domina's words, spoken in the oubliette. Perhaps the question had been rhetorical, perhaps Russo had petitioned her for a miracle.

'This all feels so unreal.' Agostina had appeared in the doorway on silent feet. She looked down at the floor, where the remains of both the clay jug and the wine glass lay in shattered pieces.

Sneaking up on armed people is a very bad idea.

'We have news of Medea. She ... They ...' It hardly needed saying. Agostina's eyes filled with tears.

I broke into Demesne itself to rescue her. She was my friend, my ally. Anea stood up, closing with the woman until there was barely space between them to sign. *Marchetti is gravely wounded, Virmyre broken with exhaustion. If you have any suggestions now is the time to voice them.*

The disciple took a step back. 'I'm sorry,' she said finally. 'I thought ...' Agostina looked down at the floor and shook her head. 'I thought and I hoped and I prayed that you'd rescue her. Now I feel like those prayers were in vain. It's not just that we've lost Medea, I feel like I've lost Santa Maria too.'

'I was wondering when you would reappear, Highness.'

Anea found Virmyre sat up in bed as she pushed open the door. *You look terrible.*

'And you, my dear, are a shining exemplar of health.'

Anea shrugged.

'They tell me you entered Demesne. Alone.' The last word loaded with disapproval. Anea nodded, slumping into the armchair beside his bed.

'Couldn't think of anything more damn foolish to do while I was unconscious, I suppose?'

I had trouble sleeping.

'So you thought you'd take the Myrmidon armour from the old *sanatorio* and infiltrate the Central Keep?'

Anea shrugged. *I get bored easily.*

'Yes, it seems that way.' He paused to take a sip of water, the movement slow and awkward.

'Is it done?'

Anea nodded. *They hanged her while I was inside Demesne. I was too late.*

Virmyre let that revelation settle in before he spoke again. Medea had never been a close friend but they'd always shared common goals, espoused the same values. A mutual yet quiet admiration had existed.

'Did you discover anything new while you were inside?'

Simonetti was still alive, though I fear he may have given his life so that I could escape.

'Unfortunate. Though I can't imagine Erebus will be overly concerned with the condition of his libraries.'

The Domina is dead.

'Russo?'

Anea nodded. *I think the impostor killed her. Why she did is a mystery. I had hoped I might persuade the Domina to join us and free Medea.*

Virmyre pressed fingertips to his brow and rubbed slowly. 'Perhaps you should finally give some consideration to leaving with the sisters. They intend to depart tomorrow.'

I am not leaving Demesne. I will have my revenge on Erebus, and his impostor too.

'No one can say you didn't try, Anea.'

I am not leaving. Not after we have lost so much, and so many.

'You could be at the coast in two or three weeks.'

Anea glowered at the old man. *The Domina gave me a parting gift*, she signed, keen to change the subject. *The silver staff.*

'She was still alive when you found her?'

I held her hand as she bled to death. Her fingers were so cold. Like stone.

'How was she?'

Filled with regret. It seems to be the fashion lately.

They sat in silence for a while. No words could sweeten the loss. Anea blinked and blinked again, resisting the deep lull of slumber, the jerk and twitch following the sensation of falling.

She opened her eyes, unsure how long they had remained closed. Virmyre was asleep, settled down beneath thick blankets. A candle stood amid a pool of spilled wax on a chipped saucer. The golden flame remained constant and would do so for many hours to come. Eventually it would burn down to a blackened wick drowning in translucence. The flame would flicker and vanish without a sound, just as Medea had.

How can anyone rescue us from this darkness? Russo's words again. Anea imagined there had been desperation in her tone, a plea from the lost. The Silent Queen stood, pausing only to press her forehead to Virmyre's. What use a departing kiss from someone with no lips? She smoothed the veil over her mandibles, wondering if the assassin had recovered.

Marchetti had not woken. His cell bore the scent of sickness; a sheen of perspiration made his face waxy, his veil damp and clinging. She took a moment to wipe his brow, smoothing back the locks of hair plastered to his face. His forehead was hot to the touch, a feverish heat much like her anger. The scar through the assassin's eye appeared more vivid than she remembered. Anea turned to footsteps sounding in the hall.

'I've come to change the dressing.' Sister Consolata stood in the doorway, unwilling to meet Anea's eyes. She fussed with prayer beads and chewed her lip. Anea stepped to one side and gestured for her to begin.

'I should warn you.' Sister Consolata paused. 'We don't expect him to recover. He's very weak.'

Thank you for trying.

'I will pray for him.' Consolata looked at Anea, a pensive look in her eye. 'Is it true he killed Margravio Contadino?'

What?

'I heard that Marchetti led the underkin before the formation of the Myrmidons. He led the raids against Demesne.' Consolata faltered. 'He must have been present when Margravio Contadino was murdered.'

Anea exited the cell, struggling to breathe, her worst fears realised. It wasn't enough that Marchetti had ambushed Emilio Contadino; the suffering he had inflicted on Medea and her children was too much to bear. A hand reached out to the wall to steady herself.

Sister Consolata stood in the doorway of the cell. 'I'm sure he wasn't directly responsible.'

Anea glowered at her and fled, struggling to make sense of Marchetti's changing loyalty and the things he'd done for Erebus.

*

She dressed for night in shawl and furs, descended the stairs with reverent care. The nave was watched over by sisters bearing lanterns and knives, who nodded a greeting and continued their vigil. Anea nodded back and slipped outside. The temperature had dropped with the setting of the sun, a crisp chill that made her breath steam on the air. Flakes of snow fell from starless skies, white on black.

Perhaps each flake is a failed prayer to Santa Maria, she thought. Tomorrow they'll melt or be stamped underfoot.

The streets were covered with a blanket of white, a sheet pulled over the corpse of the town. Anea marched toward the gallows, footprints in the virgin white following her. Medea Contadino still dangled from the noose, a pathetic trophy, a grotesque expression of power. Snow had begun to collect on her shoulders and the top of her head, her limbs damp rags. No semblance remained of arms that had once held a husband or cradled children with love. Where were the hands that had tended to roses and signed letters in flowing script? Not these frigid claws that emerged from grimy sleeves.

Anea spent some time with only a halo of anger protecting her from the night's chill. Medea Contadino was just the latest in a series of deaths, deaths that Anea could not bear to be responsible for.

'Not the best weather for a funeral, Highness.'

Anea turned on her heel, almost losing her footing on the snow-slicked cobbles. She frowned at Virmyre, who looked back with the same steady pale blue eyes she had always known. The *professore* had dragged himself across town after her, guided by the trail of her footprints, no doubt. His chest rose and fell with the effort. He was leaning on the silver staff for support.

'I took the liberty of venturing out of bed to take a look at this old thing. Do you know that the base of the staff is as wide as both of my fingers?' He held up his hand and wiggled two digits at her. Anea could not reply, her hands numb with chill. What interest had she in old relics when Emilio Contadino's killer slept just a few rooms away from her cell?

'I only mention it, Highness, because it would seem to be a good fit for the depression in the chamber.'

Anea shook her head. *What?*

'The chamber with the sarcophagi. The disc of metal with the hollow at the centre.'

Anea stepped closer, feet crunching in the snow. She wrung her hands together, willing warmth and feeling into her extremities.

'The staff,' continued Virmyre, 'has a tiny aperture in the base. It was obstructed with dust, but I think I've cleaned it sufficiently.'

Anea's mind raced with questions, struggling to understand why the staff was of such interest to Virmyre.

'And the top is loose. I always thought the staff strange. Only now I realise it is nothing short of miraculous. Why create such a perfect object without decoration?'

Unless the staff is not decorative at all, but shaped by function.

Virmyre nodded, clearly revisiting the old pleasure of lecturing a favourite pupil. 'This depression reveals a section that slides up. The tip of the staff houses a battery of tiny optics. Extraordinary really. Craftsmanship the like of which I've never seen.'

The craftsmanship of something like an artefact. Anea felt as if the ground beneath her feet had shifted. The importance of what Virmyre was saying almost shook her free of her senses. *Virmyre, you found the artefact.*

'No, Highness. That would be you.'

Anea shook her head. *What?*

'You found the artefact. A long time ago, before Lucien set off to found San Marino. You knew the staff was important so you gave it to someone trustworthy for safekeeping.'

The Domina.

'And keep it safe she did, and made it part of her attire, the trappings of her office.'

And then I forgot the staff might be important.

'Because you were more interested in medicine and improving the lives of the *cittadini*. We had no time for this.' Virmyre eyed the staff.

And then I forgot that I had ever given it to the Domina. Another memory lost to the oubliette. Anea shook her head. *Giving the Domina that title was the worst decision I ever made.*

'Don't call her that,' said Virmyre. 'She was Russo when you gave the staff to her, just as she was Russo when she gave it back.'

Anea eyed the silver staff. *Can it really be the artefact?*

'I don't know for sure, Highness. I suppose we should apply scientific rigour and conduct a trial.'

What do you propose?

'Well, jamming the staff into the hole might work.'

That is a singular definition of 'scientific rigour'.

'So you'll stop mourning in the snow and accompany me?'

I do so love to spend time in the dark underground.

'Sarcasm at this time of night, Highness?'

I have been keeping exceptionally bad company of late. It seems sarcasm is contagious.

Virmyre encircled her with his arms, the action made awkward by his grip on the staff. Anea returned the embrace and for a single moment she could forget being Orfano, forget her deformity, forget the burdens of shame, guilt and despair. Even the soundless howl of her fury abated in that moment.

'For someone so fearsomely intelligent I really am surprised you visited the gallows. You could have been caught.' Virmyre's voice was a deep rumble in his chest. She took a step back and began to sign.

It will be me up there next, and no one will know whether to mourn me or celebrate my passing. My reputation has been blighted beyond recognition. Perhaps Simonetti would write a fair account for historians to argue over, but he may well be dead himself.

'There is one solution, Highness.'

Which is?

'Stay alive to write history yourself.'

They began to walk back to the church, retracing the footprints in the white.

Do you remember when you took me to the cemetery?

'Of course.'

Anea took the silver staff and imagined the horrors she could unleash against Erebus and his hateful army of Myrmidons.

This is the hairpin, the sliver of metal I need to strike back.

34

Consequences

Eris stirred, eyes fluttering. Unnatural faces looked down, none lacking for kindness despite their strange features. Had she been asleep? Had she fallen? Why was she on the floor? The underkin lifted Eris before she had a chance to ask, fussing and fanning her, offering words of concern. A Myrmidon filled the doorway, departing only when she had recovered. Eris stared at her bedroom with glassy eyes, trying to make sense of everything: the susurrus of concerned whispering, bright candles shedding golden light, all things neat, the room itself immaculate.

'Such a contrast to Demesne,' she slurred. 'Every corridor a bad memory, every hall a regret.'

Her chamber had been transformed, a refuge attended by the broken and the twisted. She felt outside herself, like an enchantment from the old tales, soul set free of the body.

'Perhaps rest is in order, Domina Eris.' An underkin smiled with a mouth full of jet-black teeth.

They removed her clothes with dreamlike ease, and all the while she felt an acute awareness of her difference. Every helper bore traces of corruption, marks of otherness, yet if they resented her for being human they did not show it. Eris made eye contact only when necessary, thanking them in a dazed and quiet voice. She was bathed, dried and put to bed with utmost tenderness. Clean sheets and a warm room conspired to lull her asleep, even as thoughts turned to the many underkin, reverent and obedient in equal measure. Not so her next visitor, passing through her chamber door as the clock chimed the hour, six peals amid the deep hush of pre-dawn.

Eris woke to the sound of weeping. Her limbs were curled about one another, sheets forming a warm cocoon. An unfamiliar weight pressed down at the end of the bed. Eris lifted her head to find Isabella sitting, yet bent double, one hand pressed to her eyes.

'Isabella?'

The girl was undone with grief, immobile with it. The majority of candles in the chamber had been extinguished. Isabella turned, pulling her legs onto the bed. Something terrible lurked behind her bloodshot eyes, a sad smile over clenched teeth.

'You took him from me.' Isabella shuffled forward, knees now either side of Eris's legs, the blankets pinning her limbs to the mattress beneath. 'You could have saved him, could have spared him.'

No trace of peaceful slumber remained. Eris was awake, not simply aware, but present and aghast. 'Isabella, what are you doing?'

'You took him from me.' The maid moved further up the bed, ungainly on all fours. There was something in her right hand. Eris fought to escape, confined by the blankets. The maid pushed down with one hand.

'Just stay still now. This won't hurt. Much.'

'Wait! I don't understand.'

Isabella was astride her chest, knees pressing down on her arms. 'You took him from me.' Isabella held up the stiletto, just inches from her face, inches from her eyes. Eris pressed herself against the mattress, inching away from the metal spike held to her face.

'Who? Who did I take?'

'Paolo Allattamento.' The fury in Isabella's eyes cooled. 'You had him thrown in the oubliette.'

Eris shook her head as best she could. 'Not me, Erebus.'

'By your design. Your testimony saw him cast down.'

Eris had no answer.

'It was you!' And for one awful second Eris believed the maid intended to gouge out her eyes. The stiletto point hovered, a threat that filled her vision.

'I simply told the truth.'

'I know,' whispered the maid. 'I was there, hiding up on the gallery. I heard every word. You sent my poor Paolo to the oubliette.'

The stiletto was so close Eris struggled to focus on it. Her entire existence balanced on that dark blur, the woman holding it shaking with each word.

'You, you of all people in Landfall. You, who lost your brother. It wasn't my Paolo who let him die. It was Erebus.'

'I know,' breathed Eris. One slip or sudden move and she would feel inches of steel slide into her brain.

'You took him from me.' Isabella was a ruin of tears, wild-haired and trembling with fury.

'I can get him back for you,' breathed Eris.

'Like Medea Contadino?' Isabella's disgust was tangible.

'We can get him back, out of the oubliette. But I need your help.'

'What?' The stiletto edged back from her face by the slightest of margins.

'There are robes in my sitting room. The Domina's robes. You could take them, command the Myrmidons to free the *dottore*.'

Isabella knelt upright, disbelief in the tight set of her shoulders and the wordless question that parted her lips.

'Go and rescue your man,' said Eris. 'Save him and keep him and love him.' If you can, she wanted to add. 'You can be the Domina for all I care. I simply want to leave.'

'I'll take your robes, but you can keep the title,' scowled Isabella. The stiletto point was still directed toward Eris.

'So you and the *dottore* ... ?' Eris pushed herself up from the blankets, rubbing feeling into the creases of her elbows. 'This whole time?' It made a certain kind of sense. He'd always favoured the woman with smiles and a kind word.

The maid nodded. 'He's the only *nobilii* who was ever kind to me. So I was kind to him in return.'

Eris snorted a laugh, which she cut off when Isabella glowered at her. The point of the stiletto rose a few inches.

'Not in the way you're thinking. I simply listened when he was troubled. I dined with him when he was lonely. He renounced his family some time ago. He has no one else.'

'Viscount Datini has always been a keen patron.'

'Paolo enjoyed his money but never shared his views or ambitions.'

'And you?'

'I wanted to be someone, someone he could turn to.' She sucked in a breath, wiped at her face. A glimmer of a smile touch her lips. 'And to my surprise he treated me as an equal. I'm not so naive as to ignore his failings, but I'll not let you take him from me. He's all I have.'

The maid slipped from the end of the bed, backing away one uncertain foot at a time.

'I'm unarmed,' said Eris proffering empty palms. Isabella continued retreating until her back pressed against the door.

'Unarmed or not, I wouldn't trust you if you were the last person in Landfall, human or otherwise.'

The maid slipped through the door without a backward glance. The wood rattled in the frame as it slammed shut. A click of the lock confirmed Eris was a prisoner in her apartment, in her bedchamber. She rose from the bed and tried the handle, but the door remained closed.

'Well, that's the last time I give a woman a blade to protect herself,' she muttered, then began to laugh, shoulders shaking until they shook for another reason. Tears tracked down her cheeks as she convulsed with shock and relief, producing tears anew. 'There's not a soul in Landfall who would avenge me,' she whispered to the looking glass. 'Not a single person who would miss me if I perished. Not one man, woman or child who would bring flowers to my grave or remember me on my birthday.'

The tiny spark of her resolve wavered and ceased, a flame starved of oxygen. No single event extinguished the light, rather the sudden shock of her loneliness and the consequences of her deceit.

The room became dark.

The door rattled on its hinges as someone tried the handle

'Are you, ah, locked in, my lady. I mean, Domina?' Simonetti's familiar voice.

Eris didn't answer. The longcase clocks had just announced the eleventh hour. Let him think she was asleep.

'Are you still abed?' he called through the door, as if reading her mind. It was no secret Eris loved to sleep, reason in part that sessions of the Ravenscourt began at midday. The lock clicked open and the archivist pushed his head around the door to her chamber, key in hand. He blinked a few times, trying to make sense of the chaos. It was dark and the bed sheets were strewn on the floor.

'Sorry to intrude, but I thought it best to pay you a visit.'

And still Eris said nothing.

'The Myrmidons at the door insisted you were here. Perhaps they were mistaken.' The archivist stepped on the shattered remains of the looking glass, a constellation of silver shards reflecting the candlelight. He picked his way across the room, lighting more candles.

'Well, I, ah, appear to have wasted my time.' And then he saw her. 'Oh dear.'

'There's nothing wrong,' she said calmly. 'I just don't want to be here any more.'

'Well, quite.' Simonetti cleared his throat. 'It's a fashionable sentiment of late, what with people leaving both Demesne and Santa Maria in their droves.'

'I just don't want to be here any more,' she repeated, voice flat.

'Still, there are, ah, better exits from Demesne.'

Eris was sitting on the windowsill with one leg dangling beyond. She'd wrenched the curtains down, the rail lying on the floor.

'I think this way out suits me perfectly.' She tried to smile but the attempt prompted tears. 'You'd think my body would have dried up completely by now. I've cried so much lately.'

'Why don't we get you back in the warm?' said the archivist in a mild voice. He took a tentative step forward. Eris responded by swinging her other leg over the windowsill. Her hands clawed at the frame, preparing to thrust her out into the bleak daylight. 'Or I could stand over here and, ah...' Simonetti backed off a step.

The tension ebbed from her arms and neck.

'We could leave the window open for as long as you like.' He rubbed his hands together to ward off the chill. Eris looked down at the streets below; no people hurrying home to loved ones; no stray dogs looking for scraps; no windows cheered by lanterns; all doors locked shut. Not one soul.

'What do you want?' she said finally.

'I came to see if you were still alive.'

Eris said nothing, then began to cry again.

'I, ah, sorry. Bad choice of, ah, words.' Simonetti held out a hand, took a step forward, then thought better of it and stepped back. 'I didn't mean to upset you.'

'What did you just say?'

'I said I didn't mean to upset—'

'No, before that.'

'Oh. I simply came to see if you were, ah, still alive. To see if you were well. I assumed Erebus would kill you, but Viscount Datini told me otherwise.'

'Yes.' She slipped one leg back into the room. 'Erebus didn't kill me.'

'Although, I must say, you seem to be doing an awfully good job of that by yourself.'

'Thanks,' replied Eris. 'I've been giving it serious thought.'

'I would imagine no other thought would suffice when one intends to kill oneself.'

'Are you growing that beard again, Simonetti?'

The archivist probed his face with his fingers and cleared his throat. 'Not intentionally. My grooming has been lax lately.'

Eris turned from him, looking down at the town once more. 'Well, you must do what you think best.'

'Good counsel indeed, Domina, never more so than on the subject of beards.'

'Is there something I can do for you, Simonetti?'

'I don't think so, but I need to share, ah, a concern with you.'

She shook her head, then shrugged. 'Concern?'

'Well, you see, ah ... The problem is we're on the fourth floor. Now, while Demesne is a lofty edifice, and the street

289

below is undeniably cobbled, there is a small chance you won't actually, ah, die.'

'Really?'

'I'm afraid so. That's not to say you won't be horrifically injured, permanently crippled or left so reduced in faculties to resemble nothing so much as a nervous rabbit.'

'I quite like rabbits.'

'But I'm afraid outright death is unlikely, Domina.'

Eris ducked her head back into the room and slid off the windowsill. She crossed the room to the archivist. 'And I suppose you have books and research that can back up the veracity of your claims.'

'Domina, I am the archivist.' He managed to sound affronted. 'I have a plethora of sources.' Simonetti stepped around her and closed the window.

Eris narrowed her eyes. 'Was anything you just said true?'

'I possess some small knowledge of physics and biology, but honestly? I haven't the slightest idea.'

Eris sighed, looking around at the desolation beneath her feet, regretting the sack and ruin of the room. 'It's very cold in here.'

'Yes.' Simonetti rubbed his hands together. 'I expect some damn fool servant left the window open.'

Eris nodded and wiped her eyes. 'Did you really come to see if I was still alive?'

The archivist nodded and gave a brief smile. 'Yes. And I may have found something to help us in our current predicament.'

'Which predicament would that be? I've lost count.'

'The issue of the Myrmidons, and their, ah, steadfast loyalty to Erebus.'

'Go on.'

'I've chanced upon something I think you'll want to see,' said the archivist, eyes intent behind his optics. 'At first I thought it was *tinctura*, but the vials are marked *sottomesso*.'

'I've not heard of it. Where did you find these vials?'

'They were in crypt beneath House Erudito. Many of the king's possessions that failed to pique Anea's interest ended up there.'

'They *were?*'

'Well, I thought it, ah, prudent to move them to my apartment when I discovered *sottomesso* induces complete obedience.'

'What do you mean?'

'I'm not sure there are many variations on "complete obedience", although I, ah, appreciate one such as yourself struggles with the concept.'

'You found vials of a solution that instils obedience?'

'Yes. I believe I've said that already. Do keep up, Domina.'

'And you stole them?'

'Let's say they are in my safekeeping. Stolen is such an ugly word, and besides, possession is nine tenths of the law.'

Eris stared at the archivist and took a deep breath. 'And I suppose you're thinking my newfound authority as Domina combined with this alchemy will make the Myrmidons compliant.'

'Well –' Simonetti opened his hands as if pleading innocence '– when you piece it together in such a way it seems, ah, almost negligent not to act accordingly.'

'I was intending to throw myself from a window just a moment ago. Now you're suggesting I stage a coup?'

'I appreciate my timing could be, ah, better.' Simonetti smiled, removing his optics to polish them. 'The advantage is that you'll still be dead if we fail.'

'Oh.' Eris blinked. 'When you put it in those terms it seems irresistible.'

'Excellent. So you'll join me?'

Eris entered the sitting room. 'It's good fortune the underkin made three sets of robes.'

Simonetti followed her, picking up a pile of fabric from the low table. 'This one seems to have, ah, a stain on it.'

'They were Russo's robes,' said Eris, her eyes fixed on the crimson garment.

'Oh.' Simonetti dropped the robes as if stung. 'Did you . . . ?'

'Yes. She attacked me in the Central Keep. I didn't mean to do it, but . . .' She opened her mouth to say more. 'I never killed anyone before. Not myself, not directly.' Eris swallowed.

'I see.' Simonetti nodded and placed his optics on his nose.

'Well, you may be able to prevent more, ah, deaths in future if we can render the Myrmidons obedient.'

'Bring the robes with you. I have an idea,' said Eris.

'I'm not wearing—'

'That's not what I had in mind,' she replied.

'There are only two sets of new robes here,' said Simonetti, confusion in the set of his brow.

'I gave one set to Isabella. We've all been having so much fun dressing up. I didn't want her to feel left out.'

'How very charitable of you.'

'I wonder if she's succeeded in persuading the Myrmidons to pull him from the oubliette?' Eris smiled. 'This whole time, her and the *dottore*. Right under my nose, and I never saw it.'

'He went to great pains to keep the affair secret.'

'But you knew?'

'I had my, ah, suspicions. Lately suspicions are all I seem to have. But I've known Paolo a long time – we both served House Erudito once.'

The archivist and the Domina left the apartment, Simonetti unhappy about carrying the bloodstained robe.

'I hope this plan of yours works, Simonetti.'

'It has to be better than throwing oneself from a fourth-storey window, Domina.'

'I'll remind you of that when the Myrmidons turn on us.'

35

A Ghost in Amethyst

Anea had not expected to find Virmyre administering *tinctura* to himself when she entered his chamber. She'd not suspected he possessed a single vial.

Care to explain?

His pale eyes betrayed nothing.

What are you doing, Virmyre?

'I'm fifty-nine, Highness. These old bones are hardly soldier material any more.'

You are using tinctura *again?*

'Not again. Just today, just to get through the next few hours.'

She folded her arms and glowered at the *professore*. He ignored her and started attiring himself in the Myrmidon armour.

I think we are long past disguises.

'Who said anything about disguises?' said Virmyre. 'It's dangerous being your adviser; I need all the protection I can get.'

Anea paced the corridor outside his cell, occasionally pausing to shoot dark looks through the open door.

'Did you remember anything about the protocol or the staff?' asked Virmyre, voice flat.

Memory has not been my greatest asset lately. I was hoping you might remember, if you have a single straight thought in that drug-addled brain of yours. Anea continued her pacing, teasing at some rosewood beads as she did so.

'Counting your blessings?' said Virmyre with a hint of a sneer.

The beads belonged to Medea.

Virmyre declined to speak as he attached the remaining

pieces of the dark brown armour, buckled on over a leather jacket and britches. Anea by contrast wore the white robes of a Sister of Santa Maria with a scapular and veil in the same colour, but with the silver headdress she had taken from her apartment.

'Strange clothes considering what we're about.'

Anea shrugged. *This is the closest thing I have to a crown. As for the clothes, they are the most practical I could find.* Her eyes came to rest on the silver staff, propped up against the wall in the corner of the cell.

And you really think it will work?

'We can't know until we try.'

And if the only choice is to unleash the Huntsmen to wipe out the Myrmidons?

'I'd really appreciate it, Highness. I'm not sure I can fight all of them.'

Anea clenched her fists but said nothing as he fastened the last clasps on the armour. Sister Consolata approached carrying some white fabric. Anea watched the sister guide Virmyre's arms through holes in the material. A surcoat, she realised. A sword dangled from one hip, another belt encircling his waist. A canvas bag was slung from one shoulder, bulky with oddments for the task at hand.

The surcoat is your idea?

'Sometimes it becomes difficult to tell people apart when the fighting starts. I'd hate it if anyone killed the wrong Myrmidon.'

There is no one else.

'Fine. I'd hate it if *you* killed the wrong Myrmidon, Highness.'

Anea nodded, then turned to Sister Consolata.

Marchetti? Her fingers formed the name of the assassin with hesitation.

'He's still alive.' The sister looked wary. 'And still asleep.'

Anea couldn't decide how she felt. She struggled to accept that the assassin had tried so hard to free the wife of the man he'd slain.

We should go.

Virmyre nodded, blue eyes distant, no expression on the crags of his face.

*

The piazza in front of the church was filled with a procession of carts and wagons. Agostina and the sisters were supervising the cart drivers, who were attending to their tasks with grim or weary expressions. Drago Romanucci directed the operation, cajoling when the men idled. Few if any did, but he harangued them all the same. Anea watched the quiet women pack their possessions with growing anger. A few of the sisters eyed the silver staff with curiosity. Anea felt ridiculous holding it.

'We should give them time to depart,' Virmyre intoned, watching the exodus with a stern expression. Agostina appeared from the crowd, dark circles shadowing her curious eyes.

'You're not coming with us, my lady?'

Anea shook her head. *There is a possibility we may yet destroy Erebus.*

'As you wish, my lady. Send word to let us know when it's done.'

I intend to come to Santa Maria at the first possible moment.

The disciple stared at the Silent Queen with her haunting gaze of jade and cyan. Anea wondered if Agostina saw through the fiction.

'The blessings of the Saint be upon you, my lady.'

Demesne is likely to be unsafe in the months ahead. Be sure to let everyone know.

Agostina nodded. 'Are you sure won't you come with us? Let Duke Lucien defeat Erebus.'

Lucien will not march his army through winter, assuming he has the permission of the council at San Marino.

'We can't wait for spring.' Virmyre's voice was a deep rumble. 'Erebus rose to power unchecked. Now is the time to ensure he rises no further.' The *tinctura* leached all intonation from his voice, but there was a chilling quality to the words that left no doubt as to his commitment.

'May the blessings of the Saint go with you,' said Agostina, and she was gone, lost amid the crowd in the space of a few heartbeats.

'We'll need more than just blessings,' said Virmyre, watching the carts. Forlorn eyes stared from above veils, faces marked with anxiety.

Anea hefted the staff. *Time to see if the Domina's gift is really as useful as we hope it is.*

The walk across town was a sullen one, neither of them having much to offer in the way of comfort. Anea's anger at Virmyre for resorting to *tinctura* had subsided to icy indifference. Virmyre seemed oblivious to her disdain, marching toward their appointment with the chamber.

They spent some time transporting bricks from a collapsed wall with a discarded wheelbarrow, Virmyre dumping them at the mouth of the tunnel.

'I'm not sure this will hold, but it might deter them.'

We need to stop them getting out if we can. We need the creatures to swarm through Demesne itself, not the town.

Anea's hands shook as she started on the makeshift wall. Blocking the mouth of the tunnel was an onerous task. That they were sealing themselves inside Demesne made it that much harder. The longer they worked, the darker it became, the meagre light of day dwindling with each brick set upon the ones below. Anea paused to retrieve the lantern and lit it. Virmyre continued building the wall, grunting every so often as he struggled to move in the armour.

'Almost done,' he said between laboured breaths. 'The sisters should be a few miles down the road now.'

Anea held up the lantern so he could complete the wall. He fussed and packed the bricks against each other so there was no give. The last one grated as Virmyre pushed against it. Anea struggled to keep the flame of her anger alive. The familiar fear of being underground began to seep through her, a spiteful chill. Anger would see her through the hours to come, if indeed they had hours. Virmyre turned, then drew his sword and headed along the tunnel. Anea hurried after him with lantern and staff, the curving walls making looming phantoms of their shadows.

The chamber held no surprises for them yet the sombre drone filled Anea with dread. Her fascination with the sarcophagi gave way to anxiety. Was the silver staff the artefact they needed? And would they survive once they had unleashed the sleeping creatures?

Virmyre approached the metal disc at the centre of the chamber with glassy-eyed reverence. He set down the canvas bag and produced a rag.

'Let's find out what you are,' he rumbled, dropping to his knees and wiping down the metallic surface. He cleaned the aperture with devout care.

'The artefact.' He held out a hand, barely looking at her, consumed by his task. Anea passed it to him, then cast wary glances over her shoulder. Virmyre polished the end of the Domina's staff fastidiously. Anea stood over him, ghostly white in her gown, haloed in the light of the lantern, held at face height.

'Do you know what you're doing, Highness?' His baritone was barely audible above the mournful song of the chamber. Anea set the lantern down on the packed earth.

I have read about the Purge Protocol extensively in the few notes and instructions that exist.

'Yes, I know that, but do you know what you are doing?'

I am attempting to awaken dangerous creatures. I suspect they are the same creatures that nearly defeated our army during the Verde Guerra. And I am doing this using an artefact I have no memory of in the faint hope these creatures will destroy the Myrmidons. She released a breath, causing her veil to ripple.

Virmyre stood up, cradling the staff in both hands.

What could possibly go wrong?'

'I'm afraid I didn't think to pack any optimism in my bag.'

We need more than optimism, we need a miracle.

'Perhaps now is a good time to invoke Santa Maria?' He gestured to Medea's prayer beads, which were wrapped around her wrist.

Anea shook her head. *Santa Maria does not concern herself with unleashing monsters. Give me the staff.*

Virmyre passed the artefact to her, then stepped back from the disc in the floor. Anea took the length of silver metal in both hands, planting her feet either side of the aperture. Guiding the tip to the lacuna of darkness was made difficult by nervous hands, a tremor of anxiety running through her to match the sombre pitch of the room.

'Highness, is there no other way? Lucien will rally the houses, I'm sure of it. We could dispatch messengers to every corner of Landfall, encourage them to come to our side. The king only ever intended this protocol as a last resort.'

Anea sighed, fearing what she did next would sign her own death warrant. There was the scrape of metal on metal as the staff slid into the hollow, followed by a faint click.

Nothing happened. Anea wanted to scream.

'I think you might have it upside down, Highness.'

Anea turned her most withering gaze on the *professore*.

'It's just a suggestion.'

You told me it was supposed to—

Virmyre raised a hand and pointed at the staff. It was sinking into the floor, disappearing like a conjurer's trick. Anea stepped back as the top descended, inch by inch, to eye level and then lower, waist height, then to her knees, her ankles. The Domina's staff slid from view altogether, leaving Anea staring at Virmyre in a stunned silence.

The sound has stopped.

Virmyre nodded. The chamber had indeed ceased its monotonous hymn. Anea looked at the rows of unchanged sarcophagi. Cyclopean eyes of purpled light continued to stare into darkness.

What now?

'Perhaps you should step off the disc, just until we know—'

Too late.

There was a violent hiss. The disc shuddered, dust billowing up from its circumference. A whining like a chorus of insects emanated from the surface. The disc edged upward, the movement laborious.

'Anea, quickly! Step down!'

She was above him now, the disc a rising platform. Virmyre stepped forward and seized her hand as the aperture filled with an amethyst radiance. The light intensified, reaching to the ceiling in a column of stilled lightning. Motes of dust swirled and danced in the brilliance. Anea clung to Virmyre as she stepped down.

What have we done?

Virmyre had no answer as the column of amethyst light warped and coalesced. Anea blinked and fought the urge to run. A phantom appeared on the silver dais.

Santa Maria save us, she signed. But Virmyre was not paying attention to the gestures she wove, entranced by the hooded figure of amethyst light. The edges of sarcophagi could be seen through the folds of its cloak and the curve of its shoulders. The face, if there was one, remained unseen.

We have raised the dead.

'You may be right, Highness.'

'It has been many decades since anyone summoned us.' The voice came from beneath their feet, Anea felt it in the soles of her boots. There was an antiquated quality to the dialect, the tone formal to the point of disguising the gender of the speaker. Virmyre looked to Anea. She began to sign, he translating without pause.

'How should we address you?'

The spirit on the dais shimmered, a hissing sound filling the chamber as if a thousand snakes slithered and complained. Anea stepped closer to Virmyre, clutching at his surcoat, eyes wide.

'I am Alecto, one of the three proud and ancient Dirae. My sisters are Megaera and Tisiphone, who even now watch Landfall from their places in the firmament.' Slender hands emerged from voluminous sleeves, pulling back the hood with a fluid grace. The face revealed was human, but the hair that swept back from the brow was arranged in thick cords. Hers was a striking beauty, hard angles, a strong chin, straight nose. The eyes were merely absences amid the amethyst lines of the Dirae's face, as if eternity lurked behind that hollow gaze.

'Identify yourself and state your wishes.'

'I am Aranea Oscuro Diaspora,' supplied Virmyre.

'Yes. We know who you are. We wait, we watch.' The Dirae paused a moment. 'And you are the *professore,* Falcone Virmyre.'

'How did you know—'

'We wait, we watch,' said the Dirae, 'we listen.'

For a moment none spoke, Anea transfixed by the menacing shade on the dais. Then she began to sign, her pulse racing.

'I was the ruler of Landfall,' translated Virmyre, 'but I have been ousted from my throne.'

'We are aware that Demesne has undergone many changes in the last decade,' said the Dirae. There was the faintest sound of hissing beneath each word. 'It is unclear why we were made to endure such a long silence. What fate befell the king?'

'Madness.' Virmyre translated. He raised an eyebrow at Anea, who shrugged in response before signing again. 'He had to be removed. His experiments were cruel and immoral.'

'The Dirae approve. We do not tolerate immorality; we punish it, even from kings. Or queens.'

The subtle warning gave Anea pause. After a moment she began again.

'A usurper called Erebus has raised an army. He has taken Demesne from me and driven away the people of the Diaspora.'

'I am aware,' said the Dirae. 'We are all aware. We wait, we watch. You summoned; I came. What would you have the Dirae do?'

'What can you tell me of the Purge Protocol?'

An outraged hissing filled the chamber, and Anea clutched Virmyre on instinct.

'The Purge Protocol releases the Huntsmen. They are not discriminate killers; they wreak vengeance on the innocent and guilty alike.'

'There's few left in Demesne that anyone would call inno-cent,' said Virmyre.

You are supposed to be translating, not providing a commentary, she signed.

Virmyre shrugged and mouthed, 'Sorry.'

'You share a bloodline with the king,' said the Dirae, 'but so does Erebus. By what right do you claim the throne?' The hissing had become muted, as though expectation muffled the sound. The nasal whine from beneath the dais had also become quieter. Anea regarded the phantom on the dais, staring into eyes that revealed nothing. For long moments she had no idea how to respond. Finally her fingers began to move, and Virmyre lent voice to her thoughts.

'I claim no right, only that I serve the people. Service is the greatest power, to tend the sick and raise the poor, to see justice for all people. I have always enshrined fairness and wisdom, knowledge and humility. Erebus cannot lay claim to any of these ambitions. He seeks only war.'

The Dirae pulled up her hood and pressed her hands together. Anea and Virmyre stood on the packed earth of the chamber as the figure on the dais stood in deep communion. The dirge of the chamber returned in increments, louder and louder still. The whine from the dais matched its intensity. Underneath both sounds came the irritated hiss of serpents.

'Very well, Aranea Oscuro Diaspora,' replied the Dirae. 'It will be as you say.' The slender hands pulled down the hood. It was not a woman's face regarded them, but that of a wolf. The cables of hair were in motion, writhing and coiling, each terminating with the head of a snake. Anea signed frantically.

'When?'

'It has already begun,' said the Dirae.

And then the ghost in amethyst was gone. The only light in the chamber came from the lantern by their feet. The single eyes of the sarcophagi had all winked out, surrendered to darkness.

'I think it's time we left, Highness.'

Anea nodded, retrieving the lantern from the floor and thrusting her free hand into Virmyre's palm. They hurried toward the door at the far end as a series of exhalations sounded behind them. The same sounds issued from each side and yet more ahead. Virmyre squeezed her hand tight and Anea held the lantern a little higher. The door ahead welcomed them as growls and yelps became audible over the chorus of sighing sarcophagi.

'Come on,' said Virmyre, breaking into a run. There was a scuffing sound, but Anea dared not look over her shoulder, too consumed with panic to do anything but run. They emerged into the corridor as the first of the Huntsmen burst through the door, knocking Virmyre from his feet as he sought to close it.

36

Revelations

The Herald stood before the windows of the sitting room, silhouetted by the sun's ascension. The sky was a tumult of reds and oranges, afire behind diffuse clouds. Wisps appeared like steam across the hellish firmament. A smear of yellow declared the position of the sun.

Eris flashed a glance at Simonetti. She had not expected the Herald, too surprised by her promotion to Domina to spare him much thought. The archivist closed the door behind him, turning the key in the lock.

'Is this a trap?' she whispered, but Simonetti refused to answer, holding up one finger to his lips. She flashed him an angry glance, eyes alighting on the door handle. The key rested in the lock.

'You can leave if you want to,' said the archivist softly.

'I thought he was dead,' whispered Eris.

Simonetti shrugged, as if this were sufficient answer.

The walk from House Fontein to Erudito had been tense. The Myrmidons they encountered saluted, holding open gates and unbolting doors. Two of the armoured soldiers had escorted them, waiting in the corridor outside Simonetti's apartment. Eris hid her bewilderment beneath an imperious mien, one of Russo's mannerisms, she realised. Now they stood in the presence of the Herald, who showed no reverence, not even deigning to acknowledge them, intent on the violent sunrise. Eris couldn't forget his promise to kill her should Medea die.

'We are returned,' said Simonetti quietly.

The sky beyond the lead-latticed windows filled the room

with a sanguine light. Eris blinked. The vision of Russo staring down at the hilt of the stiletto protruding from her chest with disbelief retuned to her. The old Domina had fallen back against the white doors of the Ravenscourt, smearing a trail of blood as she slid to the ground. Perhaps Eris would share her predecessor's fate.

'Are you unwell?' Simonetti pressed her shoulder.

'I'm fine,' she whispered.

'There are books,' said the Herald in his ravaged voice, 'old books the king never managed to destroy. Some survived intact, others merely as fragments.'

Eris was unsure if the words that issued from under the hood were addressed to her or Simonetti. She listened all the same. Russo had always insisted knowledge was power.

'There is one fragment in particular that tells of locusts with the tails of scorpions, creatures of the sea with seven heads, stars falling from the heavens, poisoned waters. The book tells of the end of the world. The end of people.'

'Perhaps that's the outcome Erebus desires so keenly,' replied Eris. 'The end of people. An eternity of underkin.'

The Herald pointed through the window to a nearby street. His gloves were heavy, the leather thick, the gesture difficult to ignore. Two people were making their way along a derelict street, one sat on a horse, the other leading the beast.

'Dottore Allattamento,' said Eris. She snorted a laugh, incredulous and bitter. So unfair he should survive when so many were denied the luxury of living.

'She rescued him,' said Simonetti. 'Another deception in your favour.'

'Perhaps,' said Eris. 'But I'd gladly exchange places with her. I'd rather take my chances in the provinces.'

'Even if you had to marry Allattamento?'

'Let's not be hasty.'

The Herald turned, crimson light reflecting from the crosspiece of the great sword slung across his back, glinting from the carnival mask with its delicate sneer. The dappled cloak looked saturated in blood; only the raven was missing. Eris shrank back from the imposing figure, her robes clutched in tight fists.

'Medea is dead,' he said. Each word accusatory.

'Yes. I promised I'd help free her.' Eris swallowed. 'And I failed.' She couldn't recall a single occasion when she had owned up to her shortcomings. She couldn't say she really cared for the experience, but it was an improvement on the tawdry business of making excuses. Simonetti cleared his throat. His presence behind her offered scant reassurance.

'We all failed,' said the Herald in a quiet voice. 'I rode into town on a black horse with the promise of war on my lips, but not at the cost of Medea Contadino's life.'

'I thought you wanted war?' Eris had no doubt the Herald would be in his element, his fearlessness making him a warrior of legend. The great sword on his back was not for show.

'There was a time I'd have greeted the end of the world with open arms.' The Herald sounded desolate. 'Now I just want to go home.'

'We had a deal,' said Eris.

'Thinking you were the key to saving Medea was foolish,' said the Herald. 'You're just another pawn in this endless game. I can't decide if I feel disgust or pity for you.'

'Well, now that we're all friends again . . .' said Simonetti.

'Who are you?' Eris took a step forward. 'I mean really.'

'I am the *capo* of House Vedetta, successor to Delfino Datini, answerable to Duke Lucien Marino. I am his Herald.'

'Hiding behind cloaks and masks and titles is one thing,' said Eris, stepping yet closer, 'but there is always a person underneath.'

The Herald raised his hands to the hood, took a moment to unclip the mask, then pushed back the heavy fabric, revealing a handsome face. Serious grey eyes regarded her from under dark brown hair. His clenched jaw was thick with stubble; a terrible motley of scar tissue crossed his throat.

'I am Dino Adolfo Erudito, brother of Aranea Oscuro Diaspora, lover of Massimo Esposito, since murdered by the underkin.'

'Dino?' said Simonetti, breaking into a smile. 'I had no idea. I was told you had, ah, died.'

The Herald turned back to the blood-dimmed sky.

'Misdirection. I was found by a cart driver. He took me to the coast, and to my brother. I'd have died if not for him and the benevolent fortune of Santa Maria.'

'You're, ah, a believer, my lord?' said Simonetti, incredulous.

'No. But I placed a small marble figurine beneath my jerkin on the night I tried to escape with Stephania Prospero.' A ghost of a smile touched his fine lips, but it was a sad, small thing that brought no joy. 'They tell me the figurine was shattered when they stripped my armour from me. A sister of San Marino told me the Saint had turned aside a fatal blow. I'm not sure I can marshal the cynicism to deny an explanation like that.'

'Far be it for me to argue matters of faith with a, ah, heavily armed man,' replied Simonetti.

'A wise course.'

Eris took a step toward the Herald, Dino Adolfo Erudito, one of the finest swordsmen in all of Landfall, *invertito*, assassin, Orfano. He regarded her with cool grey eyes. This was the man she had framed for the murder of Fiorenza. This was Dino Adolfo.

'It was you all the time,' she said, 'hiding beneath the cloak.'

'Amusing that you accuse me of hiding. Each time we meet you're dressed as someone else, someone you're not.'

Eris looked down at the Domina's robes, her robes, made just the night before. 'I'm as weary of subterfuge as you are, I can assure you.'

Simonetti removed his optics and polished them. 'You think you're confused? I advise against being short-sighted. It's small wonder I recognise anyone at all any more.'

The business of counting the vials of *sottomesso* took some time. The cases themselves and the straw within were dry from long storage. Dust clung to everything, making a relic of Eris, crimson robes smeared with grey. At one point the Herald produced a knife and for a dry-mouthed second Eris feared he'd changed his mind. Or his heart. Perhaps he would kill her after all? But the knife blade sank into the groove between lid and case, the vials rattling inside as the Herald levered the wood apart. Eris released a breath and took the case from him with a nod of thanks. The vials were long thimbles of glass, perfectly smooth. The fluid within a jaundice yellow.

'How old are these exactly?' said Eris, wrinkling her nose at the cloudy mixture.

'The king neglected to stamp the crates or the vials with the, ah, date of production.'

'And if they go off like milk or meat?' asked the Herald.

'Then we'll find ourselves trying to persuade nearly two hundred loyal Myrmidons to stage a coup against Erebus.' Simonetti blinked. 'I, ah, imagine that will be a fairly short conversation.'

'Your talent for understatement is alive and well,' said Eris.

'Let's try and keep it that way, shall we?' said the archivist.

The first two Myrmidons entered the room at the Domina's summons. Eris, who had always assumed she could command the soldiers, realised she had never actually bothered to try during her time as the Silent Queen.

'We're administering another round of *tinctura*,' she lied, 'to bolster you after the recent upheaval.'

There was a moment of dread as neither soldier moved. Simonetti's sitting room was an unusual location for such an event. Dino waited in the bedroom, sword drawn should the plan go awry. Simonetti cleared his throat and wiped his optics on his robes. Eris flashed him an anxious look as a single bead of sweat broke free of her hairline, descending to a cheekbone. Did they suspect the ruse? Could they have learned of *sottomesso* somehow? Eris held herself immobile even as the slow creep of panic constricted her gut and lungs, an unbearable tightness in her shoulders.

The Myrmidons knelt as one and removed their helmets. They tilted back their heads and fixed stern gazes on the ceiling. Both appeared human, lacking the twisted marks that blighted so many underkin faces. Simonetti wasted no time, administering first one cloudy vial and then another to the soldiers. The Myrmidons closed their eyes and breathed a moment, heads bowed. Neither of them shook or trembled, so often a tell of *tinctura* taking effect, their stillness absolute. Eris wondered if they still drew breath. She looked at Simonetti and mouthed, 'It's not working.' The archivist shrugged, casting a wary glance at the scores of vials and their yellow contents. Eris watched the kneeling soldiers, mind racing with a litany of possible failures. Had the alchemy lost its potency, as the Herald had suggested? Perhaps the *sottomesso* had never been tested? Was there a missing ingredient or another preparation needed to activate the first? Did *sottomesso* behave the way Simonetti assumed it did? Might it be slowly killing the Myrmidons as she waited, unaware and unable to reverse what they had done?

'Stand up,' whispered Eris in desperation. 'Stand up!' she all but shouted.

The Myrmidons resumed their feet with a stately calm, faces blank of expression as the *sottomesso* coursed through them. Eris stepped back, wondering how she'd let Simonetti talk her into such a foolhardy endeavour. She drew herself up to her full height, raising her chin and clasping her hands together.

'You will take orders from me, and me alone. I am Domina Eris, and you will address me as such.'

The Myrmidons nodded, yet Eris felt only relief that neither of the soldiers had gone for his sword.

'Our Lord Erebus has succumbed to old age and madness,' she explained. 'His intentions are dangerous, so we must safeguard ourselves and Demesne in the times ahead.'

Again the Myrmidons nodded, faces blank with no hint of opinion or protest, nothing to give away their thoughts.

'Do you understand me?'

'We understand, Domina Eris.'

She blinked in surprise, then extended a hand toward Simonetti. He passed her two strips of crimson fabric, scraps from the old Domina's robes, now shredded to ribbons. Eris tied a length of fabric about the right arm of each of the soldiers.

'Now split up and find the nearest Myrmidons, relieve them and send them to me.'

The soldiers nodded, replacing their helms before saluting. They departed without a word.

'I need a very large brandy,' rumbled Simonetti.

'Make sure to pour a second glass,' said Eris, watching the

archivist root around among the many piles of books crowding the sitting room. Dino appeared in the bedroom doorway, face grave, blade still free of the scabbard.

'How many Myrmidons are there?'

'No one knows,' replied Simonetti in a mournful tone.

'At least a hundred.' Eris crossed to the doorway and looked into the corridor, then back to the Herald. He would always be the Herald, she realised. Dino was the name of a small boy who clutched the skirts of his nanny. Dino had a shy smile and enjoyed ripe apples, or so she imagined. Dino was a teenager in love with his best friend. If that boy had ever survived into manhood then no trace remained, not in the black-cloaked figure standing before her.

'At least a hundred, you say?' Simonetti had abandoned the search for brandy and was looking at Eris from beneath a worried frown.

'Viscount Datini said reinforcements were on their way just yesterday – a hundred Myrmidons. Surely they must have arrived by now?'

'Well, let's hope so,' said Simonetti.

'Otherwise we'll have rival factions of Myrmidons to contend with,' added the Herald.

Eris crossed to the crates and took out another vial of *sotto-messo*.

The afternoon spooled away from them, lost to the task of subverting the Myrmidons. Armoured soldiers arrived and obedient soldiers left, always with orders to fetch more, always wearing strips of crimson on their sword arms. The anxiety never left Eris, the ruse a constant worry, discovery threatening with each sound of footsteps approaching the door.

'How did I let you talk me into this?' said Eris during a lull.

'Once it's done it's done.' Simonetti sighed. 'It's like re-ordering a library.'

'Only books don't kill you if you shelve them incorrectly.'

'Depends how heavy they are,' replied the archivist, 'and from how high they fall.'

Simonetti's longcase clock chimed four times. The sky had

grown dark, an implacable dark blue which would soon swallow the world, the horizon a sickening bruise. Eris clutched a vial of liquid obedience in her fingers as she looked to the sky, eyes fixed on the first star of the night. It shone amethyst, so unlike the smattering of silver that appeared in greater numbers.

'What is that?' she asked.

'One of the old goddesses,' said the Herald, 'asleep in the sky.' He leaned on the door frame, arms crossed. 'Pray that no one wakes them.'

'Goddesses?'

'Alecto, Tisiphone and Megaera.' The Herald fixed Eris with serious grey eyes. 'All distinctly less benevolent than Santa Maria.'

'Do they predate the king?' asked Simonetti, rapt with interest.

'By a significant margin,' replied the Herald.

'How do you know this?' asked Eris.

'Forgive me if I don't reveal all my secrets to my sister's impostor. I don't entirely trust you yet.'

'Even after all I've done?'

The sound of booted feet in the corridor indicated more Myrmidons had arrived, interrupting their conversation. It would take many hours to treat all of them, but then Demesne would belong to Eris. Erebus' rule would be finished in hours and she would have avenged Sabatino. The purple star in the sky shimmered and winked. Eris decided the old goddess approved, sleeping or not.

37

Awakening

Anea wasn't sure what came through the doorway after them, only that it bore the face of a wolf, much like the Dirae who had woken it. Its limbs were many and spindly, elegant spider legs some seven feet long covered in chitin. Matted hair grew from the torso, deep brown and flecked tan. The tiny nub of a malformed tail twitched as the creature bore down on the supine form of Virmyre. The *professore* threw up his sword arm to protect himself, the impact of the attack sending the blade tumbling from his grip. Steel clattered on the flagstones by Anea's boots. The Huntsman's jaws foamed with saliva, teeth impacting with the breastplate mere inches from Virmyre's throat.

'What in Nine Hells?'

Anea set the lantern down on the floor and retrieved Virmyre's sword. His pale eyes were no longer dulled by *tinctura* but bright with the shock of adrenaline. Anea felt it too, and a great reservoir of anger. The sword hilt felt good, it felt right. The *professore* had thrust his right hand beneath the Huntsman's jaw, the left pinned to the floor by the point of a spidery leg. She swung the sword with a two-handed grip, taking off the limb pinioning Virmyre's hand. A shower of clear fluid jetted from the severed limb, causing the Huntsman to rear, a shrill whine replacing its frenzied growl. Anea slammed a booted foot into the side of the creature's muzzle, then stepped back and slashed down in an overhead strike. The blade sank deep into the creature's torso, eliciting a yelp. Virmyre pulled himself to his knees. He lashed out with a gloved fist and struck the Huntsman on the snout.

'We need more swords,' he grunted.

The creature retreated a fraction, allowing Virmyre to stand. Anea struck again, forcing the Huntsman back in a blur of flashing teeth. The corridor filled with a furious growling. The *professore* grabbed the opened door with both hands, slamming it against writhing, spidery limbs, the dull sound of wood on chitin, a crack of shell, the spatter of fluid on flagstones. The Huntsman withdrew further, dodging away from the next sword stroke, a clumsy thrust. Virmyre pulled the door open and slammed it again, catching the Huntsman's head as it backed over the threshold, dazed and unsteady. Virmyre leaned against the door and got it closed, hand scrabbling for a key.

There was none.

'*Figlio di puttana!*'

Anea snatched a stiletto from a sheath on Virmyre's waist and dropped to her knees, sliding the blade under the door and hammering the pommel with the flat of her hand. The door would not remain wedged closed for long, but it would buy them a few seconds at least.

'I'm constantly baffled why men are intimidated by intelligent women,' intoned Virmyre. 'I for one would like to see many more of them.'

They fled, not knowing how long the door would hold or how badly the Huntsman was hurt. Anea imagined only the most grievous of wounds would stop such a nightmare. They ascended staircases and turned corners with only the light of Anea's lantern for guidance.

'Up,' said Virmyre between laboured breaths. 'We must go up.'

The weight of armour was exacting a high price from the old man despite the stimulus of *tinctura*. He clutched his fist to his chest, eyeing the corridor with caution. Anea paused and turned, hanging the lantern from a hook in the wall, freeing her hands. The walls were rough and unfinished – she supposed they were still below ground level.

Where are we?

311

'House Fontein, I think.' Virmyre checked over his shoulder. 'The Fonteins were ever the keepers of the king's secrets.'

And now they are all dead. She noticed a spot of blood drip from Virmyre's clenched fist and spatter on the flagstones.

What happened to your hand?

'Those legs are rather sharp on their inside edge. It cut through my gauntlet.' A glance along the corridor revealed he'd left a trail in scarlet. 'Come on, in here.' Virmyre indicated a door along the passage. Rusty hinges announced their entrance more thoroughly than any courtier, the wood of the door complaining as it scraped over flagstones. The golden glow of the lantern fell on empty shelves and narrow beds. The chamber was long, a repeating arrangement of wardrobe, bed, wardrobe, bed on each side.

'Barracks.'

And not disused, signed Anea, noting rumpled blankets. Virmyre closed the door, grasped the nearest wardrobe and dragged it across the doorway. Anea chose a sword from a rack as Virmyre worked, belting it over vestments streaked with grime.

'It suits you,' said Virmyre. 'Perhaps we can recruit the Sisters of Santa Maria as our new army if we survive this.'

The tinctura *must be wearing off. I think you are starting to be funny again.*

'You sound unconvinced.'

What are you looking at?

'Your robes, they're blue?' Anea's white robes were flecked with cyan: Huntsman's blood. She thought of Lucien, the way he would bleed clear fluid, only for the blood to transmute to a sky blue.

We are unlikely to survive this, are we?

'I had hoped we might have a chance to get away before the Protocol took effect,' said Virmyre. 'It's a cruel irony the very forces we've set against Erebus might . . .' He gestured with his good hand, unwilling to say the words.

Kill us too, thought Anea. She struggled to keep her composure, tracing the blue blood on the vestments with her finger. The realisation she would not see Lucien again settled about her, a dismal shroud. Virmyre began rifling through drawers, opening wardrobe doors with noisy abandon, breaking the spell.

What are you looking for?

'Bandages.' He held up his left hand, the leather ragged, sodden with blood. The barracks held a great many swords, oddments of armour and even keepsakes, but no bandages. Anea couldn't tell if the mementos belonged to House Fontein soldiers or the Myrmidons that had replaced them. She told Virmyre to stop his search and used a knife to cut up a bed sheet.

Sit.

A bed creaked under Virmyre's weight as he obeyed. She knelt before him on the floor while he removed the glove with gritted teeth. Crimson spotted his armoured thighs, the sheets, Anea's hands.

'At least we know they're suitably dangerous. Even weak with starvation.'

Starvation? Anea began binding the hand.

'They've been down there for decades. How they've remained alive in those sarcophagi I have no idea.'

Given time they will only grow stronger.

'Time and food.' Virmyre tried not to wince. 'I'm surprised they woke so quickly.' Anea tied off a knot before replying.

I do not believe they did. I think the one that attacked us was woken weeks ago, when I stumbled against the sarcophagus.

'And the others?'

There's no telling how long they need to reorient themselves after such a long sleep.

They exchanged a wary look as Anea tied the final knot in the dressing.

'What shall we do now?'

Return to the church and bar the doors. We can watch from the balcony.

Anea got to her feet as Virmyre flexed and clenched the wounded hand.

'Have you thought of joining the Sisters of Santa Maria. You tie a good dressing.'

I already have the vestments. Being a canoness must be easier than ruling Demesne.

'I'd hope so,' rumbled Virmyre. 'It can't be any worse.'

We should try and find a way back to the church.

'Before the rest of them wake up.'

A scuttling sound beyond the door startled both of them, then the door rattled on its hinges.

'The wardrobe should buy us some time. Come on, the far end. Barracks always have two doors.'

The barricaded door burst open, not one but three Huntsmen clamouring to press into the chamber. Terrible growls and the clash of chitin on chitin followed Anea and the *professore* as they fled. Reaching the far door, Anea snatched the key from a shelf and ran through, Virmyre following with sword unsheathed. He stumbled into the corridor as Anea slammed the door into the fanged jaws of the nearest Huntsman. The door was locked with a trembling hand, the key cast down the corridor.

'We're in Fortuna's lap now. Unless you feel like praying to Santa Maria.'

Praying is good, but running is better.

Up they went on staircases that echoed with the sounds of fighting, along winding corridors that led nowhere. Twice they thought to escape the lower floors of House Fontein, and twice they found themselves lost.

'I always hated this place,' grunted Virmyre.

I thought you had studied it, made a map.

'Not now, Highness.'

The clang of steel on stone and the shouts of Myrmidons sounded from the floors above them.

How can the Huntsmen be above us already?

'We spent longer than we thought in the barracks, perhaps?'

Hardly.

'Something in the sarcophagi, like *tinctura* perhaps, to bring them out of their torpor?'

But above us?

'They have eight legs, Highness. Neither horizontal or vertical hold much of a challenge for them.'

Where do we go now?

'The Central Keep, and then back to the church as fast as we dare.'

Let us hope the creatures have not escaped beyond the castle walls yet.

'I'm sure they're busy feeding,' said Virmyre. 'And they will have met some resistance by now.'

Can we make it? Anea looked into Virmyre's eyes and saw only a grim resignation. *Lead on.*

Virmyre took her hand and ran, turning sharply down spiralling stone steps. They spilled out into a corridor lit by a brazier near the main gate that led to the Central Keep. Two Myrmidons lay dead, each bearing several wounds, none of them inflicted by swords. The nearest had been all but decapitated by powerful jaws. The corpse of the creature lay nearby, congealing in faint blue fluid.

Anea turned and swung one of the double doors closed and Virmyre followed her lead. They sweated and strained, pulling them closed behind them as they withdrew into the circuitous corridor.

'With any luck the Huntsmen will kill all the Myrmidons in the other barracks before finding the side doors and venturing further afield.'

The doors rattled and boomed as something slammed into them on the other side. Anea flinched away and Virmyre reached for his sword on instinct.

Do you think they can perform basic tasks?

'Such as?'

Opening doors?

'I think I'd prefer not to be here in case they can,' replied Virmyre. The impact came again, followed by another a second later. Anea turned and ran toward the vast double doors of the Central Keep, her eyes searching for the unlocking mechanism. Virmyre pushed against the doors but nothing moved. He turned his back to them, pressing against the wood with his shoulders. The white doors of the Ravenscourt loomed on the opposite side of the corridor, still smeared with a crimson stain.

'Was that where Russo ... ?'

A hiss escaped Anea as she found the device. She jerked a

lever and the rattling of chains drowned the sound of their frenzied breathing. But as the outer doors began to swing open the forelegs of a Huntsman slipped through, stiletto blades forged in chitin.

'Close them!' shouted Virmyre. 'Close the doors.'

The legs pressed in between the doors, the muzzle of the wolf's head followed, snapping at Virmyre, who drew back with sword unsheathed. Anea struggled with the mechanism, using both hands to yank at the leather-wrapped handle.

'There are at least four of them out there,' said Virmyre, swinging his blade at the Huntsman. The creature flinched back and the doors edged closed. Then two more legs slipped through the opening, wedging apart the heavy oak. The Huntsman howled, straining to hold the counterweighted doors apart before Anea took its head off with a two-handed strike. The doors slammed shut, forcing the twitching corpse of the Huntsman outside. Virmyre raised an eyebrow as he regarded the head on the floor at his feet.

'Thank the Saint you're here to protect me.'

Anea sheathed her sword. *Are you being sarcastic?*

'For once, no, Highness. Most certainly not.' They caught their breath, taking a moment to check the gatehouses of Erudito, Contadino and Prospero. All were barred from the other side.

'What now?' said Virmyre. 'Our way back to the church—' The sound of snarling Huntsman from beyond the outer doors interrupted.

We can wait here and hope nothing finds us.

'Unlikely, to say the least.'

Or we try the Ravenscourt.

'My guess is they're tracking us by scent.' Virmyre held up his bloodied hand. 'If I'm going to be bait I'd rather lead them to Erebus than you.'

And once we enter the Ravenscourt?

'We can leave the way we did before, from the balcony and on to the roof.'

That doesn't sound like much of an escape.

'Would you rather die up there or down here?'

They ascended the stairs of the Central Keep, into the library full of slumbering secrets, and further still until they stood outside the Ravenscourt itself. The tang of corruption assailed them as they crossed the threshold, a nauseating scent. An underkin lay beside the open doors, throat ripped open, shock and fear frozen in each of his four eyes.

'We didn't seal the doors to House Fontein quickly enough,' said Virmyre.

How are they in the Ravenscourt already?

Anea pointed to the centre of the chamber, where three of the creatures slashed at four Myrmidons with a hungry tenacity.

'At least we might live long enough to see Erebus dead,' said Virmyre.

Blades rose and fell, a Myrmidon was knocked from his feet, collapsing with a muffled clang. Another Myrmidon was skewered through one thigh. He fell back screaming then bled out in a series of whimpers.

'We're doomed,' said a voice from behind them. As one, Virmyre and Anea turned, swords pointing toward its source. Viscount Datini regarded them, a grey pallor about his wizened features.

'It's no more than you deserve, you miserable fuck,' replied Virmyre.

'What have you done?'

You ended my world, now I have ended yours. Fair is fair, Viscount.

The sound of fighting intensified. One by one the Huntsmen were slain, slender limbs rent from muscular bodies. The Myrmidons were poorer for the exchange: two remained bloodied yet standing, one dead, only one of their number remaining unharmed. Their armour and discipline had protected them, fighting in pairs, assisting each other in the face of savagery. The Myrmidons pulled back to the dais, where Erebus still presided, a monster beset by monsters. The many underkin and wretches clung to his legs like frightened children. Viscount Datini used the distraction to slip away from Virmyre and Anea, hobbling up some steps that led to the gallery above. Virmyre made to pursue until Anea rested a hand on his arm.

Leave him, we have much bigger problems. She pointed to the aberration on the dais. Anea fought a chill of dread as she regarded the sheer size of Erebus once more.

'What is that sound?' asked Erebus, armoured head casting about.

'That's the sound of your precious Myrmidons dying,' said Virmyre. They'd walked to the centre of the Ravenscourt. The *professore* prodded the corpse of one Huntsman with his boot, then grimaced. They were standing amid a lake of pale blue. Erebus raised the blunt helm and its mandible blades toward Anea.

'What have you done, hateful child?' he droned in a voice loud enough to make the underkin cower. 'What have you unleashed?'

Virmyre turned to Anea. 'Highness?' She began to sign.

'You left me no choice,' the *professore* translated. 'I needed something to destroy you and your Myrmidons at short notice.'

'We're doomed, my lord,' called Viscount Datini from the gallery.

'BE QUIET!' shouted Virmyre and Erebus in unison. A silence settled over the Ravenscourt while the sound of muted violence reached them from elsewhere in Demesne.

'You enacted the Purge Protocol.' Erebus said the words without anger or shock, only a weary resignation. 'Impressive. I thought that particular intervention had passed from memory.'

'From memory perhaps, but not from the king's machines,' replied Virmyre.

'You realise you've sentenced yourself to hell?' sneered Erebus. Anea signed, Virmyre lending his voice to her gestures.

'You sentenced me to hell, my lord. There is no reason you cannot come with me.'

'I've heard enough,' spat Erebus. 'Kill her, and kill this idiot *professore* too.'

The Myrmidons approached them, barely recovered from the encounter with the Huntsmen, one of them limping.

'Remind me why we came here,' said Virmyre as he hefted his sword.

We have nowhere else to go.

318

'Sounds perfectly reasonable. Whose suggestion was that?'

Yours.

'You should give serious thought to retiring me as your adviser.'

Noted.

Anea drew her sword and spread her feet, feeling ridiculous in the vestments of Santa Maria. She raised the blade before her, noticing Medea's rosewood prayer beads wrapped about her wrist. She glanced at Virmyre and he nodded, a stern expression on his face.

'For Medea,' he said.

They stepped forward to meet their fate.

38

All That Is Lost

Domina Eris had recruited thirty-three Myrmidons, all departing into the depths of Demesne with crimson tied about their
sword arms. The current intake stood before her, dreamy
expressions on their warped faces. The taller of them looked at
the world through a face littered with eyes, all different shapes
and colours. His comrade had mandibles but lacked ears, a
ragged hole where his nose should be. Eris breathed a sigh of
relief as they replaced their helms, obscuring faces best seen
only in nightmares. The taller addressed her, head cocked to
one side.

'Did you lose your staff, Domina Eris?'

'I . . .' She had no answer. None of the other Myrmidons
had struck up a conversation, much less questioned her. And
the silver staff of the Domina was a recognised symbol of her
office; without it she might struggle. The Myrmidons paused by
the door, regarding her. The blunt and curved helms betrayed
nothing, yet Eris felt the terrible weight of accusation. Where
was the staff? Why didn't she have it?

'Domina Eris has forgone the, ah, trappings of her predecessor,' supplied Simonetti. Eris released a shaky breath of relief as
the Myrmidons nodded. 'Please, gather more of your comrades,'
continued the archivist, 'so we may administer *sottomesso* to
them.'

'*Sottomesso?*' Eris struggled not to hiss, a knife edge razoring
her nerves. A painful second of silence passed. Eris opened her
mouth to speak but her mind remained resolutely blank.

'Ah, did I say *sottomesso*?' Simonetti smiled weakly. 'I meant *tinctura*.'

Eris waited for the Myrmidons to draw their swords and fall on the archivist, slashing him to bloody pulp.

'What is *sottomesso*?' said the Myrmidon nearest the door. Eris staggered back a step as her worst fears were realised. Their plans for obedience were undone, and all by a slip of the tongue. The Myrmidons turned to face each other and gave a tiny nod.

'Nothing. I am mistaken,' said Simonetti. 'It's been a long day.'

Fists curled about the hilts of swords, short wide blades slipping free of scabbards. The next few seconds could spell the end of the short-lived plot against Erebus.

'Send for more Myrmidons; we can't afford to waste any time.' Eris did her best to force a note of command into her voice, but the last word emerged shaky and pleading.

'Come on,' said the Myrmidon in the doorway. They abandoned Simonetti's chamber without a backward glance.

The archivist stared at Eris with sick relief. 'I'm sorry.'

A commotion sounded in the corridor, much too close.

'Never mind.' Eris scowled. More sounds echoed through the open door: steel ringing against stone, growling, a shocked cry of pain.

'What now?' muttered Simonetti, but it was Eris who crossed to the doorway and looked out. The darkness did much to make a confusion of the scene unfolding just a few dozen feet from where she stood. Soldiers in low stances jostled against each other, blades held out. Beyond them, rearing up on slender legs, was a creature from nightmare. The Myrmidons parried or ducked beneath a series of strikes, blurs in the flickering lantern light. A Myrmidon lay on the ground, unmoving.

'It has the head of a wolf,' she whispered, stepping back inside the apartment.

'What did you say?' said the archivist.

Eris turned to him ashen-faced. 'It has a wolf's head, but its legs are—'

One of the creatures slammed into the door frame, a single leg smashing into her, sending Eris sprawling into the archivist.

'What?' Simonetti almost choked on the word, eyes blinking furiously behind the optics. The monstrosity shook its head, squeezing its tawny eyes closed. Simonetti helped Eris to her feet as the creature lurched back on spidery legs, issuing a low growl of complaint, black ears pricked up.

'What is it?' shouted Simonetti. The creature attacked, jaws open, fangs slick and sharp. Eris screamed as the aberration sped toward them, promising a ragged death, ripped apart. The sound of cracking chitin filled the room as the creature spun sideways. The Herald, waiting in the bedroom, had returned for the promise of violence as if summoned. The creature, close enough to turn a snarling maw on Eris, gave no mind to its sundered legs. Eris jumped back, desperate for a weapon. Hard legs scrabbled and scratched, snaring in the crimson folds of her robes, pulling her to the floor.

'Get it off!' she shrieked.

The Herald stepped in and struck again, another leg severed. Then a parry that caught the Huntsman's jaws with the flat of the great blade. The creature snarled and bit down on instinct; the Herald replied with a kick, catching the creature in the throat with the heel of his boot. The sword came free, wrenching teeth with it, foam spilling over black lips. Eris scrambled back on hands and heels, heart hammering in her chest. The creature lunged for the Herald before a blur of steel stilled it, mangling the skull in one mighty strike. A spatter of clear blood flicked the length of Eris's robes, where it transmuted to pale blue seconds later. Eris and Simonetti looked at each other dazed and incredulous as the Herald wiped his sword clean.

'Well, you took your time,' spat Eris.

'You're still alive, aren't you?'

'Barely! I thought that thing was going to rip my throat out.'

'That's what they usually do.'

'What is it?' whispered Simonetti, one hand pressed to his jugular as if reassuring himself.

'Huntsman,' said the Herald. 'Anea woke the Huntsmen.'

322

'And how in Nine Hells did she do that?' asked Eris, looking at the ruined corpse at her feet.

'I suspect she asked one of those sleeping goddesses I told you about.' The Herald slung the great sword over his back and drew the smaller sword at his hip. 'They'll destroy the Myrmidons and anything else that crosses their path.'

'How do you, ah, know all of this?' Simonetti frowned.

'Secrets from San Marino,' said the Herald. 'Old spirits bound to the will of the king. Lucien would never invoke the Dirae. It had to be Anea.'

'We'll never escape,' said Eris, regarding the corpse with disgust. It oozed viscous fluid, no less horrific in death than it had been in life.

The Herald started for the door.

'Where are you going? You can't leave us.'

'If Demesne is lost then I want to be sure Erebus is lost in the process.' The Herald glowered at her. 'I won't die knowing he might survive this.'

Their journey through House Erudito led them to the upper floors, keen to escape the sounds of fighting below. Higher they climbed, up coiling staircases, along disused passages and higher still. The journey was not uninterrupted. The next Hunstman they encountered was savaging a fallen Myrmidon, its jaws clamped around the soldier's neck. There was a hungry gleam in its eye which verged on madness. Black-furred ears pricked up at their footfalls. The creature turned to face the new threat. The Herald refused the Huntsman the space it needed to charge, lunging forward with startling speed. The great sword remained across his back, the smaller sword drawn in the space of a heartbeat. The Huntsman reared, filling the corridor with a growl that made Eris want to flee back to Simonetti's apartment. She clung to the archivist, who clung to her in return.

The Herald was not so perturbed, severing limbs as they thrust forward. He turned the Huntsman's parries aside, catching its limbs at their joints, slashing with such force the chitin cracked and split. The creature staggered forward, snapping at the cloaked figure with glistening fangs, but the Herald ran sideways, a boot planted on the wall thrusting him back the way he'd come and up. A half-turn in the air, the sword spinning to a reverse grip, both hands about the crosspiece, and he landed atop the Huntsman. The full length of the sword slid through the creature's thorax. The Huntsman snarled and trembled, legs thrashing as the Herald twisted the blade, levering through vitals, grinding across chitin. Gradually the growling stopped. Spidery limbs stilled, and the eyes stared sightlessly. Everyone took a shaky breath.

'I think I'm going to throw up,' whispered Eris. 'That was disgusting.'

'Agreed. But preferable to being, ah, eaten,' said Simonetti. The Herald stamped a boot down on the creature's muzzle, pulling the blade free of the corpse before wiping it clean with a rag.

'Achilles,' he said in a whisper.

'You're so fast,' said Eris.

'Training helps,' replied the Herald, 'being Orfano helps more.'

'What do you know about these . . . things?' said Eris.

'I've seen them before,' replied the Herald, 'but not in years.'

'Where?' she pressed.

'In the Foresta Vecchia,' said Simonetti, 'during the Verde Guerra.'

'You fought these during the war?' said Eris in a hushed voice.

'It would be more accurate to say they hunted us, and we did whatever we could to survive. We thought we'd exterminated them.'

'It seems you thought wrong,' said Eris, frowning.

'Anea thought it best to keep their existence secret from the *cittadini* lest panic consume Landfall completely. Little did we know they slept beneath House Fontein.'

The Herald gestured them onward. Wooden stairs rickety with age complained beneath their feet as they fled. A door burst open, disgorging them onto the rooftops of Demesne.

'How wonderful,' said Eris. 'Now we can freeze to death.'

324

'Perhaps you'd prefer it back in the castle, Domina? With the Huntsmen.'

Eris turned a sullen glare on the Herald before retreating a few dozen feet.

'Stay here while I look for a way in,' said the Herald, not pausing for a moment. Simonetti slumped down on the lip of the roof and dangled his feet over the edge, shivering in his ashen robes. Eris sat beside him, following his gaze. The winding streets and courtyards of Santa Maria lay beneath them like a skewed map. It might have been majestic once, beautiful even, but destruction had reached down, scarring every home.

'I always hated the town,' said Eris. 'The press and stink of it. All those market traders haranguing passers-by.'

'It is an acquired taste,' said the archivist. 'Still, the town is empty now. No one is going to harangue you today.'

Far below, a lone Myrmidon staggered along the street obviously wounded, feet scuffing on the cobbles. One arm was held across his body. His sword dangled from his other, its weight slowing him. His journey was short. A blur of the impossible, eight-legged and vicious. One moment the Myrmidon travelled the street; the next he was thrust into an alley, providing a feast for a Huntsman.

'Perhaps there is some, ah, haranguing after all,' said Simonetti. Eris felt the bile rise in her throat as she stared down. The Huntsman continued savaging the corpse for long minutes, mercifully just out of sight.

'I was just thinking how hungry I was,' said the archivist, 'but now . . .' Simonetti cleared his throat and thrust his hands into his robes.

One more person dead. She'd not known the Myrmidon, and yet she still felt a tiny spark of something. Was it conscience? Grief? Guilt? Was this a feeling of misplaced responsibility? The cycle of thoughts maddened her. She opened her mouth to be free of them, surprised at the words edging from her lips, tiny, fragile things.

'Why are you helping me?'

Simonetti looked up from his maudlin inspection of the city. He gave no answer, wiping his optics on robes far from clean.

'You've always been neutral,' continued Eris. 'Politically, I mean. So why help me, after everything I've done? Everything I've been a party to. I'm more complicit than most.'

The archivist nodded but gave no answer.

'We lost the moment we hanged Medea, didn't we?'

Another nod. 'I think you'll find you lost a long time before that.'

Eris clenched her hands into fists – to ward off the cold, she told herself.

'When. When did we lose?'

'Ah. Well, the moment you set yourself against Anea, I'd say.'

Eris nodded and snorted a bitter laugh, then crossed her arms, hunching down against the cold.

'You admire her.' Not a question.

'Of course,' replied Simonetti. 'She enshrines the things I hold dear.'

'Such as?'

'Making education available to all, the library, researching science in order to improve the lives of the *cittadini*, not just the *nobili*.'

'And?' Eris wasn't enjoying a single word of this, but she needed to hear it. She wanted to know what Anea had done to command such respect.

'Ah. Well, she made me Viscount, and that's a very rare thing. Usually a man like me would have to strap on armour and, ah, murder a score of people with a sword. But Anea made me Viscount on account of my long years of service to the archives.'

'Because she cherishes knowledge.'

Simonetti nodded. Eris looked down upon the vista of Santa Maria. Screams clawed the air, made faint by the distance. Ranks of townhouses and endless pantiles, covered wells and lonely streets, arches and passages in profusion. Each window shuttered, every door locked.

'All of these plans, these plots, they went badly wrong, didn't they?'

Simonetti gave a weary nod. 'So many plans and secrets, all undone.'

326

'Anea unleashed those creatures, just to be rid of me.'

'To be rid of Erebus, I suspect,' said Simonetti.

Eris coughed a bitter laugh. 'I never thought I'd see the day when Anea would act more ruthlessly than Erebus.'

'For all her kindness there is a certain –' the archivist groped for the word '– implacable quality to Anea. Steely, you might say. She was never the most likeable of the Orfani. At first I thought it was on account of her being, ah, mute, but I realised her intelligence sets her apart. It's as if she, ah, occupies a space three feet above everyone's head, looking down at us.'

Eris shivered. 'That sounds like a lonely place.'

'I think I've decided,' rumbled Simonetti, after a moment.

'What?'

'Why I'm helping you.'

'Because you're keen to consort with people who are guilty of high treason?'

'Yes, that must be the reason.' Simonetti smiled. 'When I began work at the library we barely knew where to begin. So many books. Books we didn't even know existed. The king kept so much from us for centuries. He had the books privately scribed. Often, ah, killing the transcribers afterwards.'

'That's not much of an incentive to deliver a manuscript on time.'

'No, I don't suppose it was.' The archivist chuckled. 'So, we had all these tomes, and Anea was keen to transform the *sanatorio* into a library. I spent every waking moment uncovering new caches of books, deciding what they were and where they should go. Then we let people start reading them, and we had to keep track of each one. We had to make sure they were put away or repaired when damaged. Occasionally, Anea would find tomes which needed to be incorporated into the, ah, collection. The shelves were soon groaning under the weight of all those pages. I loved it.'

'Then what happened?'

'Well, people would come in and we'd try and help them find the, ah, information that was useful to them. Metallurgy for the smiths, books of unusual fashions for the tailors.'

'You still haven't explained why you're helping me.'

'Because I specialise in lost things, misplaced tomes. And you –' he held her gaze a moment then looked off into the town '– you're just another lost book. A lost girl from the Foresta di Ragno with no family and not enough common sense to know better.'

'How do you know I'm from the Foresta di Ragno?'

'Something in the way you speak. My mother hails from there.'

Eris nodded. 'So I'm a lost book?'

'Yes. But there's barely anything written in you, and most of what has been, ah, scribed so far shouldn't be read. All of those blank pages, well, something good could be written on those. But it's up to you, Eris. You have to be the author. Not Erebus and not me. It has to be you.'

Eris shivered and felt tears bloom at the corners of her eyes. She brushed them away angrily.

'I've spent so long pretending to be Anea, I'm not sure what I'd write in that book. It's been so long since I was that girl from the Foresta di Ragno. I wouldn't know how to write my own future.'

'That's what, ah, concerns me.'

'And if I did learn to write my future? What then? Would you place me on a dusty shelf, high up somewhere.'

'Even if I did, I doubt you'd stay there for long.' Simonetti smiled. 'I think I'd, ah, keep you somewhere close to hand, just so I could check your grammar.'

'Probably for the best.' Eris smiled. It was a comfort to think Simonetti could have an iota of faith in her, but doubt remained. Even his avuncular optimism couldn't pull her from the shadow of Erebus.

'I've found a workman's hatch.' The Herald had drawn close on silent feet. Eris flinched so hard she all but slipped from the edge of the roof. 'It took some work but I prised it open.'

'Might we return to my apartment?' asked Simonetti, pulling himself to his feet. 'I'm sure the creatures have moved on by now.'

'I'm going to the Ravenscourt. I still have a score to settle with Erebus,' said the Herald.

'But we'll be killed,' said Eris.

'And we'll die of cold if we stay here,' replied the Herald. 'Besides, it won't take long for a Huntsman to find its way up here.'

'So we just march into the Ravenscourt.' Eris had stepped close to the Herald, a gleam of anger in her eye, hands balled into fists. 'Do you really think—'

'None of us will survive this,' replied the Herald. 'I just need to make sure Erebus dies before I do. Come with me. Or don't.'

They trekked across the tiled rooftops, drawing closer to the vast dome at their centre. Arched doorways four feet tall beckoned them, flickering beacons in the night.

'Quickly now.' The Herald pressed on, breaking into a jog. They were close, perhaps twenty feet from the door, when the scuttling form of a Huntsman crested the dome. A deep growl issued from behind bared teeth. The Herald drew the great sword from where it lay across his back.

'We waited too long,' mumbled Simonetti.

39

The Shard

'Not feeling so clever now, eh Virmyre!' rumbled Viscount Datini from the gallery of the Ravenscourt. The Myrmidons were closing in, the soft thump of their boots on the black and white flagstones.

'If we survive this –' Virmyre flicked a glance to the gallery '– I'm going to kill Datini first.'

Anea nodded, but couldn't relinquish her grip on the sword to sign a more detailed response. She wished she had taken *tinctura* that morning, with danger so close at hand. Her instinct was to run but run where? Fear itself stalked the corridors of Demesne. Alecto had seen to that. There would be no surviving what came next, but the urge to fight, to remain, to hold on, was not so easily abandoned.

The Myrmidons edged closer, short wide blades held in low guards, ready to enact the will of Erebus. These Myrmidons had recently dispatched three Huntsmen. One limped, the other was missing some armour from his thigh, ripped free by the savage tenacity of chitin and fangs. The *professore* looked calm and confident in surcoat and armour, the blade in his fist held with familiar ease.

'I wish Lucien were here,' said Virmyre quietly. Anea nodded. Lucien in a temper was a worthy opponent.

'You were never supposed to rule,' droned Erebus from the dais. 'I never wanted you for the Orfani, but the king insisted.'

Anea shuddered at the truth of it. She would have been raised with the underkin if not for her hated father. Years spent in the darkness of the oubliette, the chill waters her only home.

'Now you're the architect of all my woes,' continued Erebus.

'I can't decide who likes the sound of his own voice more,' said Virmyre, 'him or Datini.'

Their opponents approached. Anea wondered how she must look to these battered Myrmidons. A young woman with a swathe of corn-blonde hair, a halo of silver playing about her head even if it were a only nimbus of metal, artifice rather than divinity. The vestments of Santa Maria would provide no protection, only the sword in her hand might parry the blows to come. She was a shard of the Saint herself, not quite a champion, nothing like an avatar.

'I had hoped for Lucien,' continued Erebus. 'I'd have settled for Dino, despite his disgusting preference.'

Anea stiffened at the mention of her brothers.

'I definitely wish Dino were here,' said Virmyre, eyeing the Myrmidons. Anea raised her wrist, lifting the rosewood prayer beads to her veil in the imitation of a kiss, before advancing toward her opponent. The sword whipped up above her head as Anea surged forward, spinning as she went, the blade a blur of steel in the darkness. The soldier threw up a parry, slowed by the armour, his vigour tested and found wanting. The Myrmidon staggered back, clutching his breastplate. He dragged in a wheezing breath and caught Anea's next strike on the flat of his blade. She withdrew, falling in beside Virmyre. The other Myrmidons adopted cautious stances.

'You need to teach me that move when we have a spare moment,' said Virmyre.

'So strange that you Orfani have always opposed me.' There was a note of self-pity in the maddening drone of Erebus' voice. 'You were supposed to be the ruling class, kings of the under-kin, and yet here you are, playing goddess in borrowed robes.'

Anea hissed. This wasn't a holy war, it wasn't even a war of ideologies. This was survival, the fate of humans versus the grinding ambition of Erebus, keen to see the underkin ascendant.

Virmyre glanced at her. 'Three versus two really isn't in our favour, Highness. If you have any tricks up your sleeve now is the time to use them.'

331

The Myrmidons closed in on three sides. Anea ducked beneath a swipe from her left that would have snapped her collarbone like kindling, then formed a riposte that saw her own blade meet the faceplate of her attacker. There was a stifled grunt. She ducked, turned, spun away and lashed out again. The blade caught another attacker across his thigh, the steel point skittering from armour. A glance over her shoulder revealed Virmyre was locked, forte to forte, both hands grasping the hilt of his sword. Anea threw up a parry and sidestepped. The outcome, always bleak, now looked inevitable.

'I never did like Myrmidons,' snarled Virmyre. Another glance confirmed the *professore* was starting to sag, his opponent's strength greater than his own.

Anea thrust her blade forward, the tip went skidding from a bracer, impacted with the Myrmidon's breastplate, snapped and clattered to the floor. Virmyre was almost on his knees, his sword scraping against sword. The other Myrmidon was edging behind him, hoping to deliver a *coup de grâce* while Virmyre's blade was held fast.

Just then Marchetti appeared on the left side of the curving balcony, hopping the railing with nimble feet. Anea wanted to cry out with relief. The assassin was a fleet shadow, tumbling down a broad banner of cloth hanging before a Doric column. A stiletto in his free hand punctured the fabric, slowing his descent with a tearing sound. Three underkin standing near the dais marshalled their courage, urged on by the complaints of Erebus. The underkin shambled towards him in their borrowed finery, a variety of short weapons clutched in pale hands, ceremonial in the main, more filigree than military. Marchetti landed on the dusty black and white tiles, rolled and returned to his feet with languorous ease. Only a half-step betrayed he was wounded.

The assassin gave a casual flick of the wrist, his sword circling out and returning to a close guard. The first underkin didn't know he was finished until he turned his head to see the dark blur beside him. His throat erupted in a flood of gore before a desperate hand pressed to the wound. The underkin sank to his knees, weapon slipping from fingers, slumping forward onto his puzzled face. The second underkin at least had the chance to parry. His blade went high to block the assassin's feint with the stiletto. Marchetti sidestepped, a twist of a shoulder, the extension of an arm. The underkin's innards came free of his torso as a cry of dismay escaped his lips.

The Myrmidons attacking Anea and Virmyre saw none of this, helms hindering their vision. It was only the direction of Anea's gaze that betrayed the newcomer and his bloody work. The Myrmidon bearing down on Virmyre surrendered to curiosity, turning to see the commotion. Anea needed no further invitation. The *professore* was all but on his knees; he would not last much longer. Anea ran, hefting her broken sword in both hands. Four inches lower and she would have decapitated the Myrmidon – blood splashed from the bottom of his faceplate as her blade smashed into it. The Myrmidon fell back twitching, sword falling from fingers desperate to tear off the battered headgear, voice a ragged wail of anguish.

Virmyre stood, turning on instinct and thrusting low, steel sliding through the unprotected thigh of another Myrmidon. There was a scream as Virmyre twisted and wrenched the blade loose, a bright spatter of red across the white and black tiles of the Ravenscourt.

'I hope you're not the sort to gloat about saving another's life, Highness.'

Anea advanced toward the Myrmidon with the dented faceplate, now collapsed on the floor. She discarded her broken sword and adopted his. The Myrmidon pulled off the damaged helm revealing a ruined face: he had looked human once, had a tongue to create words and a mouth to kiss those he loved. Anea envied him, clutching the sword tighter. The Myrmidon raised his hands to his broken nose and smashed cheekbones. Anea didn't spare him the time to lament his looks, removing his head with three quick strikes.

Marchetti dispatched the last of his attackers with a callous ease, sword scoring a series of wounds that reduced the underkin to bloody meat. Only the paleness of his skin and a sheen of sweat told of the assassin's struggle. Marchetti wrenched his opponent's head up, slamming a stiletto through one eye socket, then looked up at Erebus in defiance.

'Impressive,' droned Erebus, 'but futile.'

Marchetti removed the steel from the underkin's head and wiped it clean in one fluid motion. The underkin twitched and slumped to the floor, blood pooling across the flagstones as his boots drummed a pathetic rhythm.

If the last of the Myrmidons was perturbed by the fate of his comrades he declined to show it. Anea respected him for that. She watched as the attacker drew close, using his momentum to force Virmyre off balance. The old *professore* stumbled.

'Kill him!' shouted Viscount Datini from the gallery.

'You may have to kill Datini for me, Highness,' grunted Virmyre. The Myrmidon struck, batting aside Virmyre's blade. Anea's heart lurched as the next strike followed. The *professore* threw up his wounded hand to deflect the Myrmidon's blade, which slammed into the bracer, skittering off. Virmyre buckled at the knees, pulling his arm across his chest in barely suppressed agony. The Myrmidon's blade was already falling for the killing blow.

Anea caught it on her own blade, turning it aside, wrists aching with the impact. She stepped inside her opponent's reach, using the crosspiece to smash the faceplate, but the angle was wrong. Instead of delivering a staggering blow she merely removed the Myrmidon's helm. A woman's face looked back her, ashen and grave. Was this the Myrmidon who had smuggled the clay jug into the oubliette? Anea held out her sword, ready to parry, but made no move to attack. The woman spared a glance over her shoulder, confirming Marchetti's approach bearing death in each hand.

'Remind me not to parry with my arm in future, Highness,' intoned Virmyre. He winced as he struggled to his feet. The Myrmidon woman edged away from Anea, distancing herself from Marchetti as she did so.

'It seems the odds are somewhat reversed, wouldn't you say?' Virmyre rolled his shoulders and winced. There was a boom and rattle as the door slammed against the wall at the back of the chamber. Three Myrmidons appeared behind the looming presence of Erebus. Virmyre said the very thing Anea and Marchetti were unable to.

'Fuck.'

Anea sheathed her sword and pressed her fingers together. *We cannot fight so many. Get to higher ground.* She pointed to the balcony and headed toward the stairs. The Myrmidon woman took advantage of the break in the fighting, retreating to the opposite staircase.

'There's no escape,' shouted Viscount Datini from the opposite side of the chamber, where he clung to the gallery railing like a doomed captain preparing to go down with his ship. 'You will all be executed.' Anea found the notion of Demesne sinking into the ground appealing – perhaps the oubliette would swallow them, Huntsmen and all. Anea continued toward the stairs, keen not to be caught out in the open. She had no wish to be surrounded again, not even with Marchetti and Virmyre at her side.

'Anea, wait!' Virmyre was trudging after her, slowed by his armour.

Suddenly two underkin sprang from behind a column, choosing that moment to obey their master's exhortations. The hunched and pallid creatures thrust with fencing blades looted from nobles. Anea didn't pause, throwing up a block with her heavier blade, kicking an exposed knee and surging past. She turned to deliver a slash across the shoulder blades of the first underkin, who howled. Virmyre sank his blade into the juncture of neck and shoulder, bones breaking. The second underkin's nerve abandoned him, but his retreat was short-lived, his run an ungainly shuffle. Marchetti twisted past him, blades flickering, once, twice, three times. The underkin stopped his frenzied flight, shuddering to a halt as he released a despairing cry. Anea felt a pang of pity for the fallen underkin. Might she be fighting in the service of Erebus had things been different?

Marchetti gestured toward the stairs but headed toward the centre of the Ravenscourt.

'Where's he going?' muttered Virmyre.

Gone to buy us a few seconds to climb these stairs, for all the good it will do.

'Slow down, Highness.' The vitality the *tinctura* imbued had left Virmyre, leaving him ashen and unsteady.

The view from the top of the stairs provided an uninterrupted panorama of allies and enemies spread out across the Ravenscourt. More Myrmidons had entered, ragged and wounded. The underkin on the dais had dispersed. No longer content to watch, Erebus clearly intended to join the melee, stalking forward, towering over his subjects, the unseeing gaze of his helm locked on Anea.

'It's a strange thing to fight for your life when we're all going to die anyway,' said Virmyre.

A flicker of darkness and a fluttering of wings snatched their attention. A raven had found its way into the chamber, black wings beating the air beneath the dome.

'What does it mean?'

The Herald, signed Anea. War had come to Demesne and would crush every one of them.

40

Resignation

The Herald hefted his great sword in both hands, intent on the Huntsman. The curve of the dome proved no impediment to the creature's spindly legs. Weathervanes wailed as the wind gusted across the rooftops, whipping Eris's hair about her face. Simonetti held up one arm to shield his eyes. The stars had slunk from hiding to bear witness, an amethyst eye in the dark firmament brightest of all.

'I think I'd rather die of cold,' said Eris. The creature continued growling.

'You may get your wish if you stay out here any longer,' said the Herald. 'Run. Run now.'

Chitin leg followed chitin leg as the Huntsman traversed the dome of the Ravenscourt, black lips curling back from sharp teeth, pointed ears laid flat against its skull. Simonetti pressed a hand to her back and they sprinted forward, the Herald running alongside them. Eris's eyes were fixed on their destination, a small maintenance door, while at the top of her vision the Huntsman was impossible to ignore as it surged towards them. Eris wanted to stop, to turn, to flee, but Simonetti's hand continued pressing between her shoulder blades, urging her on. A glint of moonlight from the Herald's great sword distracted her, and then she was hurrying into the doorway, waiting to feel sharp teeth snag and tear as the Huntsman dropped down, slashing through the muscles of her neck. She stooped and threw up an arm, stumbling into the gloom of the Ravenscourt. The irony that she had fled here for safety was not lost on her.

'Surely there's some other corner of this castle we can hide in?'

Simonetti was close behind, but paid no heed to her words, eyes throwing panicked glances over his shoulder. The Herald turned to the door too late to slam it shut. The creature forced itself through the cramped doorway, close enough to tear them to bloody ribbons on the threshold. The Herald sidestepped the lunging Huntsman, stumbling but keeping his feet. Heavy strikes from his great sword descended, missing the creature time and again. Teeth flashed and limbs scythed the air, promising a quick end should the Herald's attention waver.

'More of them will come unless we shut the door,' Simonetti managed between ragged breaths. Eris tugged the archivist's sleeve, shocked into wordless silence by the vignette of insanity and suffering below them. Erebus lurched from the dais, leaving a score of wretches milling about, seemingly unaware of the chaos. Underkin scurried from beneath him, mindful not to be crushed by his rancid bulk. They wailed in despair or offered anguished prayers to their Myrmidon god.

'Look!' Simonetti pointed at two Myrmidons rushing the stairs on the opposite side of the room, attempting to reach one of their kin who had lost her helm in the fighting. Viscount Datini stood behind, urging her on with a maddened gleam in his dark eyes. His sabre drawn, the wizened viscount resembled a young boy, whooping and hollering.

'I think I, ah, preferred the previous *capo*,' said Simonetti.

'At least he had youth on his side,' said Eris, before pointing to the middle of the chamber.

'Oh dear,' mumbled Simonetti.

The centre of the Ravenscourt was host to three Huntsman corpses, shattered playing pieces on the chequerboard flagstones. They were not unique; others had also been expended in the bloody game. Fallen Myrmidons spilled crimson, deep brown armour dented or ripped free, swords slumbering in dead hands or lying forgotten in shadows.

'Marchetti is still alive,' gasped the archivist. A flicker of movement in the shadows drew her eye elsewhere, a silhouette of deeper darkness in the struggle. Marchetti was all but invisible but for the bright steel he clutched in each hand. He slipped between Myrmidons at the centre of the Ravenscourt, delaying, parrying, eluding blades with fluid ease. He performed a dance of atrocity. His music was the ring of steel on steel, the grunt of the wounded, tortured cries. More Myrmidons crowded in to slay the traitor, but earned only wounds for their troubles.

'There's no way he can fight all of them,' breathed Eris.

'He's giving ground. Soon he'll be up against the main doors, assuming Erebus doesn't reach him first.'

Eris remained entranced as the hideous form of Erebus advanced on the assassin, failing to notice the Huntsman surging along the balcony behind her. It came on slender legs, jaws wide, eyes agleam with frenzied hate. No more than a blur of movement in the corner of her eye, a profusion of limbs bent to the effort of speeding toward her. Eris turned just as the creature came within arm's reach. There was not even time to scream.

Simonetti was thrown to the wooden floorboards of the balcony, the Huntsman crashing into him, eliciting an anguished cry. His optics fell and spun away. Eris could only watch as the creature performed the task it had been bred for. She reached out with empty hands to help, yet shrank back from the violence, found herself wishing for a sword or the Domina's staff. The snarling Huntsman sank its jaws into the base of Simonetti's neck, then began to shake its head from side to side. The archivist called out, hands scrabbling on the wooden floor. Eris waited for the stink of fresh blood, for the man's thrashing feet to go still, but the folds of Simonetti's hood confounded the sharp teeth. The harder the Huntsman tried the more the fabric snared its fangs. The creature jolted and sagged, releasing the hapless archivist with a growl of frustration. Standing behind the aberration was the Herald, both hands about the hilt of his sword. Two of the creature's legs lay nearby, leaking pools of translucent fluid. The raven rejoined its master, chiding the Huntsman with a raucous cry.

'You stepped into my parlour, fucker,' said the Herald. The Huntsman turned to face its attacker, slipping for the lack of hind legs. The Herald's blade was already cleaving the air, reaching an apex, descending in a dull blur. The Huntsman dodged aside, growling, then lunged forward uncaring of its wounds, jaws ready to seize the Herald's thigh. Eris cried out, concern shaking the sound from her. A sidestep, a redirection of the blade, a twist of the body, of the shoulders.

'*Figlio di puttana*,' said the Herald.

The Huntman's head sailed up to the rafters still snarling. Eris could only watch, empty hands shaking, eyes twitching from Simonetti, still supine, to the Herald and back again.

'Oh dear,' sobbed Simonetti. 'I cannot see.'

Eris fell to her knees and retrieved the archivist's optics.

'I cannot see. I cannot see.'

'Here.' She pressed the lenses into his hands. 'I found them for you.'

'Oh, thank you, a million times thank you,' he breathed, the words running together with relief. They pulled each other to their feet in an awkward lurch, finding themselves face to face with the Herald. His great sword rested point down on the floor, his left hand proffered the hilt of his other sword. The pommel glittered in the light, the head of a cataphract drake in fine silver, onyx eyes dull.

'This is Achilles.' Eris took the blade with trembling hands. 'Don't lose him.'

'Wait,' she said. 'You can't mean to leave me here to protect . . .' But the Herald had turned away, running back to the doorway from the rooftops, which threatened to disgorge another Huntsman into the frenzied panic of the Ravenscourt. He hefted his sword like a spear and thrust it, forcing the creature back, splitting flesh and drawing more translucent blood.

'This is safety?' Simonetti looked from the melee of the Ravenscourt to the palms of his hands, now flecked with splinters. 'I think I'd like to resign as archivist now, Domina.'

'I think I'd like to resign as Domina,' she replied. 'Let's get away from the door. I don't want to be here if the Herald fails.' Eris led the still trembling Simonetti along the curving balcony. Several underkin stood before them, crowding together, bearing mournful looks. Some had surrendered to despair, uttering

340

pitiful cries through distorted faces. Eris hefted the sword, struggling under the unfamiliar weight.

'Do they have to make these things quite so heavy?'

'I wouldn't know, Domina,' said the archivist with a wary glance at the blade in her hands.

A lone underkin produced a dagger, holding it before him in an uncertain hand. 'We will protect Lord Erebus unto death!'

Eris frowned. 'Oh, do get the fuck out of my way, you horrible little man!' she bellowed. To her surprise the underkin acquiesced, shuffling from her path, browbeaten and cowed, keen to be spared the wrath of an armed and furious Domina.

'You certainly have a way with people, Eris.'

'Shut up, Simonetti.'

'Yes, Domina.'

The underkin on the balcony departed, some climbing down the drapes to the relative safety of the Ravenscourt, where they shared fearful glances with their friends. Others fled past the archivist and the sword-wielding Domina.

'I didn't think I was that intimidating,' mumbled Eris as she looked over her shoulder.

'I don't think they're fleeing from you, but her.' Simonetti pointed to where the balcony ended.

Standing at the top of the staircase just ten feet away was Anea Oscuro Diaspora, the Silent Queen, the *strega* princess, rightful ruler of Landfall. Eris could only watch as a Huntsman lunged onto the balcony from above, dropping from the ceiling like a spider. The Silent Queen didn't flinch, burying her sword in the creature's gaping maw. A cold fury emanated from Anea, light radiating from her headdress like a halo, the steel in her hand a divine verdict for any stepping too close. There was something resplendent about her despite the gore and the grime. If Santa Maria wished her will to be done on Landfall she had no better conduit than the Silent Queen. Anea struck again, forcing the creature over the balcony's edge, the Huntsman's legs scrabbling for purchase. It trembled with agony and fell to the floor below, impacting with a wet smacking sound.

'Ah, I forgot she'd learned the blade,' said Simonetti, a note of pride in his voice.

'Perhaps we should rejoin the Herald?' said Eris quietly.

'Slow down, Highness,' shouted Virmyre from below, once Anea's champion of the sciences, now her champion in battle. Eris envied the devotion the woman inspired in her subjects; it transcended duty, was more powerful than love, greater than the most hateful of rages. Virmyre fought at the base of the stairs, freeing his blade from the neck of an underkin with a jerk and twist. The unfortunate slumped to the floor convulsing, hands pawing as translucent blood flowed from the wound.

Virmyre failed to notice the Myrmidon flanking him as he sought to climb the stairs.

'Look out!' screamed Eris, pointing a finger. The Silent Queen turned to see Virmyre dodge the attack.

Not quickly enough.

Blade met pauldron, smashing the dark brown armour free of Virmyre's shoulder with a bell-like chime. The *professore* staggered, the Myrmidon pressing the advantage. Eris ran down the stairs past Anea, swinging the drake-headed blade with all her strength. The steel glanced off the armour but knocked Virmyre's attacker off balance. Anea stepped in a second after, swinging with equal fury. An arm flailed up to turn the blow aside, but was severed at the elbow. There was an awful moment where neither Anea nor Eris nor Virmyre moved, spellbound by shock. The Myrmidon spasmed, staring at the stump of his arm in sickened fascination, then fell face down with a crash. Eris flinched, saw Anea do the same. Simonetti edged past the two women and went to Virmyre's aid.

'And who's side are you on today?' said Virmyre. The archivist pulled him to his feet with a groan.

'Side? Do you honestly think I can tell which side I'm on?' said the archivist. 'I simply want Demesne restored and war averted. And to, ah, keep my optics.'

'Sounds like you're on our side then,' said Virmyre, expression stern.

'Did you have anything to do with these... things.' Simonetti gestured toward a corpse smattered in blue blood.

'The Huntsmen? Well, it was Anea's decision, but ... yes, I helped.'

'And you're questioning my loyalty?'

'Good point.' Virmyre shrugged in his armour.

'I'd like to resign as archivist, if I may.'

'I'll need your resignation in writing, I'm afraid,' intoned Virmyre.

Eris listened to their banter but felt no joy. Her gaze had not left Anea, seeing only hatred reflected back in eyes that had watched Demesne taken from her. Eyes that had witnessed a kingdom subverted for dire purposes. No wonder the Silent Queen raised her sword to strike.

'My lady! No!' shouted Simonetti, hands held up in supplication. Eris raised her blade, hoping to fend off the killing blow.

It was at that moment that Erebus charged from the centre of the Ravenscourt, an angry misshapen god bringing the promise of damnation with every footfall. As one they turned to face him, Silent Queen, impostor, archivist and *professore*. Eris glanced at her sword and the swords of Anea and Virmyre. The steel seemed inadequate for the task ahead.

41

Old Scores

Anea looked at the sword she had taken from the Myrmidon. It was well crafted: the forte would turn aside the heaviest of blows, the hilt bound tight in calfskin. It was not a long blade, suited for fighting in the confines of corridors and rooms. The weapons of her childhood had been a strange ceramic, less heavy than the steel she now wielded to defend herself. All of these considerations were small comfort as Erebus crossed the Ravenscourt on six legs of mottled chitin. He towered over Myrmidon and underkin alike, knocking his subjects aside in his temper.

'Anea! Get behind me,' said Virmyre, but she would not use her most loyal friend as a shield. Anea hissed, dropping into a low stance, the rosewood beads clacking about her wrist. The impostor took a position beside her, wielding her blade like an amateur. Simonetti could only back away, edging toward the entrance of the Ravenscourt, lacking both weapons and advice. No one had anything to say; no words could encapsulate the horror of Erebus as he lumbered towards them in an ungainly lurch. The same scene played out across the Ravenscourt, small groups of Myrmidons and underkin fending off attacks from multi-legged Huntsmen.

Erebus bellowed an incoherent dirge. A foreleg rose, longer than the tallest of them, slashing down with shocking speed. Anea danced to one side and returned the attack, her blade not meant for Erebus himself, but the offending limb. Virmyre ran forward and tried his own blade against an insectile leg. The impostor joined the attack, much to Anea's surprise. The

344

woman swung the blade, teeth gritted, slashing at the nearest leg. All scored the chitin but failed to cut deeper. Erebus shifted his weight onto his rear legs, lashing out with great scythes of chitin. Anea was sent skidding across the dusty floor. She pitched forward but saved herself with an outstretched hand, settling into a low crouch. Virmyre thrust his sword up into the belly of Erebus, and was rewarded with a dull, wet sound.

'I've got you now, you old bast—' But he was wrong. A chitin leg smashed into the *professore*, knocking him off his feet, sending him sideways. He lost his footing and collapsed, sword skidding across the tiles near the double doors. The impostor stepped towards her former master, unleashing an attack that made up for its lack of finesse with unrestrained fury. Anea heard the woman call out 'Sabat—' but anything else was drowned out but a bellow of pain from Erebus. The impostor's blade removed the tip of one foreleg, perhaps a few inches of brittle limb. Translucence jetted and spattered the floor.

'You?!' snarled Erebus, turning his blunted helm in the direction of his attacker. He stabbed at the red-robed woman, missing the impostor by a small margin. She shrieked and fell back, landing on her backside, then rolled away beyond the reach of the jagged limbs.

'You, who I took from nothing!' bellowed Erebus. 'You, to whom I gave everything!'

Anea ran to Virmyre, helping him to his feet. He held his wounded hand to his ribs and winced.

'This isn't working, Highness.'

They stared as Erebus lurched toward the impostor, looming over her with one raised leg. Seconds away from shattering ribs, puncturing lungs, rupturing her wicked heart.

'She saved my life,' said Virmyre, unable to wrench his eyes from the unfolding tragedy.

It was then Marchetti landed on the grotesque's back, flinging himself heedlessly from the balcony. The assassin used his stiletto like a piton, sinking it to the hilt between plates of insectile armour. His other hand slashed ineffectually at the Myrmidon god, chopping at the mottled shell. Erebus lurched sideways several feet, carrying him away from the impostor. She

345

slipped away, clutching her sword to her like a babe. Erebus shook and bucked like a wild horse in summer, but Marchetti was resolute. His sword slipped from his grasp as he struggled to stay astride the vast insect.

'We cannot defeat him,' whispered Virmyre as they watched the assassin cling to the monstrosity. 'He's impervious to our weapons.'

Perhaps he can help? Anea pointed to the stairs, where the Herald descended, throwing back his hood.

'Dino?' whispered Virmyre.

Anea stared, held immobile by a trinity of feelings: disbelief that Dino had ventured here as Lucien's Herald, relief that he lived at all, and greatest of all, terrible fear he'd be taken again. Grey eyes flashed silver as Dino closed with Erebus, bearing the largest blade she had ever seen. Dino swept the great sword up and across his body, raising it above his head, where the steel shone with a cyan glimmer. Erebus, occupied with the unwanted passenger on his back, failed to notice the Herald's approach, rearing and twisting. The Herald struck, and a shudder of destruction passed through Erebus. Everyone watched, stunned, as one thick limb fell away. The sound that filled the Ravenscourt was unnatural. Myrmidons stopped their battles and even the Huntsmen stalled their fury. Anea watched the impostor clamp her hands to her ears, wretched with fear.

Simonetti had retrieved Virmyre's weapon during Dino's attack and returned it to him, not daring to tear his eyes from the towering form of Erebus. 'Your sword, Professore,' he said in a fearful whisper. 'For all the good it will do.'

'Thank you,' replied Virmyre, eyes fixed on Erebus, who wheeled about to attack Dino. The giant vermin lurched toward them on five ungainly legs. Anea stepped back, ducking beneath a flailing limb even as Virmyre dodged the other way, a desperate parry with both hands. Simonetti was not so fortunate. Erebus bludgeoned him, knocking him clear of the fight. The smooth floor and dust conspired to spirit the archivist away, his robed form sliding to a halt by the Ravenscourt doors.

'Simonetti?' called the impostor, running to him. The man didn't move. 'Simonetti?' Still no reply. The impostor turned from the archivist's broken form and screamed with fury, a blur of red robes and steel. Dino followed her lead. She ran forward, sword above her head, but the strike was parried by a mottled limb.

'Foolish girl,' sneered Erebus. 'Best you return to the Foresta di Ragno.' But Dino's blade was not so easily turned aside, fracturing the shell of his corpus.

Marchetti had locked his legs around the abomination's abdomen. He held the stiletto in a reverse grip, puncturing the hard shell, single eye shining bright with hatred.

'We need to help them,' said Virmyre, limping into the melee. Anea nodded, advancing with him despite wanting to run to furthest corner of Demesne. The Ravenscourt filled with the agonised howl of Erebus as Marchetti continued to stab him, the piercing blade relentless. Erebus lurched sideways, colliding into the balustrade of the staircase. A leg scythed though a Myrmidon hard pressed by a Huntsman, but Erebus did not notice, intent on jarring the assassin from his back. Marchetti fell. The assassin's head smacked into the smooth tiles and all resistance fled his body, reducing him to a tangle of limbs.

'Now we're really in trouble,' said Virmyre before lunging in, only to find his blade turned aside by the thick shell of Erebus once more. 'I really must get a bigger sword next time we do this.'

'Next time?' said the impostor, blinking.

'Figure of speech.'

Erebus filled the air with a dirge of complaint, striking at Dino, who turned aside the limb with his great sword. The blow elicited a pained grunt, Erebus' attack sending the Orfano to his knees. A Huntsman broke from the melee, lunging at the kneeling figure, but was cut down by Erebus. The creature collapsed, head a ruin.

'He's mine!' roared the monstrosity. 'I can unmake anything the king made. I'm twice the ruler he ever was.'

Anea rejoined the fray, sighting a join between the first and second segments of a rear leg. She clutched the sword with both hands, raising the steel above her head and imploring Santa Maria for aid. Erebus snarled, his attention focused on

347

Dino, who threatened to remove another leg with his great sword. Anea's blade found its mark, sinking into the joint with a spatter of translucent fluid. Then the steel stuck fast. Anea tugged at the hilt, hissed in frustration.

Erebus howled and stumbled. Anea, divested of her weapon, could only shrink away as he wheeled about. She threw her arms around her head and knelt down, praying she would not be trampled. Virmyre pulled her up, swinging her to one side. She looked over her shoulder to see a sad smile cross his lips. Unarmed, all she could offer was a word from her slender fingers. *Run.* But it was too late.

Anea felt as if she were outside time. It slowed to a sickening throb like her pulse as the scene unfolded before her. Virmyre turned to face their great enemy as Anea watched, powerless to intervene.

Erebus towered over the *professore*, one limb gone, another crippled by Anea's sword. Dino appeared at Virmyre's shoulder and gave a grim nod. They moved in concert, meeting the threat with blades in motion. Dino's sword extended to the limit of his arms, sweeping up in a wide arc of bloody violence. Virmyre's blade sank into Erebus' abdomen, where the shell had been shattered. Only the hilt protruded. There was a moment where the only sound was of raven wings flapping in agitation. Dino's blade ripped through the soft meat of Erebus' neck, rending muscle, tendon and jugular alike. The blade tore free of the flesh, a shower of translucent ichor following the steel. A tremor passed through the colossal form.

'Dino, what have you done?' rasped Erebus, but the words were half formed and barely audible. Insectile legs convulsed, then surrendered to gravity. Dino leaped to one side, cloak flaring out behind him. Anea gasped as the bleeding corpse crashed to the ground, burying Virmyre amid collapsing limbs. She wanted to scream, hands held out as if she might pluck the *professore* from beneath the tyrant he'd fought so hard to defeat.

No one spoke.

Anea used a discarded sword to lever at the gigantic corpse, frantic. Dino worked with her, his great sword proving the better tool. The impostor joined them, straining with the effort.

Together they pulled Virmyre's body free, his surcoat a mottled blue, drenched in the blood of Erebus.

Is he still alive? Anea could barely make the words. Adrenaline had given way to shock, leaving her tremulous. Dino felt for a pulse, pressed his face close to Virmyre's nose. The Orfano looked up, grey eyes blank but for the hint of red that bloomed at the corners. He swallowed and said nothing.

Is he still alive?

'I can't feel a pulse.' Dino kissed his fingertips and pressed them to Virmyre's forehead. Anea clung to her brother, falling into his arms as he stood. The impostor knelt beside Simonetti, shaking her head in disbelief.

'I'm still having trouble believing you're you, really you,' said Dino, looking at his sister. 'I've become so used to hating you. Now I've got you back and I'm not sure what to say.'

Cruel that I lose Virmyre the same day I get you back from the dead, signed Anea.

'I'd send for a *dottore*, but I doubt you'll find one for twenty miles.'

Erebus twitched, a single limb clawing the black and white marble flagstones. Anea flinched, a hiss escaping her.

'I will rule.' The voice was a pitiful protest. 'And all my children will feast on your souls.' Erebus rose once more, drawing himself to his full height. 'Lucien couldn't kill me; you will not kill me.'

Finish it, signed Anea, taking a step back from the warped form of the Majordomo. Dino swung the great sword in a wide overhead arch, hacking the head of Erebus free from the insectile body. For a moment the corpse remained standing, taking a few tentative steps toward Dino, then collapsed once more. Anea stared at the monstrous corpse before them, her stomach a knot of misery, throat thick with emotion.

'Lucien and I –' Dino wiped the blade clean '– are not same.'

Wounded and dead Myrmidons lay beside Huntsmen staring at the ceiling with dead eyes, tongues lolling from canine mouths. The underkin who had entered the fighting were no more than broken corpses. All across the Ravenscourt the same story of carnage, death and sacrifice. A few underkin survivors peered at the charnel scene from behind columns, too afraid to venture out, too afraid to seek an exit.

Anea released a breath and wanted to feel joy or victory, but Erebus' death provided no comfort. She stared at the decapitated head, almost afraid to believe he was truly dead.

'Erebus is over,' said Dino as if reassuring himself. 'It's done.'

Anea shook her head, fingers sketching words on the tainted air.

It is not done yet. She turned to the impostor. *There is one last thing that needs doing.* Dino turned to see Marchetti rise to his knees just a dozen feet away. The assassin crawled to his sword and took the hilt with shaking hands.

'More than one thing.' Dino pointed with a bloodied hand, the words pure accusation in the silence of the Ravenscourt. 'You ambushed Emilio Contadino.' Marchetti looked back, single eye clouded with confusion. 'It was your men who killed Massimo.'

He came over to our side, protested Anea.

Dino shook his head. 'And that will bring Emilio back, I suppose?'

Of course not.

Marchetti climbed to his feet, a sheen of sweat on his grey features.

'Please!' A voice from near the double doors. Simonetti dragged himself to his feet using the door frame. Pale and bloodied, the archivist stared at them through one lens of his optics, the other shattered. 'This is hardly the time to settle old scores.'

'Be quiet,' said Dino, 'or you'll be shelving books in the afterlife.'

The archivist bowed his head.

'Simonetti is right,' said the impostor. 'We came together to defeat Erebus, and we're free of him. We have the opportunity to begin again. Isn't this what you wanted? To free Demesne, to free the *cittadini*?'

Anea signed, the gestures large enough for everyone to read. *You killed Russo, took my throne, destroyed the town I helped flourish, turned back the clock on all my good deeds.*

'I was coerced,' said the impostor. 'Bought and bribed and blackmailed.'

If it was not for you Virmyre would still be alive. I will have justice.

The impostor flinched from the words as if struck, then turned and fled toward the dais, red robes fluttering as she retreated. Anea drew her sword and followed, leaving Dino staring down at Marchetti in a ravaged Ravenscourt.

42

An Angel of Vengeance

Eris sprinted the length of the Ravenscourt, the drake-headed sword still in hand, the grip slick with sweat. The Myrmidons defending Erebus had fallen to the Huntsmen, who had in turn been overwhelmed by the underkin. The cost of the exchange was steep, many of the sham courtiers dead. The dais was a charnel scene of sundered limbs and split torsos. Agonised expressions lingered on the faces of the dead. The floor was slick with blood, blue and red alike. The underkin who remained had lost all stomach for the fight, clutching their weapons and wounded limbs fearfully. They parted before the fleeing Domina, thinking she charged them in a berserk rage.

Eris spotted the open door at the rear of the Ravenscourt, leading somewhere else, somewhere beyond this dire crucible and its many consequences. Only Viscount Datini presented an obstacle. He'd clambered down from the balcony during the fight, as if standing upon the dais might confer on him ultimate authority over Landfall. The old man levelled his sabre, adopting an imperious mien.

'I command you to stop,' he shouted, the dark pits of his eyes devoid of anything close to reason. Eris's left hand slipped around the hilt of Achilles, where it met her right. She gritted her teeth and lifted the blade to waist height. 'You will stop!' shouted the viscount. He took a step back but it was too late.

Eris launched herself into the air and swung, knocking the sabre from his fingers, then ploughed into the old man, shoulder to chest, knocking him onto his backside. She stumbled and slipped, but kept her feet. The viscount blinked in surprise, mouth open, bereft of words.

Anea closed with the dais, no less intent, an avenging angel amid the carnage.

'Bloody women,' muttered the viscount.

Out through the doorway at speed, slipping on blood-slicked boots, Eris careened from a wall, knocking the wind from her lungs. Her legs didn't fail her, carrying her on, fuelled by desperation and the desire to be free. The stairwell spiralled down. Twice her feet betrayed her in the darkness. Twice she grasped the handrail, averting the promise of broken bones should she survive the fall. Footsteps followed, echoing down the stairs, foretelling a sharp end should she falter.

Eris flung open a familiar door leading to a concealed passage. No light here, only a darkness between places, a limbo separating the Central Keep and House Fontein. She'd walked its length many times, but never without lantern light. Her robes snagged on the stonework, grey teeth snaring crimson. A rectangle of gold shone before her, light pushing past the edges of a door. Eris wrenched at the handle and dashed through, no thought to what might lie beyond, losing Anea in the labyrinth of Demesne her only priority. Her lungs ached with exertion, legs leaden. She dared a glance over her shoulder but the curving corridor remained empty. It was the backward glance that cost her the collision.

Two Huntsmen snapped and growled at a lone Myrmidon, cornered outside a training chamber. The first Huntsman had seized a thigh, the Myrmidon's flesh spared its hateful fangs by dark brown armour. The second Huntsman was attempting to grasp an arm, fended off by the desperate parries of the doomed soldier. Time and again his sword opened slashes on the Huntsman's muzzle.

It was the second Huntsman Eris blundered into, its spindly legs splayed across the width of the corridor. She fell head first over the lunging creature, hands stretching out on instinct, reaching for the floor. The blade she carried dragged her forward, speeding her descent. The Huntsman turned, jaws snapping at the flurry of crimson robes. Eris rolled onto her side, the blade held up despite the numbness of her arm, elbow singing with pain. The Myrmidon turned to look at her, face concealed by the sinister helm. A rough sash of scarlet was tied to the soldier's sword arm.

'Domina Eris?'

The struggle paused as all present sized up their opponents. Growling filled the corridor as Huntsmen eyed Domina and Myrmidon. Then the Myrmidon lifted his sword, a dull grunt escaping his lips. The creatures fell on the Myrmidon, and Eris drew her sword arm back. Gathering her courage, she slashed at the Huntsman nearest to her. Achilles descended on legs and body, opening deep cuts with each blow. Eris stepped to one side as she'd seen the Herald do, then struck again, caving in one eye, the skull breaking through the pelt in bloody shards of white. With every motion the Huntsman slowed, unable to weather her strikes. A pitiful whine escaped the Huntsman as it sank to the flagstones with twitching limbs.

Eris ran. The Myrmidon would have to deal with the remaining attacker alone. Something worse than Huntsmen was coming. A snatched look down the corridor confirmed the truth of it. Anea, sword in hand, lantern in the other, head surrounded by a silver nimbus. The Silent Queen ignored the fight between Myrmidon and Huntsman, continuing her pursuit. Eris considered losing the sword, its weight an unwelcome burden, yet she couldn't bring herself to cast the weapon aside. An arch offered stairs leading downward, with the hope they might lead outside, away from the terrible madness engulfing Demesne. She took them.

The glint in the darkness confused her at first. She slid to a graceless halt, stooped and snatched the key from the floor, puzzled why such a thing had been so carelessly misplaced. Behind her was the clang of metal on stone, Anea descending the spiral staircase at speed.

Eris ran to the nearest doorway and tried the key with frantic fervour. The resulting click of the lock was the sweetest sound. She gasped with relief. The door swung in and Eris crossed the threshold, Anea close behind in a swish of grimed white robes and blazing light. Eris withdrew the key, slamming the door in her pursuer's face. The door jolted and edged open a few inches. Eris pushed back. 'Leave me alone!' she all but screamed.

Anea hissed with frustration, hammering on the wood. The door rattled in its frame as Eris leaned against it, hand forcing the key into the lock. Metal slipped on metal, then slid into the dark eye of the keyhole. She turned her wrist and dared not breathe. The door rattled on its hinges but the wood remained steadfast. Then a strike that could only have been steel on wood, Anea's fury vented. It would do no good; a sword was not the tool for breaking down a door.

Eris began to laugh, at first quietly, then hysterically. She had outrun the Silent Queen's justice. The sound of Anea's temper increased, Eris was helpless with laughter, relief and shock overtaking her. The blows stopped; Anea had given up.

The room was lit by a single lantern, her destination, her beacon in the black. Eris passed the many beds, finding shredded sheets and spatters of blood on the floor. She paid them no mind, her only thought to safeguard the light in the room. Fingers folded over the hoop extending from the lantern top. She hissed as her chilly fingers clutched heated metal.

'How I am supposed to carry this if it burns my fingers?'

The response was a low growl from the far end of the barrack room. A terrified tremor passed through her as she turned with reluctance, holding the light up. The door at the opposite end of the room yawned open; a wardrobe lay on its front nearby. A hasty barricade, she decided, and one that had not held. The wolf head of the Huntsman was visible at the limit of the lantern's reach. It hung in the darkness as if disembodied, fangs a jagged series of shards that promised slow death. The eyes were discs of yellow in black, as furious as the look Anea had borne.

Eris edged to the centre of the room until she stood between the beds. The light was ample invitation, the Huntsman needing no further incentive. Eris raised the blade, wishing she'd used just an hour of her time as ruler of Demesne receiving some instruction. The aberration scrabbled over the downed wardrobe, the now familiar eight-legged arachnid run no less appalling. Her skin crawled with the strangeness of it. There was a gleam of madness in the creature's eyes, hunger but also intelligence.

She lashed out with the sword as the Huntsman drew close. The blade removed the tip of a lupine ear as the Huntsman reared up, forelegs thrashing out with shocking speed. The first turned aside the length of steel, the second knocked the lantern from her grasp. The glass and metal container settled in the join between abdomen and thorax, illuminating the creature's nightmare anatomy. Eris kicked the Huntsman in the snout, bringing the sword down with a scream, the blade a blur of silver.

The lantern buckled and split, oil leaking, igniting, flaring as bright as her desperation. Tongues of yellow and orange consumed the matted fur of the Huntsman, its grey and tan turning to black. The barrack room was filled with a frenzied howling. Eris stepped back and mounted a bed, skirting around the creature, now engulfed in flame. The Huntsman turned to follow her from the room, a fiery spirit from the abyss. Eris fled through the door even as the creature struggled to pursue her, heedless of the flames.

The corridor was no safer than the barrack room. Anea had not been denied by such a thing as architecture. She had found a way around. Not locked doors or even the walls themselves would stop her. Eris ducked forward on instinct, Anea's blade missing its mark, likely slashing Eris's throat to her very spine had the blow connected. Anea hissed and withdrew, raising the sword once more.

'I know you want rid of me –' Eris adopted a stance she'd seen Virmyre take, but knew it was mere imitation, raising the sword to parry '– but I want rid of you just as much.' The Huntsman burst from the door still aflame before either woman could attack the other. Impostor and Silent Queen rained strikes upon the creature, Eris's blows frantic while Anea struck with precision. The creature succumbed, jaws slamming onto the flagstones as it died. Eris fled, leaving Anea behind the obstacle of the burning corpse but knowing it would not delay her long.

One turn, another corner and another corridor. Eris wrestled a lantern from a wall, its flame burning low. She listened for the footsteps that would surely follow. Shallow stairs led down into the bowels of the earth. How far had she descended? How much longer would the light last? And where was Anea? The dimming light revealed a dead end, a greater curse than any Huntsman she might meet, a corridor with only a sinkhole. She turned just as the Silent Queen rounded the corner, chest rising and falling from the chase.

'I did what I had to do to save my brother. Surely you of all people can understand that.'

Anea set the lantern down by her feet and sheathed her sword, head hanging low as if contemplating. *And where is your brother now?* she signed.

'He's dead. Sabatino is dead. Erebus took him from me. You know only too well the pain of losing a brother. Except Dino's not dead.'

Are you expecting sympathy? Anea's gaze hardened further. *From me?*

'No. No sympathy. Only a trial.'

Anea hissed a laugh behind her veil. *You want a trial? Very well. I, Aranea Oscuro Diaspora, charge you with the impersonation of Landfall's rightful ruler. I charge you with conspiracy and high treason against the kingdom of Landfall. I charge you with complicity in the illegal hanging of Medea Contadino and the assassination of Emilio Contadino.*

'That wasn't my doing.'

I charge you with the murder of Russo Maria Diaspora. Anea looked impossibly terrible, lit from below, a column of right-eousness in white. *I spent ten years reforming Landfall; all my work was undone in a handful of treacherous months. By Erebus. And by you. How do you plead?*

'Does it matter?'

It matters to me.

'I plead not guilty. I plead coercion.'

The sentence is death.

Eris lunged forward, sword describing an arc of silver in a wild swipe. Anea drew on reflexes only an Orfano could summon. The Silent Queen parried with both hands, the tip of Eris's sword clashing with Anea's at the forte, the sound thunderous in the forgotten corridor. Eris stumbled back, shocked at the Silent Queen's speed.

Anea started in with two light strikes to test her defences and Eris knew she was outclassed. Twice she turned aside thrusts that would have gouged her flesh; the third strike was a heavy slash she was unprepared for. Her arms shook with the impact, Achilles falling from her numbed fingers. Eris watched her last hope of survival clatter to the flagstones. The Silent Queen was no more than a silhouette, the lantern far behind her. All trace of holy light was extinguished, making her an avenging shadow.

'I never did like wearing your dresses,' said Eris, 'you pompous bitch.'

The Silent Queen raised her sword, and Eris flinched back on instinct. But it was not the sharp shock of blade parting flesh that caused her to gasp. Feet slipped at the sinkhole's edge, tumbling her into darkness, lost to the oubliette.

43

The Teeth of Winter

Anea watched the impostor slip from view. One moment she was there, empty-handed and desperate, the next swallowed by darkness. A flurry of the Domina's red robes, a tearing sound as they snagged on the edges of the sinkhole then a dull splash from below. Silence crowded in with the darkness like strangling hands. Anea blinked and caught her breath, strength and fury fleeing her, leaving her spent and shaking. The constant fighting through Demesne, facing Erebus and the pursuit of the impostor had all taken their toll. There was relief that Dino was still alive, joy that Erebus had been overthrown, but also a pervading sadness that they had lost so much, and so many.

Anea retraced her steps to the lantern, a wavering golden light at the junction of the corridor, lifting the flickering light from the floor with a trembling hand. The oil within would not last much longer, yet she returned to the scene of the impostor's disappearance. The flagstones yawned open, the maw of an abyssal creature.

'Help me!' The words were fractured and pitiful. Anea clenched the hilt of the sword tighter, frown deepening.

'Please. It's freezing down here.'

Anea drew close to the edge of the sinkhole and sheathed her blade. Eyes of onyx looked back from the silver head of a cataphract drake; Dino's sword lay on the flagstones. She knelt beside it, curling fingers around the hilt, lifting the bright steel before laying it across her thighs.

'I think there's something down here.'

Anea lowered the lantern over the sinkhole, illuminating

a portion of the oubliette below. Light dappled the stagnant water, a mound of earth and flagstones rising above the underground lake. The impostor had dragged herself atop it to be free of the frigid waters, but was clearly injured. Eris clutched at one wrist, stifling sobs.

Did you ever stop to think what it was like for me, trapped where you are now?

'I'm sorry. Please don't leave me down here.'

And if I had begged you, just a few weeks ago, would you have let me go free? I think not. Anea looked from the impostor to the glossy gaze of the silver drake, then her eyes drifted further, settling on the rosewood prayer beads about her wrist.

'Please? I helped you kill Erebus. I tried rescuing Medea. Surely that's worth something?'

What did I ever do to you that I deserved to be cast down there?

'Nothing,' whispered Eris. Anea glowered into the Stygian depths, removing the prayer beads from her slender wrist.

Too little, too late, signed Anea.

'Please don't leave me here.'

The rosewood beads fell through the darkness, splashing into the waters of the oubliette by the mound. The impostor fished out the beads, peered at them in the gloom and looked up, curiosity etched on her tear-stained face.

'What am I supposed to do with these?'

Pray to Santa Maria. The same way I prayed that Medea would be spared. Perhaps the Saint will grant you clemency, but I doubt it.

'You can't just leave me down here.'

Yes. I can. I am Lady Aranea Oscuro Diaspora, and I sentence you to the fate you inflicted on me. Enjoy the oubliette. Soon you will not remember any of this. Sleep well.

Anea stood and turned her back on the sinkhole, the oubliette and the impostor, taking the light with her. The screams escorted her until she was far from the oubliette.

The lantern all but guttered out as she drifted through the corridors of House Fontein. A sombre hush had settled, like a fall of fresh snow that silenced and chilled in equal measure. The Huntsmen had vanished, the sound of their predations ceased. Anea glided along the corridor like a phantom, Dino's sword in one hand, the spent lantern in the other. No matter. She was at the doorway to the Ravenscourt. How many times had she stepped through this arch as Demesne's rightful ruler? How many times had she stepped onto the the dais to address her subjects? It felt good, but the throne would have to go.

'So good of you to join us, my lady.' Viscount Datini was waiting for her, adopting his usual pose, hands clasped behind his back. Two of the larger underkin stood beside him, Myrmidon swords in the hands of amateurs. They'd procured helms from the fallen which only served to make them look like the ragtag pretenders they truly were.

'I had wondered if you would meet your end at the hands of Eris —' the viscount smiled '— but you are ever resilient, my lady.'

A single Myrmidon knelt beside Virmyre at the centre of the Ravenscourt, cradling his head. Dino stood over them, a guardian in black, his great sword resting point down, close in height to the man who bore it. The raven was silent, perched on his shoulder with accusatory looks for all. None of the thirty or so underkin dared look at him directly, standing around in a loose semicircle. Marchetti stood with them. The assassin was anything but imposing, one hand pressed against the back of his head, unfocused eyes regarding the scene with a weary resignation.

'It seems your efforts to retake the throne are for nought.' The viscount coughed up a bitter laugh, his deep-set eyes twinkling with bleak humour. 'You are quite outnumbered. I doubt even the great Dino Adolfo Erudito could slay thirty opponents single-handed.'

Anea walked up to the viscount and buried the sword in his chest with a single thrust. He looked down in shock at the finely crafted pommel that protruded from his ribs and opened his mouth to speak. No words emerged.

Anea signed, and Dino translated the sentiment.

'You stepped into my parlour, fucker.'

The ambitious viscount collapsed on his face, startling his

two protectors. They edged away from Anea's unflinching violence.

'You're starting to sound a lot like me,' said Dino.

Anea heaved the viscount's corpse over with one boot and drew out the sword, slick to the forte with noble blood. The underkin on the dais withdrew, lacking the skill and the will to attack the vengeful angel of Santa Maria. They joined their fellows on the floor of the Ravenscourt. Anea pointed at the female Myrmidon kneeling beside Virmyre. There was a deep scratch along the top corner of her breastplate.

'You,' translated Dino as she signed. 'It was you who brought me the clay jug in the oubliette.'

The Myrmidon nodded. 'And the blanket. You looked so cold, my lady.'

Anea nodded. She drew close to the Myrmidon, standing beside Dino. Her fingers flickered more gestures.

'What are you doing to Virmyre?' supplied Dino.

'I bound his wounds, my lady. I think he still lives, but his pulse is very weak.'

Anea swallowed and blinked away tears, taking several seconds to compose herself before sketching out new gestures on the air.

'Take these underkin and claim the Datini estate for yourselves,' translated Dino. 'I'm tired of death, tired of this constant violence. Perhaps one day underkin and humans will live side by side.' Anea sighed, then continued signing. 'But not today.'

The Myrmidon opened her mouth to speak, shock robbing her of words. She cleared her throat and tried again. 'My lady. How will we escape with those creatures abroad?'

'You may wait here for a week,' said Dino, eyes fixed on Anea's fingers. 'Then you must leave. These are my terms. No harm will come to you. You have my word.'

The last Myrmidon nodded. 'As you wish, my lady.'

Anea couldn't miss the direction of Dino's gaze, locked on the slumped form of the assassin.

'And you'll spare him too, I suppose?' he said.

I cannot stop you killing him, Dino. That choice is yours. But remember, he tried to free Medea. Marchetti turned his back on

362

Erebus. How many Myrmidons did he kill so we might prevail? We have suffered greatly, but so has he.

Dino regarded the assassin, eyes drifting to the ruin of Erebus, then back to the Myrmidon who tended Virmyre. 'And were you so lenient with the impostor?'

She still lives.

Dino raised an eyebrow in surprise. 'He was responsible for the attack.'

I know.

'The attack that killed Emilio. And Massimo.'

Emilio was supposed to come alone, Marchetti signed. *It was never my intention to kill Massimo — he was simply another casualty. They all were.*

'And yet Massimo's dead.' No anger in Dino's tone, just exhaustion and disgust. 'And scores of innocents along with him.'

I for one have had enough killing for one day, signed Anea. She glanced back at the dais, where Viscount Datini's corpse continued to bleed. *For a lifetime.* She stood before the carcass of Erebus, which resembled a five-fingered claw clutching at the Ravenscourt and the power it held.

'The underkin will need Marchetti to survive the journey to the Datini estate,' said Dino with a shrug. Anea hugged him and did not let go. Wanting to cry with relief, with exhaustion, with the sour sickness of death.

'But if I release him, you have to have to show mercy to the girl.

No more miracles today, Dino.

The last few hours of that night were fitful and laden with anticipation of the day to come. The sky bore the first streaks of golden light when Anea was roused from a dreamless torpor.

'Is there any wine?' said Virmyre.

She blinked and looked around. They had settled behind one column of the Ravenscourt, pulled down the drapes and used them as blankets.

'I said, is there any wine, because frankly I deserve to get unreasonably pissed. I dare say I'm entitled to it.'

Anea got to her feet and crossed to where Virmyre was sitting propped up against the wall.

Entitlement is such an unattractive quality.

'I am largely defined by my defects,' said Virmyre, stifling a cough.

There is no wine, but it would please me to share the sunrise with you.

'Some queen you are,' said Virmyre, mock affront on his lined face. 'Imagine running a kingdom without wine. There'll be a revolt, you know? And I'll be the one to lead it.'

That is acceptable, especially as you cannot stand without my help.

'Good point. Sunrise then?'

It took them some time to reach a good vantage point. Dino bore the brunt of Virmyre's weight as they stumbled across the rooftops of House Contadino. The sun crested the horizon revealing a landscape dotted with a few dozen Huntsmen. The creatures lacked leadership, not forming a pack but hunting alone.

What have I done?

Virmyre cleared his throat as Dino set him down on a stubby chimney pot. 'It reminds me of the time Lucien defeated the king.'

How so?

'The king's chamber was alive with spiders. You couldn't set foot in there without stepping on a handful of the things. Disgusting. And of course, once the windows to the king's chamber were broken the whole of Demesne was infested. They were everywhere. It seemed as if the king's madness would never end.'

But those days did end.

'Of course.' Virmyre coughed and winced as his ribs troubled him. 'The spiders that remained on the rooftops were eaten by ravens. Those spiders roaming the corridors were consumed by cataphract drakes, hence their popularity in the years after the king's death.'

'Achilles,' said Dino, rubbing a corner of his cloak over the silver face of the drake that adorned his sword.

'Yes, like Achilles.' Virmyre looked troubled, then continued. 'Other spiders were squashed by the squeamish, or cast from windows by those with parchment and cup to hand.'

The Huntsmen are hardly the same as the common house spider.

'No, I quite agree. But they will succumb to the same fate, picked off one by one.'

I doubt there is a cup and parchment big enough to capture one of them, let alone a window to throw it from.

'I do so love it when you're literal, Highness.'

The sun had edged higher, decorating the lines of the land in soft gilt, making the horrors of the night seem less severe.

'Perhaps they will help with your escaped spiders, Virmyre?' said Dino. He'd raised one hand to point at the southern road, where it led to the Terminiello Inn.

'There does seem to be a great deal of activity there.' The *professore* squinted into the distance.

Lucien, signed Anea, wanting to laugh until she wept.

'Damn fool marched his army through the teeth of winter to reach us,' said Virmyre, grinning.

Did you have anything to do with this?

Dino shrugged, then nodded. 'I am Duke Marino's Herald, but I didn't come alone. Delfino Datini and his man Corvino waited at the inn for my signal. When it seemed war was unavoidable I sent them back to San Marino.'

'It seems Duke Lucien still suffers from a deficit of patience,' said Virmyre.

'Anyone else would have waited until spring,' said Dino.

Does he know about the impostor, about my imprisonment?

Dino shrugged. 'Hard to know. I'm sure he has other spies, and word travels.'

Anea pushed her fingers into her brother's hand and rested her head on his shoulder. They watched a group of horsemen ride down a lone Huntsman with spears. The creature flailed and bucked, but was quickly overcome, trampled by hooves and rent apart by bright steel.

'Everything will be fine, Highness.' Virmyre was old and

bruised and broken, and yet the familiar sparkle lingered in his pale blue eyes. 'Duke Lucien's men need only mop up the survivors, instead of facing a hundred Myrmidons or more.'

We did it together, Virmyre.

'Regardless, I am proud of you, Anea.'

She hugged the old *professore*, then wiped tears from the corners of her eyes with the back of one hand.

'Do you think we could go back inside now?' asked Virmyre. 'I'm quite old and these bones feel the cold more than they should.'

The Silent Queen sat on the throne of Landfall, regarding the Ravenscourt through heavy-lidded eyes, lost in thought. The legs of that great seat were fashioned from four helms in the style of the Myrmidons lest any forget who had opposed her rule. The arms of the throne were two scabbards, holding the short wide blades of the soldiers who lay ripped apart across the four Houses of Demesne, while the back was formed from a Myrmidon breastplate. A sunburst made of beaten copper formed the top, appearing to halo her head. This was not a throne that had been crafted so much as welded together, assembled from the very fabric of violence. A violence she had survived. There was no chance of falling asleep mid-session in a seat such as this. It was designed to awe, not to comfort. Aranea Oscuro Diaspora drowsed despite the shortcomings of the throne, awaiting the arrival of Duke Lucien Marino.

44

Scouting

'Shouldn't we be fighting?' said Delfino, pulling himself onto the battlements above the Contadino gatehouse. Climbing had never been Delfino's preferred method of transit, his lack of ability all the more stark when compared to Corvino; the man rarely bothered with a rope.

'There'll be fighting inside,' said the *aiutante*. He perched on the wall regarding the courtyard below, abandoned and strewn with detritus.

'What a mess,' said Delfino. A glance over his shoulder revealed the slim crescent of the morning sun. Lucien's troops had fought late into the night, falling back to an encampment where they rested in uneasy shifts. It had been a taut few hours of darkness, grim-faced veterans' memories of the Verde Guerra painfully real beneath the stars. The newer recruits were ashen-faced at the horrors they fought.

'I still can't believe we're facing Huntsmen. Again. Once was enough,' muttered Delfino. Trios of horsemen had risen at dawn, circling the town with weary vigilance. Lucien had made clear the imperative: they must contain the creatures else they slip away across Landfall, preying on fearful *cittadini*.

'There's one,' whispered Corvino. The creature emerged from a fire-gutted house, scuttling along the shadowed side of the street, pausing every few feet to listen. Strange to see a Huntsman from so high above, looking no larger than a house spider at this distance, curiously malformed.

'We should be down there, killing that thing,' said Delfino.

'If you don't keep your voice down it will be up here killing

367

us.' Corvino watched the creature skulk away, turning a street corner and venturing beyond. Lucien's army had killed two dozen of the aberrations, losing a score of men in the process.

'I don't understand why you're so keen to enter Demesne,' said Delfino after the Huntsman was lost from sight. 'I thought you despised the place.'

'I do.'

They headed along the narrow wall, breaking into Demesne through a window to save them a long climb to the cobbles below. The room was thick with dust and stillness, the corridors beyond much the same, haunted by a chilling absence. The door hung from its hinges, barely attached.

'Servants' quarters,' said Delfino, lifting a cobwebbed hairbrush from a table. 'What exactly are we doing? Shouldn't we be outside with the others, riding down Huntsmen?'

'Scouts, aren't we?' replied Corvino. 'We're scouting.'

'But we need to kill the Huntsmen, and we need to find out where they've come from.'

'That's what we're doing,' replied Corvino. 'Finding out.'

House Contadino was abandoned but for the memories that lingered in each room. Forgotten belongings told stories of people hasty to depart, unsent letters told stories of their own, and all the while the accretions of grey dust made the previously great house indistinct, smeared by time.

'Do you know where you're going?' asked Delfino. He reckoned they'd spent an hour wandering. Rarely did his *aiutante* demand anything, so he'd no problem humouring the man, but patience was never Delfino's strongest suite.

'Towards the centre.' Corvino shrugged. 'I'm not familiar with Demesne, I only lived beneath it.'

'This way.' Delfino turned a corner and led them through the gloom, listening at doors and waiting at junctions. Huntsmen were just as content to wait for their prey as to run them down. Corvino followed with a lantern, his frown sullen more than angry, movements stilted.

'What's got into you, today?' whispered Delfino.

'Just anxious, is all.'

Before long the scouts had reached the circular corridor of the Central Keep and were standing before the white double doors of the Ravenscourt. A smear of crimson sullied their perfection, a matching stain on the flagstones.

'I wonder who died here?'

Corvino shrugged.

'Think they made it to the other side of the doors?'

'Not after losing that much blood,' replied Corvino.

There were other bodies in the corridor, Myrmidons ripped open or gouged at the joints of their armour, all clutching weapons, tenacious to the last. Slender spider legs lay severed from their owners, slumped in pools of blue ichor. Wolf heads stared with maddened eyes at the ceiling, furious even in death.

'Why are there Huntsmen here at all?' whispered Delfino. The question had been gnawing at him since they first sighted the creatures. No one had expected them, the initial horror subsiding to quiet wariness. The veterans knew Huntsmen could be killed from horseback. Away from the forest the advantage was very much with the cavalry.

'Just glad we're not fighting these armoured thugs,' said Corvino, a boot resting on the breastplate of a Myrmidon missing both legs below the knees.

'Do you know another way into the Ravenscourt?' asked Delfino, searching the dead for a key he might use on the locked doors. Corvino shook his head. Delfino crossed to the doors and raised a fist.

'Don't!' gasped Corvino, but Delfino hammered at the wood, then looked over his shoulder and shrugged.

'At least we'll find out if they're alive in there.'

'Whoever they might be,' muttered Corvino, pulling his swords from their sheaths. Delfino drew his own blade and they waited.

'You just told every Huntsman with half an ear where we are.'

'They'll all be outside by now,' replied Delfino.

'Sure of that, are you?'

Delfino declined to answer and kept his eyes scanning the dark corridor. Twice they feared something scuttled beyond the limit of the lantern light, but nothing ventured forward to rend them into bloody pulp.

'Come on,' whispered Corvino. 'Time to leave these old stones.'

Delfino thought he detected a note of sadness in the scout's words.

'What were you hoping to find?'

'Don't you think it strange we said goodbye to Dino nearly a month ago and we've neither seen nor heard from him since?'

'Dino.' Delfino's eyes widened. 'I'd forgotten about him in the rush to assemble the troops.'

'We all did.' Corvino's frown deepened. 'And he's been here all this time.'

'He can handle himself. I'm sure—'

'And if he was cornered by three of those things? What then?' Corvino sheathed a sword and pulled down his hood. Delfino had never known his *aiutante* and the Herald to share more than five words. The depth of Corvino's concern was puzzling.

Chains rattled behind the walls; the white doors creaked and shifted on their hinges, opening inwards.

'Delfino?' The word was rough and loud on the still air.

'My lord. We were just talking about you. Corvino was worried you'd met an untimely end.'

'Sorry to disappoint you both.'

'Not disappointed,' Corvino blurted.

Dark circles around Dino's eyes and an ashen pallor told of hours of lost sleep. His clothes were torn in several places, his cloak more ragged than Delfino remembered. The raven on his shoulder was gone, but his right hand gripped the great sword, reflecting gold in the lantern light.

'You'd best come in,' said the Herald. 'I've a lot to tell you, and none of it straightforward.'

45

Instrument of Woe

The girl in crimson curled about herself, twisting about a stomach empty of everything except jagged pain. Her lips were dry as drake skin, mouth parched. Twice she'd sampled the waters; twice she'd regretted it. Caught between wakefulness and sleeping, she drowsed through numbing cold and cramps that racked her stomach. Her refuge from the frigid lake was a crude mound of earth and shattered stone the width of a shield and no more. All light had faded after the woman had cast her down here. Aranea Oscuro Diaspora. Other facts had slipped away, yet this name was hammered into her, as sharp as any nail. Aranea Oscuro Diaspora, the Silent Queen. As if there were a kingdom to rule any more. The slow writhe of thoughts and the torment of fractured memories robbed her of past and future, leaving only a maddening present.

Absolute darkness being the rule, she kept her eyes open only as a matter of instinct. A glow in the distance set her pulse racing. The oubliette was the absence of everything: warmth, light, company, food, clean water. Even hope had abandoned her. Now it returned as a golden light approached. The gentle slap and swish of disturbed waters reached her ears. The prow of a gondola edged through the darkness, the illumination making the figure aboard a chiaroscuro. The girl in crimson tried to speak, her voice a forgotten croak, dying at the back of her throat.

'You'll need this if you want to think straight.' The man on the gondola handed her a stoppered clay jug filled with water. She searched the face for some clue to his identity. Fine lips underlined by a neat goatee, black hair shot through with grey. He'd be attractive if he wasn't so stern. His clothes bore none of the hallmarks of nobility, nor was he attired for battle.

'Thank you,' she managed before turning her attention to the jug.

'Sip it. You'll want to make it last.' His voice was a pleasant baritone. She paused before drinking, a wary glance hardening to open distrust.

'It's not poisoned,' he said, 'if that's what you're worried about.'

'I just...' She shrugged and pulled the cork free, but could not bring herself to drink.

'I'm not supposed to be down here. Do you understand?'

The girl in crimson nodded, not knowing if she did. Had she known him before she'd been cast down? His name eluded her. Her memories were fleeting on the occasions they returned. The vision that stayed with her most was of a woman hanged from a rope on a cold winter's day. The woman's name, like the man in front of her, had been stolen away, though it seemed the sight would always remain.

'You should drink,' said the man. 'It will help your memory if nothing else.'

The water was fresh, tasting like a miracle after the rank liquid that threatened to drown or freeze her. She drank, trying to sip as instructed, seeking the eyes of the stern man on the gondola. He'd retreated a way and had picked up a hammer from the seat. Next came a long metal rod, the tip folding back on itself and back again to form a hook. She watched, a crease of curiosity at her brow. The stern man planted the rod into the water and raised the hammer. The sound shattered the deep silence of the oubliette, reduced to echoes in mere seconds. He tested the rod to see if it remained firm, then lit a lantern and hung it from the hook, a disc of pale light amid the gloom.

'So I can find you again.'

It was not the only marker he left. More hammering. A trail of lanterns on poles stretched into the darkness after he'd gone. She was grateful for the light they gave, but knew to follow them would lead to a locked door, and guards too. Hadn't she kept someone down here once in the same way? The girl in crimson watched the lights, clutching her stoppered clay jug, thankful for the water. The man had departed, not sparing her a backward glance. He had concentrated on poling the gondola back to the entrance and the world above. The girl in crimson closed her eyes and waited for his return.

'Virmyre,' she whispered.

The gondola woke her as it returned. Her second visitor also offered a stoppered clay jug, exchanging it for the first, now empty. She blinked in confusion. This was not the older man from before, yet he bore an equally stern expression. His hair was raven black and yet to see the first strands of grey. He'd grown it long, much longer than was fashionable.

'So you're Eris.' A strong voice, one used to giving orders and being heard.

'Yes.' She waited a moment as several memories surfaced, none of them good. 'That's what Erebus called me. I can't remember my original name.' Eris drank, grateful for the water. The man dipped the pole into the water as if testing a spear, his balance on the gondola absolute. He wore a rich brown frock coat with immaculate turquoise detailing, matching britches tucked into riding boots. Eris eyed the short sword resting at his hip, the many medals pinned to his chest. This was a man who knew the cost of victory and its rewards.

'Did you come all this way just to give me fresh water?'

The man snorted a laugh, breaking into an easy smile.

'I didn't think so,' said Eris.

'We've never met, in case you're having trouble remembering.' He looked over the rank surface of the gloomy lake. 'Though I've been down here before.' A frown darkened his face. 'And not willingly.'

'You're Duke Lucien Marino,' said Eris.

He sketched a bow so gracefully the gondola did not rock, the water beneath undisturbed.

'I told the Domina that the Orfani were well versed in escaping death. But she wouldn't listen.' Eris sighed. 'She couldn't

373

bring herself to kill your sister. I think she loved her until the end, in her own way.'

'The Domina lost her mind to ambition and *tinctura*. Don't try repainting her as your reluctant accomplice.'

Eris looked down at her feet, the hem of her robe ragged and filthy.

'Why are you here?'

'I wanted to see you for myself.' Lucien pushed the tip of a thumb to his teeth for a pensive moment. 'The actress, the deceiver, the wolf in queen's clothing.'

'You wanted proof. You wanted to see the impostor with your own eyes.'

'I suppose you do bear a similarity.' Lucien chewed his lip. 'Not that I'd ever admit that to Anea.'

'And here I am. The instrument of all your woes.' Eris rose to her feet, careful not to slip from the tiny island of her incarceration. She bobbed a curtsy.

'Instrument is a pretty word for it.' Lucien's smile was bitter. 'Erebus made you his tool for a purpose. And then discarded you.'

'He made me Domina.'

'Only because you killed Russo. You're dangerous. He needed to keep you close at hand.'

Eris looked away, unable to meet Lucien Marino's gaze.

'Russo should be down here with you. The death you gave her was much too quick a punishment.'

'I was trying to defend myself. I never meant to...' Words failed her. She couldn't bring herself to say it.

'That, at least, I can believe.' He stabbed the pole into the chilly depths. 'Enjoy the water. I can't guarantee there will be any more.' Lucien frowned. 'Ah, I nearly forgot.' The duke crouched in the gondola. 'I brought this for you.' He passed a blanket of unbleached wool to her, a weight at its centre. No sooner had Eris taken it than he pushed away, guiding the gondola back along the trail of lights Virmyre had set out in the darkness.

She called after him, 'Will she ever set me free?'

Lucien declined to respond, leaving Eris to inspect her gift.

The blanket contained half a loaf of bread, a small pot of olives and two wings of cooked chicken, now cold. She fell on the food like a Huntsman, sating her hunger in minutes. It brought small relief, quickly turning to discomfort. Her stomach was not used to such fare.

The shadowy half-life of the oubliette dragged and crawled. Time passed in the dimming of the lanterns, flames flickering then dying with each passing hour. She picked at the remaining food, no matter how she tried to hoard it. Best to eat now than let it spoil. Only the blanket remained constant. She shivered beneath it, thanking Lucien Marino over and over. Darkness reigned again before the her third visitor appeared.

Anea resembled a work of art. Her gondola was not untreated, mouldering wood, but painted a splendid white, a handful of lanterns hanging at prow and stern. An avenging angel more perfect than Eris remembered, scrubbed clean of the grime of battle, a column of white demanding attention. Her gown was layered and intricate, decorated with silk and embroidery. There was something of the Saint about her, made divine by the semicircle of silver that swept back from her brow. This was a woman who had risen from the abyss to reclaim her throne.

A lone scout poled the gondola across the waters, an older man with a sour look. No words escaped him, and Eris was glad of it. Not a scout, she realised, but Nardo. The steward of House Contadino.

The gondola drew closer, just beyond arm's reach.

If only you had come alone, thought Eris. It might be me leaving on the gondola.

The Silent Queen sketched symbols on the air and Eris was surprised to find they made sense to her. The oubliette had not taken that knowledge from her. Not yet.

Some think me overly cruel for keeping you here, Simonetti chief among them. And Lucien. Virmyre too.

'Simonetti is a good man.' Eris stood, thrust out her chin in challenge. 'Is he well? Did he survive his wounds?'

Anea nodded. *I am still no closer to deciding what to do with him. Though he saved my life when I found the Domina. More of your handiwork.*

Eris swallowed, legs shaking, weak from incarceration. 'Simonetti tried to save Medea. And I never intended to kill the Domina.'

Her name was Russo. Russo Maria Diaspora. Anea looked away.

'Simonetti accepted that Erebus manipulated me. Something you can't conceive of for all your wisdom and intelligence.'

I can conceive of many things. Loyalty is the one that interests me most.

'People are loyal only to themselves,' Eris sneered. 'Perhaps you should remember that in future.'

I disagree. Virmyre remained here. Dino came back, not out of loyalty to me, but to Lucien. Lucien in turn brought an army through the teeth of winter. Perhaps you should reappraise your view of loyalty.

'So you'll not release me? Even knowing how Erebus used me, how Dottore Allattamento trained me for the task. You'll not release me despite the Domina's betrayal?'

And if I let you go free? Am I to spend my waking moments waiting for you to deceive us once more? Waiting for the next murder, the next scheme?

'I won't. I swear it. Lucien said the Domina lost her mind to ambition and *tinctura*. Can't I plead the same? I only wanted to protect my brother. You of all people can understand that.'

Anea shook her head slowly then gestured to Nardo to depart.

Eris was sure these would be her last visitors. If she could seize the gondola ... If she could slip out of Demesne ... If she could find her way to Simonetti's estate ...

But Nardo had poled the gondola back, no doubt guessing her intentions. Fortuna would not bestow the gift of escape, it seemed.

'Say you'll think on it,' said Eris. 'I beg you. Don't abandon me down here.' No more words came, and she succumbed to near-silent sobs of hopelessness.

Anea departed, a vision in white gliding effortlessly over the

Stygian waters. Darkness closed in once more, the food gone, even the slivers between her teeth just memories. In time Eris drank the oubliette's water, cupping handfuls of the icy fluid, knowing to do so would wash away all her memories. It would wash away her failures and regrets, wash away her grief for Sabatino. She didn't have the courage to drown herself, but the memories of all she had wrought would fade and die.

'Perhaps it's better this way.'

The girl in crimson sat alone, burdened by forgetfulness and incomprehension.

46

The Revelation Coda

'You seem to be on your own, Highness.' Virmyre was waiting for her in the corridor that joined the Ravenscourt to House Fontein. He leaned heavily on a cane; the mere effort of being out of bed had leached the colour from his face. Delfino Datini stood close to the old *professore* under the pretext of being his bodyguard, though the concern in his eyes was that of a nurse.

I dismissed Nardo; he's heading to the Ravenscourt by the usual route. Anea gave a curt nod, signalling the conversation was ended, but the *professore* was not so easily deterred.

'I wasn't speaking of Nardo. We agreed she should go free.' Anea flashed him an angry glance but Virmyre continued: 'Erebus was an arch-manipulator, and she was just a lost girl with a sick brother from the provinces.'

She made her choice. She chose Erebus.

'After everything that's happened,' Delfino released a sigh, 'you can't find some clemency for someone in the oubliette?'

Anea pressed forward, forcing the men to part before her, grasping the door handle to the Ravenscourt. She marshalled her thoughts with a calming breath. Eris was too dangerous, she told herself over and over.

'Have you decided what you'll say to them?' said Virmyre, his voice soft.

Anea nodded, then pushed through the door without further pause.

'So much for sharing one's plans,' said Virmyre.

'Let's see what she has to say,' said Delfino, his tone soothing.

Anea stepped out onto the dais and looked over the vast

chamber. Gone were the corpses of Huntsman and Myrmidon, gone were the shattered forms of misshapen underkin. Gone was the rank horror of Erebus, who even in death had perturbed the scouts of House Vedetta. The men had removed his remains, offering up prayers to Santa Maria and asking for protection from the Myrmidon god.

The blood had been mopped away though stains persisted. The flagstones had been swept and the windows opened to the fragile winter light. All around were the tells of conflict: scratched marble, broken balustrades, chipped columns. The broad swathes of fabric, drenched in blood or reeking of smoke, were gone. Anea stifled an impatient hiss. It would take months to repair the Ravenscourt, but it would never fully return to its former splendour. Much like herself, she imagined.

Lucien stood at the centre of the Ravenscourt, careful not to mount the dais lest it send the wrong message. Dino stood beside him, locked in conversation with Corvino. The two had been inseparable since the scouts had retaken Demesne. Nardo stood nearby, sharing tales and moonleaf with the younger scouts. One by one the men and women became silent, all eyes turning to Anea, splendid in her white gown and silver headpiece. Virmyre followed her out on to the dais, anything but steady, Delfino close behind should he fall.

Sit down. You look awful. Anea frowned.

'Where do you suggest, Highness. The throne? What will people think?'

I do not care. Just sit.

Virmyre did just that, perching on the Myrmidon throne, prompting a few laughs from the scouts. A lone voice called out, 'Hail the king,' but the crowd settled quickly.

Anea ushered everyone closer, noting the reverence in the eyes of the men and women who had fought for Demesne, and for Landfall. A pause, and then she began to sign, explaining the whole tale. Virmyre translated, stopping every so often to wet his throat with water or wine according to his taste. Little by little, the tale of deceit and betrayal was laid out. Every skein of ambition, every whorl of confusion, every loose thread

379

woven back into the whole. The abductions, the disguises, the murders.

There are some who say this story should end with Eris remaining in the oubliette for ever more, while others claim mercy makes the better ending. All I know is that it is a dangerous thing to have a double walking free.

The scouts muttered to themselves, in agreement in the main, although some accepted Virmyre's view: a young girl from the Foresta di Ragno, lacking the sense or bravery to escape Erebus' influence.

What I do now is to show you that what I am does not make me different. I am and always will be a cittadino *of Landfall. And not birth or gender, or appearance, will stop me caring for the people I serve.*

Virmyre frowned as he formed the last of her words, a glimmer of suspicion in his eyes. Anea untied the veil and revealed her true face to the room.

Her heartbeat eclipsed all sound in the chamber, unsurprising on account of the shocked silence.

'Hell of a thing,' said Nardo, breaking the spell she had cast over the scouts. Anea's hands trembled so badly she barely made the next gestures legibly.

If I do not speak it is not because I am haughty. If I do not tell you how grateful I am it is not because I am arrogant. If I fail to communicate with you in a way less obscure it is not because I wish it. This – Anea gestured at her face, the warped jaw splitting into mandibles, the lipless mouth and absent chin – *is my vow of silence. Not a choice but a curse. I have told this tale so you may tell others in turn. Tell them of Eris, and my lost memories. Tell them of a Silent Queen who only ever wanted a republic. Tell them of Medea Contadino. Tell them how brave you were to retake Landfall when I thought all was lost.*

Silence.

So often the quiet had been an oppressive weight, bowing her shoulders, yet the silence in the Ravenscourt was one of calm. Understanding filtered through the crowd, a hundred minds putting the pieces together.

'What now?' shouted a voice from the back.

Anea gestured and Virmyre coughed in disbelief. Three attempts were made before he managed to convey what Anea had wanted to say for what seemed her whole life.

Now we will have elections, the first elections for a new republic.

The applause rumbled through the Ravenscourt like thunder and did not stop for some time.

'Here you are,' said Virmyre, stepping out onto the church balcony. Lucien and Dino smiled at the old man. The three Orfani crowded about the sole brazier and drank hot wine, heavy blankets around their shoulders. Breath plumed on the chilly air.

'So glad we're outside on a temperate night,' said Delfino through a forced grin as he followed Virmyre through the door. Corvino snorted a laugh behind his fist.

Medea loved it here, signed Anea. All nodded and shared a moment's peace.

'And in just a few short months,' said Lucien after a pause, 'the kingdom will be no more. What will you do now, Sister?'

Anea considered this. *I will become a canoness. In time I hope to improve our medicines, without resorting to anything that clouds my judgement.* She gave Virmyre a significant look. *What will you do?*

Lucien smiled. 'I've a town full of cart drivers, fishermen, farmers, sisters and merchants, all vying for influence. But more than that I have a wife and child who miss me, and I them much more than they know.'

'They know,' whispered Virmyre with a slow smile. 'They know.'

And you, Dino?

Barely a trace of the Herald remained; the man who stood before them was not dressed for war. The great sword did not sleep at his shoulder, the mottled cloak had been cast off.

'I thought I'd fall in with Corvino.' There was a ghost of a smile on his lips. It had been much too long since any had seen it there. 'Delfino, I mean. Lord Datini, to give him his full title, is about to settle down, or so I hear.'

'The things we do for love,' said Delfino, his hands reaching for his pipe. A sigh of frustration escaped his lips and he shook his head, then snorted a laugh.

'Something amusing you?' asked Lucien.

'It occurred to me I lost both my father and my estate in this war, but in truth I lost them years ago. It just seems more real somehow, now that he's dead.' Delfino sipped his wine, a faraway look in his eyes. 'How did he die?'

After we killed Erebus – Anea's hands shook as she made the symbols – *he staged a coup of his own, commanding the underkin once the Myrmidons had fallen. He was so desperate for Datini to be a great house.* She paused.

'I think I'd rather not know,' said Delfino. He crossed to the parapet and looked out. 'Will it ever be the same again? Santa Maria, I mean. The town looks awfully bleak from here.' There was no denying his words; the town, like Demesne itself, had endured grave wounds.

It will never be what it was, signed Anea, *but perhaps one day it can be something better.*

'You know, with the coming election –' Lucien regarded his wine, not meeting Anea's eye '– and you as canoness...'

Assuming the sisters return to Demesne, signed Anea.

'Assuming they do, and with you no longer queen, it doesn't make much sense to leave Eris in the oubliette, starving to death, does it? It's not as if she can impersonate you any more, not after today.'

I never said she should starve.

'Lucien has a point,' said Virmyre. 'Giancarlo and Erebus himself once consigned you to such a fate. You're not casting yourself in a good light by leaving her down there.'

I am sending a message, signed Anea. *If I do not make an example of her then how long before we suffer another betrayal?*

'I'm not convinced the punishment fits the crime, Sister,' said Lucien, his voice low. 'Demesne exacts a cruel price from even the best of us, even those of us who were born here.'

'Especially those of us who were born here,' said Dino. Corvino nodded and looked towards Demesne and its many dark windows.

'What hope is there for someone drawn in from the outside?' said Lucien.

'Lucien has the truth of it,' agreed Delfino. 'Do you really want to be remembered as the queen who sentenced a commoner to the oubliette?'

'It doesn't matter that she's a commoner,' said Virmyre. 'It matters that she's a person.'

Anea shook her head and crossed to the parapet, turning her back on the conversation. She clutched at the chilly stone, frowning at the vast ivy-covered mass, barely lit in the twilight. It was the usual flurry of emotions: anger that so much damage had been done, embarrassment that she'd lost herself to *tinctura* and let her kingdom be stolen, fear that whatever she did in the years ahead would not compensate for such a fall from grace. She knew the prime mover of the plot against her had been Erebus, yet he was dead while Eris remained alive. But vengeance was not so easily cast aside, even the idea of forgiveness made her want to scream.

No one had much to say in the moments that followed. One by one they departed the balcony. Only Anea and Delfino remained, staring out at the star-strewn sky, a single amethyst glimmer among the points of white light.

How did you meet Corvino? He is an underkin, is he not?

'He is. I found him on the road south. He escaped the oubliette the same night Dino saved you and Lucien. He used the same rope to climb out, if I remember rightly.'

The actions of that night bore so many consequences.

Delfino smiled and rubbed a hand across his stubbled jaw. 'He was just a scrawny youngster with some terrible scars and those black fingernails that are common to the Orfani. I took him on as my *aiutante* and never looked back. Never regretted it either.'

Anea eyed the scout and waited, but Delfino looked away.

Go on. I have a feeling you have more to say.

'Well.' Delfino forced a smile. 'I took Corvino under my wing. That was good fortune, for him and for me. Seems to me that Eris had the bad fortune to be taken in by Erebus. There's no wrong and no right to it, just blind fate.'

Anea turned away. Delfino performed a small bow and headed to the door. He pulled at the handle, but Anea had followed him and touched him lightly on the arm.

Could I ask one more thing of you?

'Anything,' replied Delfino.

Bring Simonetti to me at first light tomorrow.

Delfino frowned but declined to ask why, content to bid the Silent Queen goodnight. Anea returned to the balcony's edge and released a long sigh. She was so tired she wanted to weep, but her bed would bring no rest. Her mind would crawl and stumble and run circles and always it would return to the same question. What to do with the impostor?

47

The Exiled Coda

The cart jostled her awake, shaking her from a hateful dream. The only sounds were the steady plod-plod of hooves, the creaking of wood and the soft exhalations of the wind. She'd been far underground, alone and afraid with only darkness and incomprehension to keep her company. Disoriented moments passed as she blinked the sleep from her eyes, turning this way and that. A tentative hand pushed the tarpaulin from her face, revealing the pale grey sky, the winter wind gusting hard. A heavy blanket was swaddled about her body. There was no sign of the mangy red robes she'd been attired in; she wore the britches and blouse of a messenger.

'It wasn't a dream. They cast me into the oubliette. So am I dreaming now?'

'Ah, you're awake,' said Simonetti. 'I wasn't sure you were going to make it.'

Eris sat up straighter, watching Landfall's countryside roll past.

'Where am I?' she breathed.

'A few miles south of the Datini estate. I, ah, had some help getting you out of Demesne.'

'The last Myrmidon? The underkin? Surely not Virmyre?'

Simonetti smiled. 'Ah, no. Anea herself. She decided that as long as people believed she'd cast you down for all eternity it was as good as the same thing.'

'So she freed me?' Eris watched her breath steam on the winter air, clutched the blanket tight and dared herself to feel some vestige of hope.

'Not exactly.' Simonetti looked over his shoulder, then turned his attention back to the reins. 'You're an exile, which sounds, ah, terribly exciting, doesn't it?'

Eris shrugged. 'I'll settle for not starving to death.' The cart rattled along the road and the Datini estate loomed in the distance. The thirty or so underkin marched in a ragged line behind the cart, led by the last Myrmidon. Eris squinted. Another armed underkin brought up the rear, but she couldn't remember his name, only that he was very dangerous.

'So we're going to live here, on the Datini estate?' Eris smiled and shook her head in disbelief. 'Can you imagine what the old viscount would say?'

'Yes. Yes, I can.' said Simonetti. 'Expletives in the main.' It was strange to see the man driving the cart, strange to see him beyond Demesne's walls. A pang of sorrow for the archivist made her catch her breath.

'Did she . . . did Anea exile you too?'

'Ah, no, not really.' Simonetti forced a smile. 'A man can only look after a library for so long, and I've a feeling the underkin will need an envoy to deal with the other houses.'

'An envoy?'

'Apparently so.' Simonetti smiled. 'There are worse jobs.'

'I can't believe she released me. I was certain I was going to die down there.'

'Anea took the, ah, unusual step of revealing her face to the scouts. A brave move considering what lies beneath the veil.'

'Mandibles,' said Eris.

'Should she ever need to prove who she is—'

'She merely has to show her face,' said Eris. 'That's one thing I can't emulate.'

'You and I, my dear, are both, ah, retired. I as archivist, and you as imposter.'

'I don't mind giving my profession up, but what of you?'

'I'm having my possessions brought here from the Simonetti estate as we speak. I may have given up my library but a man should never be without his books. They provide a good means of staying out of, ah, trouble.'

The archivist smiled and Eris smiled back. She turned to

stare at the road that spooled out behind them, down gently twisting lanes hemmed in by hedgerows. She imagined the many miles they had travelled from Demesne, the many miles between herself and the people she'd hurt and betrayed. She imagined Paolo Allattamento and Isabella in a small farmhouse, living quiet lives. She imagined Dino, finally at peace without the shadow of war threatening the land. And she imagined Sabatino's grave and the lonely cemetery watched over by ravens.

'I've just remembered something,' said Eris.

Simonetti looked over his shoulder and blinked. 'That's good. The effects of Lethe are well documented, but you weren't in the oubliette for such a long time. What have you remembered?'

'My . . .' Tears sprang to her eyes. 'I've remembered my name. My name is Sabina.'

Acknowledgements

So that was three books. I can't quite believe it.

As ever, a roll call of people who have helped shape, hone, and deliver *The Erebus Sequence,* as well as those who have provided inspiration and support.

Many thanks to Matt Lyons and Matt Rowan, who have been test-readers, cheerleaders, and sounding boards throughout.

Huge gratitude to Juliet Mushens for signing me up in the first place, but also lending me her keen editorial perspective. Also Sarah Manning for tolerating how bad I am with forms of any kind.

I am incredibly lucky that *The Erebus Sequence* found a home at Gollancz. Thanks to Simon Spanton, Gillian Redfearn, Sophie Calder, Charlie Panayiotou, Mark Stay and Genn McMenemy.

A small cadre of friends have always been onside for me; thanks to Rebecca Levine, Magnus Anderson, Jon Morgan and David Bailey.

Fellow authors who kept me sane: Jen Williams, Tom Pollock, Emma Trevayne and Chess Haig.

A quick call out to Lou Abercrombie, who did me proud with her photographic skills, and to Alejandro Collucci for providing the look of the series.

And lastly, thanks to you, the reader.